SUNROPER

A GODDESSES RISING NOVEL

Also by Natalie J. Damschroder

Under the Moon

Heavy Metal

A Kiss of Revenge

If You Believe in Me

Sunroper

A Goddesses Rising Novel

Natalie J. Damschroder

This book is a work of fiction. Names, characters, places, and incidents are the product of the author's imagination or are used fictitiously. Any resemblance to actual events, locales, or persons, living or dead, is coincidental.

Entangled Publishing, LLC
2614 South Timberline Road
Suite 109
Fort Collins, CO 80525
Visit our website at www.entangledpublishing.com.

Edited by Danielle Poiesz and Kerri-Leigh Grady
Cover design by Kim Killion

Ebook ISBN 978-1-62266-048-3
Print ISBN 978-1-62266-049-0

Manufactured in the United States of America

First Edition December 2013

To Jim, whose love, support, and belief in me make all of this possible.

Chapter One

The secrecy in which we have dwelled for centuries is threatened not only by modern technology, but by the actions of our members.

—Numina internal documents

Many things had changed since the day six months ago when a single touch altered Marley Canton's entire life forever. But she was still not the kind of woman who would typically be found in a trendy dance club in downtown Boston. She could play the part, though, if she needed to—and tonight she needed to.

"Jameson," she said, holding up two fingers at the bartender, who nodded and reached for the whiskey. Marley gave the guy eyeballing her a polite but standoffish smile as she turned to study the dance floor and scan the clusters of tiny, clear tables along the sides of the room. She didn't immediately see her prey, so with her drink in hand, it was time to prowl.

Lights flashed in time to the pumping music as she moved through the room. Bodies arched and ground and bounced on the dance floor, generating a steamy heat combated by the icy air-conditioning. As she eased her way toward the far side of the room, she glanced at every face, concentrating on the younger men. The guy she was looking for was twenty-three, arrogant, and slim. She'd studied enough pictures of him online and in the tabloids to be able to recognize him even in here. Once she got close enough, she would know her target.

She paused at the corner and angled her shoulders back to rest against the wall, sipping her whiskey to cover how closely she watched a group entering the club. It felt good to be on a mission. A few years ago, she'd lived a quiet, content life as the owner of an inn in Maine, giving lost souls a place to heal and figure out what they wanted to do with their lives. She'd been whole, happy, a middling-powerful goddess surrounded by her natural energy source, crystals, that helped her channel her power. Not that she'd used her abilities for anything special back then. But she'd fallen in love and stupidly given that man a piece of herself as well as a dose of power, allowing him to rip the rest—and more—away from her and four other goddesses before he'd been stopped. She'd helped to build a new educational program within the Society for Goddess Education and Defense, which had given her purpose for a little while, but the events of the past year had only shown her just how worthless she'd been.

Not anymore.

Marley glanced at the door as a woman tucked away her ID and a new group of clubbers pushed into the crowd. No sign of the guy Marley sought, so she moved on, too, striding down the long side of the club's main area. This side was darker and filled with couples making creative use of their tongues. Marley closed her eyes and tuned in with the rest of her senses. The usual ones combined in a natural awareness of the bodies around her, but over the last few months she'd developed a new ability to detect guys like Josh, the kid she was after, because of differences in his personal energy related to his generic heritage. Almost like reading his aura, except inside rather than outside.

She sighed and opened her eyes. All the guys over here were normal. Relatively speaking.

"You want to say that again?"

She stopped short and swung her drink out of the way as a tousle-haired guy in a silk shirt shoved a shorter, burlier guy into her path. Everyone around them halted—or at least paused in their dancing and flirting—and the sweet, hot aroma in the air sharpened with their interest in a potential fight.

Burly guy shook his head slowly, a smile twisting one side of his mouth. "Yeah, I'll say it again. *Suck. My—*"

Silk-shirt guy launched himself at Burly, and chaos erupted as friends staggered around trying to separate the two. They sprawled at Marley's feet, failing to land effective punches on each other. She wrinkled her nose against the blend of yeasty beer and fruity alcohol wafting from spilled drinks all around her, and her body curved and swayed to avoid the flailing limbs. She tried to ignore the hand-wringing laments of the guys' dates or friends or whatever the women were. The tears streaming down their faces were an uncomfortable reminder of how it felt to be useless in a fight.

Marley weaved toward the wall, out of the way of the bouncers pushing through the crowd, those feelings strengthening despite how poorly they fit into her current reality. She wasn't worthless anymore. She may have accidentally created a leech by giving the man she loved a bit of power, but now she could take it away from those who didn't deserve it.

Bestowing power on the son of a goddess—someone who had the genes but not the legacy—was a dangerous game. Marley had misjudged her fiancé's intentions. She'd wanted to bring them closer, to share something so vital to her identity. But she'd been played. He didn't want her, just her power. Limited as it was, it had been enough to allow him to steal from others and keep on taking until her sister Quinn—along with Quinn's now-husband Nick and assistant Sam—had stopped him. Quinn had drawn all the stolen power out of the leech and stored it inside her own body until a few months ago, when she was finally able to return most of it to its original goddesses.

Except Marley. She was too damaged, and for a couple of years she'd struggled to adapt to being powerless, to being part of a community she no longer belonged in. Just like those women as they watched their boyfriends brawling on the dirty floor of a club.

Marley straightened up, skimming her gaze across the room. The girls still stood to the side as the bouncers took care of the fight, just as Marley had stood by, helpless, when Quinn and a young goddess named Riley had been abducted by descendants of the gods, young men who wanted to steal their power.

Marley would have been a liability in that fight. Not that she'd ever been a warrior, but the first time, when she and Quinn and the others had defended her inn against attack, the energy she'd channeled through crystals allowed her to disorient and even knock out the attackers without even touching them.

But after being leeched, she had nothing. She would have become another victim to be rescued, so she'd stood by and let everyone else do the job. When it was all over, she'd vowed she'd never be that weak again. Yet here she was, standing by during a fight—never mind that this one had nothing to do with her—and struggling not to feel worthless.

This is not why I'm here, she reminded herself. She focused on reaching out with her senses, searching for her target.

"He's here," said a familiar voice in her ear.

She shook away the memories that voice dug up and touched her earpiece. "I'm kind of stuck back here. Where did he go?"

She tilted her head up and spotted Anson at the rail around the second floor. They'd been working together for five months now, but she still had to brace for the cascade of split-second reactions he caused, the ones telling her to run as fast as she could.

He'd been her fiancé, her enemy, the man who'd leeched her. And now he was her unlikely partner, a chameleon who managed to blend in wherever they went.

"I'm not leaving!" Silk Shirt shouted, yanking his arm away. Burly jerked forward to shove him, and the whole thing started all over again.

Anson caught Marley's eye and jerked his chin toward the rear of the building. "Straight back. Looks like a group of them have taken over one of the nooks."

Marley took a swallow of whiskey. She was still corralled against the wall, with no clear path to get where Anson indicated. She relished the woody burn in her chest and the warmth that seeped through her body. "Keep an eye on him. Let me know if he tries anything."

"Will do." Anson raised a beer bottle to his mouth and kept his gaze on an area Marley couldn't see.

She stood still, balanced on her ridiculous six-inch heels. The clutch she held in her left hand vibrated. She wasn't going anywhere and couldn't see past the tangle in front of her, so she popped open the clasp to check her phone's display. Crap. It was her sister.

She snapped the bag closed again and took another, bigger mouthful of whiskey. Avoiding Quinn never worked, but this wasn't a good place to take scolding phone calls. Quinn was going to try one more time, no doubt, to get Marley to go to Riley and Sam's wedding tomorrow. But Marley couldn't do it. As much as she wanted to be there when her friends celebrated their well-deserved happiness, she couldn't face them. Not when all she could do was imagine the pity and resentment they must harbor for her after all that had happened.

The noise level around Marley dropped as the bouncers finally hauled the fighters away, their pack trailing behind them. Her gaze fell on a handful of young men standing around a tall table near the dance floor. They were lanky and slouchy with long arms and legs, wearing carefully distressed jeans and short-sleeved shirts. She checked their faces and jolted when she recognized two of them.

"What's the matter?" Anson asked over the comm.

She cursed to herself and drained her glass, setting it on an empty table. She shouldn't have let him see her reaction. Their partnership only worked if they never referenced the past, and these guys were part of it. "Nothing. Burst of air-conditioning." She rubbed her arm to illustrate. "You're supposed to be watching our guy in the back. He still there?"

"Yeah, just hanging out, but he's talking up a couple of girls."

"I'm on my way. Keep your eye on him." Her path was going to take her by the guys she'd just recognized, and she didn't want Anson to spot them. They were young Numina, men descended from gods who'd kept themselves secret for years, and these particular kids had been part of the group that had abducted Quinn and Riley on Anson's orders when he was still Marley's enemy. She didn't know if these guys were Deimons like Josh and his buddies, lazy bastards who wanted the power of their ancestors without having to do the work, but they were definitely Numina.

Goddesses weren't secret like Numina were. There weren't many goddesses in the world, and people who heard about them didn't always believe in their existence, but many goddesses used their abilities commercially, and they even had a professional association with the Society. They were open about what they were. But the descendants of the gods? Everyone had thought those bloodlines had disappeared thousands of years ago. It turned out they'd just taken "secret society" very, very seriously.

The legacy of the gods was far subtler than the power goddesses wielded, much easier to keep secret. Numina had "influence," an enhanced level of charm, charisma, and the golden touch that brought them unimaginable success in business and politics. That influence varied, though, and was sometimes trumped by greed or laziness, especially in the younger generation. Hence the Deimons, who'd named themselves after Deimos, the god of fear. They had somehow discovered a goddess who would dole out her own power like a drug, a potentially easier path to the fame and fortune of their fathers.

Marley and Anson had stumbled across the group while researching Numina as a whole. "Flux," as they called the drug, provided a surge of energy that also gave them abilities of the goddesses, like telekinesis or increased strength. Marley didn't know if it also made them stupid, but one group of fluxed-up idiots had robbed a casino recently.

That was why she was hunting them. Deimons were irresponsible at best and potentially dangerous, and the only good thing about her void of power was that she was now able to take the flux away from them, to nullify them. As far as she knew, she was the only one who'd ever had that ability.

Tonight's target, Josh, was seriously high on flux. Marley didn't know if he was connected to the kids huddled in front of her, but with their history, she needed to know what they were up to.

She eased closer and caught the attention of a passing server. "Whiskey, please. Jameson," she added close to the woman's ear.

She nodded and yelled to Marley, "You gonna be here?" She pointed at the floor where they stood.

Marley nodded back, satisfied. Now she had an excuse to stay where she was and lurk for a few minutes. The music covered a lot of the conversation, but nullifying the flux had enhanced her senses somehow in the last couple of months, and she caught snatches of it.

"...to the beach house one more time before closing up..."

"...with third-quarter returns better than last year, we can monetize the..."

"...man, I need nachos..."

"...I swear, gozongas out to here, nipples the size of..."

She screwed up her face, wishing she'd missed that last bit. She was wasting her time—there was nothing useful here, and she didn't detect any flux.

The server slipped between a couple of sweating bodies and handed Marley her drink. She gave her a twenty and waved off change. The woman's face smoothed from annoyed at the inconvenience to pleased with the high tip before she hustled away. Marley sipped and was about to move on when the young men's conversation stopped her.

"Did you hear what Gashface is doing tomorrow?"

Marley tensed at the nickname of one of the guys who'd kidnapped Quinn and Riley a few months earlier. So his friends were calling him Gashface now, too? Riley must have called him that in front of the others after she'd sliced up his face. Interesting that they'd adopted it.

"Don't call him that, he'll pound your face in," one of them retorted.

A snicker. "Yeah, right. He's a total pansy."

"You haven't seen him lately."

Out of the corner of her eye, Marley saw the guy who'd mentioned Gashface lean on the table. His voice hushed a little, but the DJ lowered the music to call out something garbled, leaving a sound gap she could easily hear through. The other guys at the table leaned closer to the one talking.

"That stuff is doing something to him. He claims it's the cleanest high you'll ever get—no crash, no freakiness, but he's got an edge now, man. He says he's gonna kill the bitch that cut his face."

Marley froze. She didn't just stop moving—she went so cold on the inside that her teeth chattered once before she clamped them together. Her numb fingers could barely feel the glass she was holding.

Gashface was on flux, and the "bitch" was Riley.

"Yeah, right," another kid scoffed. "Says who?"

"Delwhip." The first guy took a casual pull from his beer bottle, clearly relishing having the floor. "His dad's got everything figured out. Gash will take out the bitch and her friends, and then he'll move on the board. We'll be back on top in a matter of days."

Marley's head spun, the implications almost too much to absorb. Tomorrow was Riley and Sam's wedding. Gashface was going to attack her at her freaking wedding?

Of course he was. *Take out the bitch and her friends.* That was what the kid had just said. Marley knew the name Delwhip, too. Both Delwhip senior and junior had been involved in the kidnapping—among other things—and the plan she'd just overheard was huge for so many reasons. Marley had to do something.

In the few seconds she'd tuned out, the conversation had moved on. One of the guys raised his voice.

"Get me some freaking *nachos*!" He slapped a pile of napkins onto the table to punctuate his demand.

"Hellz yeah!"

"I'm starving!"

"Nothing happening here anyway."

The guys finished their drinks and headed toward the exit, either unconvinced or uncaring that someone they called friend might be capable of something so horrible. Marley followed them, unable to be as cavalier.

She had to call Quinn and warn her, but of what? What if it was just a rumor? Sam would stop the wedding at any hint of danger to Riley, and Marley had hosted enough ceremonies at her inn to know what a hassle that would be. A false alarm would be one more black mark on her record.

"Where the hell are you going?" Anson asked. "He's in the other direction."

"I know. I'm following a lead." She said the words, but her steps slowed. She doubted these guys knew anything real, and trying to get information from them would risk her greater mission. They weren't her target right now, and following them was unlikely to take her to Gashface. She watched them for another couple of seconds, uncertain, but decided to let them go.

First things first. She'd finish the job she was here to do, then figure out what Delwhip was planning and stop it.

She was about to pivot when another guy came through the cascade of crystals covering the doorway to the entrance. He paused to look around, and their eyes met, locking for a second. A zing shot through Marley's center in a way it hadn't for…well, years.

He was tall, wearing straight-leg jeans and a golden-brown, distressed leather jacket over a navy T-shirt, all as expensive as the custom-made boots on his feet. He had dark blond hair, cut just long enough to brush the bottom of his neck. Its well-formed waves told her a professional stylist got her hands in it on a regular basis. The color looked natural, too, just a sun-bleached shade lighter than his eyebrows. Lashes long enough for her to see from twelve feet away framed silvery-blue eyes that practically sparked with electricity. Damn.

The eyes did it to her more than anything. Their intensity struck hard, interest flaring there as they fixed on her own odd-colored eyes. The leeching had drained most of their nearly violet color, leaving them almost white. People usually looked away half a second after seeing them. But his eyes were bright and deep, almost beckoning as they stared into hers. He wasn't unnerved.

Her body trembled a little, and she turned away, draining her glass for a second time. It was far more full this time, the burn more potent. Fire flashed through her torso and out to her limbs. She took a deep breath and slid into the crowd. She needed bodies behind her, insulation from the gaze she could still feel on her skin.

She knew that guy. She'd never met Gage Samargo, businessman-adventurer, CEO of GS Consulting, but she'd researched him—and a lot of men like him—in the last several weeks. Not only was he Numina, he was massively rich and powerful in his own right. His company was a hybrid, combining traditional business with innovation and philanthropy. He worked with start-ups whose central technology could help people or make someone rich, and he found a way for them to do both.

She'd read an in-depth article series by a reporter who'd gone with him to Africa two years ago. Gage Samargo worked with aid agencies, getting down in the dirt and blood, passing out food, teaching farming methods, and assisting doctors in the field. He routinely met with the lowest-paid government workers as well as high-level officials, and made sure to learn all about the politics of the region so the companies coming in could navigate properly.

It all sounded too good to be true, but nothing Marley had read about him had mentioned clubbing. He wasn't a playboy, and he didn't invest in the kinds of excess found in places like this. He was, however, descended from gods, and that made him a person of interest.

With enough distance to have regained her wits, she turned back and sought Gage, who now stood at the bar. The crowd bunched on either side of him, and both bartenders stood smiling in front of him. He gestured at the shelves and said something to a couple of the patrons watching him. They laughed, and he grinned back.

There went the zing again, right up her spine to the base of her skull, leaving tingles in its wake—and in parts of her that should be permanently dormant. She raised her hand to her neck, trying to smooth away the goose bumps. Even with his jacket on, his physical strength was apparent in the controlled grace of his movements, the ripple of muscle when he turned sideways and reached into his pocket for his wallet. She couldn't stop staring, noticing things like the shape of his wrist and the golden skin in the V of his T-shirt.

Gage shifted and their eyes met again. He stilled, hand in the air with a black card held between two fingers. She couldn't see the color of his eyes now that he was in deeper shadow. In fact, she shouldn't have been able to see it when he first came in, but there was no mistaking it: the brilliance was burned into her brain.

Another man's glowing blue eyes—gleaming with exultation as he leeched her of all her power—popped into her head. A skitter of panic overwhelmed the pleasurable tingles. Marley spun and took off toward the restrooms.

"Marley? Marley! What the—You know we'll lose signal in there. Marl—"

Anson's voice cut off when Marley pushed through the door of the ladies' room. Thank god there wasn't a line. Only one stall door was open, and she hurried into it as the main door opened behind her and the voices of about half-a-dozen women filled the room.

Marley spun the lock and set her purse on the toilet-paper holder, pressing her palms against the chilled metal of the door and inhaling deeply, slowly. It was too much at once, throwing her not just off balance, but into a completely discombobulated state. She needed to pull herself together.

Gage Samargo might be Numina, but he's not a leech. He has no reason to be one. And he'd be no threat to you even if he was.

Marley took another deep breath. He might not be that kind of threat, but her body told her he wasn't harmless. Her knees were still a little shaky. Even though she couldn't be leeched again, physical damage hadn't been all her ex had done. She doubted she'd ever be able to trust a man again. Worse, she wouldn't be able to trust herself.

Focus, Marley, she told herself. *Think about the facts.* Gage wasn't just Numina, he was the son of the damned secret society's leader. His presence here couldn't be coincidence, but he didn't even come close to fitting the profile of the Deimons.

Goddess abilities manifested in physical ways, but Numina influence was a special kind of intelligence, a way of looking at the world, seeing paths and making connections others might not, as well as an aura of charisma and charm. These were the men who were considered “natural leaders.” They held audiences mesmerized and made everyone love them and want to be near them, even when they were assholes. That got them whatever they wanted and could lead to huge levels of success in business, government, and other arenas of power.

But there were interrupted lines of descent, some families were weaker than others, and sometimes greed and corruption led to scandal and loss of status. Splinter groups had formed, like the one Delwhip ran, and the one that had abducted Quinn and Riley. That’s when the Society got wind of their existence and intentions.

Quinn, president of the Society, was now in careful, delicate negotiations with the Numina leadership—Gage’s father, in particular—to set up a summit so they could form a mutually beneficial relationship and decide how to deal with the splinters. Delwhip and others like him had been trying to undermine their progress toward the summit for months. And from what Marley had just heard in the club, he’d grown tired of throwing wrenches into the works and was going for a big play, using Gashface as a tool. She had to stop it.

But she had to finish what she was doing here, first. She couldn’t leave here without nullifying Josh. Marley was determined to keep the fluxed Deimons under control and off the leadership’s radar so they couldn’t do more damage than the splinter groups had already done.

A high-pitched, furious voice penetrated Marley’s reverie. “Did you see how drunk she was? How can he be into that?”

Marley glanced at her watch, stunned at how long she’d been hiding. She was surprised Anson hadn’t stormed the castle, ready to shit a brick. She picked up her purse and pulled out her phone. He'd texted her, and she hadn't heard it. She tapped out a quick reply that she was on her way out and stepped out of the stall. The two women at the sink gave her dirty looks, and as she strode out the door, she heard something about not flushing the toilet.

Oh well. She'd been less concerned about pretense than she had about regaining her composure. She pulled it around herself now, setting aside everything but the reason she was here.

Pausing at the end of the hall, she scanned the club instinctively. No sign of Gage Samargo anymore. Josh, however, stood a couple dozen yards away in a pseudo-VIP area filled with plush couches and chairs. He had one hand braced on a pillar, all the better to lean over the young woman pressed against it. His mouth moved rapidly, as if he was trying to talk her into something, and the woman looked a little freaked. Her eyes darted around, and she kept easing sideways. Josh moved with her, keeping her in place.

Marley tensed all over, her free hand curling into a fist. She needed to get this done without anyone noticing, and that was going to be hard the way things were set up. She only needed one touch, but between her and Josh were a long sofa, a couple of tables, and a couple dozen people.

"Servers heading your way," Anson told her through the comm, sounding disgruntled. "What the hell were you doing?"

"I had to go to the bathroom," Marley murmured, looking for a dark spot where she could wait for the right moment. She eased behind one large group of clubbers and then slipped between two threesomes who were too busy to notice. That put her next to a tall potted fern, of all the convenient clichés, where she could wait for the servers to finish doling out drinks and for the group to refocus. She cast out mental feelers to make sure Josh was the only fluxed Deimon in the bunch. She detected three other guys who were Numina but no more flux. Josh remained her only target.

Most goddesses could sense life and even differentiate between energy signatures, recognizing goddesses versus regular humans in an instant. Riley had also been able to tell when someone was Numina, a seemingly rare gift. Before Marley was leeched, detection of any kind hadn't been one of her greater abilities. Now, she had it in spades.

Maybe she always had it, she just didn't know, but the day she had accidentally nullified Sam, everything clicked into place.

Her displaced power had gone toxic inside Quinn, unable to return to its proper host, and they'd used Sam as a filter to save Quinn's life. It had been horrible watching Sam take in the poison. The screaming, the torment none of them could do anything about. Desperate, knowing she was ultimately responsible for Sam's pain, Marley had touched him, helpless to do anything but offer comfort. But then it *stopped.* The toxic energy disappeared—she'd felt it happen and so had Sam.

With the action came an awareness that she'd never had before, and she'd understood for the first time the extent of what Anson's leeching her to nothing had done. He'd taken away her power, but he'd also created something new. He'd carved an emptiness into her that wasn't static as they had thought—it had a purpose, its own power.

She had become a null. A black hole. She could remove power, energy, ability from someone who wasn't supposed to have it. Someone like Sam. Or like Josh, the Numina kid a few yards away trying to get in the pants of a woman who clearly didn't want him to.

Josh shoved the woman's shirt up to her rib cage and stuck his hand under it. She pushed his hand away, but he didn't let her go. Furious, Marley moved out from behind the plant.

His Numina signature was a faint hum on a singular frequency shared by three other guys in the vicinity. This close, the blue shine of flux that Marley could detect with her brain rather than her eyes almost stung her with its intensity. When the young woman tried to shove Josh away again, Marley's sense of the flux changed. It felt similar to touching a live wire, jagged and uncomfortable.

A handful of people headed toward the dance floor. This was Marley's best chance, and she should do it now, before Josh got more aggressive. She swept the area again, not seeing Gage or anyone else of importance.

"I'm going in," she told Anson in a low voice.

"Roger that."

She moved smoothly, careful not to bump anyone or draw attention by walking too quickly. Within a few steps she was behind Josh. His hands in the air, he'd somehow hauled the woman against his body without touching her. A faint, airy scream escaped her, but Josh bent toward her neck as if he were a vampire.

Marley kept moving, brushing a hand against his elbow as she passed. She felt the flux disappear as somewhere deep inside a brief, sharp pain throbbed. She stifled a gasp and faltered before moving toward the back door. Behind her, Josh gave a low moan.

The room seemed to dim, even more than it already was, the lights going faintly green. She squeezed her eyes closed for a second, trying to clear the haze. Another blink and it was gone.

"Meet me out back," she managed to whisper to Anson. She didn't want to linger in the back alley waiting for him. She should have said it sooner, but the unprecedented pain had distracted her.

"Already on my way," he assured her.

With her hand on the door's crash bar, Marley turned back. Josh was on his knees, his face in his hands. A couple of his friends stood over him. One looked around, scowling. At least the young woman Josh had been leaning over was on the other side of the room, huddling with her friends and casting a look at Josh that was both disgusted and worried.

Marley had to get out of there. She pushed at the door, but a new figure loomed in front of her. This time she couldn't hold in her gasp.

"I think that door's alarmed," said Gage Samargo, gesturing at a sign. "If you're going to yack, the bathroom's that way. Or you can use that plant." This time he pointed to the fern she'd hidden next to earlier.

Marley's heart thundered. Had he been watching her? Why?

She straightened, letting her hand drop. She knew the alarm was disabled—Anson had done it when they first got here, and she'd intended to reset it as she went through. But in front of Gage she pretended she hadn't noticed the sign, or hadn't cared.

"I'm not going to yack," she assured him. "Just need some air."

"I bet." His easygoing demeanor disappeared, though he stood relaxed, hands tucked in his jeans pockets. His navy T-shirt was snug across his chest, looser over his abs but in a way that still showed how taut they were. She was close enough to see the bright blue of his eyes even better than before, silver threads adding a unique shine that she could never confuse with a leech's glow.

Marley swallowed—or tried to. Her throat had dried up.

They stood for several seconds, eyeballing each other. She wondered what he was thinking, since he didn't have the same look of uneasy curiosity most people wore when they first saw her eyes up close.

"I'm looking for my brother," Gage finally said. "Do you know him?"

Her brow tightened. Why would he ask her that? Did he somehow know *her*? Even if he did, what connection did he think she had to him?

She responded the way she would if she had no clue who Gage was. "I don't know. Who's your brother?"

"Sorry. Aiden Samargo?" He reached into his jacket and pulled out a phone. After waking the screen, he showed her a picture.

Marley kept her face blank as she looked. "Is he missing?" She recognized Aiden and knew the other guy in the photo with him. He was also Numina, though she couldn't recall his name.

"In a manner of speaking." He swiped to another shot. "How about these guys?" He showed her more photos of men, most in their twenties, that Marley had seen before. Their fathers were all involved in the summit negotiations.

She shook her head. "Sorry." She didn't meet his eyes, not wanting him to see that she was skirting the truth. But her gaze landed on his full, unhappy mouth, and she imagined using small, soft kisses to loosen it up until he had no choice but to kiss her back.

Ugh. Not the time or place for that.

"Wish I could help you," she managed, taking a step to go around him. "Good luck." She hoped she could get past Josh without him spotting her and figuring out what she'd done, but Gage shifted to block her. Her head snapped up, and she braced her feet, ready to deal with him physically if she had to.

He noticed, judging by the way his gaze sharpened and his weight moved from his heels to the balls of his feet.

Marley raised her eyebrows at him. He smirked and stood down, his shoulders relaxing before he turned to the side to let her pass.

She managed to keep her pace normal as she moved, even throwing an extra sway into her hips because she had no doubt he was watching her leave. She had no idea why he'd even approached her, but a sense of dread told her this wasn't the last encounter she'd have with him.

As she left the club and went out into the crisp, smoke-saturated fall air, she admitted it wasn't *all* dread.

CHAPTER TWO

The man is full of relentless charm, but where his peers may wear it as a surface glamour, Gage Samargo's runs bone deep. He works tirelessly from predawn to midnight, eagerly taking on any necessary task. In a typical day in central Africa, this might include digging wells, conducting business meetings, assisting a local doctor with field surgery, and playing footie with schoolchildren.
—*Wall Street Journal* article series

Instinct told Gage to just let the woman go, but it also told him she was hiding something. Her hips had swayed as she strode away in her snug dress and impossibly high heels. Her dark red hair was piled tightly on her head, and her movements had a graceful athleticism and strength. She could easily use those feminine wiles to trick any man.

Gage hesitated. He'd seen her touch Josh before he'd collapsed on the floor, too. He didn't know what she'd done, but she'd done something. She'd been too fast to use a syringe, though, and he'd have sworn her hand was empty when he'd watched it all go down.

His skin crawled as another thought struck him. If his theories on the research he'd done for his father were right, then flux was energy based, not a typical street drug. With a single touch, this woman could have just passed Josh some of the drug. Josh's reaction wasn't completely unlike an addict's right after a hit, either. And this woman…well, she was pretty enough, mysterious enough, and confident enough to be a goddess. Just like the one rumored to be dealing the flux.

Maybe she was worth following…

But Josh was Numina, and Gage had known him for years. Sure, he and his friends were younger than Aiden, but they were close enough to be worth questioning. Josh was even on the interrogation list his father had provided for Gage, after sending Aiden undercover to learn about the Deimons had backfired so badly.

Aiden hadn't just failed to give their father information for his talks with the Society for Goddess Education and Defense—he'd practically disappeared. He'd called twice: once to say he wasn't following through on the assignment, and once to tell their father he was okay but wouldn't be in touch for a while. He hadn't responded to any of Gage's text messages, e-mails, or phone calls, and Gage had been unable to track the GPS on his phone. His brother's silence told him that something was very wrong. They hadn't been out of contact for this long in their entire lives.

Gage blew out a breath, looking from the group around Josh to the entrance and back. He probably *should* stay here and ask Josh and his friends about Aiden and the flux. But he'd already been stymied by others just like them. No one would talk about it, and if they knew anything about Aiden, they were obeying some bro code of silence. Gage's expectations of getting anywhere with these tactics was low as it was, and with Josh's current state, Gage might not get the most productive answers.

Decision made, it didn't take him long to catch up with the redhead, hindered as she was by her tight dress and tall heels.

She sent a text or e-mail on her way outside and then stopped at the curb, looking back and forth as if waiting for someone. Gage handed his ticket to the valet and hovered behind a group congregating near the podium while he quickly called his father with an update.

He picked up immediately. "Son. You learn anything?"

"I don't know. No sign of Aiden, but something happened…" He described the incident with Josh.

"The woman had white eyes, you said?" His father sounded as excited as he ever outwardly showed. "She could be the goddess providing the drug. I've heard murmurs about a woman with white eyes."

"What kind of murmurs?"

"I'm not sure. Nothing concrete, and I can't remember any specifics. It might not be something I heard directly, just background conversation. But it's too coincidental—she must be involved."

A small black SUV pulled to the curb, and the woman opened the door. Gage watched her hemline rise high on her thighs when she climbed up and swiveled her legs inside. "That's what I was thinking, too. I need to find out more."

"What about talking to Josh directly? He's on the list. He might have some information on her."

"I wouldn't count on it. You know they've all been closemouthed about everything."

"I don't know where everyone learned to be so secretive," his father growled.

Gage watched the SUV angle to pull out into traffic, but it had to wait for a stream of cars. *Come on, come on*, he urged silently as the valet approached way too slowly with Gage's car, parking behind the SUV.

"You're kidding, right?" Gage asked his father. He passed a tip to the valet and, using the loitering club-hoppers as cover, circled behind his car to get in. Since it was already running, the Bluetooth paired the phone and transferred the call to the speaker.

"Of course I'm kidding." His father sighed. "Well, keep me posted. We don't have any meetings tomorrow. Quinn Caldwell and her team have a wedding or something, so I'll be in the office."

Of course he would. It was Saturday. Forget the idea that he could take a day off when the leader of the goddesses did. All the more reason for him not to, in fact. Harmon Samargo, CEO of one of the largest shipping and transportation conglomerates in the world, was focusing all his time on the summit negotiations with the Society these days. Protecting Numina was his top priority next to his sons, and a handful of bad seeds had damaged his ability to do so. Gage guessed it was no surprise that his father wasn't taking a break.

He grinned and gunned the engine of his crimson Viper, passing a slow-moving minivan but keeping a couple of cars between him and the SUV. His sports car was too unique for stealth activities, but hopefully the woman had no reason to think he'd follow her.

"Be careful, son. And don't be misguided by my interest in the goddess. Your priority is your brother."

"Got it, Dad."

The car beeped as his father disconnected their call, and Gage concentrated on the SUV. A few minutes later, it pulled into a hotel parking garage. He watched the gate swing down behind it with GUESTS ONLY written across the striped bar.

Okay, so he'd become a guest.

He drove around the block to the front of the hotel and waved off the valet when he got out. He'd need immediate access to his car later.

Inside, Gage approached the clerk smiling at him from the check-in desk.

She poised her hands over her keyboard "How can I help you, sir?"

"Hi…Allie." He read her name off her tag. "I need a room,

please."

"One night?" Her fingernails click-clacked on the keys.

"Indefinite."

She frowned at her screen. "I can give you until next weekend. Then I'm afraid we're fully booked." She flashed her perfect teeth. "Family weekend for a few of the area colleges. But I can certainly let you know if something opens up before then."

"That's fine. It probably won't be that long." He handed over his Black Card. "Listen, a friend of mine is staying here right now, too. She didn't give me her room number, but I'd like to be on her floor. Can you arrange that?"

Her sunny expression dimmed a bit. "I can try. What's her name?"

He smiled, rueful. "It's under her boyfriend's name, and I don't know him. I'm supposed to meet him for the first time this week. She's a redhead, and she's got unusually light eyes."

The woman perked up. "Oh, I remember them! And his name was unusual, too. Like a hurricane. No, tornado. Let me find you an appropriate room." She winked and went to town on the keyboard, gave Gage a paper to sign, and ran his card. Less than a minute later she handed him his keycards, leaning toward him with a knowing look and lowering her voice. "They actually have adjoining rooms on the twelfth floor, not a shared room. You might still have a chance." She winked and turned to someone behind Gage.

Bemused at her assumption that his "friend" was more than that, he crossed the gleaming lobby to the gold-colored elevator and hit the up button.

The elevator took him straight to twelve and let him out into a hallway that smelled faintly of gardenias. He frowned at the arrangement on the table in front of the elevator bank. The flower had been his mother's favorite, and there had been a ton of them at her funeral. He'd only been nine at the time, but it was the kind of thing that stuck with a guy. He hoped there weren't any in the hotel room.

The hallway was empty as he made his way to his room, his footfalls silent on the thickly padded carpeting. The floral scent faded with distance, and he breathed easier. His room was just past the corner where two halls met. As he unlocked his door, the one next to his opened. The redhead stepped out, luckily with her back to him, carrying an ice bucket. Gage darted into his room and eased the door closed. Allie had earned herself high marks for putting him right next to his "friend."

Gage stood just inside his door until the woman returned. This was a quality hotel, but he could still hear the clatter of ice in the plastic bucket when she set it on the table next to their shared wall, followed by the *click* of a light switch. Satisfied that he'd know when she left—and pretty sure that it wouldn't be immediate—he left to park his car in the garage and retrieve his duffel.

• • •

Saturday afternoon found Marley lurking in the shadows of the unoccupied side balcony of a centuries-old church, unseen by the people waiting below. She stifled a yawn, resenting the wasted hours she'd spent digging for information that was nowhere to be found. Her only option had been to show up for a wedding she'd had no intention of attending.

The whispered conversations hissed off the stone walls, echoed by the polished wooden pews and getting caught in the high, raftered ceiling. She'd been here since long before anyone else had arrived, even before the florist and the rep from the historical society that represented the church. Luckily, no one had ventured upstairs.

Anson was stationed in the cemetery outside with a wide view of the area so he could warn Marley when Gashface approached. Since they'd been unable to find any information to confirm or disprove what she'd overheard in the club, she had no choice but to operate on the assumption that it was accurate. She'd warned Anson to stay out of sight. His presence would be as disruptive to the wedding as Gashface's. Quinn and Nick, and Sam and Riley would never understand why Marley was working with Anson Tournado, of all people. It sounded ridiculous even to her, despite how well it had worked so far.

She hadn't known when she'd run away what she was going to do with her newly discovered ability to nullify power. She just knew everything had to change. She went home to Maine and sold her inn—the amount of land, worth even more than the building, had sold for enough money to cover her expenses for years. Then she'd spent some time meditating, trying to understand herself better, to be more in touch with her body. She'd trained physically, growing stronger and learning to fight. Goddess-Marley had lived a passive, quiet life and barely knew how to throw a punch. No matter how successful Quinn was with the Numina summit, Marley knew the battle wasn't over. She knew that she had to do whatever she could to protect the goddesses and the Society, even if she didn't truly belong there anymore.

But she hadn't known how she was going to help, how to turn her new ability into something beneficial. Or even if she could do it again. That was why she went after Anson in the first place.

She had to test the nullification, and he was the one man she knew she could test it on. Though Quinn had rendered Anson unable to leech anyone again, there had been a residue that she hadn't been able to remove, leaving him with a tiny bit of toxic energy that had obviously made him sick like it had Quinn. If Marley could nullify power, she'd be able to get to it.

Anson had grown up in LA, so after property-record searches, Marley prowled around his neighborhood until she found him outside a seedy bar, practically in the gutter. She'd touched him and cured him. The toxic energy disappeared.

She'd intended to leave him there once her test was done, but he'd followed her and made a pest of himself until she agreed to let him help her. At first, they'd done mundane digging into all things Numina, learning everything they could about the leadership and anyone else who might be relevant. Anson was as skilled as Sam at research and possibly better at hacking. Besides, it was better than being completely alone. Anson did everything she asked and never made a suspicious move. Maybe he wanted redemption as much as she did.

She and Quinn had exchanged information, with Marley dodging all personal discussion and pretending that little bit was involvement enough. Then she'd stumbled across mention of the Deimons in a disturbing Facebook post. They'd dug deeper, and she'd found her purpose. She couldn't tell Quinn about that part though—it'd only make things worse. Marley had to handle it on her own.

The church's side door opened, and a man in a suit carrying a Bible entered, followed by Quinn and Nick. The suited man, probably a justice of the peace, took position in front of the altar. Quinn and Nick stood on either side of him. Marley's eyes prickled when they smiled at each other, love apparent in both their gazes, even from this distance. They'd been married a couple of months ago in a quiet civil ceremony in Ohio. Quinn had asked Marley to attend but hadn't seemed surprised when she said she couldn't.

Her throat tightened with regret, but she swallowed hard. It was too late now, and she doubted she'd have done anything differently anyway. It didn't matter how sincere Quinn was about wanting her there. Marley doubted Nick felt the same, and she would have felt like a fraud the entire time.

Nick's driving motivation was Quinn's well-being. He'd never said anything directly to Marley, but she could tell he held little regard for her. She'd put the woman he loved in danger. He was a legacy protector, with protector parents, assigned essentially as bodyguards for goddesses who didn't have access to their power source and were in danger. He'd recently taken over as leader of the Protectorate, an organization as old as the Society. It wasn't surprising he didn't like Marley after her role in the leechings.

Sam Remington, Riley's groom, had also trained as a protector after he quit his job as Quinn's assistant. He was more compassionate than Nick, more tolerant, and if he suspected Marley had anything to do with taking away his pain, he probably looked at her more favorably than Nick did. His tolerance dried up abruptly, however, the second there was a hint of danger targeting Riley.

Anson had plenty of experience in just how capable those two were—and he'd experience it again should they ever find out Marley was working with him. He'd spent the morning whining that Marley should just tell them what she'd heard. There was no way Sam would let Gashface within ten yards of Riley, but Marley knew he would sacrifice himself in the process, if necessary, and that would kind of put a damper on the wedding day.

No, she had to do this for her friends. It was the least she could do for all the hell they'd been through because of her. And if *she* owed them, for damned sure Anson did, too.

She checked her watch, then peered out one of the narrow windows. With ten minutes until the ceremony's official start time, guests still straggled up the walk. Marley recognized a few goddesses. Neither Sam nor Riley had close family anymore, but Marley assumed some of the other guests were distant relatives and maybe friends from before everything turned upside down.

As long as she and Anson both stayed out of sight, Marley would never have any questions to answer.

A violinist situated down below played a short introduction. The guests settled with a rustle, and the woman launched into the wedding march. Marley moved silently to the end of the balcony to watch the main entry. The double doors drifted open, and Riley and Sam stepped through, arm in arm. Unusual though it was for the bride and groom to enter together, Marley thought it was beautiful, demonstrating their equal relationship, their support of each other as their sole family. Riley looked radiant in her simple white gown, Sam tall and strong and happy.

Goddamn Gashface and Delwhip for being arrogant, destructive assholes, but Marley was glad they'd given her reason to witness this. She pressed her lips together and clamped down on the well of sentiment threatening to break her down. She would *not* give away her presence by sniffling.

She watched the justice of the peace greet everyone and run them through the traditional service, mixing Corinthians and other stuff she recognized, until Sam cradled Riley's face and bent to kiss her.

Marley stood in her dark corner, aching at the distance between herself and the happy, smiling group below. Nothing had happened. No attack. No sign of Gashface at all. She'd put herself through this for nothing.

Can the self-pity. This was your choice. But it was one thing to know in her head how she would feel being near them again and quite another to actually live it.

Her phone buzzed. Anson's signal that Gashface was approaching, since he was too far away for their comms. She slipped over to the window. Gashface strode up the hill toward the church, opposite the parking area and the main door. He'd gotten a bit heavier since last spring and had overcompensated by graduating to larger clothing. His khakis and polo were baggy on him, but the layer of padding could be hiding enough muscle to give her a challenge. That, and the weapons he no doubt carried.

He headed for the side door she'd entered through earlier. Whether he would come up to the balcony or stay on the main floor depended on the depth of his intent. Which was stronger—his need for revenge, which meant he'd go directly for Riley, or the power of the guy who'd hired him? Delwhip would have stressed keeping his distance so as not to be identified.

Marley was betting on revenge, though. The scar Riley had given him blazed an angry red—three parallel tears across his left cheek. He unsheathed a wicked-looking knife as he walked. Yep—he wanted revenge.

Marley quietly ran down the stairs to the tiny foyer at the bottom and pressed her back against the wall. A flare of flux approached the door, revealing his proximity. Seconds later, the door latch clinked and the door swung open. She took two seconds to assess his position and calculate her moves, and within two more she'd kicked the knife from his hand and spun to elbow him in the nose. The blow knocked him back, out of the church, so his cry of pain hit open air instead of echoing indoors and calling attention to them. Marley kept moving forward, using her hardest parts against his most vulnerable: fist to groin, elbow to solar plexus, head to the already-bruised nose, foot to knee. His legs buckled, and he went down. Marley lifted her booted foot and brought the heel down at the base of his neck, flattening him.

"You stupid bitch." Gash growled out a few filthy curses as he writhed and twisted to get free. Marley bent to touch him, to nullify him, but this time he was ready and she was too slow. He used the flux, an invisible push knocking her off him. She stumbled a couple of steps before halting in a crouch.

He didn't waste time trying to get up. Lifting his head and shoulders off the ground, he raised his hands, palms out, fingers spread. His dark eyes blazed with fury, and his upper lip peeled back to bare his teeth, spittle strung between them. A hissing growl came out of his throat.

She threw herself into a side roll so his attempt to grab and throw her through the air failed. Her move brought her closer to him, but the knife was lying in the grass on his other side. He lunged for it, landing on his stomach a few inches from the weapon. Marley dashed at him, but he scrambled to his hands and knees and grabbed the knife just as she reached him. He roared and slashed at her, barely missing when she curved her body away. His momentum threw off his balance again. She kicked, and the knife arced through the air. A punch to his temple simultaneously knocked him out and nullified him. As the blue shine of the flux disappeared, there was an accompanying deep throb, just like the night before. And then nothing.

"Son of a bitch," Marley panted. She braced her hands on her knees for a few seconds until her pulse stopped racing and her chest no longer heaved from the adrenaline.

She walked over to pick up the knife. It was well balanced and very sharp, and now it was hers. She went back and patted him down until she found a sheath attached to his belt. She yanked it off and snapped it around her own, securing the knife before checking him for other weapons. He'd tucked a Ruger into his rear waistband. That would've been slightly more effective. No doubt he'd planned to use the flux to throw the knife, altering its course if necessary and probably adding an extra shove when it struck. Then he'd use the gun on the other three, assuming none of them spotted him. Once he was inside, Riley could have sensed his presence without looking, and the moon, Quinn's source, was close enough to full for her to use its power to disable him with a flick of her wrist.

A glance at the church reassured her they were still undetected, but that wouldn't last long. The ceremony had to be close to over, and while most of the people who would pour out of the building would have no clue who Marley was or what she was doing there, she couldn't expect that no one would recognize her and tell Quinn.

And she still didn't want anyone to know she was the one taking the flux. When they'd hacked into the Deimons' message board to track their intentions and movements, she'd learned that the first few guys she'd ever nullified had tried to get more flux afterward but hadn't been able to accept it. That meant the more Deimons Marley nullified, the bigger the group that would want revenge. Her window for finding the rogue goddess distributing the flux and figuring out a way to stop her was narrowing.

With her newly honed strength—like her senses, enhanced by the flux she'd taken in—she heaved Gash up by his collar and dragged him down the hill, ignoring his moans and weak struggles when he came to halfway there. A silver BMW was parked on the road that wound through the cemetery. She threw him against a headstone a dozen yards from his car and towered over him with her hands on her hips.

"Who sent you?" she demanded. She wanted confirmation of the gossip.

He shaded his eyes against the sun. "No one. I'm here for myself."

"Bullshit. You wouldn't have waited so many months to act. Someone showed you the carrot. Who?"

Gashface struggled upright and tried to look nonchalant, draping his wrists over his knees. But his sullenness ruined the attempt. He didn't seem to have even noticed that the flux was gone. Maybe he thought he'd used it up in the fight.

She waited. Finally, he rolled his eyes. "Tournado did. He's back in the game, and he's going after Remington in there for taking everything he had."

Marley laughed. "You are such a liar." She wasn't naive enough to think Anson would never go behind her back to get revenge on her friends, but she did know he was too smart to have let it all play out like this.

He gaped. "No, I'm not. He—"

She crouched and slid his knife from its sheath in one move, holding it with a backhand grip as she leaned into his face. "Tell me. Who sent you." She wasn't fooling around anymore. She'd use the knife if she had to, and the dangerous edge to her voice proved it.

He stopped trying to put her off. "Delwhip."

"Senior or junior?"

He shrugged one shoulder. "What's the difference?"

"Were you to kill?" Her stomach went sour when he nodded, not meeting her eyes. "Who?"

"Kordek first, then Remington, then the Jarretts if I could get to them. The woman last."

Weakest to strongest, relatively speaking, but also a deliberate order as each death would impact the others more. They wanted maximum disruption to keep Quinn from spearheading the Society's partnership with Numina. Marley doubted Delwhip really cared if Riley went down first, but it was incentive to keep Gash on track.

"Thanks." Marley jerked him forward, then rapped his head on the stone behind him. He slumped over, unconscious. She almost left him there, but she didn't know how long the wedding party would linger, so she hauled him to his car and tossed him in the trunk, kinking the inside release pull so it wouldn't work properly. He'd get himself out—eventually.

She scanned the graveyard and got ready to text Anson, but before she got a hand on her phone, an engine rumbled up the road. A moment later, their SUV pulled up behind the BMW. Marley got in, glancing over her shoulder as she did. A chill swept over her when she saw Riley standing at the top of the hill, staring down at her.

How long had she been there? How much had she seen? There was a good chance she wouldn't recognize Marley. She'd dyed her hair auburn when she'd changed her life and the sunglasses she wore hid her eyes. For sure, she'd never worn black leather and ass-kicker boots before, and Riley had never known Marley to be willing to or capable of fighting like that. But the way the bride stood, her bouquet hanging forgotten at her side, veil and train fluttering unheeded in the strong breeze…

Marley slammed the door on longing and the vehicle at the same time.

CHAPTER THREE

A global society is dependent upon cross-cultural cooperation in all realms, be they business, social, economic, or entertainment.
—GS Consulting brochure

"Where is he?" Anson gunned the SUV past the BMW, craning around to look for Gashface.

"In the trunk."

A smile played around his mouth. "Did he give you a struggle?"

"Hardly." She checked the sky, which had grown overcast in the last half hour, but it was only lightly clouded, not stormy enough to account for the green tint everything seemed to have. The wind had picked up a little, too, but not sufficiently to bend the trees along the side of the road that way. A little queasy, she focused inside the vehicle instead of looking out the window.

"He admitted Delwhip sent him and that he was supposed to kill them all."

Anson whistled. "Then I guess you did the right thing."

"And he was on flux."

His eyebrows went up again. "Did you ask him where he got it?"

Her hand clenched in her lap. "He doesn't even know I took it. If I asked about it, I'd be revealing myself. So no."

"Good thing I know where we're going then." A little of his old arrogance showed in his smirk when he flipped on the turn signal and checked for traffic before turning onto a major road.

Marley was distracted by a dark red Viper they passed at the stoplight to their left. It looked familiar. She couldn't remember where she'd seen it before. Last night, maybe? They weren't common.

And then she realized what Anson had said. "Wait, where are we going?"

"Upstate New York."

Why the hell…

She drew in a breath, understanding sweeping away her irritation. "You found her. How?"

He shrugged. "I found evidence of where she might be. Some of the data I was running came together overnight."

"Where?"

"Halfway between Albany and Hudson. On a farm in a tiny burg called North Chatham."

Marley checked the side mirror but didn't see the Viper, Nick's vintage Charger, or the Camaro Sam drove. Not even a limo or rented sedan that might be more appropriate for a wedding than a macho sports car. Riley must not have recognized her.

"Any reason to think the goddess is there now?" Marley asked.

"She could be. There's lots of credit-card activity by suspected Deimons in that area once a month, and the timing is right."

She tried not to let anticipation bubble into excitement. It was hardly proof. "Okay, then. North Chatham it is." She glanced at her watch. "How long to get there?"

"Two and a half, three hours."

"Let me know if you want me to drive." He never did, so she folded her arms, slumped in her seat, and closed her eyes to grab a nap.

Not five seconds later, her phone rang. She sighed but didn't move.

"You gonna get that?"

"No."

It rang again, loud in the confines of the SUV. Marley felt Anson eying her and sensed his amusement.

"They spotted you, didn't they?"

She ignored him, but she couldn't ignore the phone anymore. It was her own fault she'd been spotted, and now she had to explain what had happened and why she hadn't stayed.

She put the phone to her ear. "Yeah."

"You don't sound happy to hear from me," Quinn said wryly.

"Why are you calling me when your best friends are getting married?" Marley winced not just at her defensive tone but at the words themselves. She should have thought that through a little.

"So you *did* get the invitation."

"I got it."

"You didn't RSVP."

Marley pinched the bridge of her nose, squeezing her eyes closed. "Do we have to talk about this? It's a little late now."

"True, which is why I was so surprised when Riley told me she saw you at the church a little while ago."

"I'd be surprised, too," Marley said. She considered claiming Riley was mistaken, but she couldn't lie to her sister. Their parents had given Quinn up for adoption. They'd only been teenagers, and more than eight years later, they'd married, had Marley, and never told either daughter about her sister. Marley had found the paperwork when she was a kid, but Quinn didn't know about Marley until a few years ago, when the whole leech thing happened. Bad circumstances to meet family for the first time, and Marley had struggled to be worthy of the relationship Quinn offered ever since. And failed miserably, multiple times. Deliberate lying just compounded it all.

"Want to guess what we found?" A burst of sound followed Quinn's question. Laughter and cheering. Marley could picture the guests sending Riley and Sam off to the reception in a fancy, crepe-paper-decorated car.

"No," she said, again truthfully.

"Too bad. It was Gashface. In the trunk of a car near the church. Riley watched you put him there, and then she watched you get into an SUV with someone else and drive off."

Crap. Marley focused on the first part and hoped she could deflect Quinn away from the second. "He was going to kill you guys."

Quinn snorted. "You mean he was going to try?"

"Okay, yes, he was going to try. But even if he never got to the altar, it would have ruined the entire day. I didn't want that to happen."

After a pause, Quinn said, "Thank you. I know Riley and Sam will appreciate it when I tell them. Who sent him?"

"Why do you think someone sent him?" Quinn would want to know the whole story, but Marley didn't plan to tell them about the flux and the rogue goddess until it was no longer an issue.

"Riley has seen him three times since she first gave him those scars. He didn't do anything then."

Marley could have debated how circumstantial that was—questioned the conditions, pointed out the symbolism of doing it on her wedding day, blah, blah, blah. But she knew Quinn wouldn't let it go, not even to put it off until after the wedding stuff. "It was Delwhip."

Quinn cursed. "I knew it. He's fought against every stride we've made with Numina. If his brother-in-law weren't the former president, they'd have kicked him to the curb a long time ago. Or worse." She said something away from the phone, probably to Nick.

Back on the line, she asked, "How did you know?"

"Um, I overheard some guys and took a chance that it wasn't big talk by little men. Since it was Gashface, you know, I was worried."

A deep voice rumbled in the background. The phone rasped, as if Quinn had held it against her body, and Marley heard her make a sharp exclamation. The voice responded, and Marley frowned. That cadence wasn't Nick's. It was Sam's.

"Where are you?" Marley asked.

"At the church. Where did you think I was?"

"The whole point of keeping this from you guys was to avoid disrupting their wedding day. Why aren't you all on your way to the reception?"

"Why are you fraternizing with the enemy?"

Crap crap crap crap crap.

Marley played dumb. "What are you talking about?"

"The SUV. Riley got the plate, and Sam pulled the registration."

"On his wedding day? At a two-hundred-year-old church? You're telling me they have Wi-Fi?" She forced a scathing tone but knew it wouldn't work. She was so busted.

"He has a broadband card and a lot more legal access now than he used to."

She wondered what that meant, but it didn't matter. Not now. "So?"

"So, Riley wouldn't do wedding photos until he ran it."

There wasn't anything Marley could say in a phone conversation that would be an adequate defense. Anything Quinn and the others could possibly be thinking about Marley, admitting she was working with Anson Tournado would be a thousand times worse. So she sat in silence, the hiss of tires on the pitted pavement the only sound.

"Come on, Marley. Tell me what the hell you're doing with the man who ruined your life."

Before Marley could do more than open her mouth with

absolutely no clue what to say, her phone beeped a low-battery signal.

"Marley."

The phone beeped again. "Sorry, Quinn. Battery's dying. I'll explain later." She hit the button to disconnect, then held down the power button, almost breathless at the reprieve.

Which was short-lived.

"Your sister's got your number now, huh?"

Marley dropped the phone into the console next to her seat and flipped her bangs out of her eyes. "My sister has always had my number." In every way that phrase could be interpreted.

"What was she calling about?"

"You."

Anson flicked a glance at her but didn't grin or look pleased. He also didn't make any snarky comments. "How'd she know?"

"Riley saw your plates." She shook her head. "Why is this registered under your real name?"

He shrugged. "What would be the point?"

She supposed he was right. After all, hiding his identity hadn't stopped *her* from finding him.

"I take it she's not happy," Anson said.

"She wouldn't be if I'd let her get past the question of why."

He stopped at a light and looked directly at Marley. "What will you tell her? When you stop avoiding the issue."

She stared through the windshield. "You know why I'm working with you."

"Yeah, but is that what you'd tell her?"

She finally looked over at him. The conversation with her sister made her really see him. He'd lost weight, his natural slimness almost crossing over to scrawny. The bones and tendons in his wrists strained the taut skin over them. His eyes were dull and sunken, framed with bruise-like shadows, settled above sharp cheekbones and a brittle-looking jaw.

Overall, he still looked better than when she'd found him in LA, and she liked to think a sense of purpose, the opportunity to make things right, was at least partially responsible.

"I'll tell her the truth," she finally answered his question. Satisfied, he focused on the road again. Marley reclined her seat a little and closed her eyes. The radio came on, the volume low, tuned to some local pop/rock station. She let it float around her as she drifted off to sleep.

• • •

A couple of hours later, Anson woke her. She blinked back the haze of the half sleep she'd been in, surprised it had been so long. The SUV rolled slowly down a country road, fully residential with no streetlights or sidewalks but plenty of towering trees that had dumped yellow, red, and brown leaves all over the road and the yards.

She pulled the lever to raise her seat and lowered her window a little. "This is it?" The sharp tang of burned leaves mingled with wood smoke and gave the chilly air an illusion of warmth.

"The bustling metropolis of North Chatham, New York," Anson confirmed. "Or is that sleepy village?"

Most definitely the latter. Some of the homes lining the street were close to the road, others set back a little. Most were on the large side, colonial in style, with a few Cape Cods thrown in. Cheery lights glowed next to painted front doors and from homey windows.

They passed a house with a UNITED STATES POST OFFICE sign, a single white church, and tiny Colonial with a long handicapped ramp and a sign proclaiming it the North Chatham Free Library.

Five seconds later, they were on their way out of town.

"That's it?" Marley twisted to look through the back window, surprised at her nostalgia. The village reminded her of home, the inn she'd owned in Maine.

"For the center of town, yeah, I assume so." He glanced at the GPS in the dash. "The farm is a couple more miles."

Marley settled back in her seat and turned an alert eye to what was ahead. It was nearly eight thirty at night, late enough to be dark but not so late there weren't other cars around. They'd have to do a quick scope now and come back later to really check out the place. They had a lot to learn if they were going to find a way to stop the goddess from giving out flux.

"There it is." Anson pulled the SUV into a gravelly cutout on the side of the road and turned off the engine. It ticked slowly down while they studied the open land across the street.

Not that they could see much. Two silos towered against the sky, which glowed a faint orange from the lights of Albany half an hour away. Marley assumed the long, shadowed building near the silos was the barn, set back a few hundred yards from the road. She couldn't see a farmhouse, but there were a few smaller buildings speckling the property. Despite the lack of visible details, the whole place gave off an air of abandonment. Marley listened hard, but only crickets and katydids sang their songs at deafening levels, too loud for her to hear anything else in the distance.

They sat for a few minutes, watching nothing happen. Not even a breeze stirred the nearby underbrush. Then lights flashed in the rearview mirror. Anson grunted and started the truck, causing Marley to focus on the car that rolled slowly past them. The car that said DEPUTY SHERIFF on the passenger-side door.

"Hell." Marley adjusted her seat belt as Anson got back on the road. "Let him get farther ahead and just turn around. We'll get a motel and come back later."

As soon as a curve in the road hid them from sight, Anson did a three-point turn and headed back the way they'd come. About ten minutes later they drove into the nearest "big" town, Valatie, and found a quaint little motel. Anson checked them in—it was too dark for Marley to wear sunglasses to hide her eyes, and they made her too recognizable.

"Want to grab something to eat?" Anson tossed his bag into the room he'd just unlocked and prepared to close the door again.

Marley glanced across the parking lot to a shopping strip across the street, anchored by a brightly lit pizza joint. "I'm just gonna order in. We'll go back about midnight."

He nodded and stuck his room key in his pocket before strolling toward the sidewalk.

Marley went into her own room and locked the chain behind her. She dug through the small pile of brochures next to the phone and called the pizza place to order a meatball sub for delivery. Half an hour later, showered and fed, she stretched out with her laptop to review the information Anson had sent her before they'd left for the wedding that morning. He'd gathered credit-card transactions, travel data, and property search results and fed them through some kind of program that sorted and compiled the info, then laid it all out in charts. Slick.

As he'd said, the information indicated clusters of young Numina—some they'd suspected of being Deimons and some that didn't surprise her even though she and Anson hadn't had them on the list—spent a couple of days here around this time every month.

The farm he'd pinpointed was currently owned by AS Services. Marley had never heard of it, but it was probably a DBA or a holding company or something. The guy who'd handled the sale a few months ago was a manager for a real estate investment trust, half of whose board of directors were Numina.

None of this connected them to the rogue goddess directly, but Marley had gleaned enough from the cryptic Deimon discussions Anson had hacked into to know that new initiates had to go to a remote location and prove their worthiness to receive flux. It wasn't just a pay up, take it, and leave sort of thing. The farm, as rundown as it was, fit the bill.

An icon flashed in the corner of the laptop screen and a chime signaled an incoming video call. Marley frowned at it. She used the program to instant message with Anson but had never done a videoconference. Her default setting must be "Available," but who would know how to find her?

She rolled her eyes. That was a stupid question.

She touched the icon to accept the call and the program swept over her screen. A tiny box with her chin and chest in it popped into one corner, and Riley's and Sam's faces crowded the center.

"Hi, Marley." Sam's voice rumbled through her speakers. "Hey, adjust your camera. We can't see you."

She didn't move. They didn't need to read her that closely. "You guys are supposed to be on your honeymoon. Or at least on a plane to get there."

"We leave in the morning." Riley scowled. "Come on, this is annoying. Fix the screen."

Marley sighed and pushed the top of the laptop back until the camera was aimed at her face.

Riley squealed. "I love the red! When did you do that?"

"Seriously?" Sam turned to look at his wife. "We've got an assassin on lockdown and you're talking about her hair?"

"Sorry." Riley sobered. A little. She had a twinkle in her eye that didn't fit the reason Sam just gave for their call.

"Why the hell are you guys calling me on your wedding night?"

Riley raised her eyebrows. "Because you have a lot to tell us."

Marley sighed again and shoved herself back to lean against the headboard, pulling the computer onto her lap. "Not really."

"Oh, come on," Riley scoffed. "We don't see you for months, we barely hear from you. Then rumors start floating around about a vigilante going after baby Numina—"

"Deimons," Marley cut in. "They named themselves after Deimos. Personally, I'd have called them Numinauds, but they didn't ask me."

"Numinauds?" Her brow wrinkled as she worked it out. "Numina frauds. Ha! Pretenders to their fathers' legacies. Anyway, these kids have gotten into something not so good, and you're involved somehow. You don't RSVP to our wedding—"

"That hurt our feelings, by the way," Sam interjected.

"But you still show up to thwart an assassination attempt with a freakish show of strength. All very nice, except you're with *Anson Tournado*." Riley paused, thinking, then moved the finger at the corner of her mouth to point it at Marley. "Let's start there."

Marley shook her head. "That's in the middle. The whole story would take hours, and you guys—"

"Are on our honeymoon. Stop saying that." Riley scowled. "Quinn's worried about you and a little fed up. She's not here," she went on, obviously anticipating Marley's question, "because she's due in New York for another meeting with the Numina board, and she's got one of Delwhip's pawns in hand as ammunition to remove him from the summit negotiations."

"This could be an important break in the talks, a way to silence Delwhip," Sam added.

"How are things going down there?" Marley asked, partly because she didn't want to talk about what she was up to and partly because she really wanted to know. What with dodging Quinn's calls, she hadn't been updated in a while.

Sam and Riley gave her identical looks that said they knew what she was doing.

"Slow," Sam admitted bluntly.

"We've established which guys have broken away from the main," Riley added. "And now we're starting to discuss what those splinter groups want and how they plan to get it. Which means rehashing everything that happened in the last five years. Which brings us," she said pointedly, "back to Anson."

Marley drew a deep breath. This was her fight. Her chance at redemption for all the pain and fear she'd made possible. Telling them, having them come to her rescue, would negate everything she'd done to earn back their trust, to be worthy of it. And they were on their friggin' honeymoon!

She reached for the top of the laptop's touch screen, a little desperate to disconnect the call and escape. But before she could close the program, Sam said, "I know where you are. If you hang up on us, we'll just come there and *really* get involved."

"All right, all right." She thudded her head lightly against the wall behind her, tears prickling her eyelids. It almost overwhelmed her that he knew her so well.

She missed them. Missed having people to share with, ones who cared about what happened to her.

"I'll tell you what I'm doing, but you have to promise not to tell Quinn. Unless you have to," she added, not wanting to ask them to full-out lie. "She doesn't need the distraction or the worry with the summit."

"If it's vital information, I won't keep it from her," Sam said. "Especially if it's putting you in danger."

"I don't want her position weakened," Marley insisted. "I'm handling this." When they both nodded, she took a deep breath.

"If you're going back to the beginning," Riley said softly, "what happened the night you left? Sam won't talk about it."

Marley stared at him, surprised that he'd withhold anything from Riley.

His jaw came forward, his gaze off to the side of the screen. "There's nothing to talk about. I don't know what happened."

But the fact that he wouldn't look directly at Marley told her he had his suspicions.

And, she realized, he deserved to have them confirmed. "I don't understand what happened, either," she said, "but I think our magic is broader than we ever understood."

They gaped at her use of the word "magic," which was an undeclared taboo in the goddess community.

"Giving Anson my power, then having the rest of it ripped away from me, created some kind of void."

"Hmm." He curled his hand around his chin. "Okay."

"I didn't really know it was there. Quinn could sense it, but she called it my empty vessel. I thought it made me permanently normal," she said. "I never realized there was anything else to it until after that last transfer."

"And what about Sam?" Riley looked between them, but her expression didn't change. So she, too, had figured some things out. "I didn't see anything happen during the transfer, but there was something later, a shadow or…" She shook her head. "I don't know, I thought I was imagining it. But…" Her voice cracked slightly.

Marley wrapped her arms around herself and pressed her lips together, remembering the horror of that night. Sam, the son of a goddess, the only one capable of accepting Marley's poisonous energy, had insisted that Quinn give it to him. He'd been so sure he could handle whatever it did to him. He'd been wrong.

"I didn't expect touching you to do anything," she said to Sam. "I just wanted to let you know you weren't alone."

"But you took it away when you did," he marveled.

She shook her head. "Not intentionally. I thought at first it totally disappeared, but it's more that it became inert, and maybe…infused me? It's made me stronger without giving me any goddess-like power."

"And?" Sam pressed. "You can suck the energy out of other people now, too?"

She nodded. "I can nullify it, remove it from anyone who's not supposed to have it."

"That's…incredible." Riley looked amazed and maybe a little envious. She leaned forward, eager. "How do you know who has it and whether they're supposed to or not?"

"Well, the energy—the Deimons call it flux—has its own

signature," Marley said. "Once I found the first one of them and nullified it, I could tell who was regular Numina and who was *different*. I don't know how, but I can sense the flux."

"And how did you learn this?" Sam demanded. He didn't sound thrilled with her revelations so far. Too bad, because it was only going to get worse.

Unless she didn't tell them. Her finger brushed the track pad. The part of her that craved their approval, that couldn't handle their disappointment, wanted to just shut down the computer and claim technical difficulties later.

But dammit, she was supposed to have changed. What happened to never being a victim again? That meant not making herself one, either.

If she wanted to be different, she had to do things differently.

She folded her arms and looked directly at Sam. "I tracked down Anson and nullified him the same way I nullified you. I wanted to make sure it worked."

"That was the stupidest thing you've ever done," Sam barked.

Marley kept her expression still. "And I've done some very stupid things," she said softly.

Riley elbowed Sam, who looked abashed. "I'm sorry. But why wouldn't you come to one of us? We'd have gone with you if we couldn't find another—"

His wife, who seemed to have intuited a lot from Marley's response, talked over him. "Why did you stay with him, though? After everything he did to you? To Quinn?"

"I needed help, and he wanted to give it. Make up for the past, I guess. Plus, he had hacking skills and inside information, and he knew at least some of the parties already."

"I have skills," Sam grumbled. "Why didn't you *come to me*?"

Riley blew out an exasperated breath but this time stayed silent. How could Marley answer without sounding accusatory or at least hurting their feelings? The problem wasn't them. It was her.

"It turned out to be mutually beneficial with Anson," she finally said, trying to steer the conversation away. "We researched everyone associated with Numina. I figured my ability was only worth something if one of the kids we dealt with last spring got ambitious enough to become a leech."

"That's always a risk," Sam agreed. "We have a database of potentials, but—"

"Not enough time to track them all," Marley finished. "I had to act on instinct."

Riley sat back, looking serious. "We knew something was going on, but had no clue what until we interrogated Gashface. Well, Nick interrogated him. We were dancing." She flashed a tiny grin and motioned between herself and Sam.

"I'm sorry," Marley said. "I didn't want anything to interfere with your wedding."

Riley waved it off. "Never mind that. So this flux is like bestowing power? Like my great-grandparents did?"

Marley had helped Riley research her family when she first came to the Society. They'd figured out that her great-grandmother had given power to her husband regularly, draining herself to such a point that her daughters never came into their own abilities. Neither did Riley's mother. They weren't sure why the dormancy ended with Riley, who was a very strong goddess with metal as her source.

"Exactly like that," Marley confirmed. She couldn't sit still anymore. She spun the laptop sideways and got off the bed to pace in front of it. "It took us a long time to piece together how they were getting the flux. It was clear nullifying them individually wasn't going to work for very long. There were always going to be more than I could get to, and I was worried about how far some of them would be willing to go. We had to stop it at the source. We eventually determined that a goddess is bestowing small amounts of power to these guys."

"So she's like a drug dealer," Riley said. "Who would do that?

"And in return for what?"

Marley spread her hands at Sam's question. "We don't know. We know she's probably the one who went rogue so many years ago. That goddess's power source was the sun—that's the only thing I think is strong enough to give someone so much power to dole out."

Sam's jaw tensed even more. "Cressida Lahr," he ground out.

"What?" Riley turned to him, surprised.

"Her name is Cressida Lahr," he repeated.

"How do you know that?" Marley asked. "We haven't been able to track down any detailed information about the goddess. We've had to come at this from the Deimons side."

Sam rubbed his hands over his face. "I've done a lot of reading while we digitized more of the archive files. I knew about the rogue goddess from when we first went after the leech, and since the Numina splinter groups are kind of a rogue organization, I wanted to see how the Society had handled her back then."

"And what did you find?" Marley prodded.

He shrugged. "Not much. She had access to a lot of power, obviously. She started using it against anyone who displeased her. When the Society tried to discipline her, she disassociated. She did something unforgivable, too—they didn't document what, but it had to be the equivalent of felonious assault, at least, because they sent a security team after her. Probably would have done the same as they did with Anson and turned her over to the mainstream authorities, but she'd disappeared."

"And now she's bestowing power on these kids." Marley paced faster. "The amounts I've taken from them have been small, probably too small to give them the ability to leech anyone. But that could change."

"As long as she provides a regular supply," Sam said, "there's no reason for them to consider turning leech. That would be dangerous, not to mention a lot of work."

"There could be another reason." Marley's hands curled until her nails dug into her palms. "I knew Gash was going to attack because his friends were talking about it. They said he's changed since he started taking the flux, that he had a new edge."

Sam's brows puckered. "Did you see that in him?"

"Oh yeah. He was crazed. It didn't help him much."

"How much flux is available to them?" Riley put a hand over her eyes. "Please stand still, Marley. You're giving me a headache."

"Sorry." She stopped in the middle of the floor and faced the computer. "It might be unlimited. I don't know. We don't have anyone to ask."

"There aren't any other goddesses who use the sun?" Riley looked to Sam, but Marley knew the answer from her days managing the goddess roster and non-member records in the Society's offices.

"Barbara was the only one." Barbara Valiant had been president of the Society when Anson first went on his leeching spree, and she was the only one in a century—besides, apparently, Cressida Lahr—to have the sun as her source. She'd been very old, very controlled and contained, and could have been invaluable in this quest. "I wonder if Lahr waited to do this," she mused, "until after Barbara died. If she thought Barbara was the only one who could stop her."

"It's logical." But Sam didn't seem to be thinking about Barbara. "Who else knows about all this?"

Marley shrugged. "No idea. I doubt the higher-ups in Numina do, or they'd have nailed the Society over it already. That's another reason I'm trying to stop her before it gets any bigger."

Anson's usual triple knock hit the door. Crap. She'd lost track of time.

"I gotta go," she told the others, bending to pull on her boots.

"Where?" Sam demanded. "It's midnight. Where are you going?"

"I'm just checking out the site we found. No big deal."

"What site? Marley!" Riley actually reached up a hand as if she could stop Marley from closing the laptop.

"You guys have been a huge help," she told them, shrugging on her jacket. "Knowing her name should make a big difference in tracking her. I'll let you know when we've taken care of her."

Not that she had any clue how they were going to do that.

CHAPTER FOUR

Any goddess who becomes aware of rogue activity beyond the guidelines of the Society and the Protectorate should contact the office immediately.

—Goddess Society for Education and Defense internal memo

"So what's the plan?" Anson started the vehicle and backed out. "I didn't see any good place to hide the truck."

"I used Google satellite to see if there were any other ways in besides the main road and didn't see anything," Marley agreed. "You can just drop me and cruise around until I signal you."

He frowned at her. "Not a good idea."

"I don't think anything's going to happen tonight. I just want to scout the place, see what the layout is, if there's any evidence that she uses it."

"What makes you think nothing's going down tonight?"

"Ah...because the sun is her power source? And there's no sun at night?"

He didn't respond. Marley was being disingenuous, but she didn't know if he knew it. They'd *guessed* that the sun was her power source and that she needed a direct line to the sun to be able to use it to channel energy. But what Lahr was doing had never been done before, so they couldn't assume anything about her was typical. She might be able to store the energy for longer periods and could, therefore, transfer it at night.

The roads were quieter now, some houses already dark. Anson paused half a mile from the farm, and Marley jumped out to slip into the woods on the other side of the street. The SUV's engine gunned, and darkness returned as the vehicle disappeared down the road.

Leaves crackled in the thick underbrush with every step she took, but she didn't try too hard to be quiet until she could see the farmyard through the trees. Then she moved more slowly and carefully, easing up to the edge of the property.

It was as still as it had been earlier. Nothing moved. No vehicles crouched in the weed-filled gravel lot or near the long building or the silos. She made her way along the curving tree line toward the barn, eyes peeled for movement or shadows. She was too far away to sense anyone's presence inside the building.

She eased up to the end of the building. Weathered, rotting wood alternated with gaps where it had completely broken away, but paint clung in enough spots to show it used to be white. There wasn't any kind of door along this wall, so she found a big enough gap and ducked inside.

The space felt open and empty, but it was close to pitch black. She twisted on the LED beam of her flashlight and aimed it at the floor, slowly raising it in front of her—and was glad she hadn't kept moving in the dark. She'd have walked right into the solid wood-frame wall two feet in front of her. A sweep of the flashlight showed the wall extending all the way down the building and about fifteen feet up. She couldn't tell if there was a ceiling or if it was open to the rafters above. Two-by-fours were backed by plywood rather than drywall, a crude but effective structure. It would block light and at least some sound, preserving the abandoned atmosphere of the place while allowing them some freedom and maybe even comfort.

Marley didn't see a door here, either, so she walked around the interior wall to the other side of the building. Her flashlight revealed animal droppings, a few glowing pairs of eyes that blinked out just before she heard scurrying feet, and the same unending wall. She clicked off the flashlight and stood listening, letting her eyes adjust again. There were no voices or sounds of movement. She peered carefully around the corner. Nothing.

When she turned the flashlight back on it illuminated a simple, hollow-core door about twenty feet away, a gold-colored doorknob gleaming in the beam of light. The barn's outer wall, perhaps more sheltered from the elements on this side, looked more intact. The ground had less debris and a clear path worn into the dirt from steady foot traffic. Marley shone the flashlight along the slight indent from the door all the way to the far end of the building and a chained entrance. What was the point in a chain with all the holes in the walls?

Everything was still except for the occasional rustle of leaves in the light evening breeze. A few long strides took her to the door, but she didn't touch the handle. She slid on a pair of leather gloves from her jacket pocket and twisted the knob.

Anticipation welled as she nudged the door open and peered into more darkness. She closed it behind her and felt for a light switch. The bare plywood snagged her gloved fingertips before they landed on a two-inch-wide rocker switch. She clicked and light filtered into the room, dim and orange but growing brighter. The compact fluorescent bulbs were attached to the corners where the walls met. There was no ceiling—Marley could see stars through holes in the barn roof. The ugly, chipped-wood walls were bare and flat, the dirt floor swept clear, the only furniture a crude, throne-like wooden chair with a tall back and wide arms. Red velvet had been tossed across it, discarded.

Marley couldn't imagine what they did here. Assuming this was, in fact, where the transfers took place. Hardly a typical setting for a drug deal.

She stepped out into the middle of the room, studying the ground. There were a multitude of small, round depressions in the dirt. When she moved back for a wider view, she saw an uneven half circle made up of rows of these dots, then another behind the first.

Aha! Folding chairs. Those were from the feet of folding chairs. They'd been arranged facing the throne. Now she could picture the scene. Cressida Lahr holding court over the Deimons. *If* they were right about her coming here. It could just be a meeting place for the group, something to make them feel secretive and superior. Like a college secret society meeting in a tomb or cellar.

An owl hooted softly in the rafters above her, and something rustled just outside the wall. She crossed to the throne and picked up the velvet. It wasn't very good quality and was too small to drape over the whole throne. Carefully, she sniffed it, but it didn't smell any different from the barn overall. Okay, so if Cressida did sit here, if she bestowed flux from here, would there be residue?

She draped the velvet across the seat and arms of the chair and climbed up into it, closing her eyes. But the light glared overhead now, stark and very nonatmospheric. She couldn't concentrate. After turning off the lights and returning to the chair, this time when she closed her eyes she was able to sink down into her consciousness and reach out with all of her senses.

The property itself had a sense of weight, of purpose. Nothing dramatic, like some people might feel in an ancient cathedral, but something suited to the work ethic of a farm. The air around her was still. Not a void, but empty of detectable remnants of who had used this space.

She zeroed in on the throne under her, concentrating on the stiff fabric against her palms and fingers, the solid wood supporting her body. A faint blue shine seemed almost detectable, but it was *so* faint she doubted it was real.

And then a sharp awareness of Numina struck her, followed by the faintest hint of dark, spicy aftershave. Her eyes flew open, but even adjusted to the darkness, she could see nothing. Slow, almost-silent footsteps came from outside the door. Whoever it was would be in the room any second, and there was nowhere for Marley to go.

The doorknob rattled as it turned, the hinges squeaking slightly as the door opened. Marley held her breath and kept perfectly still. Maybe he'd leave the light off and move on because he thought no one was here. She was capable of stillness to a degree that rendered her part of the furniture, but that would only work if he never looked in her direction.

The lights came on, still warmed up and therefore still bright. And Gage Samargo's silver-blue eyes landed right on her.

• • •

Disappointment punched Gage in the gut when he saw the woman with the white eyes sitting in a throne-like chair inside the barn. The implication was that his father was right, and she was the goddess dealing flux. He hadn't realized how much he didn't want her to be until now.

They stared at each other for a few seconds. Then the woman rose and jumped off the base of the chair. Her tall black boots kicked up puffs of dust when she landed. Gage followed the rising dust up her snug jeans to the short leather jacket she wore over what appeared to be a black tank top. Her dark red hair was down tonight, and with the aggressive angle of her chin and the fire in her eyes, she looked very different from the woman he'd met in the club.

He'd followed her when she and the guy with the tornado name left the hotel. There was no way he could get close to the church they drove to without being seen, so he'd found a spot in the cemetery on the other side of a hill for the Viper and moved as close as he could through the headstones.

He'd dug a pair of high-powered binoculars out of the bottom of the tiny trunk—one of the pros of being a "businessman-adventurer"—and for a long time, nothing happened. Then he'd watched people walk into a church. He about died from boredom by the time he saw a figure stalking toward the building, possibly with a weapon. The distance meant Gage could do nothing, and his pulse had raced through the brief fight. If this woman had been the one who took down the figure, dragged him to his car, and stuffed him in the trunk, she *had* to be a goddess. No normal woman could have done all that.

Gage had managed to follow them again, all the way to upstate New York, where they'd stared for a few minutes at a ruin of a barn before getting a motel room in Valatie, home of Washington Irving.

Ichabod Crane Central High School on the town's main road had triggered memory of a mention of the headless horseman on the Deimon's online message board. In the last few hours, Gage had done some guided digging and found that the broker who'd handled the sale of this property was Numina. That was enough actionable evidence for him. He was done with the wait-and-see approach.

"Where's my brother?" he demanded, shoving the door closed behind him and blocking her path to it.

The woman didn't react outwardly to his aggression. She stood where she was, her expression unrevealing. "I don't know."

"You know who he is."

"Yes. But I've never met him, and I don't know where you can find him."

Gage narrowed his eyes. She could be lying, but he could usually tell when someone was. It was an important skill in business, and she didn't have any of the typical tells.

"If you know who he is, then you know who I am, and that puts me at a disadvantage."

"Yes, it does." But she didn't offer her name.

Okay, then. He tried a different tack. "What's the going rate for a dose of flux?"

Finally, a reaction. Her eyebrow went up, and she said, "Why are you asking?"

"Because I want some, obviously."

Damn, he felt clumsy. He didn't usually approach a meeting so awkwardly, even those he wasn't prepared for.

She laughed. He tried not to frown and didn't ask what was funny. Awkward was bad enough, but he wore defensiveness even worse.

"You don't want flux." She folded her arms. "You don't need it. But do you seriously think I'm the one who has it?"

Yeah, he had…until now. "If you don't, who does?"

"Why do you want to know?" She shifted to lean against the chair and crossed her ankles, obviously to convey how little of a threat she considered him.

Frustrated, Gage moved away from the door and studied the room they were in. It was unremarkable, even down to the markings on the floor. Chairs, boat shoes, a few loafers, and even a couple of pairs of boots. He spotted footprints that had to belong to the woman and followed their path to the throne. She hadn't moved, just stood watching him.

He thought about how easily Allie, the hotel clerk, had accommodated him. He was taking the wrong approach. Demanding and posturing was not his preferred MO, but *this* woman was too shrewd to fall for an abrupt change in his attitude, so he'd have to modulate it gradually.

He strode across the barn and stopped a couple of feet from her. Close enough to nudge her comfort zone but not so close as to be threatening.

"The other night you said you didn't know my brother."

"As I said just now, I don't know him. I do know who he is, but as your family is part of the billionaire club, many people do."

He glanced around, then back to her. "I thought only men could receive flux."

That surprised another laugh out of her, but she quickly schooled it. "And?"

"If you're not dealing it, you must be looking to get some yourself. Why else would you be here?"

"I have no need or desire to receive it. My reasons for being here are personal." An edge was detectable in her voice now, though barely.

Gage had to admire her ability to avoid answering his questions without lying or sticking to obstinate silence. He took another step closer, and it was as if he'd stepped into another realm. The air surrounding her was warm and filled with a sweet, light fragrance, enticing enough to make him inhale deeper. He thought of fresh air and meringues. The scent was very unlike the tough persona she wore and much more innocent than the luscious femininity she'd presented the other night in the club. As he inhaled, it sent a curl of desire through him.

He had to know who she was.

"Tell me your name," he murmured, staring into her purple-flecked eyes. They flickered uncertainly. "Just your first name." He raised a hand, knowing if he touched her, the spell would break.

"Marley," she almost whispered, but as soon as the word was out of her mouth she backed away, her eyes darkening and anger filling her expression.

"Don—" He cut himself off when noise from outside the barn interrupted. Voices. Then a chain rattled and hit the dirt. The voices got louder. It was a big group.

He cursed and looked wildly around, knowing there was no

place to hide. Marley twisted to look up and behind the throne. She didn't want to be discovered here, either. Instinctively, Gage knew she wasn't who his father had surmised, but maybe she could be an ally.

The only place to go was up. Marley had already climbed onto the pedestal base, but she would be too short to get into the loft that overhung the wall. With one leap Gage was on the seat and pulling himself up to the top of it. His boots braced wide against the protrusions on either side of the seat back, he reached up for the top of the plywood wall. Thank god he was tall. And that he'd dabbled in parkour at college. He bounced up to balance on the two-by-four at the top of the wall, crouched, one hand touching the wood to help his balance.

"Who the hell left the lights on?" said an annoyed voice in the outer hall.

Gage could see the group filing in through the previously chained outer door. They looked straight ahead, down the hall, but in seconds they'd be in the main room and easily spot both of them. They had to hurry. He stretched to reach the edge of the loft. Below him, Marley stood on the chair. Twisting his wrist, he found a convenient stopper strip nailed to the edge of the loft. He grabbed with both hands and kicked sideways and up. It took two tries to catch the edge with one foot and drag himself to the loft floor. He rolled and swung around, reaching down to grab Marley's wrist. To his shock, instead of letting him pull her up, she just used his leverage to grab the loft herself. In seconds she was at his side, and a lot more quietly than he'd done it.

They both flattened themselves as much as they could and still see into the room below. And then the door opened, and eight men in their early to mid-twenties entered and milled around in the empty space. Gage examined every face as they came in, the wood of the loft edge digging hard into his hands as he squeezed. His brother wasn't here. His mind raced. He could take all their pictures, figure out who they were, and track their activities to try to pinpoint where Aiden could be. Or after this meeting—or whatever it was—he could follow them.

Marley's hand closed hard over his wrist, and he realized he'd started to push himself up. She shook her head and glared at him.

She was right. Better to learn what he could first, then decide how to act. He settled back down to watch. A couple of the guys lugged a big case to the middle of the room and started unloading folding chairs. They set them up in a semicircle, then draped them all in that same cheap red velvet that had been heaped on the throne. One of the guys rearranged the fabric to cover the raw wood, then draped a white fur down its center. They laid a red-and-white runner from the throne to the door and set up a folding table, covered in more velvet, before unfolding a gold-colored stylized sun and hanging it on the wall.

He and Marley exchanged disgusted, incredulous looks. Okay, some of these guys didn't have the money they used to, but inexpensive didn't have to mean tacky. Gage didn't look away as quickly as Marley did, and he caught a slight smile she probably hadn't meant him to see.

The camaraderie might be odd with someone he'd been suspicious of only minutes before, but he liked it anyway. Being allies definitely worked for him.

The guys settled nervously on their chairs, all except for one. He stood by the door, aiming his flashlight down the hall every few seconds. Gage didn't recognize most of them, even on closer inspection, though one looked familiar enough that he was probably a sibling of someone Gage knew. He suspected a couple of them were regular guys, not Numina but hangers-on. There were some in every group, wannabes who weren't let in on the secrets but were allowed to tag along because they would fetch drinks, carry notes to girls, and clean up after the ones who couldn't hold their liquor. Gage hadn't been part of that scene for a very long time and was ashamed of the brief period when it had made him feel important.

Behind and below him, the outside door creaked. Gage inched forward and leaned over, but the walls cut off his angle and all he saw was moving shadow. The kid with the flashlight hissed excitedly to his friends and then stood at attention, shining the light down the outer corridor.

Gage finally recognized the next person who entered the room. Brad Carmichael had gone to prep school with Aiden and, like Gage's brother, was probably a couple of years older than most of the other guys in here. Gage's heart began to race, and he stared at the door, not sure if he wanted his brother to come through next or not.

Brad stepped into the room a few feet, looked around importantly like some kind of Secret Service pretender, and nodded back at Flashlight Kid. Gage recognized the next two people, too—Tony Dicenzo and Christopher Wilson. Chris was Aiden's best friend. So where was Aiden?

The boys lined up about two feet back from the edge of the runner. Exactly eight beats later a woman glided in. Her steps were so slow and graceful Gage wished she'd lift the hem of her long, billowy, golden dress so he could see if she was literally gliding. His heart beat harder, but this time not from nerves. *This* had to be the goddess, the provider of flux.

He couldn't define her ethnicity, some exotic blend of many races, and had to guess at her age. She didn't have the soft look of someone in her twenties, but her face was unlined. She could be anywhere from mid-thirties to mid-forties. Her dark gold hair rippled and flowed down to her elbows, in curls over her chest, and past her waist in the back. She held her hands loosely clasped in front of her at first, but as she moved along the runner they spread slowly out to the side, her hair rising into the air without a breeze, and she flew the last few feet to the chair.

Gage blinked, dazed. The goddess stood for a moment, her arms still upraised as she faced her acolytes, who stood in half bows so they could keep their eyes on her but still pay her the respect she commanded.

Her hair had dropped, and Gage frowned at it. Less of a glowing gold, it was now simply blond and not as long as he first thought. She sat, and Gage wasn't nearly as dazzled as he'd been a few moments ago. He canted a look at Marley, who scowled fiercely at the scene. He hoped she hadn't noticed his temporary trance. He'd met a few goddesses in his life, and none had had such an effect on him. Hell, even the most powerful Numina, who claimed the strongest influence, couldn't use it at will like that.

Flashlight Kid shut and locked the door before joining his friends while the three older guys stood at ease behind the group, looking smug and superior. When the goddess spoke, all of their eyes widened and jaws went slack. Looking at them, Gage would have thought she had the most melodious voice and said the most incredible things they'd ever heard. But her voice sounded pretty normal to him, if slightly rough. Like she'd lived hard, maybe drank a lot.

He wanted to ask Marley if she was similarly affected but had no way to do so. He doubted she'd give him a straight answer, anyway.

"I see new faces," the blond goddess said, gesturing with one arm and a closing sweep of the hand. Gage frowned. The movement had been reminiscent of how she'd moved across the barn, but instead of graceful, it struck him as melodramatic.

"Please stand and introduce yourselves." She nodded to the first kid on her left, the youngest looking. "Tell me why you are here."

The boy stood and wiped his hands on his khakis. He glanced down at the person next to him, who nodded encouragingly. Curls flopped into his eyes when he faced the goddess. He shook them back, looked terrified, and let them fall in his eyes again.

"Madame Cressida. I mean, Madame Lahr. Um…Cres—" He stopped and cleared his throat. "Ma'am. I'm Ricky Pettle, and I'm here because I want…" His voice jerked higher when his friend punched him in the leg. "I mean, I'm here to learn from you. My brother told me ser-serving you was the best thing he ever did."

She inclined her head. "As indeed it was. I read that he leads the NFL in kickoff returns."

Gage shook his head, sure he couldn't have heard such a line from someone like her.

But she continued, "His Rookie of the Year status seems a foregone conclusion, young as the football season is."

Now Gage knew who the kid was. He had two older brothers, one a year older than Gage. He'd refused to go into the family business, which had collapsed with the real-estate crash in 2007. The middle brother had been an undrafted free agent—meaning no team wanted him at first—but now he was wowing everyone with his abilities. His performance so surpassed his college achievements that rumors of drugs were rampant. But no one would find anything—they couldn't test for flux.

"Uh, yeah," the kid agreed. "So, that's why I'm here."

"You seek to play football?" She sounded skeptical and with good reason. The boy was scrawny. Gage suspected if he dug up photos of himself at that age people would say the same about him, and he was built well enough now. Not NFL level, though.

"No! I'm more of an artistic type. A writer, actually."

"Ah. Come forward." She stood as he approached, his head bowed. "Look at me, please." He raised his head, and she brushed the curls out of his face. His eyes closed, as if her touch was pure ecstasy. Was she giving him flux already?

No, he looked disappointed when she released him.

"Have you paid your tribute?" she asked.

"Yes, ma'am," he rasped.

"And what are your goals? What type of writer do you wish to be?"

"An essayist. I have a contract with a publisher, and there's a tour…" His voice trailed off.

It wasn't hard to figure out what he wanted. Interviews and book signings wouldn't be successful if he was as tentative and dorky as he presented now. Gage didn't know if flux could make him confident and attractive, but the kid clearly hoped it would.

Silence filled the room while she seemed to consider. "The potential returns have value," she acknowledged. "Agreed."

She made a swooping motion with her hand, and the kid shrieked as he flew into the air, arms and legs flying backward. He flipped head over tail and hung over his friends, as if being held up by some invisible giant.

Gage gaped, glad the kid had made so much noise and covered his own indrawn breath. Marley had clapped a hand over her mouth, her eyes wide above it. Cressida lifted one arm as if holding the boy in the air. She flung the other toward him, and a shaft of yellow light shot across, striking him in the chest before it expanded to surround him and then sink into his body. His second outcry was more a shout of joy.

The kid lowered to the ground. He landed on his feet but didn't stay on them, crumpling into a heap that everyone ignored as Cressida took her seat again.

"Who's next?" she asked in a pleasant voice that sent a shiver of dread down Gage's spine.

Another of the attendees stepped forward. Gage wasn't sure he wanted to watch this again, and clearly Marley didn't either as she slithered backward, tugging at his arm. When she was far enough back, she rose to a crouch and beckoned him with an impatient hand. Slowly, quietly, he followed her to a gap in the wall where doors obviously used to be. He supposed they'd have tossed hay from here onto trucks or something. Marley leaned out, nodded, and swung over the side. By the time Gage looked, she was halfway down a wooden ladder attached to the wall. She had to skip rungs that were broken or missing, and for a third of the drop, there was only one side rail.

Gage's mouth dropped open watching her navigate the mess without hesitation. She looked up at him from the ground, fists on her hips. No way he could do that. He was a lot heavier than her and was missing whatever gene or superpower let her be so frigging silent.

She widened her eyes and firmed her lips in a "come *on*!" expression. His ego wouldn't let him refuse.

Far more slowly than she had, he lowered himself onto the first couple of rungs. His hands ached from gripping the splintery wood until he was sure the support under his feet would hold. He had to bite back a yelp when a large splinter punctured his palm. He had about twelve feet to go.

Screw it.

Pushing off hard so he'd hit a grassy area instead of the harder ground at the base, he absorbed most of the impact with his legs, bending his knees deep and letting his momentum take him straight into a roll. He came up on his feet and was immediately dragged toward the woods by Marley, who ran almost too fast for him to keep up. Or at least with his sleeve bunched in her hand.

"What the hell?" he hissed when he thought they were far enough away not to be heard. He yanked his sleeve away. "What are you doing?"

"We couldn't be caught in there." She motioned to him to follow and kept going, somehow seeing a path through the trees in the very dim light.

"No shit. I'm surprised you didn't leave me there."

She cast a speculative look over her shoulder, one that swept over his entire body. "It was pretty clear you weren't part of all that. I assume you followed me thinking I was her." She finally halted in a gap between a giant oak tree and a tangle of vine-choked shrubbery.

"Yeah," he admitted. "You're obviously not."

"No."

"But that doesn't mean I can trust you. What's your goal here?"

"We don't have time for that." She pulled out her phone and began typing on the screen. "I'm not going to have much of a window to do this. You should just stay out of the way."

Yeah, that was going to happen.

"To do what? Who are you texting?"

"My getaway driver." She slid the phone into her back pocket and stared back the way they'd come. Her stance shifted, as if she were preparing to run again.

Gage blocked her. "What are you going to do?"

Her jaw tightened. "Look—"

"No, you look. I'm not getting out of your way unless you tell me what's going on. I know some of those guys. I don't like what's happening in there, but I won't let you attack them."

She rolled her eyes. "I'm not going to—Okay, fine. I'm just going to take what they were just given. That's all."

Something he'd read from Aiden's laptop—an e-mail exchange or something posted on the message boards—filtered into his head. A guy complaining that his flux had been taken or something. On top of it came his memory of her brief touch on Josh's elbow.

His head spun. This was so not the world he lived in. "You can steal their flux?"

"I nullify it. It goes inert. They can't use it, and they can't accept any more. And I'm not letting those guys get out of here with it."

Gage had seen Josh on flux, and he suspected the four Numina who'd been arrested for robbing a casino had been on it, too. So he understood where she was coming from. But that wasn't *his* primary goal. He had to find and extricate Aiden from whatever involvement he had in this.

His father's needs, though, weren't so specific. He wanted the summit to succeed, and from what Gage had just witnessed, having information on the goddess wasn't going to provide the even playing field his father hoped for. If some of those guys' fathers found out what was happening, they'd want to bury the goddesses.

"Let me help," he said.

Marley shook her head. "I don't want this to become a big fight, and those are your people. You're better off—"

"I'm not standing back here while you put yourself at risk," he growled. "I don't care how capable you are."

She smiled. "I was going to say you're better off following the goddess. I expect the guys who came in with her will leave with her, too. They might lead you to Aiden. Or to their headquarters where I can pin her down and figure out how to stop this."

Gage settled, recognizing the logic in what she was saying. "You could still need backup."

She shook her head. "I have it. We'll meet back at my motel. I have a feeling you know where that is."

He quirked a sheepish smile.

"Okay, then."

Something banged in the direction of the barn, wood on wood, and voices filtered through the trees. They weren't close enough to see much, but the goddess in her gold dress headed off into the woods with three figures.

"Go," Marley whispered. "Good luck."

Gage hesitated, but this was her world, not his. He'd have to take a chance and hope to hell it didn't bite him in the ass.

"Be careful," he said. But as he headed off to follow the goddess, he had the uneasy realization that his path might be the more dangerous one.

Chapter Five

The energy of the mind is the essence of life.
—Aristotle

Marley didn't spare more than a moment worrying about Gage. Somehow, in the short time they'd spent in the loft, everything had changed. They'd shared the same appalled reaction to Cressida Lahr's actions, and even though Gage hadn't said it outright, she could see that he was on board with stopping it.

Sending him after the goddess might not have been the best move, though. Marley didn't know if he could find out her destination without being seen, and that woman was powerful enough to detect his presence even if he was stealthy. She could hardly believe they hadn't been detected in the loft. Maybe Lahr didn't have that particular ability, or maybe it hadn't occurred to her that anyone could be there who wasn't supposed to be. Either way, they were lucky.

She hunkered down in the brush as the group of men from the barn passed nearby, presumably on a path. They came close enough for her to detect their signatures. Most of the eight were Numina. The regular guys hunched and acted furtive as they walked, but a few of the others surrounded two in particular, jumping around and arm-punching them. Those two were practically vibrating in her head with the flux they'd been given. They'd either received more than the ones she'd nullified before, or those guys had used some up by the time she'd found them.

She couldn't let these two get out of her reach. If she lost them, they might hurt someone. She crept through the darkness, following them. They'd grown a little louder, their movements more obvious, but they still spoke in whispers and low voices she couldn't make out. Within two minutes she spotted the glint of moonlight on metal in what appeared to be a large clearing. A parking lot? Once they reached their cars, she'd have less chance of success. She had to make her move now.

She snuck closer, pinpointing the two with flux, looking for openings. Damn it for being October. They had long sleeves and long pants, so only faces and hands were exposed. And the others still crowded around her targets.

She hesitated as they approached the final bend before the clearing. This was going to completely expose her. There was no way to do it that they wouldn't notice. After tonight, they'd all be on high alert.

Marley dashed out onto the muddy path and toward the crowd, plowing through a gap between two of the boys. She shoved them to opposite sides, registering the crashes that told her they'd landed several feet into the woods. Three guys in front of her turned—one had flux. Marley reached for his face. His eyes widened, and he fell back with a scream. His buddies moved in to protect him. Marley dodged a punch and blocked a kick before tossing both boys out of her way.

Her target had recovered from his surprise and stood in a fighting stance now, his feet dancing. Marley flew toward him, able to place her feet firmly despite the mud, her weight balanced perfectly to prevent slipping. He misjudged and threw his punch too late. Marley was already inside his range, so his fist went past her ear. She wrapped her hands around his arm, twisted, and threw him over her shoulder. But she hadn't managed to touch skin, so she had to move in again, trying to get to a vulnerable spot.

He groaned from the ground and tilted his head back, looking for her. She loomed over him, reaching for his face, and he raised his hands to stop her. Marley slid her hand across his palm, and it was done.

His cry of loss and outrage was almost heartbreaking. But she steeled herself against it and turned to seek his much-smarter buddy. Marley had noted the positions of the three remaining guys through the last few seconds. One of the sober Deimons had run for the vehicles. Another stood with a switchblade, but he hovered nervously on the sidelines, breathless and scared, holding the weapon so loosely he couldn't cut butter. The fluxed guy stood in the middle of the path, and before Marley had finished turning from the nullified one on the ground, a wave of energy hit her.

His first use of his bestowed power.

Her mouth opened, preparing a scream. She expected pain or a blow that knocked her on her ass like Gashface's blast had. But none of that happened. Instead, she absorbed the entire wave, just as if she'd touched the man who'd used it. There was the same awareness of a void where the energy had been a split second before, but something was different. She felt it change this time, sensed it sinking into her. After that it was nothing. But she was more.

"Nice try," she said. "My turn." She started for him, half hoping he'd send another wave her way. A craving she hadn't felt in years cramped her chest, igniting a spark of fear. But she didn't have time for that. She doused it and lunged.

And missed. He turned and ran—again, smarter than his buddy. But Marley wasn't just some chick in tight jeans and heeled boots. She caught up with him at the edge of the clearing. As she emerged from the trees a sharp pain slashed across her right side. She gasped and turned to see the kid with the switchblade. He'd swept aside her leather jacket and cut her. How the hell had she lost track of him?

Through a furiously cold, green haze, she grabbed his weapon arm and twisted until it snapped. When he screamed, his friends scrambled to a halt and started back toward them, stumbling when they saw her. Marley ignored the warm wetness on her side and stomped across the old, weedy gravel.

"No!" The guy held up his hands in front of his face. "Don't kill me!"

"Shut up." Marley caught him by the back of the neck as he fell. He dropped to the ground and wept.

"Nut up and help your friend," she told him. "He needs medical attention. And listen good." She bent forward to get in his face. "If the rest of your buddies are smart, they'll learn a lesson from this and stay away from Cressida Lahr."

She straightened and turned, vertigo making her sway for a second. She thought she saw Sam standing ten feet away, and fearful rage rose up before her vision cleared and she realized it was Anson.

Who was at least seven inches shorter and about two people more narrow. She faltered, now truly scared. What was happening to her?

"You all right?" he asked when she approached.

"Fine." But her legs felt weak all of a sudden, and he wrapped an arm around her waist to help her toward the street. They only got two steps.

"What the hell?" He spun to face her and yanked her jacket away from her side. "Marley, you're bleeding!"

"Oh yeah. I forgot." She pressed her hand to her side and was a little alarmed at how much the skin gave along the cut. Her shirt and the waistband of her pants were soaked. But at least there was an explanation for her hallucination. "Let's just get back to the motel and I'll take care of it."

"We should go to the hospital," Anson argued. "That's a lot of blood."

"It'll be fine," she insisted. She let him help her into the truck and frowned as she looked around. Had he moved it? She didn't think they'd walked as far as the original parking spot. The blood loss was making it hard to concentrate.

Once they were on the road she pressed on the little map light and lifted her shirt to see the cut. Shit, that was bad. Not too deep but several inches long and still bleeding actively. Once upon a time she could have sealed it up with a mere thought.

She froze, staring at the wound. It looked…smaller? That guy had sent her that wave of energy, and she'd absorbed it. Could it be giving her back her powers? She focused on closing the edges, starting at one end.

And holy crap, it worked.

• • •

Gage checked the clock on his phone half-a-dozen times in ten minutes, when he wasn't looking up and down the road for Marley's black SUV. He was at the motel, but there was no sign of her. He paced for a few more minutes before the SUV finally pulled into the lot and stopped in front of a door halfway down the building. Gage strode over as a guy climbed out of the driver's side and hurried around to the passenger door. Marley half fell out of the truck before the guy got there, catching herself on the top of the door and hissing.

"Well, fuck. I thought I fixed that." She looked down at her side where her lifted arms had raised her jacket and shirt to expose a slice of skin. Bloody skin.

Gage hurried to support her, heedless of her friend making the move to do the same thing. "What happened?"

"You're here." Marley tried to look at his face, the motion making her sway against his arm around her back. "Did you follow Lahr?"

"I'll tell you what I learned inside."

The other guy eyed Gage for a few seconds but must have decided Marley's injury was more important than confronting someone he didn't know. He opened one of the motel room doors and stood aside to let them go first.

Gage tried to let Marley walk, but when her first step almost took them both down, he bent to sweep her up into his arms and carry her inside.

"My hero," she muttered, but she didn't fight him.

"I try." He carefully set her on the mussed bedspread and flipped on the light. It wasn't enough. "Hey, can you turn on all the other lights? I'm Gage," he offered so the other guy would tell him his name.

It didn't happen right away. "He's Anson," Marley said. "And you know my name."

Gage grimaced. "I'm still at a disadvantage, but we'll get to that. Can you take off—" But she already had her good arm out of the jacket. She pressed her lips together as she moved to pull it off the arm on the bloody side.

"Fucking jacket's ruined." She dropped it on the floor. Anson picked it up and laid it on a towel. He'd brought the whole pile out of the bathroom.

"We don't want to leave blood all over the place," he said.

"Good thinking." Marley inhaled deeply through her nose and held it while she stripped off her tank top. "Holy fuck, that hurts."

She lay back, apparently oblivious to the fact that Gage stood there staring. He didn't know how to process two diametrically opposed reactions. Her breasts, cupped in a lacy black bra, were spectacular. The primal male part of him was full of appreciation. But blood covered her side, already dried around the edges while still seeping from a long slice in the curve of her waist, just below her ribs.

"You need a hospital," he told her, his voice rough.

"Not gonna happen." She lifted her arm and twisted to look at the wound, then fell back on the pillow again. "But I can't take care of it myself. Sam or Nick could do it. They'd use floss or something." Her chuckle turned into a moan. "Hell, Quinn or Riley could heal it without even touching me."

Quinn and Riley must be goddesses if they could heal Marley like that. But he'd thought Marley was a goddess, too. "You can't heal it?"

She gave him a stern look but said, "No."

"And I suppose Quinn and Riley aren't nearby?"

"Unfortunately not." She took a deep breath and settled against the pillows.

Gage sighed and started to roll up his sleeves. "Do you have any booze?" he asked Anson. "Something with high alcohol content. Assuming you don't have rubbing alcohol," he added as an afterthought. He was getting carried away with the whole down-and-dirty vibe.

Anson brought him a hefty first-aid kit and a bottle of whiskey. Marley gave *him* a look this time, and he just shrugged. "A loaded first-aid kit seemed like a good thing to have around," he said.

Marley's lips curved approvingly, but Anson didn't see. He'd turned away to crack open the bottle of whiskey and set it within Gage's reach.

Gage flipped open the red plastic case and surveyed the contents. There were gloves and antiseptic wipes but no bottles of liquid alcohol. The wipes wouldn't do anything on a wound that size. He did find a suture kit, complete with a syringe of anesthetic, so at least he wouldn't have to resort to floss.

"Good supplies," he said. "I'm going to go scrub up." He pulled a chair over and set up the gloves and kit on the bed. "We'll probably need more towels," he said to Anson. "Lay some under her, will you? And then douse the wound with the whiskey. I'll be right back." He went into the bathroom and started soaping up his hands and forearms. He'd done rough-and-tumble medicine before, on job sites in countries that didn't have a clinic on every corner. Somehow, he hadn't expected his search for Aiden to get this physical. And he had a feeling it was only going to get worse.

He went back out to the bedroom. Anson and Marley were where he'd left them, except the room smelled like a bar now, and there was a pad of towels laid flat on the bed under her side with a rolled one, stained with whiskey and blood, pressed tight under her waist. Her arm lay across her eyes, giving him full access to her wound and arranging her breasts delectably.

Something was seriously wrong with him.

He sat in the chair and carefully put on the gloves from the kit. "I'm going to give you a shot, but I don't know how long it will take to numb you."

"Better do two," Anson said from behind him. "It's a long cut."

"Just get on with it," Marley growled.

Gage had Anson open the outer packaging and only touched the sterile syringe himself. He had no idea what the nerve distribution was in this area of the body, where to inject her for maximum effectiveness. So he just injected the contents in several spots on both sides of the wound. While he did, he probed the slice a little, trying to determine if one layer of stitches would be enough. Luckily, it didn't seem too deep. He had no idea how to do an inner layer, or even if the nylon in the kit was the right kind for internal stitches.

He cleared his throat. "While we wait for that to work, maybe we should talk about what happened in the barn."

"Tell Anson what we saw." Marley didn't uncover her eyes, and her voice shook a little. Gage hoped the anesthetic worked quickly.

He described the meeting and what the goddess had done, lifting the kid and sending energy to him in a visible shaft. "I've never seen a goddess in action before," he said. "Are you all that powerful?"

Marley peered at him from under her arm. "What do you mean, 'are you all'?"

He quirked an eyebrow at her. "Normal people don't have the strength and control you do. Or the eyes. So you—"

"I'm not a goddess." Her tone was hard, flat, but somehow full of pain.

"She used to be," Anson said.

Gage glanced over his shoulder to find the man watching Marley with some mix of regret and desperate longing that quickly faded into an implacable mask.

"What do you mean, she used to be?"

"She was leeched." He waved his hand back and forth over his eyes. "That's what bleached the color out of her irises."

"And it, what, took all her power?" He'd heard something about leeches recently, but he couldn't remember where. Before the goddesses approached Numina, so not connected with his brother or the flux.

"Doesn't matter," Marley barked, then hissed in a breath. "To answer your question, no, not every goddess is that powerful. I, in particular, have no power anymore. Not that kind." She swallowed hard and drew a long breath. "Do you know the football player Lahr mentioned?"

"A little." He wondered how much she knew about the kids in that meeting. About him. His father would kill him if he revealed anything about Numina, but he obviously had ties to them or he wouldn't be here. "He was a fringe player, a long shot to make a team. But his talent has exploded since mini camp."

"Which was when?"

"June."

She cursed. "She's been doing this longer than I thought. She must be giving him flux on a regular basis. Probably not just him, either."

Gage touched her with the needle, and she flinched away, subtly. The anesthetic obviously hadn't worked yet. He sat back, thinking about the conversation he'd caught pieces of as he'd followed the goddess, Chris, and the rest. "After seeing the barn, I'm guessing this is her opening act. She gives them what they expect. It's illicit, foreign, enhances the experience. Next time, she probably does it somewhere else, maybe somewhere a little classier. The tribute she mentioned is probably an escalating pay scale. Draw them in, make them feel like they're part of something. Convince them that someday they could make the inner circle."

"And the ones with real talent," Anson added, "something they can channel the energy into, are her stars."

"I think I heard Brad mention Vanrose," Gage confirmed. "He's a Hollywood producer. His first movie hit number one last month." He poked Marley's side again. This time she didn't move. He leaned in and tried not to wince as he stuck the needle through her skin. "You doing okay?"

Marley grunted. He slowly drew the nylon taut and tugged the edges of the cut together. No one talked while he stitched. He'd only gotten a quarter of the way through when Marley arched and yelled, "Motherfucking son of a bitch!" She flung out her arm, slamming her hand into Gage's chest.

He jerked but kept himself from puckering the wound and causing her even more pain. "I'm sorry."

"Not your fault," she squeezed out. She fisted his shirt in her hand and didn't seem inclined to let go.

"I don't have any more anesthetic."

"Just get it done."

He did, as quickly and as gently as he could. By the time he tied off and cut the final stitch, he didn't know if Marley was even conscious anymore. Her hand was still clenched against his chest so hard he wasn't sure she could let go even if awake. He swabbed her down, cleaning off as much blood as he could before bandaging her, peeling off the gloves, and gathering the trash. They'd have to find a Dumpster. If a maid found all this, the management might find it necessary to call the police. The comforter would have to go, too, and maybe the sheets under it. He'd check once they got her up.

"Marley." He said her name softly, bending over her to see if she was awake. Her hand slowly relaxed until it pressed flat against him. Not pushing him away, but almost a caress. He laid his hand over hers, suddenly aware of his heart beating in his chest. That she was feeling it, too, was strangely more intimate than what he'd just done to her side. "Are you awake?"

"Yeah," she rasped out.

"Let's move you to the other bed so you can rest. There are painkillers in the kit. I'll clean up and take the bloody stuff to dump somewhere."

"I've got it." Anson collected the pile Gage had left on the floor.

"No. We—" Marley opened her eyes and looked into Gage's, visibly shifting gears and changing what she'd been about to say. "Thank you," she murmured. "That definitely went above and beyond."

The motel room door opened behind Gage, then closed with a *click*.

"You're welcome." They stared silently at each other for a few seconds. Gage was falling in love with her eyes. Most people probably found them freaky, but they were so uniquely beautiful. Something so pale, so defined by the ring around her iris and the dark purple flecks should have been cold and empty. But they were full of life, full of emotion, and it made him want to study them to see how it was possible.

And then, even as he thought that, they went hard and cold like marble. Disappointment replaced the warmth in his chest as her hand dropped away. She lifted her head as if to rise, and Gage helped her sit up. Anson came back into the room, and Marley swung her legs over the side of the bed, her muscles tight under Gage's bracing hands. He shifted to help her to the other bed, but she shook her head.

"We've got to figure out our next move." She pressed her hand to her side. Goose bumps rose on her exposed skin, and she nodded toward a battered leather bag on top of the dresser. "Someone want to give me a shirt?"

Anson dug around a little and tossed her a button-down. She shook her head this time at Gage's silent offer to help and managed to get her arms in. "So what happened after you left the barn?" she asked him. "Where did they go? You didn't follow them very long."

Gage watched her fingers closing the buttons, hiding her drool-worthy cleavage. "I didn't need to. Brad, Tony, and Christopher talked loud enough for me to hear as they hiked to a luxury rental car near the back of the property. They were driving to Albany to get a flight to New York City."

"Crap." Marley slowly stood and stretched a little, testing her range. Anson pulled the covers off the bed and stuffed them into a trash bag. "New York. We'll never find her there."

"Yeah, we will," Gage contradicted without thinking. When had this turned into a team effort? When had he stopped being suspicious of Marley? Well, as soon as he'd seen the goddess in action and he knew Marley wasn't the flux dealer, but that didn't automatically put them on the same side. "Look, we need to step back a minute and focus on the people in this room." He included Anson with a glance, but the man raised a hand and shook his head.

"I'm support staff. This is between you two."

Marley didn't chew her lip or furrow her brow, but her eyes warmed again as she studied Gage. "What's your interest in all this?"

"What's yours?" When she didn't answer, he said, "You already know my brother is part of it. You give me something, then I'll give you more."

"Okay. My full name is Marley Canton. My sister is Quinn Caldwell."

"The president of the Society." That did explain a lot. "She sent you after the goddess? She knows about her?"

Alarm sped through Marley's expression so quickly Gage wasn't sure he'd seen it. "No. She hasn't sent me anywhere. I don't work for her. This is completely independent of the summit."

That was one too many sentences to be convincing, but Gage didn't think she was lying about Quinn's knowledge. Her tone was more about concern that he'd somehow rat Marley out to her sister.

But if Marley knew about the summit, she knew about Numina, too. "Why have you been following Numina?"

"Who says I have been?"

He chuckled. "The club. The church. Here. It's not coincidence."

Her eyes narrowed. "You're the Viper."

Uh-oh. He tried to look puzzled. "We're talking about superheroes now? Or is the Viper a supervillain."

"I saw your car in Boston and again by the church. You were following me."

He lowered his head and spread his hands to his sides in acknowledgment. "Busted. I saw what you did to Josh and decided you were a better lead."

"To what?"

"To the goddess who was responsible." He motioned in the direction of North Chatham and the barn. "My brother is involved with this somehow." He was going to keep his father's assignment to himself. Marley's loyalties would always be to the other side of the summit.

Marley nodded. "Involved in what way? Business or personal?"

He winced. "Maybe both. I was concerned before because he's been out of communication with us for a while, which is unusual. And after what we saw tonight, I'm well beyond concerned."

"You should be. Consider flux a gateway drug to a truckload of trouble." Her lips tightened, and she eased herself down on the corner of the unused bed. Anson, who'd moved quietly around them, checking drawers and packing loose items back into the first-aid kit and Marley's duffel, carried them outside.

"So what's next?" He figured they'd shared as much as either of them was inclined to, and the best way for him to learn more was to stick with her. Working together also increased his chances of finding Aiden.

"What did you hear when you followed them?" Marley braced her hands on her knees. Her breathing had grown shallower, but she showed no signs of intending to lie down and rest.

"Christopher said he'd arrange for the next group to meet them in the Pritchard Building," he said. "My father owns that building."

Marley raised her eyebrows. "That's a coincidence."

He smiled. "Not really. Christopher has an apartment there. Aiden does, too."

"So I shouldn't bother trying to get you to go away, huh?" Marley pushed slowly to her feet and let out a long breath.

"No. I think we're in this together now." He met her reticent gaze steadily, not intending to back down.

But she nodded and moved to open the door. "You said you had painkillers?"

"In the first-aid kit." He took a quick look around the room to make sure they hadn't left anything, then followed her out the door.

There was minimal basis for it, but instinct told him he stood to gain—or lose—far more in this adventure than he'd ever anticipated.

CHAPTER SIX

You pay for the granite countertops, multihead shower enclosures, and top-of-the-line security. The prestige and respect come free with the mailing address.

—Pritchard Building marketing materials

Marley stretched out in the back of the SUV, finally letting herself succumb to her exhaustion. It would take two to three hours to get to New York City, which would put them there just before dawn.

The pills she'd taken had dulled the stabbing, throbbing ache in her side and reduced her headache to barely noticeable, but enduring the stitches had taken its toll. Gage had missed the mark with the anesthesia—or it just hadn't been strong enough—so she'd felt every poke and slide of the curved needle, every tug when he tied off a stitch. She'd found other, better things to concentrate on: the slow glide of his breath, the way his spicy, woodsy scent filtered through the coppery stench of blood whenever he shifted position. His hands, gentle but decisive, making her shiver between waves of pain. The way he noticed her nearly naked body and somehow admired it without being distracted from his task. Though maybe she'd imagined that last part.

She hadn't intended to grab him. That had been a completely involuntary reaction when the needle pierced a spot not numbed by the anesthetic. But his hard, warm chest had grounded her, given her something tangible to concentrate on while he finished torturing her. Then there'd been that moment right after he finished when he'd stared into her eyes as if he found them the most fascinating things in the world. As if he found *her* fascinating.

It had been so long since Marley had felt appealing to anyone. It was intoxicating, and that made it unacceptable. She would never regress to the needy woman who'd helped Anson become a monster.

So she'd shut Gage out, ignoring how the silver of his eyes seemed to dim, and considered leaving him behind. But he'd made clear that wouldn't work. Their goals were too similar. Plus, he had inside access. They would both benefit from working together, suffer from trying to work separately. She just had to keep a tight rein on her attraction.

That wouldn't be easy with her resources compromised. The hallucination she'd had before they got back to the hotel still bothered her. For a few minutes, she'd have sworn she'd watched that cut seal closed. She'd been excited to think the nullifications had sparked her abilities again, but then they got to the motel and nothing had changed. She was still pouring blood all over herself.

Hopefully sleep would help, after the saving lives and the driving and the sneaking and the fighting and the being injured. Lack of sleep had to be the reason the ceiling of the truck kept moving, too. It twisted, rose away from her, and began to dissolve into green fog before a gust of air blew it away. A gust she didn't feel, that didn't move anything else. She blinked hard, and the ceiling looked normal, the dome light the only thing breaking the sweep of gray fabric over the guys' heads.

"I can't believe you left that car behind," Anson said to Gage in the front seat as the SUV accelerated onto the highway.

"It'll be fine until I can get a service up here to get it. I have a space in the city."

"So that's a V-10?"

Marley drifted off to car talk, the mundane chatter surprisingly comforting.

When she woke, they were mired in Manhattan traffic, inching past orange cones as road workers finished nighttime construction work. She yawned and maneuvered herself upright, twisting awkwardly to avoid using the muscles on her right side. She settled into the seat behind Gage and watched the city go by. Even at this early hour, one you could barely call morning, the street was full of cabs and cars, and people hustled up and down the sidewalks. Quinn would be here, ready to start the next round of talks at the summit hotel. If she ever found out Marley was in the city, hurt, and hadn't come to her for help, she'd give her a matching scar under her left rib cage.

Gage directed Anson to his father's building and the parking garage in the back. The entrance had a bar gate and security stand.

"How are we going to get in?" Marley's voice was raspy. She wished she had a bottle of water. She still felt weak.

"With this." Gage handed a card to Anson and passed a bottle of some kind of sports drink over the seat to Marley. "Drink the whole thing. I have a few more. You need a lot of fluids, but you also needed the rest." He leaned down so the guard could see his face. "Morning, Floyd. How'd you pull the early shift again?"

"Hey, Mr. Samargo." The fit, salt-and-peppered man flashed a white smile. "I traded with Paolo. His wife went into labor."

"Already? Wow! I've been gone too long. I'll have to send them a gift."

"It's a girl," Floyd said, handing back Gage's pass after swiping it through a reader. "According to the ultrasound, anyway."

"Awesome. Taylor wanted a little sister."

"That he did, that he did." Floyd nodded behind them. Marley turned to look out the back window. A BMW waited its turn to get in.

"Thanks, Floyd." Gage began to straighten, then leaned down again and asked, "My brother here?"

"No, sir. He's not on the log, and I didn't see him come in."

"Okay, thanks. Have a good day!" He sat up and replaced his card in his wallet, pensive until Anson asked where to go. "Up three levels. I have a space on four."

Anson wound the SUV up the ramps, the engine's roar echoing off the concrete. Marley watched Gage in the vehicle's side mirror. How someone treated those who served him was a standard test of character. Marley had known some guys, her small-town politician father among them, who knew kids' names and life events only so they could manipulate. Gage had sounded completely sincere.

"You have a space?" she asked as they reached the fourth level. "But you don't live here, do you? You said your brother does."

"My father does, too. The space goes with his apartment. All the way down on the right," he directed Anson.

Marley opened her door as soon as they'd parked. The fresh air—citified as it was—rejuvenated her a little. No one was around, but she slid a pair of sunglasses over her eyes, anyway. She walked to the open wall in front of the truck and stared at the brightening sky on the far horizon, a tiny slice between tall buildings on either side of the street, while she drank some of the sports drink. *Ugh, gross.*

Gage joined her at the wall. "Two Numina-owned businesses are headquartered here, and a lot of the descendants have apartments on the upper floors. They could be clients for Cressida Lahr. She might even be using one of the apartments for the next meeting. Chris's maybe."

"Seems likely." Marley tried to focus on the chill morning beyond the concrete barrier, but Gage was too close. He hadn't put his jacket back on, and his T-shirt hugged his shoulders. She kept looking at the way the sleeve followed the curve so perfectly, lying snug against his rounded biceps but not digging in. The long, lean muscles of his arm flexed under golden skin, leading her down to the strong wrist she'd noticed in the club.

"How are you feeling?" His voice was a low rumble that made her shiver.

"About how you'd expect." She touched her side absently.

Gage's arm came around her back. His hand slid under hers to brush the edges of the bandage. The move brought his chest against her shoulder so that she felt surrounded by him. She enjoyed the sensation far too much. Battling attraction was one thing, but attraction mixed with a desire to be taken care of? Fuck that.

"That stay on okay?" Gage asked.

Marley pulled away. "Fine. Feels damp, though. I should check it."

"Are we going to stand out here and wait for someone to drive by, or what?" Anson had pulled their bags out of the cargo area and stood frowning at Gage and Marley. "Just wondering if we have a plan. Or a place to go."

Gage moved away from the wall and slung his leather duffel over his shoulder, then hefted Marley's and motioned with his head toward the center of the structure. They followed him to an elevator paneled in mirrors but not staffed by an attendant. Marley hung her sunglasses from her jeans pocket and watched Gage swipe another card and punch in a code on a keypad before hitting floor ninety-eight, one below the top floor.

His access apparently turned the elevator into an express, because it glided smoothly upward without stopping or even indicating what floors they passed. None of them spoke. Marley closed her eyes and leaned heavily on the bar across the back wall. Her side ached and stung, making concentration difficult, but she tried to sense Numina on the floors they passed. With her narrow range and the elevator's speed, she didn't expect to. Even if she did, she wouldn't know what floor they were on or if they were relevant to their mission. Numina-owned businesses probably employed Numina, so it wasn't a valuable exercise. It just gave her something to think about besides Gage or her pain.

"We're here." Gage wrapped an arm around Marley's waist, his hand on her good side, to support her. She hadn't even noticed the doors open, they'd glided so silently. His hand slipped under the hem of her shirt, his skin hot on hers, and as innocent as it was, it sparked something restless and hungry that she barely recognized, it had been so long.

"I'm good." She moved away, letting him pass by to open the only door in the hallway. "Is this yours?"

"My family's. It's the only one on this side of the floor."

Marley frowned. "We're going to share with your parents?"

"My father prefers to stay in the hotel where they're holding the meetings." Gage turned the top lock and switched keys to unlock the bottom. "My mother's…not here."

Marley frowned. She couldn't remember reading anything about his mother. But then, she'd been concentrating her research on the men.

"Anyway, we can use this as our planning ground and stay here as long as we need to." He stood back for them to precede him inside.

Marley walked into a gray marble foyer with darker gray walls that somehow held a luster she'd never seen before. Gage tossed his keys into a silver tray that sat on a walnut table, and the overhead light glowed out of a silver chandelier.

The foyer opened into a huge sitting room in the same colors. Here, though, blue and white pillows, rugs, and decorative objects such as vases and carved animals nicely contrasted with the dark upholstery and black wood furniture. The lines were all clean and symmetrical—not showily modern but less than cozy.

And definitely not furniture Marley wanted to get blood on.

"Do you have somewhere I can shower?" She hated to waste any time, but the blood caked on her skin itched, and she felt grimy from scalp to soles.

"Of course. Down here." Gage signaled for them to walk down the hall with him. It was almost wide enough to walk two abreast. He stopped to turn on a light in a bedroom and said to Anson, "There's an en-suite bathroom in here. Help yourself."

Marley glimpsed a maroon bedspread and easy chair and the corner of what might be a desk before Anson thanked him and disappeared inside, closing the door.

Gage smiled at Marley. "Come on. You can have the master bedroom." He curved his arm around her waist again to guide her to the end of the hall. It was becoming a habit, but Marley couldn't make herself move away. She *was* still exhausted and his support *did* help, and she didn't want the sensations whirling inside her with every shift of his warm hand on her side to stop.

"I don't need the master," she said when they reached it and she saw there was another, very nice room opposite it. "I can take that one."

Gage shook his head. "That bathroom's too small. Too basic. Come on." He nudged her ahead of him into the room on the left, then directly into the bathroom before she could register anything about the bedroom/sitting room combination.

"Oh... Wow." For the first time in a very long time, Marley went girlie. The bathroom was, of course, massive. Easily as big as the parlor of her former inn. Down the left side ran a gray, granite-topped vanity with two large sinks and enough real estate between them to hold the toiletries of six people. The cabinets beneath were white but with curvy black trim that came across as both welcoming and avant-garde. A gigantic mirror ran the length of the wall over the sinks. An octagonal nook at the end of the counter held the toilet where a pocket door could be slid across the opening. On the wall directly ahead stood the shower, again big enough for three or four people, with multiple showerheads and molded seats behind clear glass. It was all too easy to imagine it as a sexual playground, and despite her pain and fatigue and griminess, the heat ignited by Gage's touches curled through her.

She turned hastily away to take in the light gray tiles on the floor, the big black armoire, and a Jacuzzi tub that was no safer for her imagination than the shower. Flowering plants cascaded out of high alcoves on the walls, and early morning light poured through the windows. She wanted to soak in that tub, indulge in scented bath oils and candles and gentle music. To take a half-hour shower, then wrap up in what she was sure would be large, thirsty towels. She even wanted to lather herself in silky lotions and put on makeup and a dress and go out for a long, normal evening with friends or on a date.

"What do you think?" Gage asked from behind her.

"I think I may never leave this room." Marley's boots echoed as she walked across the floor. "This is pretty amazing."

Gage shrugged. "It's home. My father had everything upgraded when he renovated, after—" He cleared his throat. "Anyway, it's all yours."

Marley looked at him closely for the first time since they arrived in the city. His eyes and shoulders drooped with his own exhaustion, and she realized that except for her naps in the truck, none of them had really slept. But more than tiredness weighed him down. She recognized sadness in eyes that right now held barely a hint of silver.

"Thank you," she said quietly. Her original intent had been to get right to work as soon as she was clean. Cressida and her followers most likely would have gotten to the city before them.

There was a chance that delaying would put them more steps behind, but it was too dangerous to engage anyone under these conditions. If they were going to go after Cressida as a team, they all had to be…well, if not in top shape, at least in *better* shape.

"I'm going to shower and get some real sleep," she said. "We should set a time to meet and discuss strategy."

Gage nodded and checked his watch. "How's ten thirty?"

"That's fine. Would you tell Anson, please?"

"Sure." He hesitated. "You shouldn't get the stitches wet. Infection."

Marley tried not to roll her eyes. "The bandage is waterproof, but you were there. If I'm going to get an infection, it's because of crud that was around me, not the water here."

He looked like he wanted to argue, but held his tongue. "All right. I'm gonna hit the shower, too. I'll be just across the hall, but help yourself to anything you need. Kitchen's always stocked with something, even when no one is expected."

Marley's stomach rumbled. She should eat, too, but cleanliness and sleep were more important. She'd fuel up during their meeting.

"Thanks," she said again. "Hey, mutual showers won't drain the hot water too fast, will they? I might…linger."

What on earth had possessed her to say it that way? *Be in there a while.* Now, that would've been much more neutral. Linger, especially with the hesitation first, sounded like a come-on.

If Gage took it that way, he didn't reveal it. "No, we'll have plenty of hot water. Enjoy." He closed the door behind him on the way out.

And Marley kicked her own ass for feeling disappointed.

• • •

Gage knocked on Anson's door and waited for several seconds before the man opened it. His hair was wet and he'd changed into sweats and an old, thin, ugly T-shirt. The comforter on the bed was flipped to one side, and the sheets and pillow were rumpled. He'd already been to bed.

Anson blinked heavy eyelids. "Yeah?"

"We're going to meet at ten thirty in the kitchen to plan."

"Okay." He abruptly closed the door.

Okay then.

Gage went out to double-check the alarm system. In case someone got thirsty before ten thirty, he turned on a dim light in the kitchen, an interior room with no outside windows. Then he grabbed his bag on the way back down the hall to the guest room he'd chosen. Only after he was in that room with two, maybe three, closed doors between him and Marley did he let loose the grin he'd been holding back.

He'd seen the flash of self-annoyance that had followed her words and knew she hadn't meant "linger" as an invitation. But she'd been aware of how it sounded, and he'd enjoyed the buzz of mutual attraction that had passed between them. That bathroom *did* inspire fantasies. He could imagine her soaping herself up, running her hands over those fantastic breasts, and… Okay, the blood that would run off her body and down the drain killed the image. He shouldn't have let her take a full shower but empathized too much with her desire to be clean. They'd have to get some antibiotics somewhere.

He stripped off his boots, jeans, and shirt and went into his own, much more pedestrian bathroom. He didn't need all the fancy stuff. The hot water alone was enough to make him groan. He let it pound on his head and aching shoulders, soak his hair, and revive his brain.

If it felt this good to him, he could imagine how it felt to Marley.

He braced his hands against the wall of the shower and leaned into them, blowing out water that dripped into his mouth. Had it really been less than thirty-six hours since he first laid eyes on her in the club Friday night? Yesterday she'd thwarted what appeared to be an attack at a church—he'd have to ask her about that—and then nullified the flux in two Deimons who'd obviously tried to stop her. They'd traveled three hundred miles, and though Marley was the only one who'd slept, it didn't really count given the knife wound and his not-so-gentle stitching. The three hours of sleep they'd scheduled weren't going to take any of them far.

He stayed that way, leaning against the tile, for god knew how long, unable to work up the energy to leave the shower. His mind drifted through images of the past two days until he wasn't sure he was fully awake. His mind became full of Marley's ivory skin, his hands stroking it and his mouth tasting it, her moans in his ear.

No. Not moans. Groans, and not human ones. That was the pipes. And apparently they'd tested the limits of the hot-water tank after all because his shower had gone cold. Probably a good thing since he'd dreamed himself into a decent hard-on.

He twisted off the water and stepped out onto the thick bath mat, dripping. After a few quick swipes with a towel, he took half-a-dozen steps into the bedroom and fell onto the bed naked. Hopefully no emergencies would come up before his alarm went off.

• • •

Gage dragged himself from solid darkness, through a fast-forward surge of dreams, and into bleary awareness. He cursed his noisy watch and the sadist who'd selected the alarm sound. It wasn't easy to turn off, either. He peered at the time while fumbling for the button. They'd be meeting in the kitchen in ten minutes. Marley was probably out there already, and he should scrounge up something for them to eat.

God, he was tired. But if he had any hope of finding Aiden and helping Marley stop the goddess, he had to get moving.

The alarm finally stopped attacking his eardrums. He dragged himself out of bed, pulled on jeans and a faded blue T-shirt, and headed for the kitchen. The tile floor was cool on his feet as he crossed the foyer. It was too silent, though, making him wonder if the other two had skipped out on him. Then he swung around the archway into the kitchen and relaxed. Anson wasn't there and the stainless-steel appliances appeared untouched, but Marley sat at the breakfast counter, a steaming mug of coffee next to the laptop in front of her.

Drawing in an appreciative breath of the strong brew, Gage crossed the spacious pentagonal room to the coffeemaker and poured his own cup. "Thanks for making this."

Marley gave an absent nod but didn't look up from the screen. Gage watched her, trying to decide if she was actively ignoring him or simply engrossed in whatever she was looking at. He gave her a few minutes while he let the coffee perk up his system.

He needed to call his father, to update him on what he'd learned, but he wasn't looking forward to the conversation. Gage had nothing new about Aiden. The goddess was far more powerful than his father had anticipated, and she was passing on that dangerous power to Numina. But that wouldn't give him the leverage he was looking for, because it looked like other Numina were involved in the enterprise.

His stomach rumbled. He turned to open cupboards and check the food situation. "Where's Anson?"

"Out."

"Out where? I thought he was sleeping." He found a couple of unopened boxes of cereal, but they had no milk. No eggs or bread, either. Pancake mix—but again, he found when he checked the instructions, no milk or eggs. Up on a top shelf he found a red box that triggered memories of his childhood. He pulled it down and checked the directions. It just needed water for a "hot and hearty breakfast." Behind the box was a sealed bag of raisins. That'd work.

"What are you looking at?" he asked Marley.

"I'm making a list of all the occupants of this building."

"All of them?" He set a saucepan on the stove and measured out water for two servings.

"What I can find."

She still sounded distracted, so Gage drank his coffee while he waited for the water to boil, added the grainy cereal, and stirred with a whisk until it thickened. He poured the contents of the pan into two bowls, added a handful of raisins and a sprinkling of sugar to each one, and carried them to the counter. He set one next to the laptop. After a few seconds, Marley looked down at it and frowned.

"What's this?"

"Cream of Wheat." He held out a spoon and waited for her to take it. "Healthy, hearty, and reminiscent of easier times. My mother made it when I was little."

A smile flickered across her mouth, and she took the utensil. "So did mine. Exactly like this. Thanks."

"You're welcome." He dipped his spoon into his bowl. "Is she involved with the summit? Your mother."

"Hell no." Marley blew on her cereal before taking a bite. "She was never into that kind of thing. She has far too much to do being the woman behind the man."

That sounded familiar. "Your dad's a politician?"

Marley's whole face lightened, her eyes sparkling with amusement. "I guess you know what I'm talking about. Your mother must have a similar duty. Mine has her own business and interests, at least. What about yours?"

Gage shifted on his stool and studied the furrow his spoon made through the cooling cereal. "She used to. She, uh, died when I was almost ten."

"I'm sorry," she said in a low voice. "I guess that means Aiden was just a baby."

"Yeah." He rubbed the heel of his hand against his breastbone, but the ache under it didn't dissipate. He took a deep breath and straightened, about to turn the conversation to something else. But the warm compassion in Marley's eyes caught him. He hadn't talked about this in years, but now, while they shared a meal their mothers used to make, it seemed natural to continue.

"It was postpartum depression. She drowned in the bathtub. We'd have thought it was an accident, that she just fell asleep, but she left a note."

Marley let out a small gasp. "Oh, Gage. How awful. Who found her?"

He laughed, the humorless sound cracking hard in the air. "A maid. That was always the best and worst thing. I was at school, and my dad had taken the day off to take Aiden out of the house and give her a break. He was strolling around the park with him while she did it. The maid got worried when she couldn't hear anything from the bathroom, but she went in way too late. She called the police and they had her body taken care of before my father even got home."

His eyes stung as he remembered being called to the school office, the guidance counselor meeting him in the hallway. She hadn't said anything, and he wouldn't have known from her expression that there was anything wrong. But the arm she'd put around his shoulders, the squeeze so full of tenderness, and the gentle way she spoke had scared him.

Marley's hand touched his knee, offering tentative comfort. He dropped his spoon in the bowl and laid his hand over hers, his fingers curling under. "I wasn't surprised when he came to get me from school. I'd had this sense of dread for months. She was just all wrong, you know? Dad told me new mothers cried a lot, but I knew it was more than that. She didn't want to hold the baby or hug me. There was no laughter or togetherness. Except…God, I forgot." The bowl clattered onto the countertop. Pain burned in his throat, his chest, his head. He ground his hands against his eyes.

"That last morning. She made me Cream of Wheat with raisins before I went to school."

A *thunk* on marble must have been Marley setting her own bowl down. A second later she stood in front of Gage, nudging under his hands to hug him tighter than he thought possible. He pulled her closer, burying his face in her hair. She still smelled like fresh air and sugary goodness. "I'm sorry. This is…insane."

Her body twitched, but she stroked a hand down the back of his head and rested it on the nape of his neck. "No. It's okay. Never apologize for missing her." She continued to soothe him, her hands soft and comforting on his shoulders and back, but it didn't take long for Gage to pull away from the old grief and refocus on what he held.

His arms were wrapped so tightly around her torso that one hand gripped her waist, the other her ribs above the bandage. Half an inch from the curve of her breast. Her raised arms lifted her chest against his, and her skin was warm on his cheek, close enough to taste.

He cleared his throat and loosened his arms. "Thanks. Sorry."

Marley eased back but didn't step away. Her eyes were damp. "I don't want to sound critical, but didn't anyone get her help?"

She was too close, seeing too much. "Oh yeah." He rotated on the stool to retrieve his now-cold cereal and shoved a spoonful in his mouth. Marley settled a hip onto her own stool but kept watching him. "They put her on antidepressants, and she was scheduled for counseling, but she didn't go most of the time. My father…" He trailed off. His father had been at a complete loss. He'd struggled to take care of sons of very different ages and needs and still do his job well enough to keep them going. Back then the companies had been in a growth cycle, with a lot invested and not much leeway for a leave of absence. Gage hadn't understood it then, but his father had no idea how to help his wife—or at least no true awareness of how deeply troubled she was.

But Gage wouldn't tell any of that to Marley. She was still a stranger, however much she didn't feel like one. "He did the best he could. It wasn't enough. He made up for it afterward, at least with me and Aiden. We're a lot closer than a lot of broken families."

He grabbed both their bowls and carried them to the sink, running water in them before he pulled out the coffeepot to top off both their mugs. "Anyway. That's not exactly relevant." He set the pot on a trivet built into the counter. "Let's talk about the barn."

"Yeah." She sounded resigned but more about the topic itself than Gage changing it. She stretched and sat fully on the stool. "Where do we start?"

"How about with the goddess. Cressida Lahr—you said that's her name?" Gage took a deep gulp of coffee, hoping the caffeine hit would give him back his equilibrium. "Man, I didn't think goddesses had that much power. She put them under some type of spell and then raised that kid off the ground."

Marley pressed her lips together, her hand tapping a pen against the counter. "Some of that is beyond the scope of what I believed goddesses to be capable of, too."

"Explain it to me." He cradled his mug and leaned an elbow on the counter. "How does it work? It's very different from—" Wow, had he really almost talked openly about the qualities inherent in Numina? He needed to get some control. The mother thing shouldn't have cracked him open that much. He'd been trained his whole life not to talk about his heritage, and for a second it almost came pouring out of him.

Numina power was subtle and inherent. Most of his peers took it for granted, but Gage had actually read the Numina manifesto and the book of history his people had begun centuries ago, wanting to understand where he came from.

During early American settlement, as descendants of the gods emigrated from all over the world, they'd drawn together Numina as a secret organization. The history was updated constantly, as the power of influence was explored and tested and honed. But it remained a quiet power, invisible and undetectable, and able to achieve only as much as the man was willing to invest. The stronger his influence, the greater his success, but that was about as far as it went.

Very different from what they had witnessed, however briefly, in the barn.

Marley was staring at her laptop, but her eyes were unfocused. Finally, she slapped it closed and faced him with folded arms. She didn't look like she wanted to share goddess secrets any more than he wanted to share Numina ones, but in the end, they were probably both going to have to give a little.

"Look, whatever they're doing, it's putting both sides at risk," he pointed out. "Goddesses and Numina. Just help me understand what we're up against."

She nodded. "I know. It's just…not an easy topic."

He wondered if she was referring to whatever had happened to take her own power. Leeching, Anson had called it.

"Each goddess has a source that serves as a conduit for a supply of energy. Sources vary widely, so how strong a goddess is varies, too. And we all have different…talents, I guess. Some goddesses are better at healing. Some are strong telekinetics or can affect electronics or sense and communicate with life forms. Cressida Lahr's source is apparently the sun."

She paused, and Gage understood why. "Which is the greatest source that exists, I'd imagine." She nodded, and he asked, "How many of you have the sun as a source?"

"Only two that I'm aware of. And one died a few months ago."

"What's your source?"

Her brows tightened with clear annoyance before she said, "It was crystals. Amethyst, quartz, aventurine, stuff like that."

So probably nothing that allowed the kind of access the sun

did. He didn't miss her use of past tense, and was careful when he said, "Could you store it? The energy?"

"Some. That's probably why she was able to bestow it at night, even though her source wasn't directly accessible."

Gage drank some more of his coffee, thinking. "Are we sure it's not? There's ambient energy passing the Earth constantly, even when the planet is blocking the visible light."

"I'm not sure of much." Marley sighed. "I do know that what she gave them last night would only last a little while. It doesn't give them her ability to use the sun. When they want more, she'll have to give it to them."

But that wasn't completely true. He still couldn't remember exactly where he'd heard about leeches, but more of the information was popping up in his brain. They had to have power before they could take power. "Does it allow them to get more from someone else? To leech them?"

Her expression tightened. "It can, if she gives them enough."

"And then they'd have the ability to do…what?"

She shrugged. "Pretty much whatever a goddess can do. And I would guess that it boosts your influence."

He jolted a little at hearing her use of the word. He'd only ever heard Numina—in other words, men—use the word that way. "Because of Vanrose, you mean? The producer?"

"Yeah. The football player has physical ways to use it. The producer is convincing people to make his movies, and making sure they do well. I'm not sure how, but that's gotta be an enhancement of his natural ability."

Gage agreed, and it gave him new insight into what may have caused Aiden to abandon his assignment. Too many Numina had no patience for the slow growth their grandfathers, great-grandfathers, and so on had been used to. Aiden wasn't a bad kid, but he'd had trouble figuring out what he wanted to do with his life. It made Gage a little sick to think his little brother may have been enticed by the kind of thing they'd witnessed in the barn last night.

"Why Numina?" he demanded, frustrated. "Why is she preying on us?"

Marley glared into her mug, maybe to keep from glaring at him. "It's the bloodline. Goddesses can't bestow power on a normal guy, only the son of a goddess. Numina are descended from the same ancient races we are, so the genetic similarity must be strong enough."

"What's your involvement in this?" Gage jerked his chin at Marley. "Why do you care about guys using a drug to make themselves better?"

"Because the power isn't theirs!" Marley slammed her hand on the counter. "They're not supposed to have it. Nothing good comes from such transfers."

"Ever?" Gage had fallen into playing devil's advocate. He couldn't imagine justifying the use of something like flux, even for beneficial outcomes, but maybe others could. "It doesn't have to be used for robbing casinos and coercing women in clubs. Pettle and Vanrose aren't hurting anyone, and someone could use the enhancement for charitable or philanthropic purposes."

This time Marley's glare was directed at him. "Do you see me going after Pettle and Vanrose? They're not a danger to anyone. Now. When that changes, I will."

Gage went cold. "What do you mean, *when* that changes?"

She blew out a breath. "There's some talk that the flux is more than just ready energy. It may affect them in other ways. Make them more aggressive, maybe. I'm not sure if that's universal, but it's an even greater incentive for me to do this."

Gage gripped the edge of the counter so tightly his knuckles cracked. She was telling him that his brother could be mentally or emotionally damaged by flux. And what about when there was already a genetic predisposition? Aiden was the moody, broody one. Their father had watched him closely his whole life, made him undergo more than the basic medical exam every year, and even had him assessed periodically by mental-health professionals. So far, everything had been fine, but it could be lurking, waiting. Just like his mother had been triggered by pregnancy and childbirth. Flux could be the trigger that activated mental illness in Aiden.

No. It was not going to happen. Gage wouldn't let it, and Marley seemed the only way to guarantee it. If Aiden had taken flux, she could nullify him. If he hadn't, then they had to stop Lahr before he did.

But Gage didn't understand *why* Marley was their only hope.

"Why you?" He stood and spread his hands. "Why have you taken on the responsibility of nullifying everyone?"

She whirled off her stool and paced to the other side of the island attached to the breakfast bar. "Because I can. I don't think there's ever been anyone else who could."

"So how can you?"

His obvious, simple question hung between them. Anguish darkened Marley's eyes to ivory, and for a moment he thought she was going to run from the room. But then the anguish hardened, her shoulders straightened, and calm seemed to saturate her.

"Do you know why the summit is happening? Between the Society and Numina?"

"Yes," he said cautiously. The party line was that the time had come for the related groups to recognize each other and find a way to come together. But Gage's father had told him about the splinter groups that didn't like the way things were traditionally done. Some of the men in those groups had overreached and come crashing down. They wanted back whatever they'd lost—money, respect, position—and weren't necessarily picky about how they got it.

Since he didn't know how much *Marley* knew, he wasn't going to spell it out. She didn't ask him to.

"Do you know that members of Numina paid the leech to do what he did?"

"I—" Totally clueless, Gage shook his head. "What do you mean? What he did to you?"

She pushed away from the island and started pacing. "Down-and-dirty summary: Numina hired an ambitious young son of a goddess to collect power. A woman fell in love with him and bestowed enough power on him that he was able to leech four other goddesses—five, counting me—before he was stopped. He was jailed for two years, which put a crimp in the Numina splinter group's plans, but they're nothing if not determined, so they set him on another path earlier this year. That's when the Society found out about Numina and began making efforts toward the summit."

"Okay..." Gage folded his arms and braced his feet wide, watching her pace. "That doesn't explain why this seems to be a personal quest that you're on alone."

She stopped moving, took a deep breath, and plunged both hands into her hair, pushing it all back off her face. "All of this is my fault. This goddess, Cressida Lahr, disappeared years ago. She didn't start handing out flux until after the leech was created. They got the idea of the bestowments from me. No one would ever have known it was possible if I hadn't fallen in love with an asshole and given him what I thought was a gift."

"It was a gift," Anson said as he entered the room, his arms full of bags, folders, and a large cardboard tube. "He was just too stupid to recognize it."

Marley didn't look at Anson, but his words resonated between them. More than a reassurance. An apology. Why would he apologize, unless he was the one too stupid to recognize her gift? Which meant...Anson was the leech?

Gage reeled, but the math fell apart after that conclusion. If he'd leeched Marley, why was she working with him now? Was she still in love with him?

Anson deposited everything on the counter and started emptying the bags of food. Gage couldn't ask her with the other guy in the room. He struggled to get back to the reason they'd been talking about leeches in the first place, and he remembered his original question. "So you feel responsible," he said to Marley, moving closer. "But that doesn't explain how you can nullify them. Why you're the only one who can."

She shook her head, her shoulders slumping. "Bestowing the energy isn't natural. It damaged the part of me that holds it, and the leeching made it irreparable. But it also created something like a void. When I come in contact with the energy, it goes inert—almost like someone flips a switch, rendering it completely inactive—and transfers from them to me. We don't have record of those two things ever happening before, and definitely not in modern times. So as far as we know, I'm the only one."

"Was that what you were doing at the church yesterday?" He grabbed the empty coffeemaker and dodged Anson on his way to the fridge with a gallon of milk and a six-pack of beer. "Was that guy on flux?"

"Yes, but that wasn't…" She pressed her mouth together, and he wondered if she regretted how much she'd already told him. "He was an assassin. It was my friends' wedding, and I didn't want him to ruin it. So I stopped him." She grabbed the cardboard tube Anson had brought in and yanked the plastic cap out of the end.

"Who was he?" When Marley acted like she was completely engrossed in rolling out what looked like blueprints, he said, "He had to be Numina if he had flux. Why would he want to kill your friends? Why didn't you call the police?"

"I left him for Quinn. She brought him to your father and the other leaders. It has nothing to do with us now."

He had a feeling it had a lot to do with her personally, but he recognized when it was time to let something go. He finished setting up the coffeemaker to brew another full pot, then turned to Anson. "I made some hot cereal. I can make more if you want some."

Anson shook his head and stuffed all the loose plastic bags into one. "No, thanks. I grabbed a McMuffin while I was out." He opened a cabinet under the counter and tossed the bags in.

Marley spread the papers out on the island.

Gage rinsed out his and Marley's mugs and took a third one down for Anson. "Is that this building?" He motioned to the sheets. "Where did you get that?"

"Hall of records." Anson settled against the counter next to the stove. His posture was watchful, ready. No wasted movement, though one could also assume he didn't have any energy to waste. He couldn't have slept very long before he went out for groceries and building plans.

"The hall of records isn't open on Sunday," Gage said.

"Open to the right people with the right resources," Anson responded.

"What kind of resources?"

Anson smiled, perhaps the first one Gage had seen from him. It deepened the shadows around his sunken eyes and crumpled the skin that was stretched too tight over his bones. But there was still a glimmer of something that the right person would probably see as a "rescue me" kind of challenge. Heat rushed up through Gage. Barbed, bitter heat that it took him several heartbeats to recognize as jealousy. Until now, he hadn't detected even a hint of anything romantic between Marley and Anson. But he knew women were supposed to go for that wounded-hero stuff, and Marley had extra motivation if she blamed herself for everything that had happened. He'd seen twisted logic used to justify feelings before, and the pink tint on Marley's cheeks right now made Gage grind his teeth.

He barely knew her. He had no business being jealous.

Marley came around the island to lay a 3-D architectural rendering of the building on the wide granite counter. She left a few rolled pages on the breakfast bar that Gage assumed were more detailed blueprints.

"Can you help me label this?" She pointed to the drawing and tapped the list she'd been making earlier. Gage and Anson moved in on either side of her. With a few quick notes, she marked companies on the lower floors and the residential business office for the top fifteen floors. Finally, she scrawled "here" in the apartment on the ninety-eighth floor and leaned back. "Who am I missing?"

"This is Aiden's. And here's Chris's." Gage pointed, and Marley marked them. But his brain was working faster than her hand, so he plucked the pen away and quickly scrawled the names of other residents and businesses he knew off the top of his head. "I don't know how much good this will do us. There are a lot more that I don't know." He finished the last one he could think of and handed her the pen.

"It's good to know the lay of the land," she said. "I can walk by these apartments and see if I can sense them inside." She tapped her finger on Chris's and Aiden's boxes, which were in the same hallway but not right next to each other.

"Sense them how?"

She tensed. A small movement he wouldn't have noticed if he hadn't been standing right next to her. Was it because of his question or because their bodies were touching?

"I can recognize a Numina signature, as well as whether or not they have flux." She waved a hand over the page. "Anywhere else you think is a possible place they'd stage a meeting or something?"

Gage studied the rendering and tried to think. None of the businesses or public areas would do. There were conference rooms and hospitality suites that could be rented, but they had to be registered, and he doubted they'd take that risk. Some would be cautious about getting caught and others wouldn't want to "share" what they saw as an exclusive group.

"No, the apartments are the most likely places, I think."

"The guys you asked me about at the club. The friends of Aiden's. They were all there last night, right? Brad, Tony, and Chris."

"Yeah, but Brad and Tony don't have apartments here in the city at all, as far as I know. Their fathers are partners and headquartered in Chicago with no branches here. So they just crash with Chris or Aiden when they're all in town."

Marley tilted her head and studied him. "Why do you think Aiden wasn't there?"

Gage had no clue. He hadn't told Marley about his father sending Aiden to join the Deimons to get inside information about the goddess, and he wasn't going to. He'd already gone further than his father would have sanctioned. He had to keep some family business private.

"How long has he been out of touch?"

He rubbed a hand over his face. "A couple of weeks."

"Doesn't he work? He's out of college, right?"

"He doesn't need to work." He failed to keep the resignation out of his voice. "A trust was set up in his name the day he was born, and he got access to an income as soon as he obtained his bachelor's degree." He leaned against the side of the island. "If he gets a master's or goes to work for Samargo United or any other legitimate enterprise—or turns a profit on his own business—he gets full access. Otherwise, he can't touch the bulk of it until he becomes a father or turns thirty." He shrugged. "The income is more than enough for him to ignore all the rest of that. He doesn't need the full trust."

"Yet," Anson pointed out. "We don't know the nature of his involvement with Cressida. If he's on the investment side, he might need more money."

Marley was still looking at Gage. "You didn't get this trust setup?"

Gage flushed a little. "I did."

"But you work. Hard, from what I can tell." She flicked a finger at the laptop, so Gage knew she'd researched him.

"I prefer to earn my own way. I've used some of the trust money. I'm not a saint, but most of it gets reinvested or donated to charity and stuff."

Marley's mouth curved and her eyes lightened. "It embarrasses you," she observed. "I like that."

Anson cleared his throat and pulled the 3-D drawing away. "So what's the plan?"

Marley tucked her fingers into her jeans pockets and settled on her heels. "First, I go scope out the hall outside their apartments. How big are they, compared to this?" She indicated the room they were standing in.

"About half the size."

"Should be well within your range," Anson said.

Marley nodded.

"You can't be seen," he said. For the first time, Gage heard a note of concern in the man's implacable, almost android-like tone. "They saw you this time. They know who you are. The word will have spread."

"I know. Don't worry." She folded up the drawing and shoved it into the rear pocket of her jeans.

"I should go with you," Gage called out as Marley exited the kitchen. He followed her down the hall, where she paused in front of the master suite, one capable hand gripping the molding around the door.

"That was my intention." She jerked her chin at him. "Is that how you usually dress?"

He looked down at himself. The cuffs of his jeans were frayed above his bare feet, and his T-shirt had a half-inch hole near the hem. He grinned. "No."

"Get changed. We'll head out in five. Anson will monitor us on comms."

"You have comms?" His only answer was her door closing, but when he said, "Cool!" he was pretty sure she laughed.

CHAPTER SEVEN

Uneasy times can lead to uneasy alliances. Use instinct—if a gut check makes you hesitate, seek a second opinion before shaking hands or signing on the dotted line.
—Protectorate monthly newsletter

Marley strode down a hallway with Gage at her side, swamped in déjà vu. Six months ago she'd traveled similar hallways with Sam while he'd tried to sense Riley and Quinn in the apartments they passed. At the time, she'd struggled against self-pity and regret for losing her own ability to do the job. Now it was the opposite. She was seeking Numina, and Gage was just along for the ride.

She wished he wasn't. She couldn't block out her awareness of his Numina signature, but she'd work around that when they got closer to the apartments. No, it was for purely unprofessional reasons that she was regretting not going solo.

He smelled good. He hadn't shaved so it wasn't aftershave or cologne. He must use some masculine-scented soap. It came to her in waves and threw her off every bit as much as his Numina identity did.

Since changing his clothes, he looked good, too. Not that he hadn't been sexy in ratty jeans and a T-shirt, but he'd changed into expensive black pants with cordovan shoes and a barely gray dress shirt that was obviously custom tailored. He'd rolled the sleeves and added a loosely knotted tie. Combine that with the stubble on his jaw and hair that hadn't been combed after his shower so it was a little bit wild, and he bordered on devastating.

He stayed silent as they walked, his hands in his pockets, and moved with an easy, rolling gait. He never touched her, asked her questions beyond what was necessary, or otherwise got in her way. In spite of that—or maybe because of it—he distracted her like crazy.

Maybe she shouldn't have hugged him when he was talking about his mother. The contact hadn't been sexual in any way, but it was like every cell of her body had been put on alert, waiting for an appropriate moment.

Marley slowed her steps as they approached Aiden's apartment. They were starting here because Gage had a key. Before she let him use it, she closed her eyes and focused to her left. Awareness flashed immediately, but too close. She opened her eyes and motioned Gage behind her. He complied, and she tried again. Nothing. Since her leeching, she'd lost the common goddess ability to tell the difference between goddesses and regular people, so she didn't know if there were any in the apartment. She only knew that there were no Numina.

She was still unsure why she could detect the Numina signature or the flux itself. Her first nullification had been Sam, and the power in him had been almost completely hers. He wasn't Numina—Riley, the only other person Marley knew of who was aware of the Numina signature, had made that clear. Anson had been next, and they'd established that he had no Numina blood, either. So why didn't those nullifications allow her to detect the people she'd nullified? Anson was as blank in her awareness as any person on the street.

But as she'd told Sam and Riley last night, this was magic, not science. What she'd become shouldn't have been possible at all. So who cared if the rules didn't make sense? Maybe she just didn't know enough to understand them.

She stepped back and shook her head. "No one's in there. Not Numina, anyway." Gage stepped forward and knocked hard, his easy stance gone. They waited. Nothing. He knocked again. A minute later, still nothing, and tension had slithered up Marley's body. "Go ahead," she encouraged. "Even if he's not there, we might find something that will tell us where he is."

"I was already here," Gage said. "I took his laptop, which was where he had information on the Deimons, but there wasn't anything else." He unlocked the deadbolt and handle lock and opened the door.

Marley paused at the doorway to tap her comm. "We're going into the apartment," she told Anson. "I don't think anyone is here."

"Roger that."

But Gage had frozen just inside the door. "There's a light on," he said in a low voice, both in front of her and in her ear. He'd activated his comm, too. "And the alarm's off."

Marley waited while he locked the door behind them and called out his brother's name. No answer, and she still didn't sense anything. So he either wasn't here anymore—assuming he'd been the one to leave the light on—or he was dead.

Despite the lack of communication, they had no reason to think he could be dead. But if he *was,* Gage shouldn't be the one to discover his brother's body. After what he'd told her about his mother, Marley couldn't let that happen. He took a step, but she caught his arm at the elbow and tugged him back.

"Let me." She slid Gashface's Ruger from the back of her waistband. As soon as Gage saw it, he eased back without protest.

How about that? A man who didn't let protective instincts overwhelm his intelligence. Marley's respect for him kept climbing.

She swept through the living area and a den set up as a game room. "Clear," she murmured to Anson on the comm and to Gage on her way back through the living room. She moved toward the light in the kitchen and stepped carefully through the door, making sure the gun pointed in every direction she looked. All one movement. All one axis.

This kitchen was a lot smaller and less elegant than the one upstairs, with laminate instead of marble. There was a side dining area with a wood-laminate floor and a country-style table and chairs. A lamp mounted on the wall over the table cast a golden glow on the area. Marley made sure no one hid in—or was hidden by—the kitchen's shadows. She glanced at the papers spread across the table next to a closed laptop. Her exposure to financial reports was limited, but these appeared to be projections and proposals for something.

She made quick work of the two bedrooms and central bathroom. None held any sign that someone had been there recently. The towels and sink were dry, the bed professionally made. No one had slept in it since the last time housekeeping was in. No twenty-five-year-old guy who didn't feel it necessary to work would bother with hospital corners and precisely tucked pillows.

She secured the Ruger and called to Gage after returning to the kitchen. "All clear. And there's something in here."

He appeared almost immediately. Marley suspected he'd followed her after she'd cleared the other two rooms but didn't say anything since he'd stayed out of the way.

"I thought you said you took his computer. Were these all here before?" She indicated the papers on the table.

"No, it was cleaned off. I've never seen that laptop. Maybe he got a new one." He moved to examine the papers. Marley found the main switch for the kitchen lights and flipped them on. No dishes in the sink, but the dishwasher, less than half full, had been run. She tried to reconcile that with her earlier thoughts about housekeeping. The dishes were haphazardly placed, so maybe Aiden was somewhat conscientious and hadn't wanted it to smell. Which meant he probably wasn't planning on coming back for a little while.

"How often does housekeeping come in?" she asked.

"Hmm? About once a week." He added the page he'd been perusing to a pile in his left hand and picked up another from the table. "Every two weeks if he's not here. Why?"

"Putting together pieces of the puzzle." There were no magnets on the refrigerator door, never mind convenient slips of paper with the date and time of a meeting with the sun goddess. "Is there anywhere else he'd stay if he was going to be in town?"

"No." Gage stacked the pages and tapped them on the table to align them before he set them down and pulled the laptop over. "But he sometimes crashes at Christopher's, if they're on a gaming marathon or something."

Marley opened a few drawers but found nothing but bare essentials. "So what's the paperwork for?"

"A lot of it is just investment reports from his trust and stuff, but some of it looks like he's planning on starting a business."

"What kind of business?"

He shrugged and jiggled the wireless mouse while the boot screens flashed and blinked. "Doesn't say. It's all general, preliminary stuff."

Marley would take his word for it. Her father had done most of the work setting up her inn's finances, and while he'd often lectured her on wise investing and taking care of her money, she'd cared more about the people side of things.

Gage, on the other hand, had managed to balance both. At least according to the reading she'd done on him. He looked every inch the businessman right now, his eyes focused intently on the material he scanned on the laptop, his fingers quick on the keyboard. Marley could easily picture him in the boardroom or on a golf course, schmoozing clients and investors—with or without influence.

A clock in the other room chimed. She pushed away from the counter she'd been leaning on and winced when the movement pulled at her stitches. The rest of the apartment, spare as it seemed, could still hold clues.

It was a short search, partly because she didn't know what she was looking for and partly because there wasn't much to sort through. If Aiden spent much time here—and she suspected he didn't—he was usually in the game room playing games. He had a massive collection for his four gaming systems.

The bathroom and Aiden's bedroom were clean and neat, with more clothes and toiletries than Marley had owned in her entire life, but nothing was out of the ordinary. Under the beds—in Aiden's room and the guest room—was just empty carpet. If he had a hidey-hole anywhere, she couldn't find it. Nothing was stashed inside the ventilation grates, either, at least not within flashlight range. No safes tucked behind pictures on the walls or envelopes taped under drawers or any ingenious place she could come up with.

She checked in with Anson and headed back to the kitchen. Gage looked up as she entered, his gaze locking on hers for an unguarded second. The silvery-blue flashed with pleasure, and Marley shivered.

To cover her reaction, she walked over and stood behind him to view the laptop screen. "Find something?"

He slumped a little and shook his head. "Nothing. He must have bought this after I took his old one. There's barely anything on it. Just more of this stuff"—he flipped some of the papers—"too unspecific to help."

"Okay. Let's check out Christopher's then."

A few moments later, Marley tapped her comm on the way out of Aiden's apartment and updated Anson. She swung left and checked the fancy gold numbers on the doors. She heard the *slide-snap* of the deadlock behind her, and Gage caught up a few seconds later.

"What are we going to do at Christopher's?" he asked in a low voice.

"Good question," Anson added.

"I'll decide after we get there and determine if anyone's home."

She slowed when they approached the corner to the hallway where Christopher's apartment was. She knew it was to the right and across the hall, but she wasn't sure how far down his entry door was. The plush carpeting and thick walls would absorb sound, so she couldn't tell if anyone was coming from that direction.

Alcoves set into the walls held fresh flowers, statues, or framed art at intervals, and this hallway didn't end in a bland corner but rather with a larger nook that extended past the juncture. A large marble sculpture of a naked man dominated the space. Marley shifted to stand with her back against the wall of the intersection. She motioned Gage to stay back and slowly leaned toward the corner until she could peer around it.

Christopher's door was about five feet down. She detected half-a-dozen Numina behind it, and at least one of those signatures contained the blue shine that came from flux.

She grinned, eager for action. All she had to do was wait until they left and follow them. One touch, and they'd be nullified. But no, that was shortsighted. Nullifying the flux wasn't her only goal anymore. She had to stay hidden, to let things play out until they knew how to stop Lahr. But at least they knew someone was here, and Christopher had been with the goddess last night, so hopefully she was still nearby.

She might even be in the apartment. Every inch of Marley jonesed to bust through the door and find out. She was halfway through envisioning it, her muscles bunching for action, when common sense took over again. This was a building for rich people, or at least people who wanted to live like they were rich. That door wouldn't bust easily, even with Marley's enhanced strength. If she did get through it and Lahr was on the other side, what was she going to do? Battle her? With the power the goddess had at her disposal, Marley wouldn't stand a chance.

Gage's hand closed slowly around her wrist. "What are you planning?" His whisper wasn't audible in the hall but filtered into her ear through the comm.

"Marley, what's going on?" Anson asked immediately.

"Nothing," she murmured, holding herself still. Gage must have detected her gathering tension. She had to give him credit for his awareness but wished he'd trusted her more. Then she wouldn't have to endure his warm, masculine hand that held strength and gentleness in equal parts. She wouldn't notice that his skin was spa-soft but with calluses that scraped just enough across her skin to induce shivers.

"Where are you?" Anson demanded.

Marley kept her whisper as quiet as Gage's had been. "Outside Christopher's apartment. They're in there. Six people. Five regular Numina, and I think only one fluxed."

"Okay, come back. We'll strategize."

Too late. The signatures had moved closer. They were about to come out into the hall.

Marley wrapped her hand around Gage's forearm and yanked him after her, across the intersection and into the alcove. They squeezed behind the marble statue just in time. A door opened, accompanied by a jumble of voices.

Since the marble was white and Marley was dressed in dark jeans and a black shirt, she wouldn't be well hidden if anyone looked. Gage positioned himself in front of her, clearly thinking the same thing. His shoulders barely stretched wider than the statue's, so at first glance maybe they wouldn't be seen. He laid his hands on her hips, as if to hold her in position, but turned his head to listen and seemed barely aware of her presence.

Amused, she stood motionless and listened. Two of the Deimons said good-bye, and their voices faded down the hall in the opposite direction, toward the elevator. Besides the guy with flux, Marley could detect three distinct Numina signatures now. She drew in a breath. Three *distinct* signatures. Not just separate but unique. She couldn't do that before. It had to be due to the wave of energy she'd absorbed in the woods, or maybe nullifying those two fresh fluxheads. That energy had been stronger than what she'd taken before, so maybe it had a more powerful effect on her.

Elated, she wished for another way to check how far her ability stretched. Then she realized she had another Numina right in front of her. Sure enough, when she compared her awareness of him to her awareness of the other guys, his hum vibrated differently. As unique as his voice and scent.

She shifted her weight and blinked hard to disconnect. That was way too much intimacy, no matter how unaware he was.

"I'll see you at nine tonight," one of the Numina said.

Christopher, Gage mouthed, and Marley nodded, fixing his hum in her mind.

"Hang on." The fluxhead. He kept his voice low, but Marley had no trouble hearing him. "I heard she was up at the barn. She took Barry and Damian's flux before— " He was shushed in stereo and dropped his voice even further. Judging by Gage's frustrated look, he was having trouble hearing now. Marley had to work harder but could still catch every word.

"Before they even got to the parking lot. I don't know if I want to risk this. Maybe we should all lay low for a little while, until we know the threat's been neutralized."

Christopher spoke again. "We can't reschedule. Cressida is only in town tonight. If you want the next level, you have to come to the ceremony."

"But I could go to LA," the other guy suggested. "We could just do it there."

Another guy's voice held amused disdain as he answered. "You can't get the next level in LA. This set gets done here. LA is for the stars."

"Like Pettle." He named the football player with bitter envy, then let out a squeaky kind of noise that had Gage's eyebrows rising and Marley wondering if one of the other guys had poked the kid—or worse.

"Do things the right way," Christopher said, "and you'll get to LA. Eventually."

The kid sighed. "All right. I'll be here at nine. What do I need to bring again?"

There was a collective sigh. The Numina farthest back in the entryway grumbled something Marley didn't catch, and then Christopher spoke again. "The tribute you committed to at the barn. A demonstration or description of how you've used the gift so far. A presentation of your goals."

"Right, right. Got it. See you then!"

More grumbling, then the door closed. The kid's voice trailed off down the hall. He sounded like he was reciting Christopher's list.

Marley stared up at Gage. She needed to get ears inside that apartment. They had just over eight hours until the meeting, and Cressida would be gone after that. To LA. Not that California put her out of reach. But it would be far easier to take her down tonight, or barring that, collect information that might give them some clue *how* to take her down.

Gage's fingers tightened on Marley's hips, snapping her into the present. She stood inches away from him, her head tilted back in unintentional invitation. Gage watched her as if her thoughts had passed like a video across her face. Hell, maybe they had. She hadn't been trying to hide anything in those few seconds. But now with her focus off the conversation ten feet away and back in this cozy little alcove, she felt the heat of him all the way down her body, not just where he touched her. His scent had filled her while she wasn't paying attention, enticing her until she wanted to bury her face in his neck and drink deep. See if he tasted as good as he smelled.

Her eyelids flicked down, and her gaze landed on his mouth. It curved to a centimeter shy of smug. Marley let her lips part to see what he would do. His smile covered that centimeter and more, but when he tilted forward and leaned down, she didn't move.

Her brain yelled, *Hey! Moron! What the hell are you doing?* but she didn't step back or push him away. His mouth lowered slowly, his lashes drifting over his cheekbones so she couldn't see those gorgeous, silver-swirled eyes. Then she closed her own, and his open mouth brushed hers. Hovered, not waiting for permission or rejection, but…savoring her. With a sigh he closed the gap and pressed against her lips.

Tingles sent Marley into a shiver as Gage pulled her closer and wrapped his arms around her back, careful to avoid her wound. One hand cupped the back of her head as he deepened the kiss a little at a time.

And fuck it all—she should have listened to her brain. Because all the senses she'd ignored for almost five years lit up like the Christmas tree in Rockefeller Plaza, soaking in sensory input like a sponge. No, forget sponge—she was a freaking black hole of sensation, from the skin burning under the hand that had somehow made it up under her shirt to the electric, hungry clinging of their mouths. Marley opened hers to let him in deeper. God, he tasted good.

Desire pounded a multibeat rhythm in half-a-dozen parts of her body. His tongue dipped inside, slow and seductive, and she sucked it. Gage moaned and shifted, twisting to bend her back over his arm.

"What's going on?" came Anson over the apparently still-on comm. Marley had gotten so used to the faint hiss she'd stopped hearing it.

Gage levered her upright, and she stepped back so his hands dropped away from her.

"Nothing," she reported, annoyed that her voice came out a shade husky. "We'll be right up." She tapped off her comm and waited for Gage to do the same. He did, without taking his eyes off her. Her heart rate slowed and her breathing grew less labored. Nothing happened except Gage standing, waiting. His hands flexed, and Marley wanted to step back into his arms.

Instead, she bolted, squeezing past the sculpted Greek warrior or whatever he was, and with a quick check to be sure the hall was clear, she hurried toward the stairwell. Gage was beside her in two strides.

She couldn't do this. Her judgment was so beyond questionable when it came to romance, she couldn't be openly trusting of anyone, never mind someone from the other side. However aligned their goals might be, he was Numina, and so were the enemies of the Society. His father was in charge of making sure no one damaged Numina's foundation, and his loyalties would lie with his own men, even if he didn't condone what they'd done. How could she trust that Gage wouldn't make choices against her, against the people she loved?

Getting involved with the wrong guy was a mistake she was *not* going to repeat.

"We need to get access to that apartment," she said once they were out of earshot. "I want to know more details about this ceremony at nine o'clock."

"I have some ideas about that." Gage pulled open the stairwell door and stood back to let her go ahead of him. He removed the piece of paper they'd stuffed in the latch to keep it from locking, and they headed up the stairs.

"I'm not sure if we have the kind of equipment we'd need to listen remotely," she said, thinking aloud. "Anson will know if we do or if he can get it."

Gage came even with her, easily maintaining the pace she'd set. "It's New York City. Of course we can get it."

"Fast, with no one knowing about it?" she asked skeptically. When Gage just looked at her like she'd undergone a memory wipe, she sighed. "Okay, I guess with money like yours, you can do anything."

"It's not just that." They rounded a landing and continued up. "I probably have some of it, at least, at the office."

"Okay." Gage had pulled ahead of her since he had the inside corner on the turns. She pushed herself a little faster, ignoring the renewed pull in her right side but gratified that her breathing remained normal. She checked the floor number on the next landing. Six to go.

"Where's your office, anyway? It's not in this building."

"No, I wanted my own space. It's across town." After another half a flight his voice had gone slightly breathless. "What do you think about the ceremony itself?"

Marley smiled a little. "Not much until I learn more, but I'd like to get inside that apartment and watch the ceremony in person. We need to know their weaknesses to generate ideas."

"You don't have any yet?"

She had one, but it was the stupidest idea anyone had ever had. If someone could infiltrate the Deimons and get enough flux, they could leech Cressida. But the risks were far too high, so Marley didn't even want to mention it unless they had no choice. To find other options, they needed more information. Which meant she had to get into that apartment.

Gage unlocked his door but this time didn't move aside when he motioned her in. She could have angled sideways to avoid touching him, but then they'd be face-to-face again, and she'd had enough of that for today. So she strode past, letting her shoulder drag across his chest, eyes forward, chin lifted.

Gage laughed. Marley didn't, but the sound did inspire a lightness she hadn't felt in years.

• • •

It didn't take long to take action on Marley's initial plan. Anson's endless stash of gadgetry produced wireless microphones, and Gage knew enough about the building to interpret the blueprints into reality and trace a path through access corridors and ductwork. Marley's ability to control her body to a minute degree allowed her to maneuver silently through both. She planted a voice-activated mic over the heads of the Deimons without anyone knowing.

Once the mic was planted and they'd established that it was working, they took one-hour shifts with the headset while alternately napping and discussing possible plans for the nine-o'clock ceremony. Unfortunately, four hours of listening yielded nothing but boring trash talk while Christopher, Tony, and Brad played something Gage called a first-person shooter on Xbox. During Marley's shift, it had been a struggle not to let her mind wander from the gunfire and explosions and digital yells, the repetitive *eat me*s and *take that, douchebag*s. There had been a couple of mentions of Aiden, but only vague stuff that gave them no hint of where he was or what he might be doing.

In hour five, it was Anson's turn to monitor again. He sat on the living room sofa with his laptop, holding the headset to one ear. Gage sat splayed across a hard-looking easy chair. Marley collected a bowl of water and the first-aid kit and knelt on the floor by the coffee table to change her bandage.

"Wouldn't that be easier in the bathroom?" Anson suggested.

"I can't hear from the bathroom. I don't want to miss anything." She tucked her T-shirt under the edge of her bra to keep it out of the way and felt Gage's eyes lock on to her. She picked at the adhesive holding on the waterproof bandage until she had enough to grab, then tried to pull. She was used to hiding things but couldn't help her lips rolling inward when three kinds of pain hit. Pressing against the skin incited a sharp stab of warning from her body. The cut itself throbbed harder, and the skin under the adhesive stung and burned as she tried to pull the tape off.

But then Gage was at her side, his hands brushing hers away. "Let me do it. I have a better angle."

She didn't want to let him that close, but the pain was making her dizzy. The awkward twisting to try to reach the whole area didn't help, so she let him take over. His hands were incredibly gentle as they pried the tape away from her skin, going so slowly and pressing so gently that the pain subsided to a tolerable level.

He balled up the soiled bandage and tossed it into the empty grocery bag she'd brought in for trash, and then he sat back on his heels while she studied the wound. She prodded a couple of places with her finger and detected no heat, a common sign of infection. Some of the stitch points looked annoyed, and she knew that was probably from wiggling her way through the ductwork downstairs. But those were the only spots of redness, and the edges had begun to seal in most places.

"Looks good," Gage confirmed. "You're lucky."

"She should take antibiotics anyway," Anson said. "I got some when I was out earlier."

Gage eyed him. "On a Sunday. Without a prescription."

Anson didn't answer and didn't even bother looking back. He bent to listen to the headset, then shook his head at Marley to indicate whatever he heard wasn't relevant.

After a few seconds, Gage opened the first-aid kit and pulled out a tube of ointment. His fingers smoothed on the antibacterial cream so lightly that Marley had to close her eyes to fight the waves of pleasure radiating over the top of the pain.

She needed a distraction. "About your brother's friends," she said to Gage.

"You mean Chris, Brad, and Tony?"

"Yeah. They haven't taken flux."

Gage whipped his head up. "Are you sure?"

"Pretty sure. There's no sign of it in them at all."

He scowled. "That would have been nice to know earlier." But some tension seemed to have left the corners of his eyes, and his movements were a little easier than they'd been all day. Marley watched him screw the top on the tube and wipe his fingers with a paper towel, not understanding why he was so bothered that she hadn't told him about it.

And then she felt stupid. Of course—it was about Aiden. She'd said earlier that flux could be damaging these guys, and Jesus, with his mother's history, he had to be terrified of what it would do to his brother. If his friends hadn't taken it, maybe Aiden hadn't, either.

"I'm sorry." She touched his hand, and when his gaze met hers, she let him see her regret. "That was thoughtless. I should have mentioned it sooner." She could blame the kiss for muddling her brain but that would be admitting too much.

To her relief, Gage nodded his acceptance of her apology.

"Why would they push it so hard to all the other guys and not use it themselves?" she asked.

"Plenty of possible reasons." Gage handed her a roll of tape. "A smart drug dealer doesn't use his own product."

"Because he knows it's dangerous," she agreed. She tore strips of adhesive off the roll, lining them up along the edge of the table. "So maybe they know something about flux that they're not telling anyone."

"Or it's too new," Gage offered. "Smart businesspeople don't invest in something until they know everything it can do."

"Or they're getting everything they want from dealing and

don't need it." She held the plastic-backed gauze Gage laid over her wound while he taped the edges.

"Like what? Money?"

He shook his head. He reached to loosen her shirt and let his knuckles glide down her rib cage while he lowered the fabric. She shivered, and he quirked a small grin at her before moving away to gather up the trash. "Those guys, the ones they're selling to or trading with, they don't have enough money to make it worth it. Most of them had fathers who lost everything because they were stupid and greedy."

Anson suddenly lurched forward, yanked the cord out of the laptop, and tossed the headset on the table. "Listen."

"—from upstate last month. Jared and Vincent were last-minute additions because they missed the last ceremony because of work obligations."

Marley didn't recognize the voice. Gage had told her the second speaker at the apartment had been Brad, so this guy must be Tony.

"Cress might not like that." Christopher's voice. His use of a nickname was telling. *"She needs to know this stuff in advance. She might not have enough flux to spread around."*

"No, it's okay. I talked to her upstate. She's cool with it."

Silence. Then, *"When did you talk to her upstate when I wasn't around?"*

Chris sounded possessive. Marley exchanged a look with Gage. He'd heard it, too.

But Chris's buddy didn't seem concerned. He didn't challenge or raise his voice when he replied. *"After the barn, when you were getting the car."*

"When's she coming down?" asked a third guy. Brad.

"I'm going upstairs to get her at nine twenty. We'll come down about nine thirty. You got beer and shit, right?"

"Yeah, couple a sixers. These guys are lightweights. Not like the

last batch." They all laughed. *"Some chips and dip, frozen chicken wings I'll throw in the oven. They don't need a lot."*

"So, same as always? Lube 'em up so they'll be cool for the presentations. Let them sell her on the viability of their business plans. She decides how much flux they get, then they wallow in it until we kick them out and do our thing with Cressida?"

Marley made a face. *What thing?* She blamed Gage's kiss for making her think something sexual, but Tony's tone didn't imply that. It was more like whatever passed between the goddess and her toadies was kept private. Maybe it was payment, but which way? Cressida paying the guys for bringing her new customers or the guys paying her on behalf of their friends?

How many had gone through this process and for how long? The film producer's success and Pettle's rise in the NFL meant at least a year. Depending on how many stages and little ceremonies they had and how often they held meetings, Lahr could have already done this with a lot of kids. The Deimons Marley had nullified so far might only be a tiny percentage.

A bigger picture was forming, and every piece they exposed fed her despair of ever being able to stop it. They'd just keep finding new kids to fill with illicit power, and those kids would find ways to cheat and lie and take what they wanted without deserving it. She was sure there were smarter, more discreet fluxheads who'd escaped her notice and would now have an easier time avoiding her, too, since the guys at the barn could now describe her and what she did.

It sounded like they were keeping the distribution of flux under careful control. But the kids wouldn't stand for that forever. They'd want more, and they would resent the authority and restrictiveness of this system. Eventually, they'd get enough flux to allow them to leech someone. If they didn't already know it was possible, there were easy ways to find out, thanks to Marley. That put all goddesses at risk again. And it didn't even include the possibilities if the splinter groups caught wind of this. They knew more about leeching than the Deimons did. Some of them had set Anson on that path in the first place. If they found out a goddess was actually *selling* power? That was something they could understand. Once they bought in, they could drain any goddess they wanted, upping their power and eliminating any perceived threat the Society posed to Numina.

No. She halted the spiral of doom before it could drag her down. They could prevent that. Once they stopped Cressida Lahr, there'd be no more flux to exploit. Marley could track down and nullify those who already had it. Everyone would be safe. And then she could finally, maybe, be at peace.

The discussion coming over the speaker wrapped up the final details of the evening, and then the guys apparently spread out into separate rooms. The mic kicked off for only a few seconds before music activated it again.

Anson turned down the volume and stared at Marley. "I know what to do."

CHAPTER EIGHT

The abilities that are our birthright carry a heavy responsibility and must be used with discrimination and integrity.

—Numina manifesto, revised

"I'm going in."

"I knew you were going to say that." Marley folded her arms. "I don't think so."

"I know their add-ons—Jared and Vincent. They were two of mine."

"Two of your what?" Gage asked.

Marley glared at Anson. "Let's talk in the kitchen for a minute." She tried to even out her expression so Gage wouldn't see how furious she was when she turned to him. "Do you mind?"

"Of course not." His mouth curved knowingly, but his eyes were darker, harder, than usual. Marley wondered what he thought he knew and why it apparently bothered him.

"I'll keep listening." He sat in front of the laptop and picked up a pad of Anson's notes.

She led Anson into the kitchen and stuck her hands on her hips. "What the hell are you doing?"

He shrugged and went to the counter to dig a handful of almonds out of a bag. "I'm helping."

"I don't want Gage to know who you are. He doesn't know anything about those kids you hired last spring, or what you did to Riley and Quinn. He doesn't know you were the leech." When Anson had come into the kitchen earlier and made his comment about her gift to him, she'd been afraid Gage would pick up undercurrents. If he had, he hadn't said anything, and she wanted to keep it that way.

Anson leaned against the sink and crossed his ankles. "Why does that bother you?"

She dropped her hands. "It will be more difficult for all of us to work together if he knows you're even more responsible for all of this than I am."

"I don't think you care what he thinks of me." He said it so matter-of-factly and watched her so calmly that it was clear he definitely didn't care.

"Of course I care. I've—"

"What? Forgiven me?" He snorted and brushed off his palms. "I don't deserve your forgiveness, Marley. That's not why I'm here. And if your good graces don't matter, neither do his. I think you don't want him to know because it will reflect badly on you."

She scowled and folded her arms. "That's ridiculous."

"Is it? You've taken responsibility for my actions already. What does it matter if he knows the extent of those actions?"

She was so not going to discuss Gage with Anson. "Why are you here, then, if my forgiveness isn't part of it?"

He braced his hands on the counter's edge. "Wrongs need to be righted. You have the tools to right them, and I have skills that can help you. It's as simple as that."

Nothing in his actions over the past few months belied that. At first she'd thought he was just grateful to her for nullifying him, but he consistently supported her quest to keep the Deimons from causing the kind of harm he had. She had no grounds for disputing him, but something didn't ring completely true.

And it might have to do with Cressida Lahr. "You seem pretty eager to get into the room with the goddess."

He didn't blink, didn't look away, didn't fidget. "She's the target. I have a connection."

Marley's idea now felt like the worst one ever, and she was glad she hadn't voiced it earlier. "And what are you planning to do when you get in there?"

"Gather information. Find out if she has a weakness we can exploit. At the least, we'll have someone on the inside going forward."

She didn't like it. There was no reason to think he was lying to her, but she knew he wasn't telling her everything.

"Come on." He pushed away from the counter, sweeping a small, plastic orange bottle off the surface and handing it to Marley. "Take one of these, and there are some pain pills in the first-aid kit." He passed her, heading for the doorway. "It's better if no one goes in alone anyway. Backup and all that."

"Yeah, but you're usually backup on the *outside*." She followed him back to the living room and with jerky, annoyed movements, dumped one antibiotic and one pain pill into her palm before swallowing them dry.

Gage looked up from the laptop. "The mic won't go on standby with the music on. That battery will run out before the meeting time."

Marley sank down beside him on the sofa. The plush cushions enticed her to lie back and close her eyes. The gain from her scant hours of sleep had been used up with her trip through the ducts. "Not much we can do about that."

Anson stood in front of the coffee table. "Okay, so, I'll intercept Jared and Vincent in the lobby and get them to take me up. Then I'll talk them into letting me stay."

"How do you know them again?" Gage leaned to tap the volume button on the computer and then rested his forearms on his knees, hands folded between them. It was a casual pose, but Marley was close enough to recognize that his tension had returned.

"They used to work for me. I ran a company in Atlanta until last spring."

"Uh-huh. That's an odd coincidence."

Marley took a deep breath. Gage wasn't buying it. But trying to deflect or ignore him would just make the man more determined to dig, so she wouldn't bother trying. She rocked back onto her feet and stood. The room twisted and folded like a fun-house image. She held herself motionless until everything slid back into place and told herself she'd better eat something before the meeting. Passing out in the middle of it probably wouldn't get her the results she wanted.

And if the twisting and folding was worse than typical light-headedness from low blood sugar? Well, she was just going to ignore that for now.

"I want to be in there, too," she said, "but for obvious reasons I can't do it the same way. I need to hide somewhere. If we have an opportunity to take action, it will be better if we have two on the inside, one outside."

"What kind of action are we talking about?" Gage asked, rising. "Will you kill her?"

"No!" Anson and Marley said together.

Gage looked between them, his expression amused. "Okay. Just wanted to know where the line is drawn."

Marley bent to retrieve the rolled-up blueprints from the table and shuffled them until she found the sheet with a standard apartment layout. "I can go in by the ductwork again. The grate where I hid the living room mic doesn't give me a view, though." The main duct, which was barely large enough for her to slither through, fed down into a recess and to an opening at the top of the wall. That feed was only about eighteen inches wide, and there was no way she'd have an angle to see anything. She had to find a better place to hide.

"You can't go through the ductwork," Gage said. "I can't fit in there."

"We can't all be inside," Anson argued. "Someone needs to monitor from here."

"No way. This is too far away if something goes wrong."

"Guys." Marley shook the building plans. "Stop arguing. Anson has the in, so he should use it. Gage, if I thought your brother's friends would let you in, I'd say it should be you. But we know that's unlikely."

He scowled but didn't disagree with her. "I can hide just as well as you can."

"And double our chances of getting caught." She wished she didn't believe what she was saying. She would prefer to keep Anson away from a goddess doling out power. The Deimons she'd nullified couldn't get more flux, but she didn't know if that meant they couldn't get *any* other power. By the same token, the damage Anson had done to himself, combined with Marley's nullification, should mean he couldn't take in power from any goddess.

But Cressida Lahr wasn't just any goddess, and Marley didn't want to take any chances.

On the other hand, they'd heard them tell that kid this morning that bypassing protocol wasn't allowed. So if Anson was good enough to talk his way in and get them to let him stay, he probably wouldn't get any flux even if he was able to accept it.

And if he did, she'd nullify him immediately.

She traced the lines on the sheet until she found a possible way in. "Here. I can take this one down into the laundry room. It's got a bigger intake vent. I can squeeze through there and maybe..." She thought hard. "Okay, I know this is a little adventure movieish, but do you have a silent drill I can make a peephole with?"

"You can't hide in the laundry room," Gage protested. "They'll find you. And they know who you are now. They might not have the same no-kill policy you two do."

Marley lowered the blueprints. "You don't have a no-kill policy?" It hadn't occurred to her, even when he'd asked, that he might not have any qualms about taking a life. In everything that had happened over the last five years, even with every awful thing she'd allowed to occur and Anson had actively done, no one had died as a result. Marley wouldn't let it happen now, no matter how much damage Lahr did, directly or indirectly.

Gage spoke through clenched teeth. "I don't plan to kill anyone. That's not the point. The point is that you don't know the desperation level of the people who will be in that room. They know that even newly fluxed, they couldn't stop you. One of them *knifed* you already!"

Marley's side twinged to make his point. "I won't be found," she assured him. "Do these guys do their own laundry?"

He hesitated. "No."

"Do they store the beer and snacks in the laundry room?"

"Not to my knowledge," he sighed.

"Then they won't be likely to go in there."

"Unless they hear you."

"I won't make noise."

Gage didn't argue that one. Marley knew he'd listened to every inch of her crawl through the first time, and she hadn't made a sound.

"So I just need a way to be able to see into the living room. Do either of you have a drill?" she asked again, looking between them.

Gage stood with his hands on his hips, staring at the table. He shook his head almost imperceptibly, then pursed his lips and heaved a sigh. "You won't need to drill a hole."

"Why not?"

He sighed again, the sound conveying his complete lack of support for the whole plan. But then he said, "There's a two-way mirror through the laundry room into the living room."

Marley stared at him. "No freaking way."

"A family owned the apartment before Christopher did. They had small kids, and the mother wanted to be able to see them in the living room when she was doing laundry." He shrugged. "Chris thought it was hilarious and kept it. He takes girls in there to spy on their friends during dates and parties."

"Lovely." Marley grimaced. "But perfect. Too perfect. I'm starting to think everything's going too easy at this point." She checked her watch. It was nearly six. "I'm taking another nap. I want to be ready to go at eight thirty."

"Hold on." Gage held a hand out to block her path. "I still don't like this." With an eye on the blueprints, he said, "Lahr's in this building, somewhere above Chris's floor. We could try to figure out where."

Anson shook his head. "Too many possibilities. The building's too big, and there are too many variables to apply. That kind of hacking takes time we don't have."

Marley patted Gage's shoulder. "You should nap, too." She regretted the suggestion when his eyes locked onto her, the silver in them seeming to churn through the blue. Heated mercury in icy waters.

"I'll keep monitoring as long as the battery holds out." Anson settled back on the couch with the headset and closed his eyes.

Marley tried to beat Gage to the end of the hall, but he caught her hand as she reached for the doorknob, threading their fingers together and tugging her to face him.

"I don't want to talk about what happened earlier," Marley said immediately. She kept her gaze on his collarbone. The skin there was lightly tanned, smooth. A tiny pulse beat out a normal rhythm in the hollow at the base of his neck.

"Isn't that supposed to be my line?"

Marley heard the smile in his words but refused to raise her eyes any higher.

In truth, five years ago—hell, probably even two years ago—she was the kind of woman who'd dwell on the memory of a kiss like that, fret over what it meant and what came next, and beg the guy to talk it out, no matter how clear or unclear he seemed about his feelings.

But now…

"There's no room in my life for any kind of relationship," she told Gage. "So there's no point."

"Then why did it happen?" He asked it so reasonably, without any obvious agenda besides the need to know, that she had to answer honestly.

"This." She stroked her finger over the spot that entranced her a moment ago. The pulse increased its pace, and an answering flutter kicked up in her belly. Action and reaction—or was it reaction and reaction? She should stop touching him, but she couldn't. "And this." Her finger traced his cheekbone, then brushed his lips. She tried to be matter-of-fact, neutral. "You're a very good-looking guy. You had your hands on my hips. We were in a tight spot, body to body."

His Adam's apple bobbed, and his eyes drooped to half-mast again, not seductive but seduced. "So you're saying it was circumstance and you'd have kissed any guy standing there. Like, say, Anson?"

The mood broke in a wave of regret and shame. It was Marley's turn to swallow. She dropped her hand and stepped back. "Not Anson. Not anyone else. I haven't been attracted to anyone like this in a long time."

He closed his eyes. "Why would you say that to me if you're not going to let it go anywhere?"

"I don't know," she whispered. Her throat tightened. "I don't want to lie to you, I guess. I just don't have any room for this anymore."

"Now." He stepped closer again, not purposefully, but as if he didn't even know he was doing it. "You mean you don't have room for this now."

Marley shook her head and folded her arms across her body. "Ever."

"Why?" Gage spread his arms out to his sides. "Everyone needs human contact, Marley. Why are you so determined to isolate yourself?"

"I'm not." Okay, maybe her aversion to lying to him had its limits. "I have a job to do— "

"Which isn't relevant to this conversation," he cut in. "People can do their jobs and still have relationships. Why are you pushing me away?"

"Why won't you let me?" Marley shot back. "There's no reason for you to pursue this."

Gage stared at her. "You seriously don't understand why I'm attracted to you?"

"Some things are obvious," she scoffed. Her arms tightened to pull her T-shirt snug over her breasts and push them upward into the shirt's V-neck. Typically, Gage's gaze dropped. Unfair to blame him for that—any guy's would. He yanked his eyes back up to her face immediately.

"Yeah, you're hot." His voice had gone deep and low, but passion made the words clear. "I like your body, and I've had the privilege of touching you on several occasions. But there's a lot more to it than that."

Marley refused to ask *like what?* no matter how much she ached to, but he acted like she had.

"You have such intense control I know there's passion raging beneath it." His voice lowered even more, and this time, when he moved toward her, it was with predatory grace. He didn't touch her, but his blue eyes blazed behind his long, dark lashes.

Marley stood her ground, tilting her chin to keep his face in view, but blood rushed in her ears and her lungs strained to fill, to breathe him deep.

"You're driven." The words came out gentler, more of a murmur. "Focused. Loyal. It's evident in every choice you make."

Marley barely heard what he said. Her attention was on Gage's long fingers as he reached to curl them around the back of her neck. She clenched her shirt in her fists to keep them in place, her folded arms the only barrier she had.

"You protect everyone," he murmured. "Not just your friends from an assassin and a ruined wedding, but all the goddesses, even the regular people who could become secondhand casualties."

Desperate for a change in topic, some kind—*any* kind—of wall, Marley grabbed the first thing that popped into her head. "Why haven't you pulled your father and the other Numina leaders into this?"

Gage shook his head and used the motion to close the gap between their mouths. His breath misted her face, and it took all Marley's strength not to stretch up and kiss him.

"Focus, Marley. That's not the point."

"It's *a* point."

His lips curved. "Because you're protecting them, too. All the Numina who haven't been party to the activities of a bad bunch. Even the kids with flux, or who could try to get it. I've never met a woman like you, and I want to deconstruct you." His eyes flashed. Marley's insides went soft and pliant, and the tension seeped away. "I want to understand you," he murmured, his mouth coming within a hairbreadth of hers. She savored the suspension of time for a few seconds, anticipating the heat of him, the flavor. Need rose, almost lifting her to her tiptoes.

"You even," he whispered, "protect Anson. Someone who

betrayed you, who hurt you in ways you try so hard not to show. It takes a special person to be able to do that."

Marley's eyelids snapped open. *He knew?*

He stared at her, so close, the blue in his eyes agonizingly sharp. Just as Anson's had been when she bestowed power on him the first time. The love and joy in his eyes had seemed to validate her entire existence.

And it hadn't been real.

"Stop it!" She stepped back until she hit the mirror at the end of the hall. "I can't do this, Gage." She was infuriated to hear her voice shake, and that only made it worse. "You are very good at saying things I need to hear." *Oh, lovely, Marley, that sounds quite pathetic.* Other, equally pathetic words filled her mouth—*I'm not special. I'm not worthy*—but she refused to let them out, to even *listen* to them.

She was appalled to feel tears sting her eyes. She hadn't allowed that since the day Riley and Quinn had been abducted. No one was allowed to do this to her, dammit. She forced anger to blaze up and burn away everything else.

"I'm sorry." Gage reached out to her, but his apology was obviously knee-jerk. He had no idea what hit her so hard. "I have no right to be jealous. I shouldn't have said that."

He'd shocked her again. Her mouth fell open. "Jealous?"

He winced and tucked his thumbs into his pockets. "I know. It's stupid. I'm not used to feeling this way."

"There is *nothing* to be jealous of." Letting him think otherwise would have been easier, but she was pitiful enough as it was. She refused to be seen as that weak. "Anson has plenty to atone for and helping me is a way he can do that. And that, in turn, helps me achieve my goals. Period."

"Good." Satisfaction settled the intensity in his eyes, but the silver streaks still dominated the blue. "So then back—"

"No, Gage. Not back to us. I appreciate the compliments—

they were lovely things to say—but nothing is going to happen between us." She inhaled deeply and forced herself to settle into her hard-won emotionless center. When she looked up at him this time, she knew what he saw because it was all she'd seen in the mirror for a year. If he was smart, he'd heed the cold, hard mask she presented to him now.

He didn't bother trying to hide his emotions. She could easily read his disappointment, his determination, and something like sympathy that should have solidified the walls she'd shoved up but instead threatened to tear them back down.

Gage settled back on his heels and shoved his hands in his pockets. "I'm not letting it go." He made no move to stop her when she turned toward her room.

"It doesn't matter," she told him, and closed the door between them.

But she was wrong.

Part of Marley—the old, long-buried part—almost leaned against the door to catch her breath, maybe with her hand pressed against her chest like some romance-novel heroine. But because Gage wasn't going to let it go, she gathered the strength to pretend there wasn't an ounce of that woman left in her anymore. She stripped off her jeans and left them in a heap on the floor while she climbed into the most comfortable bed she'd ever slept in and called upon another skill she'd developed over the past year—the ability to fall asleep despite the turmoil in her heart.

• • •

Gage let Marley escape because she needed to sleep before the meeting tonight. Before she put herself in the middle of a whole lot of people who probably wanted to harm her, and tried to go undetected into a laundry room. With possibly the most powerful goddess in the world on the other side of that two-way mirror.

With a curse, he whirled and went into his own room. He

should sleep, too, even if he wouldn't be in the middle of the dragon's lair. He still needed to be alert and watchful. But dammit, sleep would come hard.

He paced off the wood floor, across the hand-loomed wool rug, and back onto wood. He barely noticed the change in texture against the calluses on the bottoms of his bare feet. He snatched a maroon pillow off the bed and flung it across the room. It thudded against the wall next to the bathroom and fell harmlessly to the floor.

He pinched the bridge of his nose, blew out a breath, and went into the bathroom to splash cold water on his face. When he closed his eyes, Marley was there. Her creamy skin, her fiery pale eyes, the light, crisp scent of her. The heat that blazed when she kissed him back, her body so taut and yet so soft and feminine. He'd meant every word he'd said a few minutes ago, and his respect fed the attraction.

He might never be able to banish her, no matter how hard she tried to make him. He swiped a towel over his face and tossed it on the counter. "Sleep," he muttered. "Things always look better after sleep."

He went back into the bedroom and dropped heavily onto the bed. Seconds after he closed his eyes, his phone buzzed. He ignored it the first time, but it buzzed again, loud in the silent room. He didn't want to look. If he looked, he'd be compelled to answer, no matter who it was.

But it could be Aiden.

"Fuck." He rolled over, pulled the phone out of his pocket, and tapped the screen awake. Not Aiden. And not, unfortunately, work. This was a call he couldn't ignore.

He answered with a thumb stroke and lifted the unit to his ear. "Hey, Dad."

"Son." Disappointment saturated the word.

Gage swallowed, his heart sinking. "I was going to call you.

There hasn't been time."

"I'm sure that's true, Gage, but you probably could have taken a moment to send me a text. Last I knew you'd possibly made contact with the goddess responsible for your brother's disappearance. Can you see why I would have preferred contact sooner?"

He could have been ten years old, his father asking if he understood why he was being punished for breaking a lamp. Or sixteen and home an hour past curfew.

"Of course I do, Dad. But it hasn't been that long since we talked." Less than forty-eight hours, and it felt like a week. "I'm okay," he pressed on. "I'm in the city."

"New York?" His tone rose a little. "She's here?"

"Yes, but she's not her." Jesus, that sounded confusing. "The woman I saw with the white eyes? She isn't the goddess we were looking for. But I found them both."

"Gage. That's tremendous, son! What have you learned?"

Oh boy. He rubbed his face, trying to decide how much to tell his father at this point. Enough to show he was on track and in charge but not enough to cause alarm. His dad would call off the summit negotiations if he thought the risks had increased or if he learned what a threat Cressida Lahr was. That move could alert all the wrong people and start a cascade of events that would lead to their worst-case scenario.

"I followed her to a meeting," he started. "She is definitely giving out power in small doses." He gave a light-on-details description of the events in the barn. "Now she's in the city. There's another meeting tonight."

"Where? We can organize a raid."

"No. I have nothing about Aiden. If we move on Cr—her too soon, we could lose him. He'll hate us."

"That sounds like you know something about his situation. Has he been detained, coerced, or seduced?"

Gage hesitated, afraid to say what he really thought. Based on Chris, Brad, and Tony's actions, he believed Aiden had defected of his own free will. But telling his father that would hurt worse than a needle to the heart. "I don't know yet," he said. It was disingenuous but not a lie. "Until I know for sure, we don't know the best way to proceed."

Silence told him his father was thinking it over. "What do you recommend?"

"I have a way to observe the meeting in secret. If Aiden is there, I can confirm if he's okay and assess his situation. Then I'll decide how to make contact."

"It sounds like a reasonable plan, but you'll recommend the method of contact and we'll decide together."

"Of course." He almost added *sir* to the end, something he hadn't done in a decade. He didn't resent his father grasping at his authority; it was the mantle he used whenever he was afraid for his sons.

"How did things go today?" Gage asked, knowing what the goddesses would have brought to the table after Marley's interception of the assassin.

His father let out a hard sigh. Gage imagined him rubbing his forehead.

"We were presented with evidence that Delwhip sent Brandon Williams to disrupt a wedding in which Quinn Caldwell was an attendant. Her most trusted advisors were the bride and groom—and the targets. They stopped short of accusing the senator of conspiring to have the president of the Society murdered, as well. That was considerate."

He spoke sardonically, but Gage didn't laugh. "How much damage did it do?"

"Not as much as you would think. Delwhip Junior was part of the young group who had abducted Caldwell and Kordek in the spring. I trusted his father to keep him under control, against my better judgment. I knew he was unhappy with the direction we were taking things, but I failed to anticipate the extent of his determination. He has been removed from the situation. Additional sanctions will be addressed, of course, but in the meantime, I'm afraid it has made everyone even more cautious, if not outright nervous."

Gage was glad he hadn't told his father more about Lahr and what Chris and the others were up to. If Delwhip could cause that much trouble from the sidelines... With the sons of Harmon Samargo's most trusted advisors involved in this, that knowledge by any party could bring the whole thing tumbling down.

"I'll be in touch when I can, but don't worry if it takes a couple of days again. I don't know what I'll be getting into. If I'm in a covert situation, I can't take phone calls."

"Understood, son. Thank you. And please—be careful. This is important, but not as important as your well-being."

"Understood. Good luck."

"I love you, Gage."

"Love you, too, Dad."

After hanging up, Gage lay staring at the ceiling for a good ten minutes, worrying about the careful balance they were all striving to maintain. It felt like only half a misstep would be the downfall of everyone, and too much hinged on what they found out tonight. He went over the plan in his head, still uncomfortable with not being inside the apartment himself. Then he went over it again.

He'd never fall asleep like this. He got up and dug out a pair of earbuds, connected them to his phone, and selected a hard-rock playlist. With Wolfmother filling his head, he rolled over, buried his face in his pillow, and tried to visualize someplace calm and neutral. The beach wouldn't stick—too far away and foreign to his state of mind. He put himself at the helm of a Cessna, instead, empty sky all around, the earth a checkerboard of remoteness. That was better. Someday he'd like to take Marley up. She could use the freedom of the open sky, so far from the dingy darkness she lived in now.

His brain drifted, untethered, the way it did whenever sleep finally approached. But the images morphed, and he was no longer in the bright sky but in a dusty barn, with Marley wrapped in his arms.

Finally, his body relaxed, and he slipped the rest of the way into sleep.

CHAPTER NINE

Beware hubris, for it shall ever be our downfall.
—Ancient texts kept by the oracles for the gods

"What's your status, Viper?"

Marley rolled her eyes at Gage's inquiry over her comm but didn't mind taking a second to rest. She laid her forehead on her hands to ease the strain in her neck and stretched out her legs behind her. "About halfway there. Why am I Viper, again? Isn't that your car?"

"Yeah, and you're hot and sleek and rev my engines. Or something like that. No, wait. You're like a snake, wriggling through the ductwork. That was it."

She couldn't help but laugh. "Just call me Marley. Did Anson connect with J and V yet?"

"Negative. Cowbird has not made contact."

Gage was having way too much fun with his nicknames and spy jargon. He'd emerged from his room wearing a deeper seriousness than she'd seen on him before, but when she asked about it, he'd turned on this false enthusiasm for his role as "mission leader."

"Signal me when you reach the target," he said.

"Affirmative," she grumbled. He laughed, and she tried not to be pleased.

She lifted her head and used her elbows and knees to push herself a few more inches. She'd worn a snug, long-sleeved shirt with stretchy jeans, the clothes gliding smoothly inside the metal rectangle, flexible enough to give her maximum range of motion when she climbed in and out of the system. Her boots were clunky and noisy, so she'd kept her feet bare. Despite her nap and a high-protein dinner, this trip was more challenging than the first one. She blamed the wound, which flared each time she moved her right knee and jabbed each time she twisted her torso. She'd remembered to take the antibiotic Anson had gotten for her but had skipped the pain meds. She wanted her head clear. But it turned out pain was just as bad as medication for damaging her focus. Who knew?

Anson's voice came over her comm. "Marley, where are you?"

She frowned and halted again. "I'm at junction eighteen," she said, sarcasm dripping. "I don't know where the hell I am. Where are *you*? You're not supposed to be wearing a comm." He'd put on a lapel pin with his fraternity logo hiding a tiny camera, but an earbud would have been too noticeable.

"I'm not going in yet. I had to check something else out. Seriously, where are you?"

She gave him the markings on a nearby cross vent.

"Good. Turn left, go about twenty yards, and come down through the ceiling vent. It's an empty closet." He didn't wait for her response. "Gage, come meet us. Room VP4325."

"What's going on?" Gage asked. "We don't have time for deviation."

"We're ahead of schedule, and Marley will still get there on time. Just come now. There's something you two have to see."

Marley had never heard such urgency in his voice. She wriggled around to follow his instructions, and a couple of minutes later dropped down into the "closet." It was large and empty but lined with industrial shelving. Definitely not a bedroom closet.

Male voices at low volume came through the door. She recognized Gage and Anson and opened the door to join them.

They weren't alone. She stared, slack-jawed, at the jumble of bodies sprawled all over the floor. "What the fuck?"

The men turned. Anson's implacability had tightened into grimness, but Gage's face was contorted with rage.

"Who are these guys?" Their ages ranged from probably teenager to somewhere around midlife crisis. Some wore nice clothes in a disreputable state, while others were well groomed in threadbare rags. Marley counted at least a dozen men and boys either unconscious or drugged out. She pressed the back of her hand to her nose. The room was cool, but body odor—and worse—tainted the air. God, what were they using for facilities?

"You tell me," Gage ground out.

Marley blinked at him over her hand. "I don't recognize any of them."

"Don't just look at their faces." He jabbed a finger. "*Look*."

He had to mean look for flux, but it usually teased her awareness as soon as she got close enough. This many guys should have blazed in her head. "I don't—" But then she focused, actually looking for it, and covered her mouth in horror. There was flux in there, all right, but not in the same way she'd seen it in others. It was heavy, sluggish, dim. It reminded her of the sludge she'd had to periodically get pumped from the oil tank at the inn.

"This is… I can't believe it. They're addicts. But—" She looked harder, trying to identify any sign of Numina.

The guy closest to her rolled onto his back and blinked up at them. "Cressida?" His voice was high-pitched, begging. "Is it time? We're ready. We're hungry."

His increased alertness seemed to animate the rest of him, and Marley could detect a very, very faint hum that reminded her of

Numina.

Gage strode across the strip of open space in the front of the room and pounded a fist against a blank whiteboard. "What is this place?"

"It looks like a meeting room," Marley said, though she knew he didn't mean that. "These must be...clients. But they're not like the others."

Gage threw her a scathing look. "You think?"

"No, I mean, they're not full Numina." She swept a hand out to encompass all of the bodies. "They must have minimal Numina ancestry. I can sense it, barely, in a couple of them." Only the guys closest to her side of the room. She didn't want to wade into that mass. They writhed and rolled occasionally and were entirely too horror-movie setup for her.

"Nullify them." Gage was back at her side in two steps, his hands gripping her shoulders. "You're the only one who can help them."

"But—"

The fury fell away, smoothing out the harsh lines it had carved into his face. "I know. You don't know what it will do. They've obviously been on it longer than anyone else you've nullified."

"Yeah, exactly." But it was more than that. She didn't want that sludge inside her. The flux she'd taken before had been fresh and not all that different from the energy she used to draw through crystals when she was a goddess. But this... Her entire being cringed away.

Anson edged up next to her. "It's no different from what yours was like when you took it from Sam."

She pressed her lips together so hard it hurt. He was probably right, but she hadn't been able to sense it then. Besides, that power had been hers to begin with, so even poisonous, it wasn't the same as...this.

She crouched next to the guy who'd spoken to them and

looked him over more closely. His skin had a yellowish cast, and when his eyes rolled back in his head, the whites did, too. Before she could hesitate herself into refusal, she tapped her hand against his. He cried out, shuddered, and went limp.

"Is he—"

"He's just unconscious." Marley stepped over him and quickly made her way around the room, touching each man as lightly as possible. Some of them smelled like the sewer she'd dragged Anson out of, and every one of them had the same reaction as the first guy. Some almost screamed before passing out. One guy went into convulsions, but he'd had so little flux left he had to be deep in withdrawal, anyway.

Her focus was on getting through the room fast, not on the flux itself. Once it was done, she returned to where Gage and Anson waited. She couldn't stay in here much longer or she'd lose her lunch.

Gage wrapped his hand around her elbow and studied her face. "Are you all right?"

"Yeah. Fine." At least, she seemed to be. Instead of the throbs she'd felt with Josh and Gashface, these had been mere blips. She braced herself for room spinning or green fog but nothing happened.

She turned to Anson. "How did you know about this?"

"Right before you guys woke up, Brad said something about the meeting room and the throwaways. He sounded tense. The mic cut out before they said anything more, so I dug into the reservation information for the public rooms residents can book. And I found this." He waved a hand.

Gage tugged Marley toward the door to the hall, not seeming to realize he was doing it. As if he wanted to keep her away from the addicts. "What the hell is *this*, though?"

Marley laid a hand on her churning stomach. "If I had to guess, I'd say it was another tier of customers. Obviously not ones who rate a full-blown ceremony."

But they were still people. People being treated like trash. How could anyone treat them like this?

Don't be naive. It's done all the time.

"What are we going to do?" She stared at the men on the floor. They seemed more relaxed now, sleeping rather than unconscious. A snore rose from a far corner.

Anson looked at his watch. "Do you want to abort the plan? We've got about ten minutes before the meeting starts."

She was tempted but shook her head. "Now more than ever we need to stop her." She looked at Gage, her eyes dry and burning. "Do you think this is what they meant by doing their thing with Cressida? They'll come up here after the ceremony and dose them or something?"

"I imagine it's something like that." His rage was gone, and it had left behind a quiet coldness. "I don't know what her game is, but it's obvious that Chris and the gang are more lacking in humanity than I could have ever guessed."

"I'll call the police," Anson said. "Anonymously from a burner phone. And I'll send a picture so they don't dismiss it. We don't want to be tied to this," he said when Gage opened his mouth, clearly about to protest. "We'd get bogged down in the investigation, probably as suspects. It would alert Cressida and the others, and they'd leave town and disappear. The blowback would fling crap all over the Numina leadership, no matter how strong the barriers they've built."

"What will happen to them?" Marley fixed on one kid, the youngest-looking of the bunch. He smiled in his sleep and hugged a lower leg that happened to be in front of him like a teddy bear. He reminded her of Bobby, a young guy who used to help her at the inn. So much innocence hiding so much hardship.

"They'll be taken to the hospital, probably treated for dehydration and malnourishment. The cops will want to identify them all and make sure there aren't any warrants or missing persons reports on them. Then they'll be released to family or, if they're okay, just released."

"How do you know all this?" Gage asked. His fingers flexed on Marley's arm before he released her. She hadn't realized he was still touching her until the comfort of it disappeared.

Anson shrugged. "Are we cool? We gotta hurry if that's what we're going to do."

"Yes." Marley yanked open the door to the closet, suddenly desperate to get to fresher air. "Back to the plan."

Gage took a step to follow her, grimaced with frustration, and turned to leave out the main door. Marley used the shelving to climb back up into the vent. The effort it took to slither faster but still silently had her panting by the time she reached Chris's apartment.

"I'm in place," she whispered into her comm.

"Me, too," Gage reported in. "Anson's in the lobby with his camera pin on and the comm off. He texted me that he made the call."

Leaving those guys in the meeting room left an acrid taste in Marley's throat that had nothing to do with unwashed bodies. She accepted that she'd done what she could for them, and no way did she want to be caught up in a police investigation. Her activities over the past six months would be very suspicious in light of what was in that room. No job, no home—it would focus the investigation in the wrong direction.

Not that she knew what the right direction was. Part of her couldn't have cared less about blowback on Numina. But she did care if that blowback hurt Gage.

She had to focus on the immediate task in front of her. The apartment was silent. She really hoped that meant nothing had started yet and not that they'd missed the whole damned thing.

"Anson's talking to a couple of guys," Gage told her. "Not sure if they're his contacts. I can't see their faces; they're too close. But if it's them, they'll be on their way up soon."

"Roger that." Marley maneuvered around two corners to access the vent she wanted. After everything, the damned plan had better work.

When she got to the end of the last section, she let out a grateful sigh. The space was just big enough for her to get her body through. Now she had to see if she still had the control and precision to do this silently.

She slithered the rest of the way and peered out the vent into a dark room. The crack under and around the door gave her enough light to make out the washer and dryer below her and a shelving unit to her left.

She worked her fingers under the edge of the bracket holding the grate in place, pulling and twisting. She winced at the grooves that had been dug into her skin by the thin metal. She grit her teeth and worked the bracket until it bent wide enough to slip it off the screw. She stuck her sore fingers in her mouth to soothe them while she worked the other side.

There was a noise in the apartment. She froze. The *clunk* had been faint enough to be unidentifiable but not a random settling noise. Someone was out there.

Seconds ticked by in silence. Marley worked the metal cover out of the frame and slithered forward again until she leaned out the hole. Dammit. The drop was too far to set the vent cover on the washer and dryer without making a racket.

Cursing, she wiggled backward as far as she could, carefully turned the cover around, and pulled it inside a couple of inches, not letting it touch the metal duct. Wiggle back, pull the cover, reposition her grip. Too long later, she laid it down and belly-crawled on top of it. Panting and cursing the metal edges digging into her elbows and knees, she pushed forward until she hung halfway out the opening.

Another noise outside the laundry room—this time a whistle approaching the kitchen. Marley froze with her hands curled over the top of the washing machine. The edge of the vent opening cut into her lower abdomen, and she grunted with the tearing burn in her stitched-up side. The whistler entered the kitchen outside the room. A cupboard banged. The refrigerator door opened. After a few clatters, the whistling stopped. Then, mercifully, music blared. The Silent Comedy would cover any sound she made.

She pressed up on her toes and pulled her lower body the rest of the way out of the vent, lifting her legs up into a handstand. Her arms shook. She tightened her core and curved her legs over until gravity kicked in. Then she finished the flip and landed in a crouch on the cold linoleum tile.

Her breath rasped in and out. The muscles in her shoulders, thighs, and abs all burned. This had been the biggest test of her muscular control so far. Much harder to move her body like that than to hold still or line up a shot, but she was in.

"What's that noise?" Gage asked over her comm.

She chose to believe he wasn't talking about her ragged breathing. "Music," she murmured. "I'm in the laundry room."

"Good. Anson's on his way up."

She stood and turned to face the machines, hoping Gage was right about the two-way mirror into the living room. Yes. It was still there.

Mini-blinds bled a tiny amount of light into the laundry room. Marley slowly hitched herself up onto the dryer, flinching when the metal flexed and gonged under her weight. But the music was still loud enough to mask it.

"Tony!" the guy in the kitchen yelled. "Get the door!" He banged something on the counter and turned the music down. "They're late," he added with a note of disgust before grumbling low enough that Marley only caught a few words. "Common decency...food...cold...a schedule is a schedule!"

She took a long breath and let herself settle. They'd made it.

She got onto her knees to feel for a way to open the blinds. Her fingers brushed slick metal and sharp edges, then found a rod on the right side of the window. She rotated the blinds just in time to see a guy she assumed was Tony lead two younger men into the living room. Anson trailed behind.

Brad came into the room from Marley's left, carrying a six-pack of green-bottled beer. He handed them out and said something to the new arrivals that Marley couldn't make out. Sound did penetrate somewhere, though. She squinted and made out a type of speaker below the window. She examined it with her hand and realized it was just an opening through the wall, with a tiny slide handle. She pushed it open until the voices came through clearly. Not that they talked about anything interesting. A car chase in some movie they'd just seen was her best guess.

New energy surged into her awareness. Three fluxheads had just entered the apartment, adding to the two already there. Marley's hands closed into fists as she watched them move about the living room, exchanging wrist clasps and back slaps. It would be so easy to run in there and sweep the room, take that energy from all of them. Craving gnawed at her. She'd touch them, one at a time, and the power they didn't deserve to have would go inert and sink into her.

For a moment she saw the energy swirling around them, a green mist. She could unhinge her jaw and suck it into her soul.

She blinked, and the world resolved around her. Normal. No green mist. No craving.

Okay, that was getting a little scary. She couldn't pass that off as fatigue or low blood sugar.

She blinked again, hard, and gave her head a tiny, sharp shake. Nothing changed this time. Except Anson stood alone now, sipping a beer with one hand in his pocket. He rotated slowly, and Marley knew he was giving Gage the lay of the room. The three new guys had taken one look at Anson and cornered Tony, who was now scowling and getting in the face of the one who'd done the most talking. As angry as he appeared, he spoke too low for her to catch it.

She compared Jared and Vincent to the three newcomers. Anson's contacts seemed a little younger, maybe by a couple of years. They stood shoulder to shoulder and wore matching false nonchalance. One kept flicking his fingers against his thumb. The other would sniff and run his hand under his nose every few seconds. Neither of them wore glasses but both had the pallor and scrawniness of smart guys who lived every minute indoors, probably hunched over computers. Their Numina signatures weren't as powerful as Christopher's, Brad's, and Tony's were, and it was as if a light layer of flux lay on top of that. There, but not dynamic. Marley wouldn't bet money on either one of them achieving much success with this path. Not when they couldn't tuck in their shirts or tie their shoes properly.

Did that mean they were destined to be discarded like the ones in the meeting room?

Brad had mollified the other three somehow. Marley decided to call them A, B, and C for now. They seemed closer to the ages of the inner circle, around twenty-five or twenty-six. They had more flux, and it was more integrated into their Numina signatures, which were stronger than Jared's and Vincent's. Marley wondered if the integration meant they'd received more flux, or used it more often, or had a natural affinity for it. Just as every chemical drug impacted the user differently, and every person had a different sensitivity to, say, electromagnetic energy, flux would act differently with each person who obtained it.

But watching these guys, Marley wondered how much of the effect Cressida dictated. She had to be able to control the amount she bestowed. A, B, and C were studly, confident guys. Their polo shirts and khakis were neat and fit them well. Whether their families had been hit hard financially or not, they still acted successful. Entitled and arrogant, too, but maybe that was part of it.

A stood with his feet braced wide, his beer held loosely while he surveyed the room, making eye contact with the others around him as though establishing his authority, however much of it was in his head. B was a little more relaxed. He was the only one of the three who hadn't been aggressive to Tony. He projected quiet boredom, almost an invitation to entertain him before he lost interest completely. C, the beefiest of the three, had migrated toward the food table. He'd take a few chips, swipe them in dip, and cross the few feet back to his friends for half a minute before making the trip again to try the party mix or a chicken wing. Which one had been the whiner earlier today? Her money was on B. He was good at looking bored, but on closer inspection, his eyes darted around a lot. Like he expected her to jump out any second and take everything away.

Yeah, I'll get there eventually, buddy.

Marley wished they'd hurry up. The chatter that came through the speaker was stupid, irrelevant stuff. The ubiquitous video games and some chicks A, B, and C expected to hook up with later. She relaxed into a holding position, her vision fuzzed, her brain chill but primed to go alert the instant someone said something worth listening to.

And then it happened again. The green mist floated lazily around the five fluxed Deimons. Her craving returned, a gnawing hunger in her gut. This time, Marley held still, letting it build, trying to analyze it without letting it take over. This might be a new aspect of her abilities. The awareness of Numina and flux had never been visual before, but it hadn't been individualized or measurable, either, and it definitely was now. She struggled not to focus her eyes, afraid everything would snap away again. But instead, the image of her unhinged jaw, like the viper Gage had called her, filled her brain again. She would breathe deep and all the mist would flow into her. She'd master it and be the most powerful goddess in the world.

No. That last thought wasn't hers. She didn't *want* to be powerful. Not like that. Not raging and hungry, like a leech. Her knuckles ached, and her teeth squeaked together from her fear that if she released her jaw, it would mimic the image in her head.

The door to the apartment opened, out of sight, and all the talk in the living room stopped. The guys all turned to face the entrance. Brad joined them, wiping his hands on a towel. Christopher came into sight first, his actual command of the room making A's posturing look silly. A few steps behind him came one of the most beautiful woman Marley had ever seen.

She had paid more attention in the barn to the pageantry than to the goddess herself. Unlike the other night, Cressida walked into the room wearing normal city clothes—snug black pants tucked into spike-heeled boots of smooth leather and a peacock-blue shirt that draped from her shoulders, leaving her arms bare and flashing hints of cleavage. The shirt was cinched by a silver belt, matched by long, feathery silver earrings and silver tips on the toes of her boots. Her dark gold hair was pulled up in loops to cascade down over her shoulders, and from here, Marley could tell that her eyes matched her shirt.

But her beauty didn't come from her body or her exotic, symmetrical features and flawless skin, the way she dressed, or even how she carried herself. The source of it was an internal, intangible je ne sais quoi. Charisma, chemistry, magnetism, allure—however someone wanted to label it, Cressida Lahr had oceans of it, intangible to everyone but Marley.

For the first time since her leeching, she could detect another goddess. Not in the same way she used to identify the presence of one and not in the same way she could sense Numina. It wasn't a hum or shimmer in her brain—it was something more external.

Actual magnetic attraction. Marley couldn't tear her gaze away from the woman, even to gauge everyone else's reactions to her. She was literally up against the glass, like an insect on a lighted window.

Talk about loss of control.

Slowly, Marley's sense of reason returned. She backed carefully away from the mirror and the bent and crumpled mini-blind slats. Had anyone heard her? She found herself breathing shallowly, afraid before she knew she was afraid. She was going to be no match for this woman.

But then she had even more reason to fear when Aiden walked into the room behind the goddess.

• • •

"Marley, answer me!" Gage pounded his fist on the kitchen table in Aiden's apartment. This was all wrong. He had no eyes on Marley, no ears on Anson, no idea what was happening. She'd gone quiet about ten minutes ago and didn't respond to his attempts to communicate. He'd thought at first it was a comm malfunction, but he could hear her breathing. A moment ago, everyone in Anson's camera had turned to face the entrance, and Marley had given an almost sexual gasp. Gage assumed Lahr had walked in, based on that in-unison move and Anson's uncharacteristic failure to make sure the camera had a clear view. It was blocked by the guy in front of him.

What if the goddess could tell Marley was there? She definitely had the power. They were so *stupid*, assuming Marley could go undetected once Cressida was on the premises. They had no clue what her inherent abilities were or what was passed on with the flux. They'd never discussed the possibility that they could sense her presence the same way she could sense theirs.

"Marley!" he yelled again, shooting to his feet. He'd go up there—

"Chill, Moon Man. I'm fine."

Relief hit him so hard that he did, in fact, chill from the inside out. He sank back onto the sofa and shoved his hands into his hair. When he was sure he could talk without his voice wavering, he said, "Moon Man?"

"That's your handle. Viper, Cowbird, Moon Man."

"I don't get it." The handle, anyway. He got that she was trying to distract him into calmness.

"You're like the guy in Houston directing the astronauts on the Apollo missions. Moon Man."

He managed a chuckle. "That's weak, Canton. Try again. Later." He pressed the earpiece deeper into his ear. "I can't see anything. Anson's got the camera blocked. What's going on?"

"Hang on." A few seconds later, murmurs joined Marley's breathing in Gage's ear.

"Marl?"

"Yeah," she whispered. "I stuck my backup comm in the speaker."

"Thanks."

"She's here," she shared unnecessarily.

"I can tell that much. What's happening?"

"Nothing. They're all just standing there. But Gage…"

He didn't need to hear what she was about to say. The group shifted. Cressida stepped forward, toward Anson, and the camera picked up her incredible beauty, something between a runway model and the aura that had floored him in the barn. Her aqua eyes were focused on Anson's face, several inches above the camera, and she approached with a seductive sway.

But Gage only registered all of that in the two seconds before she shifted to skirt a chair and he spotted his brother. Any foolish hopes he'd harbored that Aiden wasn't part of this shattered.

Gage pressed his fists to his mouth and stared at the laptop screen. Aiden looked older, more serious. He watched Cressida with possessiveness and a coiled tension, as if ready to spring to her aid should anyone try anything.

"Is…is he fluxed?" Gage managed to choke out.

"No," Marley said softly.

His breath came out in an embarrassing half sob. "You're sure?"

"I promise. His Numina signature is almost as strong as yours, but that's all I detect. No flux."

"Jesus." He swept his thumb across his right eye. "I feel like Neo dodging his first bullet. But it's still not good."

"No," Marley agreed. "He came in with her and Christopher."

"They could have been in the hall at the same time."

"Could have."

But she was placating him. Gage knew better. Where would Aiden have been before going to Chris's, if not in his own apartment? The way he looked at the goddess, there was no other possibility. He'd been with her.

Gage hadn't realized how he'd hoped Aiden wasn't involved in all this, despite all the signs. Especially after what they'd seen in that meeting room, a faint voice had run in the back of his mind, reassuring him that Aiden would never be party to such abhorrence. That if he was involved at all, he'd been coerced into it, or even held against his will to keep him from reporting back to their father.

Instead, he was not only involved but obviously one of the leaders of their little group. But at least he wasn't fluxed. Maybe whatever kind of relationship he had with Cressida Lahr wasn't healthy—there was no way it could be—but Aiden hadn't yet taken that irrevocable step. Gage hadn't failed his brother.

He focused on the goddess now. No one had spoken since she arrived. She tilted her head to the left and curved her full, red mouth into a predatory smile.

"I know you." Her voice was as seductive as everything else

about her. Christ, Gage could practically feel the waves of power coming off her, and he wasn't even in the room.

"You do," Anson answered without his usual lack of emotion. His words were simple confirmation, but they were said with affection and welcome.

Marley made a noise in her throat.

"It's been a very long time," Cressida said.

"More than ten years," Anson agreed. "I had no idea this was you."

Her head slowly cocked to the other side. "You had no idea what was me?"

"This." His hand rose briefly into view and disappeared. "The gift, and the gift-giver."

"You liar," Marley whispered. "You had to know. *Fuck*."

"What's wrong?" Gage shifted to the edge of the sofa, staring so hard at the screen they could probably feel it down the hall. Marley shushed him.

"Are you here for my gifts?" Cressida asked.

"I was hoping to be. I used to lead these men." He twisted, probably gesturing to Jared and Vincent, and the change in camera angle brought Aiden into the center of the shot. He was now leaning against the archway between the foyer and the living room, his fingertips tucked in the pockets of his jeans, but the new position didn't make him seem any less likely to strike if he thought it was warranted.

"They're not very good men." Cressida didn't look where Anson had indicated. "Does that mean you're not a very good leader?"

The camera moved with his shrug. "They did what I needed them to do."

She nodded once, her smile fading. "Then, as now, apparently. You used them to gain access to my program, but you're skipping ahead. That concerns me."

Another shrug. "I knew you'd be here. So here is where I came."

She sighed, a move that shifted her shirt enticingly. Gage waited tensely to see if she'd kick Anson out or let him stay. Marley's breathing had stopped, too, and he imagined her on top of the dryer, holding herself with that incredible stillness.

"All right. We'll see what you have to offer." The goddess stepped closer and leaned up. Even with the comm filtering the sounds, the carnality of her kiss came through.

"Ew," Marley complained. "That's like porn."

"I can't see anything," Gage said.

"Lucky you. It's like she's impregnating him with her mouth."

Gage couldn't help but laugh, but his amusement disappeared quickly. "How's Aiden taking it?"

After a second, Marley said, "Hmm. Not well. I think he might tear Anson's head off if she lets him."

"Is that in a hired-thug kind of sense, or more of a 'she's my woman' way?" When Marley only went *hmm* again, Gage said, "Come on. I need to know." But her reluctance had already told him.

"The second one. I'm sorry."

His stomach cramped. "We'll deal with it. One thing at a time."

Cressida backed away from Anson, and the young men moved around, finding their seats. Christopher stood in the center of the room and called Jared up to do his presentation.

It only took a few minutes for Marley to groan about how tedious it was. Gage didn't disagree, but as a businessman, he had more insight than she did into what was happening. Lahr was making an investment. She wanted to know what they were going to do with the power she gave them because she wanted to gauge the return. He would bet anything she was getting a percentage of their income or other gains.

And he had a sinking feeling he knew where she was getting

her business advice. His gaze flicked to his brother.

"Any sign she knows you're there?" he asked Marley halfway through the third guy's pitch.

"No," Marley responded, "but she should. Unless she's not looking. I don't know. When I was a goddess—"

"You still are," Gage cut in.

"I didn't automatically know if there was someone in the next room or whatever. I had to 'look.' But she's different. We've only had one other goddess with the sun as her source, and I never actually saw her use it. I don't know what to expect from this one besides what we've already seen."

Gage studied his brother again. He and his three friends had remained on their feet while everyone else sat. Brad and Tony were a few feet behind the big wicker fan-back chair from which Cressida held court. Where had they gotten that monstrosity, anyway? Gage had to admit she looked good in it. It was a much more fitting throne than the one in the barn. Which might be the point. He wondered where she sat in LA. The decorations in here weren't much more than a grade above the cheesy ones in the barn. Gold suns decorated a dark blue linen tablecloth on the food table. A larger, giant sun hanging over the gas fireplace appeared to be made of metal. Not party-store plastic but not exactly elegant.

Christopher stood closer to the group, a facilitator without much to do. Aiden, though, stood right at Cressida's elbow. He looked ready to jump the second she ordered him, but he was attentive rather than obsequious.

Eventually, the five originally scheduled for tonight's ceremony were done. Cressida swept her hand toward Anson and nodded. He rose, ignoring Christopher's step forward to usher him into position, and strode toward the goddess until he stood a couple of feet away.

"You have no initial bestowment to report on," she pointed out. "And have had no time to prepare a presentation of how you would use my gift. So let's begin with your compensation."

"I can give you what you want."

The goddess studied him with wary interest, perhaps remembering how Anson would know what she wanted. From the look of things—the ceremonies, the acolytes, all with a "tribute" to Cressida Lahr at their core—she didn't know what she wanted, herself.

"How?" she asked.

"I don't think you want me to say it here."

She stood. "Clear the room!"

The fluxheads scurried to comply, pouring out of the living room toward the kitchen. Aiden and Christopher remained while Brad and Tony herded the others, but the goddess made a sharp move with her hand, and they followed. Aiden looked crushed when she didn't even turn to look at him.

"What the hell is he doing?" Marley murmured, but Gage had no answer.

"Well?" Cressida demanded.

Anson stepped closer, so the camera only showed her chest. Gage assumed Anson was hiding her face from him so he couldn't read her lips. But he didn't know Gage and Marley could both hear.

"I've missed you," he murmured. He stroked his hand down her arm. Gage was surprised she didn't lop it off. But her hair shifted, as if she'd dipped her head.

"It wasn't necessary to miss me."

"You left. I couldn't find you. I moved on."

"Irrelevant."

"I can see things haven't changed." Anson's hand settled against the side of her neck. "I can feel what's happening to you."

Her breathing hitched. "And?"

"And I can take it," he whispered. "All of it."

She pushed him back. "With your null? The white-eyed

woman who cancels out my gifts? She can't have an effect on me. This is *mine*." Her fist thumped against her chest.

Marley cursed.

"She may thwart my goals, but she is incapable of—"

"Not her," Anson interrupted. "Me. Let me, Cress. I can help you. Just give me a little, and I can take everything."

"No," Marley growled.

After a few seconds of silence, Cressida said, "You're the leech they've been talking about."

Marley cursed again, and Gage heard metal pop, as if she'd climbed off the washing machine. "Stand down, Marley. Those guys are right near you, aren't they?"

"I'm okay," she whispered. "But I can't believe I was such an idiot. That I let him play me like this."

"How do you know he played you?" Gage was behind but catching up. Anson knew how to leech the goddess. He wanted Cressida to bestow enough on him to allow him to drain her. But he said it like he thought that was what she wanted—to get rid of her power. What was his agenda? Playing them all to gain the power he'd always been after? That was clearly what Marley thought, and she probably knew the man better than anyone. But he could be playing *Cressida*, not them. If he convinced her to do this, Marley could nullify him. The job would be done.

Assuming any of it was possible. From what Marley had said, it shouldn't be. But then, none of this should be.

"I was," Anson admitted. "They defeated me and found a way to return all the power I'd taken. But I'm still capable. And you know you can't carry that burden much longer."

"You don't know what you're talking about." The goddess whirled and paced away, spinning back when she reached her chair. "There is no burden. My program gives me everything I could possibly want."

"Cress, come on. I know you. This whole thing, it's all about your ego. I know these guys give you a little relief, but you need more. You're finding the weakest descendants, especially guys whose absences will go unnoticed, and you're pumping them full of flux. Probably killing a lot of them." His voice lowered again. "I know you don't want to be doing that. I know you're not a villain. Let me help you. You can be happy. At peace. I know you want that."

Her hand clutched the arm of the chair. "You have no idea what I want. You never have. Get them back."

Anson remained in place for half a minute. When Cress refused to even look at him, he walked to the hallway and called to everyone else. They immediately popped out of the kitchen and followed him back to the living room.

"Line up," she ordered. She stood in front of her chair. "You first. Here." She pointed at Vincent, then each of the rest, lining them up in front of her. Without any further ritual, she held a hand toward Vincent and made an abrupt, small shoving motion. Gage didn't see anything, not even a ripple in the air, but Vincent cried out, and there was a *thud*, as if he'd fallen over.

"What's she doing?" Gage asked. "I can only see in the direction Anson's facing."

"Bestowing." Marley's voice was very tight. "Small bursts to the weaker ones. Now she's on one of the older guys." She hissed. "You can't see that?"

"Nothing. I mean, I can see her movement but not what it does."

"It's slamming into these guys. Not like what happened in the barn."

"Is it hurting them?"

"I don't think so. Knocking them over like they've been tackled, though. She gave more to the last few."

Gage had guessed that, since she used two hands. "You can feel how much?"

"Kind of like a nearby breeze. Dammit," she muttered. "I don't want them to leave here with it. Did you hear the things they want to do?"

Gage had tuned out a lot of it once he'd gotten the gist. "You're talking about the personal stuff."

"Read between the lines. Punishing people who wronged them, defeating competitors, becoming famous. There are no benign ways to use flux to achieve any of that. She's close to giving them enough to leech. I can feel it. Then it's just one small step to learning how."

Gage knew she was the expert, since she'd created Anson, but he was afraid she was going to do something stupid, especially if she was thinking about the addicts. "We'll take care of them. But—"

He broke off. Cressida faced Anson now, and her beauty had become terrible, lit with fury. Her hair waved in a nonexistent wind that also rippled her shirt. Her hands rose. Her head tipped back. There was no shoving motion, but this time Gage could *see* the energy. Instead of light shooting from her hand like the first time he watched, it gushed from her entire body, forming a stream that sent Anson staggering back. The picture went staticky, bars and flashes obscuring most of what the camera caught.

"Crap. I can't see!" Gage wiggled the laptop screen, knowing it was fruitless. "What's happening to him?"

"Stop," Marley whispered with horror. "Stop. It's too much."

The image jerked and wiggled, as if Anson was having a seizure. Cressida flung her arms back. Anson sagged to the floor, and the camera only showed the carpet. A boot came into view, lifted, and pushed Anson onto his back.

"More."

Gage didn't recognize the croak at first. She bent over Anson. His hand clamped around her wrist, and the croak came again. "More."

"You said you could take it all," she said with disgust. "This isn't even a tenth." She yanked her arm away and sent another gush into Anson, who began to scream.

He wasn't the only one. "No!" Marley shouted. "She's going to kill him!"

Gage leaped to his feet. "Marley! Don't!"

But she didn't have to. The picture went clear again, the camera motionless, providing a wide view from the floor. Gage could see half of the goddess's people, all in varying stages of shock at what was occurring in front of them. Cressida, though, was now staring at the mirror. She made a grabbing motion in midair, then jerked her hand toward her. The mirror shattered into the room, Marley's body the battering ram.

Chapter Ten

Gage Samargo's driving philosophy seems to be to find a way to do what's best for everyone, something he admits is impossible but still a worthwhile goal. "Assuming something can't be done is the only way to ensure that's true," he says.
—Wall Street Journal article series

Gage shoved past a young woman in yoga pants, ignoring her shout and the ferocious yelping of the Yorkie he leaped over. The brightly lit hallway narrowed until all he could see was the corner, then the door to Christopher's apartment. He didn't stop to think, just lifted his foot and slammed it next to the handle. Wood splintered. Metal clunked. The door flew open and Gage kept going. One of the younger guys stepped in front of him, hands up. Gage wrapped his fists in the kid's preppy shirt and shoved him to the side.

Cressida stood in the center of the room, Anson unmoving at her feet. Marley swayed by the half-broken food table, her clothes covered in dust and grime. Pretzels and chips littered both the table and floor. Barbecue sauce from the chicken wings smeared the tablecloth and one of her bare feet, and she had popcorn in her hair. A beer lay on its side, the malt pouring out of it with a *glunk glunk*.

Cressida raised a lazy hand, and Gage lurched into an invisible barrier.

"Are you all right?" he asked Marley, but she didn't look at him. Her eyes glowed furiously, her chin raised, fists tight, and her body quivered as if it was all she could do not to attack the woman.

Gage didn't understand why until he looked at Anson again, and his stomach plunged. He had seen this complete absence of animation before—his mother, and tragic losses overseas. Anson wasn't simply unconscious.

He was dead.

Gage must have made some kind of sound because Cressida started to flick her fingers in his direction. But Aiden swung in front of her, almost but not quite putting himself between Gage and the goddess.

"No, Cress. That's my brother."

Gage's heart thudded against his breastbone. Aiden wasn't completely lost to him, but he'd just become a party to *murder*. They all had, and not a single one seemed to care. The men huddled as far across the room as they could get, but Chris and the others were as steady as if a party guest had drunk too much.

Cressida turned her back on Gage and Aiden to face Marley, who lifted her chin again and balanced on the balls of her feet.

"You would have had him leech me," Cressida said calmly, clear recognition of who Marley was on her face. "Why?"

"Complicated question," Marley squeezed out. "Sounded like he thought you wanted it."

"Men think that a lot."

Marley gave a half shrug.

Gage tested the invisible barrier, but even with Cressida's attention away from him, the energy field or whatever it was remained in place. He could back away from it, but not move through it. He slid sideways, his hands pressed forward. Maybe the barrier didn't stretch all the way to the wall. He kept his movement slow so as to not draw attention and made it all the way across the archway without finding a break in the shield.

"You take from my boys." The goddess gestured around the room. "They've done no harm."

"That's debatable." Marley leaned forward and snarled. "But not the point."

Don't tell her we know about the addicts. Cressida didn't need any more ammunition to kill them all.

He had to get them out of here.

Cressida cocked her head.

"They aren't supposed to have it. Any more than Anson was supposed to have the power he stole." Marley didn't glance down at all, not even a flicker. Gage watched her swallow, saw a sheen in her eyes that disappeared with a blink. Her chest heaved, and he knew she was fighting not to react to Anson's death.

"Interesting that you call him a thief." Cressida looked down at him, her expression completely impassive. Whatever history she shared with Anson, she didn't share his emotions about it. "Isn't that what you are?"

Gage expected Marley to defend herself, but instead, she deflected.

"Why would you do this?" she asked the other woman. "What do you gain? Even if these guys reach high levels of success like Pettle and Vanrose, no one knows you had anything to do with it. It's not fame you're seeking."

Cressida grinned. "No. It's *customers*." Her emphasis on the word had an odd relish, and Gage didn't think she was talking about money. There was some reason she wanted—*needed?*—more recipients.

There was a tiny gap where the energy ended at the molding. He pried his fingers into it. The barrier had just enough flexibility to let him, but then it trapped his hand against the wood.

Aiden slid closer to Gage. "Don't be stupid," he whispered out of the side of his mouth. "Cressida doesn't care about you. Don't try to be a hero. That's what gets people killed."

Was that what got Anson killed? "What are you doing here, Aid?" Gage knew his brother was right. Whether he acted or not, it would probably be a miracle if he and Marley made it out of here without joining Anson on the floor. But his chest tightened when Aiden wouldn't even look at him.

"It's just business," Aiden said.

Yeah, right. "You're with her. I mean, *with her* with her."

Aiden didn't move, but his cheeks went pink. Gage cursed inwardly.

"This incident might cut into your business," Marley said. "Once people hear you might kill them."

Cressida didn't look concerned. She backed away from Marley, and her four top guys fell in around her, including Aiden. He wrapped an arm around her waist, the first time Gage had seen anyone touch her besides Anson. His brother's gaze was steady on Marley now, not a challenge, but content in victory.

"My boys won't tell anyone." Cress lifted her other arm and they all stood, gathered close. "They've had a juicy taste now. It doesn't matter what they do with it. They want to please me, so they can get more." She motioned with her head, and everyone moved toward the door.

Cressida twisted out of the group and closed the gap between her and Marley. Gage struggled against the wall, trying to force his way around it, anything to give him leverage. There was no way the woman would leave Marley unharmed.

"You can keep trying to stop me," the goddess said. "To stop them. But I think you'll find the sacrifice isn't worth it." She sneered and turned away.

For a moment, Gage thought everyone would leave without

further incident.

And then Cressida stepped over Anson as if going out of her way to taunt Marley. It worked.

Marley screamed and lunged at her. Cress spun in a graceful circle, picking Marley up and tossing her across the room so fast Gage barely followed the movement. He trapped his own roar in his throat and bared his teeth, trying to shove the rest of his hand and arm through. Cress stalked around chairs and beer bottles toward Marley's crumpled body.

But when she bent to heave her up again, Marley rolled and took the goddess's feet out from under her. For the first time, Cressida lacked grace and elegance as she tumbled to the floor.

Gage got his arm through. "Help me!" he ordered Aiden when his brother glanced at him. "Pull me through!"

For a second Aiden's face tightened in indecision. Then he turned away.

"*Grrraaauuughhh*!" Gage shoved his shoulder against the barrier and ground his teeth in agony, pushing his way through. This damned wall was going to slice him in half. But clammy palms closed around his wrist and forearm. He opened his eyes and saw Jared and Vincent pulling with all their might. Which wasn't much, because both alternated panting and keening, their eyes practically rolling back in their heads. In their panic, they seemed to have forgotten about the flux. Or maybe they had no clue how to use it.

"Brace your feet!" Gage ordered. He looked over at Marley. She had her hands around Cress's throat, her eyes narrowed with intent. But Cress didn't even look concerned, never mind distressed. Her hands waved in the air around Marley, whose body jerked and rolled. She tilted her head back and whimpered. It was the opening the goddess needed. She circled her arms up between Marley's, sweeping them outward and breaking the hold. Then she struck Marley in the ribs, just above the knife wound. The crack echoed in the otherwise silent room.

"Goddamn it!" Gage didn't care that he was no more of a threat than Marley was. He couldn't stand here, trapped and unable to help her. If he could just get *through*, maybe he could get behind Cressida and knock her out with a booze bottle or something.

He used the leverage the boys' hold gave him and pushed with his legs, making progress inch by infinitesimal inch. Marley somehow managed to land a punch under Cress's chin. Her teeth clacked, the blow enough of a distraction to weaken her hold on the barrier. With a pop, Gage was through.

He'd only made it a few steps when Aiden grabbed him by the shoulders. "No! Let it go!"

When the hell had his brother gotten so tall?

"Leave with us." Gage barely knew what he was saying. "Help us. Cress is dangerous. This whole thing—"

Aiden shook his head. "You don't understand. None of this would have happened if that woman"—he pointed at Marley—"didn't have a vendetta against us."

"You don't know what you're talking about."

Aiden looked at him seriously. Not with bravado or denial but a simple question. "Do you?"

Gage stared at him. His silent admonishment for Marley to not reveal what they knew resounded in his skull. He wanted to believe Aiden didn't know about the depleted addicts, that knowing would make a difference. But that woman had *killed* a man. She didn't care. And Aiden was still leaving with her.

Whatever had happened in a few short weeks, his brother was a different person. Cressida had changed him. Love or worship or brainwashing—whatever drove Aiden, Gage had no chance to overcome it. Not here, not now.

His heart broke, and he opened his mouth to make one last-ditch attempt to get through to him. But he had no idea what to say.

Marley cried out, and Gage made his choice. He couldn't save Aiden right now, but maybe he could save Marley. He twisted out of Aiden's grip and ran across the room, where Marley curled on her side.

Cressida moved away, her expression as implacable as it had been before everything started. "You." She pointed at three of the observers, then at Anson. "Take him with us."

"Leave him!" Marley croaked from the floor. She'd struggled to her knees by the time Gage reached her. He crouched to hold her back. "He's not yours!"

"He's no one's." Cress's trilling laughter trailed behind her into the hallway.

Gage gathered Marley into his arms and stood to carry her out. That she didn't struggle to stop him or even protest was frightening. She was light. Too light for her height and build. Her hands were limp in her lap, and her face pressed into his neck felt feverish. He had to get her out of here, find out how badly she was hurt. He'd take her to the hospital. He turned and jerked to a halt. Christopher hadn't followed everyone else.

He said to Gage, "You'll want to be leaving now, before I call the police."

Gage shook his head. "You won't do that. No one here is innocent."

"It's my apartment. You broke in."

Hard to argue with that. Gage's boot print was probably on the door. "I heard screams. Thought someone was in trouble."

Chris jerked his chin toward Marley. "She didn't come in through the front door."

"Can you prove it?" Gage looked around the room. "Pretty obvious you had a party here. How would the police react when I say a murder was committed?"

Christopher smiled. "No body, no weapon, no blood. They'll arrest you for making a false report."

Gage stared at him, unable to reconcile the kid who'd grown up alongside Aiden with the cold, unfeeling man standing there.

Marley stirred and turned her head toward Chris. "Where is she taking him? What's she going to do?"

Chris held Gage's gaze for several seconds before looking down at Marley, still smiling. "He'll be taken care of."

• • •

Marley twisted out of Gage's arms. Fire blazed from her broken ribs, but that just balanced the pressure building behind her breastbone, the anguish burning up the back of her throat. When her bare feet hit the floor, the impact sent another wave of pain up her legs, chased by stings from glass cuts. She welcomed it, drew on it, and it gave her the strength to get in Chris's face.

"You're used to taking care of bodies, huh? How many have you killed?"

He looked startled and backed up half a step. "We haven't killed anyone. His death was an accident."

"Yeah, because she showed so much restraint when she poured god-awful amounts of energy into his damaged body."

"We didn't know—"

She couldn't handle his protestations of innocence. Even though she knew it was stupid, she plowed on. "How many of those other guys have died? Were they overdoses, too? Or more like withdrawal breakdowns?" She moved forward when Chris stepped back, hands raised, jaw slack with surprise, but she didn't let him answer. "Do you take all their money, keep them happy with flux for a while, and when they can't pay anymore, toss them on a stretch of industrial-grade carpeting to fade away?"

Chris stopped moving. His shoulders squared and his arms dropped. "You know nothing. Get out."

A fiery blackness tunneled her vision, centering around Christopher. Her lungs tightened, every breath a red-hot battle.

But she held firm when she warned, "We are not stopping. I won't let her do this again. None of you will get what you want."

Christopher's eyes narrowed. "Are you making a threat toward Cressida?"

Marley felt Gage behind her, probably ready to catch her if she keeled over. Or maybe hold her back. "Forget threat. I'm flat-out informing you that I *will* stop her, and I don't care how. My no-kill policy has been retracted." She shoved Chris back with her left arm and followed him a few steps. "Maybe I'll start with you."

Ha. Big words from the broken mess.

Her face and hands stung from tiny cuts when she came through the glass, and some of her stitches had ripped open when she hit the table. In addition to the broken ribs, all the muscles of her back and neck had been wrenched when Cressida threw her.

But she would *not* show weakness to any of Cressida Lahr's minions. "You think I won't do it? That I'm not capable?" She brushed a hand down the side of his face, his neck. Reminding him of what she'd done to his friends, even though he didn't have anything for her to take. Her hand closed around his throat, rising and falling under his bobbing Adam's apple. His pulse throbbed against her pressing thumb.

"Marley." Gage tugged her free arm, but she didn't budge. She didn't tighten her hold on Christopher, either, just let him feel the extent of her control, both physically and emotionally. Her body shook—she was sure he could see it—but the hand on his throat was absolutely steady. She wanted him to be afraid of what would happen when she released that control and convey that fear to the others. They deserved to be afraid.

She leaned up and hissed, "See you in LA." And then she let Gage usher her out the door.

She barely held it together in the elevator up to the ninety-eighth floor. Her tunnel vision had increased, the pressure now both a vise on her head and a swelling bubble in her chest. Gage had to lead her down the hall and through the door into his family apartment. And then she lost it.

The pressure burst out in a scream of rage and grief. She wasn't aware of picking up a marble bust from a side table until it flew across the room and smashed into the brass grate covering the fireplace.

"Marley, it's okay." Gage's voice came from far away, an echo through the rushing in her ears.

"It's not okay! Anson is *dead*." The room wavered, fuzzy. She shifted her feet to brace against the pitch and roll. She clenched a fist to her gut, where acid tried to burn through. "I never fully trusted him, and he knew it. I accused him of being eager to get in the room with Cressida. And he lied. He didn't tell me he knew her." Tears piled up on her eyelids. "I won't ever know if he went in there because she could give him power or because he could take it from her."

She shoved both hands through her hair and stared wildly around. The gray marble mantelpiece spun away, replaced by the dark couch, the center cushion still askew where Anson had been sitting. The huge, square, ebony coffee table almost tripped her. Another whirl. She dodged the oncoming spear of an African native that was actually a statue and stared at the crazed lunatic on the other side of the room before realizing it was a mirror.

Panic rose and rose. Marley clutched her hair and squeezed her eyes shut, folding in on herself with a moan. Silent shrieks filled her skull, carried on wispy green wings that battered at the insides of her eyes, her ears, and down into her throat, choking her. The mist swirled into shapes, gremlins digging their long, pointed fingers into her side. Ephemeral emerald scarabs chomped at her hands, her face, her feet, hungry for the blood that oozed from cuts and scratches. Her skin itched and burned where their tiny feet clung.

Stop it. This isn't real. She did something to you. The hint of rationality grew, pushing against the panic. When she'd battled Cressida, struggling to tighten her hands around her neck—cutting off her air was the only way she could think of to stop her—the goddess had pummeled her with wave after wave of energy. Marley had been confused. It hadn't hit her like a blow and hadn't hurt in any way. Just like in the woods outside the barn, the yellowed energy had soaked into Marley, now inert. Or so she'd thought.

Inert was the opposite of whatever this was.

Don't give in to it. You're strong. In control. You will not *be a victim to anyone, especially yourself.*

Slowly, calm settled into her, followed by exhaustion so intense she almost couldn't uncurl her body. Then she realized part of the reason was that Gage had his arms around her again. His murmurs resolved into actual sound, and the rushing in her ears receded. The muffling diminished. The little monsters faded into their real-life counterparts—a headache, broken ribs, pieces of glass embedded in her skin.

"I'm okay," she tried to say. She didn't think it came out clearly, but he backed off a little anyway, and she was able to raise her head and lower her arms. He helped her rise from her crouch in the middle of the living room.

"You're not okay. You're shaking." He tried to move her toward the sofa, but she shook her head.

"I'm bleeding again," she mumbled and managed to flap a hand toward her feet. But Gage focused on her side instead and cursed.

"I'm calling an ambulance."

"No!" But she had to press her lips together to hold in a sob. She couldn't go the hospital—they'd ask a ton of questions that she couldn't, or wouldn't, answer. "Let me take a shower."

Like a shower would help her broken ribs—at least two of them, one definitely displaced. Her lungs were okay, but now that she wasn't in the middle of a batshit crazy episode, the fire in her side was approaching agony. Every muscle was on the verge of cramping. She was pretty sure all her stitches had popped, and the new cuts on her face, hands, and feet would make life unpleasant for a few days.

"What the hell do you want me to do, then?" Gage held her upright with one arm and shoved the other hand through his hair in classic frustration. It dropped back into its perfect waves, making Marley smile despite everything.

There was only one thing she could do now. Her amusement drained away on a small—very small—sigh.

"Call my sister."

• • •

"Marley never told me she was working with you."

Her name triggered a split-second transition from sleep to alertness. Or rather, from drifting unconsciousness to vague awareness. She was lying on a comfortable surface but was anything but, all of her injuries raising their hands as if responding to roll call. After a few heartbeats, Marley knew she was on the bed in the master bedroom and Quinn was the one who'd spoken.

"It's only been about a day." Gage's voice dragged with weariness. He sounded closer than Quinn had. Right next to the bed.

Marley didn't want to open her eyes. The very idea seemed to increase her pain level. But at least it was all normal, explainable pain. No gremlins made out of green mist. But her brain finished processing the words, and she forced her eyelids open a crack. Both people in the room were operating from protective instinct that would create animosity, and Marley would be in the middle.

"Hey," she croaked. Gage leaned over her, and she had to smile. His expensive shirt wasn't wrinkled or even rumpled, but one button was half out of its hole and there were a few spots near the collar that were probably her blood. His hair was now actually disheveled instead of carefully styled to look that way. The bags under his eyes were the worst, though. Like dark, baggy bruises.

"Go get some sleep." She raised a hand and laid it on his arm. "You need it as much as I do."

"Hardly." He tucked his hand around hers and stared into her eyes. His were murky, their silver tint dull. "I don't want to leave you like this."

"I'll be okay." Her throat rasped when she swallowed. "Quinn's gonna fix me up. We can't go after— " Her lungs spasmed, and she coughed, crying out when it relit the fires in her side. "Oh, God."

"I'll take care of her." Quinn's hand waved over the bed, shooing Gage out of the room. "Go tell Nick what the hell went on tonight. He won't let you go to bed until you do."

He straightened but didn't let go of Marley's hand.

"In a few minutes I'll be better off than you," she assured him. "Let me talk to my sister."

"All right." He bent and pressed his lips to her forehead, a tender, unexpected gesture that had Quinn looking so shocked Marley almost laughed. He closed the door silently behind him.

"Holy hell, Marley. First Anson Tournado and now Gage Samargo? What are you up to?"

"I'll explain everything if you do this first." Marley eased her shirt up her right side.

Quinn circled the bed. She'd barely cleared the corner when she gasped, her hand coming up to cover her mouth. "Oh my God."

Marley craned her neck to see. Oh yeah, that looked like it felt. The long gash from the switchblade oozed blood around ripped stitches. The broken sutures poked out of violently pale skin. A couple of inches above that, deep crimson edged mottled plum and indigo, some spots almost black.

"Your ribs must be broken." Quinn pulled a chair over and sat next to the bed. "What did this?"

"Probably the table." She closed her eyes and immediately began to drift away. "I could've hit the edge of the window, though."

Quinn didn't say anything, and Marley forced her eyes open again to see why. Her sister stared at her, remorse tightening the lines around her mouth, her eyes awash in sadness, but displaying a hint of awe in the arch of one eyebrow. "I want to hear this story."

"You will."

"I'd better." She closed her eyes and rested the fingers of one hand on Marley's arm, the other on her thigh. As she assessed Marley's injuries, she cataloged them out loud.

"Superficial cuts on your face, neck, hands, feet. Those will be easy. Deep laceration on your side that's older than today, but worsened from whatever broke your ribs. Three of them, by the way. One fully broken, two cracked. Organs…large intestine, gall bladder, those are okay." Her brow furrowed. "Bruised liver, and a rib-bone fragment nicked it. You've got slow internal bleeding that could kill you." Her eyes opened, unfocused, pensive. Worried.

"Is that all?" Marley murmured. What was she seeing?

"No, but…" She shook her head. "Sorry. Hang on." She put her hands back on Marley, and this time her face and hands and shoulders all tightened as she concentrated.

For Marley, the relief was immediate. Not from the pain, which didn't respond at first, but from the cool, clear rush into her body. It was like sliding into a swimming hole in the woods or entering an air-conditioned building on a hot day. She let out a long, relieved breath.

A pulsing pain deep in her abdomen faded first—the liver healing. Then a searing burn ratcheted the pain scale back up to twelve, but a few moments later that, too, began to subside. Marley's rib cage felt sturdier, her torso more supported. With a tiny little *snap*, that pain disappeared. Then Quinn must have focused on the switchblade laceration. Marley writhed a little as the sensation of a zipper closing made her itch and ache. She clenched her hands around the comforter to avoid scratching and getting in her sister's way. Tiny little *phup*s were the stitches being pushed out of their holes. Then a few seconds later, the little cuts all over tingled briefly. And then it was done.

Marley blew out a long, grateful breath. "That's so much better. Thank you for coming when Gage called you. Did we interrupt a big meeting?"

"*A* meeting. Not all that big. Samargo is stalling over something. You wouldn't know what, would you?"

Marley rolled up to sit on the side of the bed. "I don't know. Maybe. I hope not. I'll tell you everything in a few minutes," she insisted. "It's the least I can do. And—" She realized how much had happened today and that she couldn't keep any of it from Quinn anymore. People were dead and more probably dying. Cressida's threat to the greater Goddess/Numina society had become a lot more than theory. And Marley had to admit, finally, that she probably wasn't going to be able to finish this on her own.

"Let me take a shower, and then I'll be out." She stood and swallowed a curse when she swayed on her feet. Quinn grabbed her by the elbow, but Marley shook her head. "I'm fine. Just exhausted."

"Trauma will do that. I can fix the boo-boos but not the toll they took. And not—" She broke off but stared at Marley's torso.

Marley waited, but she didn't continue. "What?" She spread her hands. "What aren't *you* telling *me*?"

Quinn shook her head. "You need food. We'll talk when you're out of the shower."

"All right." Marley wanted to be clean more than she wanted to know what Quinn couldn't fix.

The shower revived her a little, but her stomach growled through the whole five minutes. She found herself squinting into the steam, trying to decide if it was green or white, and then, when she couldn't tell, blocked it out.

Her body ached as if she'd been loading feed trucks, but it was a thousand percent better than it had been a couple of hours ago, when she first told Gage to call her sister. Muscles twinged and her side ached while she toweled off, but those would work out over the next day or so.

She squeezed the towel around her hair. In a minute she had to face Quinn and Nick and tell them everything that was happening. She'd have to see their disappointment that she'd kept so much from them, and probably disapproval, too, for the way she'd been handling things. For the way they were now.

As fiercely as she'd blocked her anxiety over the green mist, she blocked the familiar encroachment of despair and self-pity. It didn't matter what Quinn and Nick thought. She'd made the choices she thought best at the time. Now she was making different ones. They could disapprove all they wanted, but they were going to have to keep it to themselves.

She found them gathered in the kitchen. Quinn sat on a stool at the breakfast bar. Nick stood on one side of the island, feet spread, arms folded, head tucked so he could glower at Gage from under ridiculously long eyelashes. Gage stood on the other side of the island, his mouth curved with amusement, his stance open and nonaggressive, his weight casually on one leg, hands in his pockets. He'd changed into jeans and a fresh, crisp button-down and his hair was damp.

Quinn smiled at Marley. "You look better. We ordered Indian. I hope that's okay."

"Of course." Marley joined her sister at the bar, sliding onto the adjoining stool. "What's going on here?"

Quinn shrugged a shoulder. "The usual. Nick's suspicious and protective. Gage has Sam's talent for silent taunting, though."

Marley grinned. "Sam usually doesn't keep it silent."

"True." She looked around the room. "Okay, who's starting where?"

Gage moved to stand next to Marley and put his hand on her shoulder. The lines around his eyes and mouth deepened, the amusement he'd projected dropping away. "Anson's dead."

Quinn stiffened in shock. Nick cursed, then showed a bitter grin. His hand came up to rub Quinn's back as he said, "Good. Just sorry I wasn't the one to do it."

"Nick." Marley couldn't help herself. She couldn't defend Anson to anyone, even now, because she didn't know if he was trying to redeem himself or playing an end game just as self-serving and destructive as his earlier plans. But none of that uncertainty made his death hurt any less.

"What? You think he was truly on your side? Did he die heroically, saving your life?"

"I don't know. And no, it was definitely not a heroic death, even if his intentions were honorable."

Nick's mouth snapped closed. He leaned his forearms on the marble countertop and threaded his fingers together. "Tell us what happened."

So she did. She started at the beginning, but when she described the events in the barn and apartment, Gage took over, though Marley doubted anyone missed that he glossed over his motivation for getting involved and never mentioned his father.

Partway through their story, the food arrived. It was perfect timing, the protein and carbs giving Marley the strength to tell the rest of what happened, the parts where it was so obvious how she'd messed up.

And the worst things—the addicts in the meeting room and Anson's death. Marley hated not knowing what had become of them. Had the police shown up? What would they think had happened when they couldn't find heroin or cocaine in their systems?

"So you don't know if he was trying to get powerful again," Quinn summed up, "or trying to put an end to everything. Why didn't you get it worked out beforehand?"

Marley kept her eyes on her bowl of chicken saag and basmati rice. Her face heated with shame. "Because I was afraid to. The possibility occurred to me when we learned about the meeting—that if he could get inside and get her to bestow power, he could leech her and then I could nullify him. But then *he* suggested he go, and I got suspicious. I didn't want to endorse that kind of a plan in case he really just wanted the energy."

Nick tore off a piece of garlic naan with his teeth and chewed, shaking his head. "You should never have let him go in there."

"Obviously." She shot him a dirty look. "But even setting aside the fact that it was unlikely that he could take any power anyway, they seemed very strict with their protocols. I thought she'd refuse to give him any flux because he hadn't followed the progression. I didn't know he knew her."

Quinn wiped her mouth with a napkin. "Well, it doesn't matter whether he was good or evil. It's over." She put her hand on Marley's and said softly, "If he was truly changing, really wanted to make things right, then I'm glad you gave him a chance and I'm sorry he died that way."

Marley drew a shaky breath. "Thank you."

"Now we have to figure out how to deal with the rest of this." She looked across Marley to where Gage sat. "You're awfully silent over there. Have you told your father what happened? About the addicts?"

He shook his head while he finished chewing. "I haven't told him anything." He studied Marley for a few seconds before straightening and setting down his fork. "But I'll have to report in soon. He knows about Cressida and the flux. He tasked my brother with joining the Deimons and infiltrating their interactions with the goddess so he could assess the threat to Numina."

Marley stared at him. He hadn't told her that. She cleared her throat and stuffed rice into her mouth. She could hardly judge anyone for keeping secrets, but after the kiss in the hall and his proclamation of interest in her, she couldn't escape the sting of betrayal.

Gage seemed to have noticed her reaction. His hand on the bar tensed and flexed. "My brother bailed, though. I teamed up with Marley and Anson to find out what the goddess and Aiden's friends had done, how deep he was in and whether it was against his will or not." His hand curled. "It's not."

"And your father is going to want to know that," Nick said. "What will he do if he believes his son and the others are in charge of this?"

"I have no idea," Gage admitted. "And seeing how extensive this whole thing is—the danger level is a lot higher than he thought at first."

"What do you mean?" Quinn asked.

Gage hesitated.

Marley shoved her bowl away. "This can stop here." She looked at Gage, then her sister. "I get that you guys are on opposite sides. You have interests to protect. I would say we should all lay everything on the table, but as I've already done that, it's easy for me." She laughed, but no one else did. Her throat tightened. "If you guys feel it's not in your interests to proceed, that's fine. I can go on by myself. That was my original plan, anyway."

She waited, the ache now making it difficult to swallow. If Gage and Quinn wanted to end this here, she couldn't blame them. But as desperately as she'd wanted to push away Riley and Sam the other night, she wanted her sister and brother-in-law to stay. To stand with her and fight, the way they'd all fought together before.

What it meant to her future if they left…she didn't want to consider.

Quinn's hand landed on Marley's again, even while she met Gage's eyes. "No. Just because Harmon and I represent different organizations doesn't mean we're against each other. You can trust me to keep this to myself."

Marley's throat loosened, and her breath came out in a noisy, betraying rush. Quinn squeezed her hand and released it. "Let's move this into the other room. If you're amenable?" she added to Gage.

He nodded but stayed where he was while Quinn and Nick left the room. He leaned toward Marley and kept his voice low. "I'm sorry I didn't tell you everything. It's not about Numina. It's about family."

Another band around her lungs snapped open. "I understand."

"Probably not enough. My dad, my brother, and I have made every decision together since my mother died. It didn't matter how far over our heads something was, Dad always brought us into it. Aiden..." He shook his head and stared off to some distance only he could see. "This situation has changed everything. It's hard not to bring my father in, and I can't promise not to tell him anything. Some things he'll need to know."

The pressure returned, though to a lesser degree than it had been a moment ago. "You don't have to do any of that. You don't have to stay. If you want to tell him everything and come at the problem from the Numina side, I have no right to stop you. Cressida is one of ours, and she's hurting yours. That's the bottom line." She hated the words coming out of her mouth, true as they were.

But Gage shook his head. "No, the stakes are higher than that. It's not black and white. Numina is not healthy right now, and if I tell my father everything, he won't be able to keep others from finding out. Some of them would use it to take the whole thing down, destroying people I care about—on both sides." He stood and gripped Marley's shoulders. "And that's the real reason I can't leave. I care about people on both sides." His fingers tightened when he said the last three words.

Marley closed her eyes, swallowed, and admitted, "Me, too."

• • •

Gage tilted until his forehead met Marley's. He closed his eyes and breathed her in, so grateful that she was whole again. He hadn't stopped being terrified from the moment she crashed through that window until she came out of the shower, walking normally with no sign of the freak-out she'd had earlier. He was really afraid he was about to lose her then, when she'd folded up into a frantic ball of pain.

"Swear you're okay," he whispered.

"I swear," she whispered back. Her lips were almost close enough to brush his, and he eliminated the gap, unable to keep himself from tasting her. Her mouth opened softly, an invitation, and he stroked inside, filling himself with her essence as she let him fill her. Her hands stroked his jaw, and he flattened his against her back to keep her close.

But people were waiting, so he reluctantly released her, catching her fingers as they walked to the other room. She didn't say anything but didn't pull away until they got there.

Quinn sat curled against Nick on the couch. There weren't any other places for Gage to sit close to Marley, so he balanced on the arm of the chair she'd selected.

"You've probably figured out," he began, "that Numina is unstable. There are certain factions that are struggling to regain power they've lost, and they're willing to use methods that we as a whole eschew."

"Yeah, we have experience with some of those 'factions,'" Nick said wryly. "I assume you're not going to tell us you and your father are part of one."

Gage ignored the sarcasm in his tone. "My father has been working hard to hold together the core of Numina without violating codes that have stood for centuries. When he sent Aiden to learn about Cressida, he simply wanted a way to level the playing field a little."

"In a 'see, you have bad people too' kind of way?" Marley asked.

He gave a nod and a shrug. "Basically. When Aiden reported that he wasn't going to follow through, though, Dad asked me to take over. Both to find out what the goddess was up to and to pull Aiden out, if I could." He rubbed his palm with a thumb. "I'm going to have to tell him some things, but it's not in anyone's interest for him to know everything." He proceeded slowly, knowing Marley wouldn't appreciate where he was going. "This situation poses risk to all of us on multiple levels. One of our early concerns was that knowledge of flux use could damage reputation and standing in normal society. Even if the general public doesn't know exactly what it is, it's a drug. Imagine if Darren Pettle was outed as a flux user."

Quinn and Nick murmured in agreement, but Marley hugged herself and drew up her knees. "I think Pettle has more to worry about than a four-game suspension by the NFL."

Gage was getting to that, but not yet. "If the splinter factions find out about flux's existence, they're going to want it. I don't know why Cressida hasn't reached out to them yet."

"She might consider them too high of a risk herself," Nick said. "She's in total control right now, right? They wouldn't be as pliant."

"True." Gage nodded. "Plus, if potential customers found her, so would fathers of her current clients and other Numina who would want to crush her for daring to taint us. They will definitely underestimate her power and that would turn bloody."

He took a deep breath and rested his hand between Marley's shoulder blades. "Then there's the flux itself. When I first started looking into the Deimons, no one had any concerns about side effects. It's just energy. But we've seen evidence that it can change people."

Marley's shoulders tightened. Gage rubbed them soothingly but felt as if he were petting a tiger.

Quinn was watching Marley, her brow puckered. "Change them how?"

"Josh in the club was overly aggressive with the girl," Marley said. "And Gashface seemed pretty wild."

"And those guys we found, they showed classic signs of addiction and withdrawal," Gage added. "But it goes beyond that." He braced himself to tell them about Marley's breakdown, but to his surprise, Quinn beat him to it.

"What's it doing to you, Marley?"

Marley shrugged and wrapped her hands around her ankles. "Nothing. I told you, it goes inert."

"You're lying." Quinn's sharp words cracked through the air, and she rose. "I can see it, Marl. It's… I don't even know how to describe it. It's like the opposite of life. It's not *you*, but it's part of you."

Gage's heart pounded harder with every word Quinn uttered. Whatever that meant, whatever she was getting at, sounded even worse than he'd feared when he started them down this path.

Marley threw her legs down. "You're just seeing the void where my vessel used to be. The part of me that was taken."

Quinn shook her head, hard. "No. That part of you originally radiated energy. After you were leeched, it was dormant and broken. This is different. It's dark and it's absorbent, and there is no way it's not changing you!"

Gage prepared for Marley to explode, to argue that it didn't matter, that she had a job to do. But when she rose, her body was relaxed, almost languid. "Well, it's not. I'm not Numina. I'm not a goddess. Whatever enables me to nullify flux deactivates it. No one can take it or use it. It's done."

She said it so matter-of-factly and with such calm that no one seemed to have a response. Gage relaxed because with the way

Quinn had taken over, his part in leading them to the possibility wasn't as obvious. He didn't think Marley would take kindly to having attention called to what she might see as a weakness and what he was afraid was something more insidious.

But he'd take her insistence at face value because he didn't like the alternative.

How someone had come to mean so much to him in such a short time was difficult to process. His first reaction as he charged to Chris's apartment had been fear not just for her but for himself. Her spot in his world was already solid enough to leave a painful hole if she left it. And now he wanted to protect her almost as much as he wanted to protect Numina and his family.

It was a little disconcerting.

Marley was pacing now, as she was wont to do, laying out her plan to go to LA and find a way to stop the goddess. She raised her eyebrows at Gage, fingers poised against her bottom lip—a thinking pose.

"I'm in, of course," he said.

Marley turned to Quinn, who shook her head regretfully. "I can't. Now is the worst time for us to leave. I'll stay here and keep a lid on everything. If I can't prevent Numina from finding out what's going on, at least I can give you some warning if it's coming your way."

"Okay, then." Marley cracked a sudden, jaw-stretching yawn that immediately triggered a matching one in Gage. He tried to cover, but Nick saw and grabbed his wife, heading for the door.

"We'll get Riley and Sam to meet you in LA," he said in the hall. "You two can't do this alone."

"No!" Marley waved her hands. "Absolutely not. They just started their honeymoon."

"Yeah, in San Francisco. So they're already close. They'll get their vacation; don't worry. I'll make sure of it. But there's no way any of us are letting you do this by yourselves."

"Appreciate it." Gage tugged Marley back by the wrist. "Don't argue. Please."

She huffed but didn't protest further. After a hug for Quinn and a kiss on the cheek to Nick, she said, "I'm going to bed. Thank you, guys." She curled her lip at Gage on her way past, but her eyes crinkled a little, too, so he knew she wasn't really annoyed.

"Keep us posted on everything." Nick slapped a hand on Gage's shoulder when they reached the foyer. "Sorry about being so suspicious and everything when we first got here. There's a history."

"I know. I get it." A pang hit when he remembered that Anson—the history—was dead. "I'm here to take care of her."

Nick winked. "Be careful. That tends to get a guy in for much more than he bargained for."

It hit Gage, as he closed the door behind them, that that was exactly what he wanted.

More.

CHAPTER ELEVEN

Shadow and light, sorrow and joy, always balance our lives.
—Goddess Society health and wellness newsletter

The aircraft-warning light from the top of a nearby building shone directly between the drapes and into Marley's eyes. She pulled herself out of bed to tighten them, hoping the darker room would help her sleep, but found herself pushing them wide instead. She folded her arms and stared out at the cityscape. Tiny cars glided up and down the roads below. Blue and red lights flashed in three different places, unrelated disturbances. Some of the towering structures glowed with light while others were mostly dark. None in her sight were completely empty, though. Even the darkest ones showed where someone was working late, cleaning or struggling to finish a legal brief or some other normal thing Marley had no clue about.

The glass held her removed from the silent busyness and should have been soothing, relaxing, but it didn't change anything. She still wouldn't be able to sleep when she lay back down on that bed. She'd close her eyes and even get her body to relax, but her brain would replay that yellow river pouring into Anson until his ravaged body gave up.

She swiped tears off her cheeks. Maybe if she could get her feelings straightened out, she could settle enough to rest, but it was impossible to separate grief from guilt, anger from appreciation. Was the grief for the man she'd thought he was when she fell for him years ago? Or what she thought he was becoming now, someone worthy of a partnership or even a friendship. Her guilt was multifaceted, too. That she always, always misjudged him. Whether he'd been trying to be hero or villain tonight, her assessment had been wrong. The anger was the only easy part, applicable to any of his possible intentions. He'd played her, regardless of his goals, and he'd risked the entire mission.

But he'd gotten them this far. He'd tracked down Cressida. Their conversation had revealed helpful information, even if he hadn't known they could hear it. And without his detour from the plan, they'd never have learned about everything the goddess and her minions were doing. She had to appreciate that.

The door behind her opened, and her heart gave an odd double beat as she turned to face Gage.

He leaned a shoulder against the doorjamb and held up two white mugs. "Hot chocolate."

Marley smiled. "Spiked with brandy?"

"Cognac. Duh."

She laughed, as he'd obviously intended, and some of the weight lifted. Leaving the curtains open so they didn't have to turn on a light, she met Gage at the bed. They sat facing each other, cross-legged, and she took her steaming mug from him.

"Thank you. It smells great." The combination of warmth, sweetness, and alcohol served to do what the view had not and she began to relax. In the soft, dim light, Gage looked less haggard. He'd changed into soft-looking sleep pants and a white V-neck T-shirt. His knees touched Marley's lightly. She sipped her drink, savoring the creaminess. "You made this with milk and cocoa."

"You need the protein, and the milk might help you sleep as much as the brandy does."

"Thank you."

"How are you holding up?" His voice was low and raspy. It curled around them in the dark, part of the comfort of the night, but also curled through her, stirring an inappropriate response.

She wrapped both hands around the mug to absorb the heat. There was only one way to answer that question. "I'm fine."

"No, you're not."

He said it with such compassion and lack of judgment that she blinked back tears, tilting her head to stare at the shadowed ceiling as if it had the power to keep the emotion at bay.

"It's okay to be sorry he's gone."

It was the perfect summation of everything she'd been analyzing a few minutes ago, and it broke her. She leaned to set the almost-empty mug on the nightstand and covered her face with her hands, suppressed sobs racking her body.

Gage's fingers wrapped around her upper arms. He pulled her into his lap, settling her effortlessly and cradling her against his chest. He even rocked her. Marley's sob turned into a giggle, a sound she hadn't made in years.

"What's so funny?"

"I might have broken down, but I'm still not a cradling kind of woman." But she used to be. Maybe it was okay to allow some of that back in. Her head fit just right in the curve of his shoulder, and his scent was as warm, spicy, and enticing as the cocoa had been. The shirt was soft, his thighs hard, and his arms encircled her protectively.

"My mistake. I thought you needed comforting." He bent his head to nuzzle her, sending a cascade of tingles over her skin. She drew a sharp breath at the desire that followed it, the need to touch and be touched overwhelming everything else.

"No, comfort's not really what I need," she half whispered.

She slowly tilted her head up until her mouth brushed over his. His tongue flicked out for a half-second taste. Marley shuddered and twisted her hand into his shirt.

"You said this was bad," Gage reminded her, but he'd shifted one hand to her rib cage, spreading his fingers to tease the side of her breast.

"It is. It's the worst idea I've had in five years." But she pulled herself up and sealed her mouth to his. God, it was such a perfect fit. And damn, he knew how to use that mouth.

For a few seconds. Then he pulled back again. "Worse than belly-crawling through half a mile of ductwork?" His free hand slid up her thigh and under the hem of her fleece shorts.

"Oh, much worse." She nipped his bottom lip. He didn't take the hint.

"Worse than taking on those kids alone and getting knifed in the process?"

"A little worse than that." Since he wouldn't give her his mouth, she twisted to feast on his neck. She tongued the muscle running up to his ear and latched onto his lobe with her teeth. Her mouth curved when he hissed in pleasure. His hands tightened on her. "I won't beg," she whispered in his ear. "But you will."

In an instant he'd lifted her, turned her to straddle him, and had her tank top off, all in almost a single motion. Impressive. While his hands stroked her back and sides, fingertips tracing lightly over the sites of her now-healed injuries, she pushed his shirt up, wanting his heat, his skin against her. His abs sidetracked her, though, and she left the shirt bunched at his chest while she counted the ridges. She'd never have guessed he was this muscled. Lean and nicely proportioned, yes. But ripped? It was a nice surprise.

She ran her hands higher, humming over his pecs and squeezing his shoulders. He reached back and pulled the shirt off over his head, giving her full access. He tasted hot and salty and masculine when she tongued his collarbone, chest, neck. When she sucked hard under his jaw he gripped her head in both hands and brought her mouth back to his. They kissed hungrily, tongues tangling, mouths open and carnal, their breaths coming out in moans.

Marley arched, the rasp of his skin against her tight nipples sharply sweet. The ache between her legs intensified to an almost unbearable level. She shifted to bring her hips closer to his and let out a long moan when his erection landed in exactly the right place. His pants and her shorts were hardly a barrier to the hot length against her. Her position didn't allow her much freedom of movement, but she rubbed herself against him, wrapping her arms around his head when he bent to her breast. His tongue, his teeth, his stubble, all created shivering sensations she'd never felt before. She cried out, part pleasure, part frustration.

Gage slid both hands inside her shorts, gripping her hips and rocking her against him.

Pleasure shot through her. "Oh, God. Gage…" She clung to him, tightened her inner muscles in an effort to put off what was about to happen. "Gage, wait." But he growled against her neck and yanked her hard against him. The orgasm hit her like a freight train. Marley could only fling her head back and cry out as her body jerked in his arms.

"Jesus Christ, you're beautiful," Gage breathed. She had risen up on her knees and he had his head back, too, so he could drink her in. "I want to see that again."

She didn't tell him that wasn't likely. She'd only ever had one at a time, and never any as amazing as the one he'd just given her. She lowered herself back to his lap and kissed him, reveling in the thunder of his heartbeat against her breastbone and the still-rigid length of him between her thighs.

This kiss was long and deep, a slow exploration of each other. Gage somehow shifted them without breaking the kiss, laying her on her back and settling over her. He reached down to bend one of her knees, seating himself more snugly against tissue that was moist, swollen, and surprisingly ready for more.

Gage kissed her eyelids, the corners of her mouth. He nibbled her earlobes and nuzzled her neck until gooseflesh rose all over her body. He ran his hands over the tiny bumps on her thigh and grunted in satisfaction while he kissed her collarbone. "Nice."

"You don't have to do this." She wrapped her hands in his hair and closed her eyes, waiting for the moment his lips and tongue and teeth attacked her nipple. But he was so damned slow to get there. "I'm good. You can just—oh!" He'd rocked his hips again, his cock rubbing her clit and making it very clear she was more than good. "Oh, God."

The ache between her legs had returned, double, and she tugged on his waistband. They were locked too tightly together for her to get his pants down. He rose up enough to wriggle them off and shove them to the floor with his foot before making equally quick work with her shorts.

Before Marley could ask the obvious question, she heard a familiar crinkle. She decided not to ask him where he'd gotten the condom and just be grateful he had one nearby. But he didn't use it yet. Instead, he rolled to her side and slid his hand down her abdomen slowly enough to build desperate anticipation. Her breath shuddered out of her accompanied by a keen that sounded very much like begging. His fingers circled through her moisture, back up to her clit, then down to plunge inside her and press upward. Marley was damned glad there was no one else in the apartment—or on this part of the floor—because she had no control anymore. Gage had taken over her body and seemed to drink in every cry she made.

She squeezed his fingers. He groaned and pushed them deeper, rolling closer to kiss her again. As their tongues wrapped and glided, Marley reached down to touch him for the first time. He was magnificent, hot and hard and smooth, and she had to have him right now. Not loosening her grip, she dragged him back on top of her and guided him where she wanted him.

Gage muttered something she couldn't understand and moved away far enough to roll on the condom before he repositioned himself and pushed slowly, perfectly, into her. From there, it was all sensation, even more intense than the first time she came. She wanted it to go on forever but it rushed toward her again, her ecstasy fed by the awareness of how close Gage was, too. She didn't know how, but she could feel that every thrust took him closer and closer. They tensed together, gripping each other so tightly they could barely move except the most important parts. Gage ground out her name, not a shout but a plea, and she gave him everything. They came together in fireworks Marley would have sworn were real, and the throbbing went on and on until they were too spent to move anymore.

• • •

She didn't remember falling asleep. She didn't dream and didn't wake until ten o'clock the next morning, still entwined with Gage. *Completely* entwined. He'd threaded his fingers with hers and cradled their hands between their chests. His face was buried in her neck, one leg wrapped around her knee with his foot hooked below her calf. As if she'd disappear if he wasn't touching every part of her.

She stared up at the ceiling. She should feel trapped. Panicky. More alone than she'd been yesterday or last year. She should have already moved away and gotten into the shower, planning what she'd say to keep him from trying to take this relationship further.

Her right hand wound up in Gage's hair, her fingers sliding through the shaggy silkiness. She was forced to admit that none of that was going to happen. The circumstances had shown her a Gage Samargo she couldn't push away. He'd called her loyal, but the trait was his to claim. Yet he didn't hesitate to compromise when that seemed the prudent action, even if it strained the relationships that were most important to him.

He hadn't judged her feelings over Anson's death or put blame on her that she deserved. He'd been ready to fight for her. He could have tried to drag Aiden away but let him go with the enemy because Marley was hurt. Then he'd taken care of her when she'd gone slightly insane.

Ah. There it was. The very logical, inarguable reason they couldn't be together. Except she'd told them all last night that she wasn't being affected by the flux. She could hardly reverse herself now and make mental illness a barrier to a relationship. How could she allow this to go further, though, knowing what he went through with his mother's suicide?

Maybe it won't get worse.

Yeah, if she never nullified another person or absorbed any energy directly from Cressida, maybe it wouldn't. But there was very little chance of that. Even if they somehow eliminated Cress as a threat tomorrow—and they currently had no idea how to do that—Marley would have to nullify anyone who had flux already. Especially if they took away the supplier. Then they'd be looking for an alternative, and leeching was the top option. If they got enough goddess power, they could have permanent access to the energy. At least, that was what Anson claimed would happen after he'd drained Quinn. Maybe the sun being the initial source would make that even easier.

Even for the guys who didn't try to go that route, what was to prevent them from becoming like the addicts they'd found last night?

"You're thinking too loud." Gage's eyelashes flitted against the skin under her jaw. "You woke me up."

"Sorry." She stroked a little more firmly into his hair and could have sworn he purred. "You sleep okay? Until now."

"I slept like heaven." He pushed himself up onto one elbow and smiled sleepily at her. It tugged at her heart. "You?"

"Like I'd been broken in six places and put back together."

His smile faded, and he looked down at their still-joined hands. His thumb traced a faint scar below her knuckles, one of the deeper cuts. A goddess could speed healing but not always reverse the damage completely. "I should have been more careful last night."

"No, I'm fine." Marley stretched, the move shifting her out from under his body. She didn't know what was supposed to come next.

But apparently Gage did. He released her leg and hand but hooked his arm around her waist and rose up over her. His look was intent, almost earnest.

"I know this is happening fast. I don't want you to feel like I'm taking advantage of you."

She couldn't do this. She twisted out from under his arm and sat up. "Yeah, well, you know what they say about extreme circumstances not being conducive to long-term relationships."

"Is that what you're going with now?" He sounded both amused and disappointed. When she looked over her shoulder, though, his eyes were sad, the silver dim enough not to reflect the morning sunlight streaming through the open drapes.

She hated hurting him. So against her better judgment, she said, "For now." Then she went into the bathroom and closed the door.

A few minutes later, after she'd turned on the shower, Gage came in and popped open the shower door. He didn't ask to join her, just stepped inside and turned on the showerheads on the other end of the enclosure.

Marley stood watching him, her arms bent to shield her breasts, her front turned away from him. He didn't touch her or act like seduction was on his mind at all, only getting clean. He put his back to the spray and ran his hands over his hair, head back, eyes closed, his body stretched out for her inspection. It wasn't a body built for hard labor. Long, lean muscles spoke of athleticism and endurance over strength and show, even with the carved abdomen and chest she'd so admired last night. His skin glistened a deep gold, darker in the water and the dim space than it was in natural light. He had very few tan lines, and Marley had to hold back a snort at the image of him in a banana hammock, playing Frisbee on some European beach. If she looked hard enough, maybe she could find a picture of it.

He snapped up the top on a bottle of shampoo, poured some into his palm, and handed her the container. She took it automatically, hesitating over the intimacy of shared toiletries. It'd been years since she'd done anything like this. Maybe, at least on some level, he understood that.

She hurried to catch up to him and scrubbed shampoo through her hair. They passed soap back and forth, sudsed and rinsed, and then Gage hit a button that switched all the showerheads to massage.

"Oooohhhh, that's sinful." Marley twisted to let a jet work out a sore muscle in her upper back. "Very bad for the environment."

"What?" Gage laughed.

"Designed to make you linger. Wasting water! I could stay in here all day."

His grin turned into a leer. "Is that an invitation this time?"

Her cheeks flamed, remembering when she used the word the first time they came in here. "Ask me tomorrow."

Reluctantly, she yanked the lever to turn off the water on her side. Gage did the same, and for a moment they both stood in the fragrant, fruity steam, half a yard between them. Water dripped into the pool at their feet, the drain gurgling.

Gage curled his fingers under the tips of Marley's and walked his way up to her wrist. A gentle tug pulled her within reach, and then he had his arms around her in a wet, comforting hug. The drain gave one last *slurp*, and the dripping slowed to one drop every second or so. Gage's voice was soft enough not to echo when he said, "I'll give you the extreme-circumstances argument but that won't hold out for long."

She sighed. "Why not?"

"Because they won't be extreme forever. Once this is over and our lives are normal and boring, you'll have to come up with something else."

She managed to give him a smile before pushing open the glass door and following the steam into the gigantic bathroom, fighting tears.

He'd found the perfect thing to say. The problem was that normal right now seemed the most impossible thing to achieve.

• • •

"Folks, we're about to begin our descent into Los Angeles's LAX, where the weather is clear and sunny."

Gage tuned out the rest of the captain's final spiel and leaned past Marley to watch wisps of clouds fly by the window. The engines whined, then roared, and the plane dropped farther. "We'll be landing early. Think your friends are there yet?"

She sighed and pressed her head against the first-class seat back. "Yeah, they were scheduled to land before us. I hate this."

"I know." Gage threaded his fingers through hers. He'd heard several times since yesterday morning how they shouldn't call Sam and Riley off their honeymoon. It slowed once he'd offered to pay for their rebookings, but it popped out a couple more times since, which made him wonder about the real reason Marley didn't want to see them.

"How are you feeling?" She was probably as tired of hearing him ask that as he was about the honeymoon thing. She hadn't rested much yesterday while they got ready to travel. This flight was nonstop but still more than six hours in the air, and Marley hadn't slept at all.

She shrugged one shoulder, leaning to look out the window and watch their approach to LAX. "Not bad, considering."

Marley had pushed to leave as soon as possible, but the earliest flight they could get was Tuesday morning. God knew how much damage Cressida could have done in the two days since the scene in Chris's apartment, especially if she took Marley's promises to Chris at all seriously. The goddess might step up her game if she thought time was a factor.

Gage was banking on her ego keeping her on track, but only because he was afraid it was only a matter of time before Aiden started taking flux, and he couldn't handle that fear.

Over the increasing whine of the engines, he heard Marley give a sharp gasp.

"What's wrong?" He leaned over her, scanning her body.

"Nothing. It's…" She frowned out the window. "Not to sound all *Twilight Zone*-y, but did you see something out by the wing?"

He leaned down to check. "No. What was it?"

"Nothing." She shook her head dismissively, but her eyes were worried. "Imagination."

He tried to watch her without letting her know he was doing it, during landing and disembarkation. She didn't show any other signs of a problem, so he let it go.

A short time later they stepped onto the escalator to baggage claim. "There they are." Marley looked grim until a tall, dark-haired guy and a petite blonde looked up. Then she couldn't seem to hold back a grin. The blonde—Riley, he presumed—waved enthusiastically and moved to the bottom of the escalator. Her husband, Sam, didn't seem to share her excitement. He eyed Gage with the same wariness his buddy Nick had.

"It's so good to see you!" Riley latched on to Marley as soon as she stepped onto solid ground, dragging her into a fierce hug.

"I'm sorry, Marl. We should never have let you deal with all that on your own."

Marley extricated herself and stepped back next to Gage, surprising him. Surprising her friends, too, from the looks of them. Sam's reserve deepened noticeably.

"I didn't want your help," Marley said. "And I wasn't on my own, anyway."

"So? We should have been there. Things might have been different." And that was apparently that because Riley turned to Gage and held out a hand. "Thanks for taking care of her."

Her grip was an obvious message, belying her statement of appreciation.

"I had ulterior motives."

"Right. Your brother." One of the baggage claim alarms went off, red lights flashing halfway down the concourse. "That's probably yours. You checked bags, right?"

"Yeah, one each." Marley fell in next to Riley, who pulled a carry-on size, hard suitcase that looked like it was made of metal. "How long have you guys been here?"

"About half an hour," Riley said.

"You didn't have checked bags?" Marley sounded skeptical, even suspicious. "For your honeymoon?"

"We shipped some stuff home, thinking it would be better to travel light from here on out."

Marley nodded, and the women moved ahead as a squabbling family shuffled between them, trying to get to the now-moving but still-empty conveyor belt.

Sam added a backpack to the messenger bag he already carried and walked next to Gage. "I did some digging while we waited for you guys. I think I know where your brother's staying."

He couldn't hope it was that easy, but Marley had said Sam was a master of research-fu, even better than Anson. "Yeah?"

"Yeah, there's a block outside Hollywood called the Fiametta.

It's mostly high-end apartments over trendy boutiques and eateries. Brad's family owns it through one of their private business subsidiaries." They wove through the crowd to an open space near the end of the carousel. "We booked a place down the street a little. Couldn't afford the same block, even if they had anything open."

"I'll finance this mission," Gage said immediately. "It's my brother we're trying to save. *I'm* trying to save," he corrected.

But Sam shook his head. "The stakes are much higher than that. Of course we want to prevent anything from happening to Aiden, but even with Quinn's condensed explanation, it's not hard to envision the potential fallout." Then he smirked. "You don't need the excuse. You can still pay for everything."

Gage cleared his throat. "Thanks. I guess."

"Sure." Sam checked his watch but used the move to examine the crowd. "We can talk more about this in private."

Gage spotted his leather duffel, with Marley's less well-traveled but somehow more battered-looking bag several feet behind it, and stepped forward to retrieve both. "There should be a car waiting," he said when he got back to the others. He let Marley take her bag and slung his own over his shoulder.

"A service you always use?" Sam asked.

Gage shook his head. "Aiden's probably watching for me, and he knows my habits well enough. Maybe better than I'd have guessed a week ago."

Sam nodded his approval and motioned for Gage to take the lead. But there was still a stiffness in his demeanor, and Gage stopped in front of him. "Do you have a problem with me?"

Sam didn't seem bothered by Gage's bluntness. "I don't know yet."

"Why not?" Gage shoved his hands in his pockets. "What have I done to make you reserve judgment?"

"You mean besides drag me away from my honeymoon and

put my wife in danger again?"

"Uh-uh. I didn't do that. Marley did. Or her sister did, if you have to put blame somewhere. Marley didn't want anyone's help. So why are you acting like her big brother or ex-boyfriend or something?"

Sam laughed. "Definitely not ex-boyfriend. Brother works, though." He sighed and adjusted the strap of the messenger bag slung across his torso, eyeing the women standing at the door waiting for them. "I don't know. She certainly seems capable of handling herself now."

"You think I'm going to hurt her?"

Sam refocused on him. "Can you?"

Interesting. He didn't ask if he would, but if he could. He was questioning Gage's feelings for Marley and vice versa. "I don't know. She's holding back."

Sam nodded, seeming to evaluate the way Gage had spoken. Maybe he even read truths Gage wasn't sure of. He'd found himself thinking far more about Marley's well-being than his brother's in the last few days. If she was able to defeat Cressida that would probably sever Aiden's ties with the goddess. And with Gage, though he'd take that over his brother being addicted, injured, or worse.

But then he'd think of Marley getting hurt again trying to save Aiden. He knew that wasn't her only motivation, but dread had settled deep into the pit of his stomach.

"I passed Nick's sniff test," Gage pointed out. "Why isn't that enough?"

Sam leaned closer, leading with his jaw. "It's been four days since she met you. Four. Days. Do you know what happened the last time she fell for someone?"

Gage had to hide the burn of satisfaction at the implication of Marley's feelings. "Yeah, I know what happened. And I understand why that would make her friends protective of her. But she's more likely to hurt me than the other way around."

He didn't know what it was. The words or the way he said them, or maybe it was the fear behind them, but Sam rocked back on his heels and grinned. "Okay then. I guess we have nothing to worry about." He took off across the tiled floor, leaving Gage to collect his bag and follow, bemused.

• • •

Half an hour later, they spread out into the motley, furnished collection of rooms Sam had rented. Gage wasn't a snob. He'd stayed places in Africa and South America and the Middle East that made Sam's choice look like a palace. He'd dealt with primitive accommodations because of custom or circumstance. But those things didn't apply here. The entire unit could have fit into the living room of his parents' place in New York. He wasn't sure it qualified as an apartment. Storage space, maybe.

He had to admit it was lighter inside than his parents', with gleaming white walls and scuffed pine floors, but he wasn't sure it was possible to sit on the lumpy, burgundy sofa or the matted area rug in front of it without contracting some disease. The living room and kitchen were actually one room split by the flooring. A doorway led to two bedrooms and a bathroom so small he could touch all four walls without moving his feet.

"Why'd you pick this place?" He tried to figure out if a stain on the arm of the couch was coffee or blood.

"Free neighborhood Wi-Fi," Sam answered promptly. He set a sleek laptop on the chipped particleboard coffee table and opened it.

Gage had to be impressed. He was involved with every aspect of his business, including security and the electronics that went along with it. Sam's laptop was an upcoming model and the stuff he plugged into it—encryption units and signal blockers, among others—wasn't the kind of equipment you bought on the open market.

"A network of surveillance cameras we can follow all the way back to the Fiametta," Sam continued, not pausing in setting up. "Proximity to City Hall if we need to get into their records. Cheap food."

"Okay, I get it." He wouldn't try to convince them to move. If things went well, they wouldn't be here very long. "What's the next step?"

"Find your brother."

Gage tried not to bark at Sam for stating the obvious in such an unhelpful way. Tired of standing, he dragged the single battered wooden kitchen chair onto the living room side. The curling, black-and-white linoleum cracked under his feet as he walked across it. He set the chair next to the coffee table, straddled it, and rested his arms along the back.

Voices rose in one of the bedrooms. Marley and Riley had been locked in there since they arrived, and this wasn't the first time they seemed unhappy with each other. "You think one of us should go referee?" They weren't quite loud enough to tell if they were actually arguing, but it was definitely too loud to be casual conversation.

"No." Sam stretched, leaning back from his laptop, seeming unconcerned about what might be growing—or living—in the sofa cushion he leaned back on. "Okay, here's what I was thinking." He focused on Gage. "If Aiden's in the Fiametta, and we can pinpoint where he's staying, we can set up surveillance to track when the place is empty. Then we can slip in and see what we can find about their program."

"How are you going to tap into the surveillance and databases you need?"

"From my work with the Society I've obtained a special-investigator's license and government clearance." He checked a setting on one of the units. "It stems from Anson's assault conviction and the reports of the board and security team. There are public databases most people have no clue exist, and I can get into utility records and the reports local businesses make to credit card companies, stuff like that."

Gage nodded. "Maybe we can pinpoint when Aiden would be alone. Instead of trying to illegally search the place, I can talk to him."

Sam looked skeptical. "Do you think he'd tell you anything?"

"Yes." Gage refused to believe that after all these years Aiden would pull away that completely, that permanently. He was still Gage's baby brother. Some part of him had to still want Gage's friendship, his approval—or at the very least, to try to recruit him onto his side. "If he doesn't, I'll convince him I want in."

Sam thought about that and nodded slowly. "Okay, yeah, that could work. It's worth a try."

"What did you get on the guys we found in the Pritchard Building?" Since Sam and Riley had only had to travel a couple of hours, he'd offered to find out if they'd identified the addicts and what their conditions were before leaving San Francisco.

"As of this morning, they haven't ID'd all of them." With the computer fully booted, he flipped some switches on the other equipment. Icons popped up and disappeared in succession on the screen. "Most were treated and released from the hospital, a few detained because of outstanding warrants. None were listed as missing persons." He turned toward Gage. "I dug around on some of the names. Marley said these guys were all Numina?"

"Yeah. Well, she said there was a trace of the hum she senses in the rest of us. She guessed they might have branched out of the major bloodlines."

Sam shook his head. "Maybe way out. I don't know how Cressida is finding them. There's no evidence they have any influence. None of them are all that successful. And they obviously don't run in your circles."

"So that's one of the questions I'll ask Aiden." Gage leaned to tilt the chair on two legs. "Figuring out how we're going to stop Cressida is our biggest challenge, but I doubt Aiden will know how, and even if he does, he won't tell me. So we need to know as much as we can about their plans and motivations. How many followers does she have? How long has she been doing this? How are Aiden and the others involved? What's in it for them if they're not taking flux?"

Sam leaned to tap a few keys. "Right. That kind of information can tell us a lot." He turned his head when the women's voices grew briefly louder again. He shifted forward on the sofa and braced his feet under him but didn't stand.

"I'll go." Gage swung off the chair. "I'm not afraid of them."

Sam hit a couple of keys on the laptop. Lines of code swept down the monitor. "Go for it."

Gage circled the sofa to go into the hallway. He halted a few steps in. Even in the pauses between bursts of clacking behind him, he couldn't hear anything from the bedroom. With flimsy walls like these, he should hear at least a murmur, even if they'd lowered their voices. He raised his hand to knock but hesitated when Riley began talking again.

"So what's up with you and Gage? He's hot."

He grinned at the compliment but backed away. No guy could resist eavesdropping under normal circumstances, but these were anything but. If Marley was going to dismiss him, Gage didn't want to hear it.

Chapter Twelve

Reality shifts are harbingers of temporodimensional travel. Or encroaching insanity.
—*LA Geek* e-zine

The moment they hit the apartment, Riley had dragged Marley through the narrow main room into one of the bedrooms, where Marley had tried hard to keep the conversation off herself. She wasn't doing a very good job of it. She and Riley glared at each other, Riley with her fists on her hips in a motherly pose.

A floorboard creaked outside the door. Typing drifted through the silence between them, but Riley and Marley locked gazes, both obviously sensing Gage's presence.

"I told you to stop shouting," Marley whispered almost inaudibly.

"So what's up with you and Gage?" Riley asked. "He's hot."

They shared a laugh when Gage moved back to the main room, and it broke the tension.

But Riley dug in again. "Stop haranguing me about my damned honeymoon and pretending you want all the wedding details. We are not leaving this room, and you are *going* to be honest with me."

Marley snorted. "Is that one of your powers now? Compelling the truth?" She pushed aside the bag she'd set on the bed and frowned. Gage wasn't as tall as Sam, but neither guy would be comfortable on a bed this small alone, never mind with another body in it. Whoever managed the apartment had tucked the off-white sheets and a holey wool blanket in precision folds around the mattress. Flat pillows leaned against a scratched and gouged wall—no headboard. The four-drawer dresser continued the orphanage/barracks theme and was the only other furniture in the room. She sighed longingly for the big comfy bed and multihead shower in New York.

"I'm serious," Riley said with less vehemence. "You know you have to stop, right?"

Why did people phrase things that way? The attempt at politeness always came out patronizing, instead.

"I'll stop when what I do is no longer necessary."

Riley rolled her eyes. "Like this is some noble quest, and you don't care what it's doing to you?"

Marley didn't have a response. Denying it was doing anything to her would be lying, and lying to her friends was getting more difficult. Mainly because she could no longer lie to herself.

After the scene with Cressida, it had been easy to pretend the sheer volume of energy Marley had absorbed had combined with her injuries and fatigue to contribute to a momentary breakdown. But after a week of rationalizing away any odd little thing that happened, of telling herself she just needed to work through it, she had to acknowledge that she'd crossed some kind of tipping point, particularly in the past couple of days.

Half an hour ago, on the drive over here, she'd blinked and it was night. All the city's lights were shining, car headlights bounced off closed storefronts, and the moon hovered at forty-five degrees. She blinked again, and it was day. The cabbie was only a few words further into his travelogue, and no one else had moved.

That was the worst one, but there had been others. More green mist drifting and swirling into shapes. A curb that seemed to disappear from under her feet, sending her stumbling into a—thankfully stationary—bus. A glimpse of...*something* out on the airplane wing, something that had been there long enough to convince her she saw it and gone before she knew whether or not it was real. Whatever it was, it definitely had wings.

"I don't know." She shoved her hands into her hair. "I get these weird...reality shifts." That sounded better to her, more fantastical than frightening, than calling them what they really were. "They're quick. Like flashes. I thought they were because of my injuries and fatigue, but they haven't stopped."

"You're talking about hallucinations." Riley's voice rose. "It's got to be the flux. Marley, you can't—"

"Shh!" Marley moved her hand up and down. She didn't want Sam and Gage to hear what they were saying. "Keep this between us."

"No way!" But she'd dropped her volume. "You know what happened to Anson when he took in foreign energy and lost it. What happened to Quinn, and Sam—"

"That was different!" Marley had to bring her own tone down. "That was all due to live energy. Do you *see* live energy in me?" She held her breath, not sure what answer she wanted to hear.

Riley's eyes unfocused and she tapped her lower lip before shaking her head. "No. I don't see any energy at all. But you're different. You don't buzz or prickle like those with power do, but you don't have the same low vibration of regular people. I could pick you out of a crowd of thousands."

It almost sounded like a compliment but felt more like a diagnosis of a brand-new disease. No, She couldn't start thinking like that. "So it can't be what's causing these flashes. Maybe I'm just cracking up," she tried to joke. "Too isolated for too long? Too much time in the company of a guy who never talked?" Whoa.

Trying to lighten the mood just totally backfired. Her next indrawn breath shook and faltered, and of course, Riley saw it.

"You cared about him." All judgment was absent from her tone, but Marley knew it was there, anyway. It didn't matter. She judged herself for it, after all.

"Surprisingly, yeah." She sank onto the end of the bed. It sagged halfway to the floor, unsupported by a frame that was obviously too short for the mattress. This was going to be fun to sleep on. "Not the same way I did originally, of course. Our relationship—the new one—was never emotional. It was all practicality. Common goals and all that." Unless she'd read him wrong, and every indication was that she had, one way or another. "It doesn't matter now," she said. "He's gone."

"Yeah, and he almost took you with him." Riley paced in front of her. "How stupid was he, to take Cressida on himself?"

"He knew her," Marley said.

"I know. Quinn told me everything you told her. But did he know it was her before he went in?"

"He told her he didn't, but after Sam gave us his name, how could he not? Unless he knew her by a different name before."

Riley whirled on her. "You wanted him to leech her, didn't you?"

She wouldn't feel guilty for that. "That wasn't the plan. I considered it but never said it out loud. It shouldn't have been possible for him to receive energy anyway, and if he could, the risks were too high."

"Maybe you should have talked about it and then not let him go in there at all. He never should have had access to that much power."

Marley stood. "What do you think I am? Stupid? I'd have nullified him immediately. He wouldn't have had a chance to go on a rampage."

"At least you recognize that he would have!"

"*Could* have. Not would have."

"Why would you defend him?" Riley cried. "He took everything from you."

"Stop yelling," Marley demanded again. "I'm not defending him. I just refuse to condemn a dead man on unfair assumptions."

"Oh, please." Riley leaned against the door and shoved her arms across her chest. "They are so *not* unfair. When did he ever do anything altruistic? Anything that wasn't part of his own grand plan? Even working for Numina was part of a bigger scheme. He never would have stopped."

"No," Marley agreed. "But you guys stopped him. He almost died. And in case you hadn't heard, that can have a profound effect on people. He wasn't operating with the same motivations anymore."

They faced each other in silence for a few moments. Marley didn't want to continue this argument. It was pointless. Anson was gone. Unless Cressida had the ability to resurrect him, he couldn't harm any of them anymore.

"There's nothing we can do about it now," she told Riley softly. "Can we please change the subject?"

Riley's chin jutted mulishly for a moment, but then she smirked. "Okay. Let's talk about that." She waved a hand in the direction of the living room. "This thing with Gage is obviously more than partnership. Again."

Marley sank back onto the bed, this time sitting on the side so it didn't threaten to dump her on the floor. "He's not like Anson."

Riley raised her hands in denial. "Not judging. These circumstances are too much like me and Sam for me to be critical." She sat next to her and rubbed her hands slowly against each other. "He's Numina, though, and his father is the man in charge. That could get complicated."

"It already has." She didn't want to discuss the things Gage was keeping from his father. "But it doesn't matter. It's not going to last." Saying the words aloud hurt way more than it should have after only four days. Four concentrated, intense days, to be sure. She was consistently aware of where he was, whether it was inches away or in another room. And any other room was too far. Her body, her awareness, sought him all the time. She didn't relax unless he was near. His smooth, deep voice resonated inside her with every word he said.

"It's too early for you to say that. I mean, not to be all 'look at me and Sam' all the time, but...look at me and Sam." She laughed, delight at the core of the sound. "Similar circumstances, though you're a lot tougher than I was when I met him."

Sometimes she felt tough, as though all her efforts to grow stronger had brought her closer to the woman she wanted to be. Most of the time, it just felt like a shell over the same old Marley.

Riley twisted and pulled one leg up on the bed so she faced Marley. "Is he worthy?"

Marley stared at her. "Of *me*?"

Her friend's eyes flashed. "*Yes*, of you. Why are you so hard on yourself?"

"Why shouldn't I be?" After so many months of keeping to herself, she couldn't hold back anymore. It felt too natural—too *normal*—to sit in a bedroom with a friend, talking about boys. "I don't even know how you can ask that after everything that happened. I was such a—" She shook her head. "I'm trying not to be that weak, useless woman anymore, but—"

"Oh, Marley." Riley leaned forward and threw her arms around her.

Marley froze, blinked, and then hugged back, gratitude making a simp out of her.

When Riley pulled away, she looked sternly at Marley. "You were never useless. Sam regales me all the time with the tale of how they met you and you all took down the leech."

"*They* took down the leech. That *I* created."

"Yeah, accidentally. Did you forget that you weren't his only victim? He fooled other women, you know. And you were a big part of stopping him. Twice."

Marley bit her tongue. There was no value in arguing. "The fact remains that I chose badly when I chose Anson."

"This time, you didn't." Her eyes sparkled. "He never stops touching you. You know, little brushes, to make sure you're still there. And when he can't touch you, he watches you. I've seen that look on two guys: Nick and Sam." She tilted her head sideways, eyebrow quirked to emphasize the significance.

Marley had to agree that she'd rarely seen two men as in love with their wives as Nick and Sam were, and she'd hosted weddings and honeymooners in her other life as an innkeeper. But she couldn't let herself hope that she and Gage were on their way to such a result.

"He seems like he's cut from the same cloth," Riley pointed out. "Loyal, smart, resourceful. Ready to take on a challenge like saving the world when he doesn't really have to."

"Stop." Marley threw herself off the bed and circled toward the door. "Don't get your hopes up." *Don't get* my *hopes up.*

"Why not?"

Marley closed her eyes, hand on the doorknob. Because she was having hallucinations. Because no matter what plan they devised to stop Cressida, she was going to have to take in more flux. And because Gage had already lost someone to mental illness. Nick and Quinn and Riley and Sam may have had obstacles—Marley didn't really know—but she did know they couldn't have been this insurmountable.

"It's just ridiculous to consider right now, with everything that's happening. I'll be right back."

She escaped to the bathroom, afraid Riley would see more, ferret more out of her. Marley didn't know what to do about Gage. She couldn't let things go any further, knowing what was happening to her and *not* knowing how deeply into insanity she'd plunge.

But god help her, she wasn't sure she had the strength to stop them.

• • •

Marley drifted awake in the dark bedroom, nudged out of slumber by noises from the kitchen. She could smell coffee and bacon, universal "good morning" greetings. This was the second day Riley and Sam had gotten up early and made breakfast. A couple more would make it routine.

If they were lucky, there wouldn't be enough days for that. Yesterday had been shockingly productive. After some early tension, Sam and Gage had connected over tech talk and strategizing. They'd collected the information they needed and today, Gage was going to try to get Aiden alone. Their next move would depend on what Aiden was willing to tell him.

She worked through the plan, still worried about letting him go into the Fiametta alone. Sam and Riley planned to hang in the courtyard, but Marley couldn't get that close and risk being spotted. She'd be nearby but not close enough for comms. Which they weren't using, anyway, because they didn't want Aiden to spot any sign of deception.

Gage was banking on his close relationship with his brother being enough to keep Aiden from turning him away. Marley was afraid Cressida's influence penetrated too deep.

Next to her, Gage groaned. "You still think too loud in the morning." He rolled over and propped himself on his elbows, rubbing sleep out of his eyes. "You sleep better last night?"

She rolled onto her side and tucked her arm under the pillow. "Better than what?"

"Better than the first night."

She hadn't realized he'd noticed. It wasn't like she'd tossed and turned, keeping him awake. She'd been too conscious of the ridiculous queen-size mattress balanced on a double frame. Either one of them could roll off the side. But with only two bedrooms in the apartment, they'd agreed sharing was preferable to the petri-dish couch or uneven, rough floor in the living room. There wasn't enough floor space in here, and no way to make it even resemble comfortable if there were.

"I slept fine," she lied. It was almost insulting how easily Gage seemed to sleep next to her when all she could think about was his body, his heat covering her, the ecstasy he'd wrung from her back in New York. He smelled so good, so rich and spicy, and the few times she did drift off, erotic dreams had alternated with nightmares about battling Cressida and losing the people she cared about, one by one.

A pan clanked on the stove outside the bedroom. The radio clicked on just in time for the DJ to proclaim another bright, clear, perfect day.

Gage shifted closer and ran his hand over her hip. "Good morning." His head lowered, lips meeting hers in a soft, tender greeting.

"Morning," Marley whispered. "What are you doing?"

"What I've been dreaming about doing for two days." He kissed her again, this time hungrier. He made a low sound in his throat when she sighed and opened to him, incapable of resisting.

One last time, she told herself. She concentrated on the glide of his tongue, his taste, the weight of his hand sweeping down her leg, the other curving under her waist to the small of her back, tugging her against his body. They fit amazingly well, chest to chest, hips to hips, his erection a long, solid ridge between them.

The kiss went on and on, dragging her into sensation, away from thought. Her hands mapped every inch of him she could reach, filing away little details like the scar on the front of his shoulder, the mole on his back, the indentation at the base of his spine, and the delicious curve of his ass.

He slid his hand up her torso, his breathing hard on her neck. She had one final coherent thought—not to let Sam and Riley hear—before Gage's hand closed over her breast. She had to bury her face in her pillow as the moan vibrated in the back of her throat.

"I need you," Gage murmured into her ear. He waited for her to nod, then rolled her onto her back and settled on top of her. With excruciatingly slow movements no one could ever have heard, not even with the stupidly thin walls in this apartment, he maneuvered off her tank top and knit shorts as well as his own pants.

His hands never stopped roaming. Up and down her body, while his bare chest abraded her painfully taut nipples, sending that sweet ache into her pelvis, swelling her. She arched, needing the press of him between her legs, desperation growing. Her fingers dug into his ass, but the heels of her hands pushed against his hipbones, keeping him at a marginal distance.

"God, Marley, I want you so much." His hot breath drifted into her ear with his words, driving her desire higher. "I've never wanted a woman the way you make me want you."

"Gage," she breathed back. Pressure built in her chest that had nothing to do with his weight compressing her lungs. He rocked his hips. His cock stroked her sensitive flesh, making her gasp against his shoulder. She bent her knees and pushed her hips upward. For several seconds they hovered that way. Gage caught his breath, braced just enough on his elbows to keep from crushing her.

"What's wrong?" she whispered.

"Just give me a second." His eyes squeezed closed. "I'm trying to remember where I put the condoms. You make me forget my own name."

She giggled and then covered her face, embarrassed. Gage shifted sideways. There was a crinkle, then a few seconds later he was back, mouth covering hers, no intensity lost in the short break. She sucked him in, loved the way he devoured her, the way he clutched her hip hard with one hand and cradled her head so gently in the other.

With one small move he positioned himself and slid into her, inch by inch. Marley screwed her eyes closed and tightened every muscle in her body to hold back her howl.

Holy *crap*, that was good.

Waves of ecstasy flowed through her, amazing in their constancy. She rolled her lips inward and bit down. Her hands clutched Gage's shoulders, holding him tight to her, as he pressed all the way in, then harder, deeper, before slowly, slowly drawing out again. Then just as slowly he glided back in.

"Oh, God," she moaned. "God, Gage, I can't—I'll never survive this."

"Hang on, baby." He slid a hand around to the small of her back and shifted her so that when he drove into her, his cock dragged against her clit. The waves intensified, focused, but he kept the pace so slow, so quiet, it went on forever, a relentless sea of pleasure. She dove deep and came with the longest, most intense orgasm she'd ever had.

As soon as she convulsed around him he jerked and gasped, joining her with tiny, frantic thrusts. His hands and arms held her tight enough to leave bruises but Marley didn't care. She'd let her entire body go black and blue if he'd do this to her again.

No. She didn't mean that. She was overreacting to good sex. Endorphins.

She clung to that as they held each other. Even as their bodies cooled, emotions settled, nothing changed. Her heart felt gigantic, full of something she refused to identify or label.

After a couple more minutes she was able to shove it inside a figurative box, slam the lid, and seal it. To be dealt with later. Or never.

Gage pulled back and looked down at her with the softest expression she'd seen on his face yet. His hair was a wild mess, and his eyes sparkled with the same electricity she'd recognized when she'd first laid eyes on him in the club.

Words clogged her throat. She didn't know what they were, but anything she said right now would be a mistake. He bent and kissed her. His mouth clung, and his hand stroked down her cheek, knuckles against her jaw. A lone tear slid out of her left eye, hitting the pillow before Gage noticed it.

He pushed himself all the way up and grinned down at her. "I didn't know you could be that quiet."

"It was an effort, but don't let your ego hear that." She managed a smile.

A knock on the door startled her. She hadn't heard Sam's footsteps, which was crazy. He was far too big to not to make these cheapo floors squeak.

"Guys, you up?" he called through the door. "Time to get moving."

• • •

Clear skies, check. Bright sun, check. Perfect? Not so much.

Marley stood on a street corner near the Fiametta, sweating her ass off. She rocked from one foot to the other, waiting for the light to change so she could cross the street. A girl about half a foot shorter than she was, with smooth blond hair exactly like the Barbie Marley had carried everywhere when she was little, strode past her and did a little tripping jog into the crosswalk, against the light. Three cars had to brake hard but no one honked. Probably because the men driving those cars were too entertained by the unbound boobs putting on a show in the chick's tank top.

Maybe that was Marley's problem. She mopped her forehead with the back of her hand and blew air up into her bangs. She was overdressed. She'd pulled on her jeans, sneakers, and olive-green

T-shirt without much thought this morning, and she didn't have any shorts to wear even if she had thought about it. But come on. It wasn't supposed to be hovering around ninety in October, even in LA.

No one else seemed bothered. The old guy in the sweater vest was probably always cold, anyway, but none of the other people standing near her were sweating or complaining. Maybe it wasn't as hot as it seemed. Maybe it was just her.

Maybe this was a fun new side effect of the flux. Hallucinations and hot flashes—magical perimenopause. Fun.

The light finally changed, and she strode across the street, then checked the time. Only ten minutes since she'd left the apartment. Gage probably hadn't made contact yet. Sam and Riley were on the other side of the Fiametta, where they could cuddle and coo by a fountain and wouldn't set off alarms if one of the Deimons spotted them. Marley was actually glad she was on patrol, even if she felt she was too far away. At least she could keep moving, work off the nervous energy, while staying as close as she could to this side of the block. If Gage needed her, she was really only a mad dash away from rescue.

She paused in front of a bookstore displaying rickety wire racks full of old paperbacks out on the sidewalk. The metal creaked as she turned the rack, flipping through romances and mysteries. The musty smell that arose reminded her of digging through boxes at yard sales with her mother.

She shifted behind the rack to avoid a group passing in the other direction. The new position gave her a better view of the street. The block was busy, full of young Hollywood hopefuls hurrying to or from auditions, or gathering in clusters to do whatever young hopefuls did together. There were also plenty of older people out shopping or walking their pets. She was on the alert for Deimons or one of Cressida's inner circle but also for anyone who fit the profile of the addicts. Sam had been unable to glean any more information about the group in New York, how they'd wound up there or what exactly had happened to them, so the "profile" wasn't exactly robust. They'd all been male and had taken enough flux to appear unhealthy and strung out. So far, she hadn't seen anyone who fit.

Her phone buzzed. She flipped it up to check Gage's text. *I'm here.* She answered and moved on, passing an empty storefront and pausing again in front of a gallery, not really registering the flamboyant flower paintings she pretended to peruse. Would Aiden let him in?

Gage was fully on board with the greater goal, but Marley knew the longer he and Aiden were in conflict, the more it hurt him. He'd continued trying to contact his brother since they'd arrived in LA, and every call, text, e-mail, and IM went unanswered. For Gage's sake, she hoped Aiden opened up to him personally, explained why he was doing this. For the sake of the rest of the world, she hoped he gave them the key to taking down Cressida.

Sunlight glinted off a passing car into Marley's eyes. She winced and held her breath against a roll of nausea. Chartreuse spots came and went in her vision, obscuring the sidewalk and the bistro tables next to her.

"Are you all right?" A young woman carrying a bunch of boutique bags stopped and put her hand on Marley's arm. "Can I help?"

Marley coughed and shook her head. "I'm fine. Thank you." But she had to move on. She was calling attention to herself. She tried to blink away the dots enough to see where she was going and started down the sidewalk again.

Then she hesitated, her attention yanked to something magnetic, familiar and yet foreign at the same time. A booted foot shot out, knocking a chair directly into Marley's path. She stumbled into it, barely able to keep from falling.

"What the—" She caught herself on the back of the chair, the metal cool against her palms, and swung around to yell at…

Cressida Lahr. Grinning as if she'd just spotted her long-lost best friend.

Marley's lungs seized. Her throat sealed and her vision tunneled again, tiny green lights flashing in the darkness around the edges.

"Oh, stop being a drama queen and sit down." Cressida nudged the chair again. "Nothing's going to happen out here."

Marley sucked in a breath and looked around, half expecting all the people to be in a frozen tableau. As if the goddess had the ability to stop time so no one would see her kill her prey. But the tables immediately adjacent to the rogue goddess's were empty, and none of the restaurant's patrons seemed to sense anything amiss.

Marley's reaction to seeing Cressida revealed more than she wanted to admit about her fear of confronting the woman again. She had no choice now but to sit and try to regain her composure.

"What brings you to LA?" Cressida asked pleasantly while Marley adjusted the chair and settled into it. Marley gave her a look, and she laughed.

"Okay, let's try 'fancy meeting you here.'" Her mask dropped away, revealing shrewdness, but there was something different about her. Marley studied the woman for a moment. Her hair was still gorgeous but pulled back in a simple ponytail that left one piece to curve around her face. Her eyes weren't turquoise today but a paler version that was still striking against her dusky skin. It all enhanced her feline features but seemed natural. Definitely not power enhanced.

The goddess wore skinny jeans tucked into her black leather boots, which were now crossed on the seat of a third chair. Her shirt was more casual than before, but not T-shirt simple. Silky material, solid red. A half-empty green-tea smoothie sweated on the table, condensation dripping through the ironwork to the concrete below. Cressida sipped it, then smiled a genuine smile at Marley.

She seemed *normal.*

"I take it this isn't coincidence," Marley said.

"Of course not. Once I tag someone, I can sense his—or her—presence for half a mile. I knew exactly when you were coming."

"Tag someone?"

She shrugged. "Identify their life force. Energy signature. Whatever you want to call it. Unique as a fingerprint and always detectable if I've been paying attention."

It sounded similar to both Riley's and Marley's more limited senses, but she could sense Marley from half a mile? That was incredible range. She had never known any goddess to have any abilities that expansive.

What else was this Cressida Lahr capable of? How the hell were they going to go up against her? The element of surprise was obviously off the table.

"Anyway, I sensed you coming and thought we should talk."

"About what? What do you want?"

"I want you to stop absorbing my energy before it drives you insane."

Marley stared at her, aware her jaw had dropped but not quite capable of pulling it back up.

"What can I get you?"

It took Marley a few seconds to switch from Cressida's mini-bomb to the waiter's question. She twisted to look up at the tall, skinny guy in a white button-down shirt and black apron giving off a perfect air of ennui. He was born for LA.

"Same as she's having." Marley nodded at Cressida's smoothie.

"Coming right up."

He walked away, and Marley rested her forearms on the table. "I don't know what you're talking about."

"Let me break it down for you. My power source is the sun.

That means unlimited energy." She ticked the facts off on her fingers as she went. "Unlimited energy is dangerous in its natural state. Living proof." She pointed at herself. "You, however, are not just absorbing it, you're changing it in a way that makes it a part of you. And it's going to drive you insane. I bet it's already started."

When Marley embarked on this quest, she'd been seeking peace. Trying to become a woman she could respect, who'd made up for her mistakes. She'd never thought about what she would do as that woman, what "peace" would look like when the fighting was over. But now even the hope of it slipped away like bubbles down a drain, irretrievable.

For a few seconds, grief swamped her. The only thing she really wanted in her future was Gage, but if some version of Cressida was her destiny now, that possibility no longer existed.

Her lips trembled, but she firmed them immediately. There was no time for wallowing. The truth left her only this mission and one goal. If Cressida was in a sharing mood, Marley would learn all she could and then use it to stop her once and for all.

"How do you know that?" she asked.

Cressida snorted. "How do you think?"

"I guess you're insane."

"Mostly. I have lucid days. Like today." She tilted her head back, out of the shade of the umbrella, and closed her eyes when the sun hit her face. Her calm acceptance struck Marley as just another aspect of the madness. "When I'm in the sun like this, everything's okay. I just soak it in, like any West Coast worshiper. I don't consciously draw energy, but my body takes it in anyway, stores it, accumulates it, and once I figured out how damaging that was, it was too late. I was already on this road."

"Tell me," Marley invited gently. She got the sense this woman needed a confidant, a peer who might understand. Why else would she approach Marley like this? Marley doubted the goddess really cared what happened her, but was she in a sharing mood or did she have a greater purpose?

Cressida stayed still for almost a full minute before drawing back under the umbrella. "When I'm out of the sun, the energy drives at me. It's not meant to be static or inactive, but I can't use or expel enough of it to take the pressure off."

"Why not avoid the sun, then?" But Marley knew it couldn't be that easy.

Cressida laughed bitterly. "What do you think I've been doing all these years since the Society cast me out?"

What, indeed… No one had seen or heard of her for decades. "Why did they?"

Cressida stared at her. "You don't know the story?"

Marley shrugged. "No one does. There are very few records of you and nothing that says what you did."

"What *I* did?" She jerked forward in her chair, slamming the heels of her hands against the table and knocking it a few inches. "I did nothing but struggle to control my 'gift.'" She sneered the word. "Did they help me? Did saintly Barbara Valiant ever spare a moment for a terrified young woman who shared her source? No. The fucking Society for *Goddess Education* and *Defense*," she spat, "they sat in their official little conference room and primly told me that my actions, my choices, had given them no option but to expel me. Every goddess was too scared to come near me." Her hair had come loose, strands falling into her face. Someone behind Marley must have been staring at her because she stiffened her spine and smoothed her hair back before resettling in her chair.

"I locked myself in a house with no windows," she went on in a carefully controlled tone. "That's a different kind of insanity, and it didn't work." She tilted her head. "Your sister's like me, you know."

"Not even remotely," Marley shot back before she could help herself.

This time, Cressida's laugh held true amusement. "I mean

she's powerful. She uses the moon, yes?"

That was common knowledge. "Yes."

"And she's aware of it all the time, even when it's not full moon and she can't directly access it?"

Marley didn't remember ever having a discussion about that with her sister. "I guess."

Cressida nodded. "When the sun's overhead in the middle of the day, it's pouring down on me, even if I'm not out in it. Light and heat aren't the only kinds of energy it sends us."

"What about at night?"

Cressida pointed at her. "I know what you're getting at. Yeah, I went to Alaska, above the Arctic Circle. Spent a few years traveling back and forth, actually, between the two lands of the midnight sun. You have any idea what that was like?"

Marley could imagine the basics. Depression, loneliness, freezing temperatures, harsh weather. It could hardly be better than what Cressida was trying to hide from, and that was without accounting for the grueling travel between locations. Marley had isolated herself from her friends and family for only a few months and was already being pulled back into their fold. She couldn't imagine living that way, at the literal ends of the earth.

The waiter appeared and deposited a wicker basket of sweet potato fries in front of Cressida, then set Marley's smoothie on the table before going back inside.

Cressida offered the basket to Marley, who shook her head.

"I ran out of money, decided living like that was as bad as dying, and if I wasn't going to commit suicide, I needed to try something else. It took me a long time to reintegrate with society." She dipped a fry in a pot of ketchup and ate it.

Marley shook her head. "You sound like a shrink." She stuck a straw into her smoothie and sipped. The crisp cold slid into her mouth and down her throat, seeping out into her body and making her draw a breath of relief.

"I sound like *my* shrink." She ate three more fries. "These are good. Sure you don't want some?"

Marley was too queasy to consider eating anything. "No, thanks. I take it therapy didn't help. What else did you try?" She cared less about the history than the future, but it took one to get to the other, and so far, Cressida was willing to share. Maybe she just wanted someone to understand—no one was a villain in his or her own story. But Marley sensed she had a more specific purpose.

"Everything—drugs, biofeedback. I became OCD about expelling the energy at the end of the day, but it's not like I can just drain it into the sink. There has to be a receptacle."

"A receptacle." The nausea increased. "A person. A specific type of person. That's why you started dealing it."

The sunlight dimmed, a cloud drifting across the sky. "It works better than anything else has, but I didn't deal it until the Deimons. Until Christopher and Aiden got involved." A smile stretched her face, too wide, and her eyelids dropped to half-mast, fluttering. "Oh, the relief. I heard about the leeched goddesses and remembered the fairy tales. How they were meant to teach us not to give our power away. I went searching for those books, to learn how to do it. And I found something better."

Marley's heart thudded sluggishly. This *was* her fault. It was one thing to believe it when it could be disputed and another to have it confirmed to her face. If she'd never bestowed power on Anson, Cressida would never have known to try it and so many other people wouldn't have been harmed. Not just the goddesses, but…

"What did you find?" she croaked, even though she knew.

"I found Numina."

Chapter Thirteen

Face your challengers in the open, with frank discussion, to draw out their intentions and create open competition.
—Numina manifesto, revised

Gage walked to the Fiametta alone. He'd sent a quick e-mail to his father, a follow-up to the one he'd sent before he and Marley left New York. Whatever Quinn was doing to keep them distracted and focused on the summit was working because he'd only gotten a couple of texts back.

His father wanted a phone call, but Gage didn't even attempt it. He'd ask too many questions Gage couldn't answer. It was hard enough keeping things from him. He didn't want to lie on top of it all.

Just before he passed through the front gate into the Mediterranean-style courtyard at the Fiametta a short time later, he tapped out a short text letting Marley know he'd arrived and was going in. He wished she were with him, but Aiden would only talk to him solo, if at all.

Sam and Riley perched on the edge of a fountain, which splashed merrily in the sunlight. Riley swept her hand through the spray, scattering droplets on Sam, who growled and tickled her. She screeched and gave Gage a thumbs-up behind Sam's back.

So his path to the condo was clear, and they would be right here if he ran into trouble. Gage nodded and followed the corridor wrapping around the courtyard. The pinkish stucco walls echoed his footsteps on the travertine tile walkway. A breeze carried soft, flowery scents from the climbing vines on trellises placed around the courtyard, sectioning off stone benches and seating clusters for private lounging. This was a definite step up from the New York apartment, luxurious as it was, and thousands of miles from the rotting barn.

Aiden was in unit 4G. Gage reached the staircase and stepped from sunshine into shade. His heart beat in time with his footsteps, ringing out his approach on the metal steps. He stopped outside the glossy apartment door and knocked. After a few seconds, he couldn't stand to wait. He turned and braced his hands against the metal rail circling the upper level. The courtyard looked great from here, the layout forming a pattern reminiscent of Italian Renaissance. Way out at the fountain, Sam bent to Riley's ear. She was watching Gage up on the balcony. He imagined her expression was worried, though he was too far away to tell. He wished again for Marley to be at his side.

The door opened behind him. He turned quickly and stepped forward so he could block the door if Aiden tried to shut it on him. But his brother just nodded, stepped back, and motioned him inside. As if—

"I knew you were coming."

Gage stepped through the doorway and waited while Aiden closed and locked the door. The foyer opened into a wide living room with tall windows that allowed sunshine to pour in. More Italian tile on the floor, white walls almost completely unadorned, all the plush furniture in ivories and wheats and browns, set off by dark antique cabinets and tables topped by ornate lamps. The coordinated pillows and blanket throws, as well as dried plants stuck in baskets in a couple of corners, told Gage the apartment was either professionally decorated or was owned by a woman. Sam had only traced the deed to a holding company.

"Nice place. Cressida's?"

Aiden nodded once and led his brother into the living room. He dropped onto a chair, leaving a matching one or the sofa for Gage. He chose the sofa for the direct line to the front door.

"How did you know I was coming?" Gage asked.

"Cress knew. She's more aware of everything going on than you'd believe."

"I don't know. I'd believe a lot." Gage studied his brother. This was the longest they'd ever spent apart. They both attended local colleges and never went more than a couple of weeks without getting together, either just the two of them or with their father. Aiden somehow looked older, taller, and more mature than he'd been before Gage left for his last business trip. He wore khakis and a golf shirt no different from his usual attire, but he somehow wore them…better. Or maybe he wore his body better.

"I'm surprised you let me in," Gage said. "I'm sure you know Dad's worried about you."

Aiden shrugged. He sat against the cushion with his arms outstretched, his gaze landing somewhere on the other side of the room.

"Did you think we wouldn't be interested in whatever enterprise you've got going here?"

Aiden loosened his fingers on the arms of the chair. The dents filled in slowly. "Yeah, you'd be interested. Interested in taking over. Telling me everything I was doing wrong. I wanted this to be mine. To succeed on my own merits."

Gage opened his mouth to protest, then closed it and looked down at his hands, loosely folded between his knees. "We'd have wanted to help, yes. You can't blame us for that. We have experience and could offer you advice."

"Yeah. Like I said."

"Okay. Well, I'm proud of you." He almost choked on the words, knowing what kind of business Aiden was running. "What prompted you do to this now? Just trying to get your trust?"

Aiden's stone face tightened into annoyance. "Actually, no. That's not the reason. I haven't been in a rush to get my trust like you were."

The unfair jab wasn't typical of Aiden, and Gage reacted sharply. "I haven't touched that money, and you know it. I believe in hard work." He stopped, took a deep breath. "The point is… I'm glad you're building something. The offer to help stands. Any time. Just let me know." For an instant, he saw something lighter, hopeful, in his brother's eyes.

But he only said, "I'm fine," in that same flat voice.

"Sure. Just offering." Gage braced his forearms on his knees, folded his hands, and clamped his fingers down. He wanted to move, to pace, to slam something past Aiden's defiant calm. But he shoved all that back behind amiable interest. If he was right and Aiden still wanted his big brother's approval, maybe even despite himself, then giving it might be the way to get him to talk.

"So what's it like?" he asked.

"What's what like?"

Good. He was responding. "The flux."

Now Aiden faced him, surprised. "Why are you asking me that?"

Gage sat up straighter. "It's the product you're selling. Taking it is good business. Why wouldn't I ask how it was?"

"Because she said you'd know—that the whore you're with can tell." Aiden's composure had been broken, and he looked around, as if hoping Cressida would step into the room and clarify the discrepancy.

Gage's vision flashed red. "If you expect me to respect your goddess, you'd better respect mine."

"What? Who?" Aiden frowned at him. "What do you mean 'your goddess'?"

"Marley. The woman who's been trying to *save* you all from yourselves. You saw her at the New York ceremony? Tallish, red hair, white eyes?"

Aiden curled his lip. "She's no goddess."

"She's as much a goddess as Cressida Lahr is. But that's all off topic. What did you think Marley would know?"

"That we didn't take it." He looked unhappy that he'd revealed anything but sighed with resignation. "The business partners—me, Chris, Tony, Brad. None of us take the flux. Not yet."

Gage couldn't stop himself from sagging into the couch cushions. It had been three days since New York, plenty of time for things to have changed. He may still be late, but he wasn't *too late.*

"Why not? She doesn't have enough to go around? You guys can't afford it?" He made a show of surveying the room. "Neither one looks true to me."

Aiden shook his head. "She has too much. But she won't let us have any right now." He leaned forward, his tone and new body language portraying a "see, she doesn't want to hurt us!" assertion that Gage didn't buy for a minute.

"Because it's dangerous," Gage said. "Because it can not only make you both power hungry and power mad but because it will carve you into nothing from the inside out."

"It's not dangerous." Aiden got up and went to a glass bar against one wall. He lifted the cut-crystal stopper from a decanter and poured two glasses. "It's just energy. It won't hurt anyone." He came back and handed one of the rocks glasses to Gage.

Whiskey fumes burned his nostrils as he accepted the drink. He had to stop Aiden from taking flux, and honesty was the only way to do that. "It's affecting mental capacity, Aid. You can't take it. Brandon Williams almost murdered someone because of the flux." The exaggeration was acceptable given the stakes.

"I heard about that." Aiden put on a regretful expression and swirled his whiskey. "But the flux didn't have anything to do with his decision. It was simple revenge."

"What if it wasn't?" Gage set his glass on the table. His hand was so tight he was afraid he'd shatter the glass. "What if the flux made him sick? Or what if he had problems already, lying dormant until the flux triggered them?"

Aiden's jaw tensed, and his eyes darted from one side of the room to the other, as if he was holding himself back from lashing out.

Gage would circle back around to that. "What's your business model? Is there a membership fee to be a Deimon or something?"

"To start with. Then they have to pay a tribute. But it gets bigger. Much bigger." Now that he'd started, he seemed to forget he hadn't wanted to talk. "Tonight, we have ten people meeting who had their second dosage last month. They've all profited from their abilities. These guys are the good ones. The ones smart enough to stay off your whor—goddess's radar. They've just boosted their natural abilities, increased business, gotten promotions. They owe us a percentage of whatever they've gained."

"And then they get more flux?"

"Yep. Once a month from here on, with commissions paid as long as they're profiting. Each dose is a new transaction, so it compounds. Brilliant, right?" He grinned, looking like his old self for a moment.

Gage wanted to tell him it was the opposite of brilliant. They might be compounding their income potential, but they were also compounding their risk. What happened when their clients got so powerful they decided they didn't need to pay anymore? Or Marley's big fear, that they'd get tired of being restricted and decide to take it from another source? And that was without degradation. Maybe the stronger the Numina bloodline, the lower the side effects. Pettle and Vanrose seemed okay so far, at least publicly, but the addicts were a whole different story.

Gage had to play it cool. He couldn't be responsible for starting a leeching epidemic if they weren't yet thinking in that direction, and he was afraid once he brought up the addicts, the conversation would be over.

"So you, what, hop back and forth across the country with these rituals and stuff? How long before that gets old?"

Aiden grimaced. "That's not our long-term plan. Chris and Tony started it, and…" He made a face at Gage that was full of wry resignation and exasperation. "Some of the things they set up are pretty stupid. But it fit the clientele. As we expand and move up the ladder, we'll refine those processes."

Move up the ladder. Which sounded as if they planned to approach older, more established Numina. Such as those who'd fallen from grace recently? Who'd formed splinter groups outside of the normal structure?

The next item in the list of escalating reasons to stop Cressida Lahr.

"Is that why you weren't at the barn? You don't approve?"

"I'm more focused on setting up the next stage."

Gage wondered if Aiden really didn't see the flaw in his master plan. "What have you calculated your plateau at?"

Aiden stammered a little and shifted on his chair, glancing around. Gage had seen the reaction many times in boardrooms and on-location meetings. If Aiden had papers, he'd be shuffling them right now. He obviously didn't see the flaw.

Maybe Gage could use this. If he could convince Aiden it would be a lot of hard work for a poor final result, there might be a chance to break the seal. Give Aiden an excuse to cut ties with this whole thing, or even to let it die.

"She can only give power to Numina, right?"

"Riiight." Aiden frowned.

Gage swallowed. So Aiden didn't know sons of goddesses were candidates, too. That was good. "Not all Numina are going to be good candidates. Some won't have any need or desire for the product."

"Well, sure." He laughed. "Can you see Dad taking this stuff?"

Gage coughed. "Or any of the leadership."

"Well, obviously, our main client base is younger, less established. The guys with dreams they haven't fulfilled yet."

The ones who wanted shortcuts.

"How many of them do you think there are?" It was a tricky question. Numina didn't hand out a roster. That was too much of a threat to their secrecy. Their leadership was appointed, not elected, and one family was in charge of keeping all the ancient texts. One of the texts held names of known Numina from that time, but there were few unbroken lines under those names. Wars and disasters and emigration caused changes. Sometimes no males were born in a generation—that was almost inconceivably rare but it happened.

Most Numina did participate in a massive, extremely well-protected digital collective, but the bottom line was that no one could just pull up a spreadsheet and say "There are X Numina in the United States." Never mind pinpoint how many of those fit Aiden's target demographic.

His brother shrugged. "It doesn't matter."

Gage thought Aiden was just trying to hide his lack of knowledge, but when he raised his glass to sip, he smirked behind it. The kind of smirk someone gives when they know something big.

"No business can last if it doesn't have growth," Gage tried.

"We have plenty of room for growth."

He had to be talking about the third group, the addicts. "Yeah, about that. How did you find those guys, anyway?"

Aiden jerked his head around. His whiskey sloshed. "What

guys?"

"The ones in the meeting room in Pritchard. You…know about that, don't you?" Angered now at his brother's lackadaisical attitude about people's lives, he couldn't mask his sarcasm. "They were discovered. Marley nullified them all, and the cops took them out."

"What?" His brother shot to his feet. "What have you done?"

Gage followed. "What have *you* done?" He took a step, towered over his younger brother. "Where did you find them?"

"She *needs* them, Gage. That's the whole foundation—" He palmed the back of his head and spun, took a step, then came back. "Don't you realize that when your goddess takes the flux, they can't get any more? What will Cress do? She needs that outlet!"

"I thought you had plenty of room for growth."

"Because of them!" He flung out his hand, pleading now. "I found the list in Dad's walk-in safe, buried in centuries of old texts. He was hiding it. They've always kept track of anyone with the merest drop of Numina blood, no matter how far from the original lines they spread. When I learned about Cress's illness, I knew I had to find a way to help her forever. This was it! And you're…" He squeezed his glass, stared at it, and carefully set it on the bar. "She needs those men," he repeated. "They're not easy to track down. We're always locating more, but…" He trailed off, staring out the window. Then he shook his head abruptly. "I'll do it. She can use me. I'd do anything for her."

Gage had stood still while his brother raged, trying to wrap his head around what Aiden had done, about the things his father had never told him. But when Aiden said he'd take their place, it jolted Gage into action.

"No!" He hauled Aiden around by the shoulders. "You can't. You are the *last* person who should ever let her give you power."

"You're crazy." He knocked one of Gage's hands away, but Gage grabbed him tighter and shook him.

"No, that's what you'll be. Remember Mom, Aiden. What if mental illness runs in our family? If you take that flux, it could drive you insane."

It was the exactly wrong thing to say. Aiden slammed his hands into Gage's chest. He stumbled, almost falling when the coffee table hit him behind the knees.

"I am so fucking sick of you and Dad telling me that! You have suffocated me my whole life, blamed me for her suicide."

Gage gaped at him. "No, we didn't. It was—"

"He pretended he was protecting me, but it was really all about him. Saving face. Not failing. Not having a flawed son."

"You're wrong, Aid." Gage remembered, all too clearly, the way their father had sobbed in the months after their mom had died, clutching tiny Aiden to his chest, his arm around Gage to pin him to his side. "He loves us. He loves you."

"Then why was it only ever me being tested? Being watched like I was always about to do something depressed or manic?"

"It wasn't. I was, too." But not to the same extent—Aiden was right. "It's because you were—are—so much like her."

"Fuck you, Gage. And fuck him."

Aiden shoved Gage toward the door, yanked it open, and pushed him through. It slammed behind him, putting much more than a door between the two brothers.

He couldn't have done that worse. He'd not only failed to coax Aiden out of harm's way, failed to learn anything that would help them stop Cressida, but he'd given Aiden reason to make the worst possible decision. Every terrible scenario they'd discussed over the past several days was coming to pass.

And it was his fault.

• • •

Marley shoved her smoothie across the table, wishing she could shove herself away from this whole conversation. But she needed to know. "How did you find out about Numina?"

An unholy light shone in Cressida's eyes now. She waved at the server and lifted her empty cup, signaling that she wanted another. She spoke faster, hands flashing in the air, punctuating the words. "Ancient texts, modern records. The fact of their secrecy is a miracle in our news-obsessed world, but little bits leak out. People know. And then I knew. And I believed that if sons of goddesses could take power, maybe sons of gods could take more. They can. And what's better—there are more of them."

The sun burst out again, uncovered, and Cressida relaxed into her chair. She held one hand out into a sunbeam, rotating it, and the sharpness slowly faded away from her body language, her voice, and her expression.

"I started with Darren Pettle. He was a college running back from a mid- to high-level Numina family who desperately wanted to make the NFL. I told him I might be able to help. We could experiment, and if he made it big, he could pay me then. It was an investment—something Numina understands." She shrugged. "And there was rent to be paid, groceries to buy. The arrangement served many purposes."

Marley cleared her throat and asked the waiter delivering Cressida's second smoothie for a glass of water.

"The relief was incredible," Cressida crooned. "And Darren's success, as well. He introduced me to friends, who introduced me to friends. Their younger siblings learned of it and formed a little club." Her mouth formed a moue of affection. "They became phase two."

Marley pressed her fingers to her temples. She knew what phase three had to be—the addicts, the fringe of Numina, sons of daughters of daughters or whatever, with bloodlines diluted to barely detectable levels. How had she found *them*?

"What's the catch?"

Tears filled Cressida's eyes. "It's not enough. It's never enough.

I have temporary relief but can't end the inflow, and my tolerance grows. So I have to find more clients. Word of mouth can make things happen slowly. So when I met Chris and Tony…"

"They started pimping for you."

The light in her eyes changed. The sun had gone behind another bigger, darker cloud. "They have given me freedom. Freedom that *you* are threatening."

Fear skittered across Marley's skin for the first time since she'd sat down. She shifted and braced her feet under her, ready to defend herself. "Did they start phase three for you, too?"

Cressida stood, her chair scraping loudly across the concrete. "Phase three is secret. How do you know about my receptacles?"

Marley rose too, gagging. "*Receptacles*? They're people! You're destroying them. And every one of them you give power to is a danger to others."

"Oh, please. Like who?" The elastic around her ponytail snapped. Her hair fell around her shoulders and then fluttered back, as if blown by a breeze. But there was no air movement around them at all.

Marley's hands tightened around the edge of the table. No one passed on the sidewalk near them, and the last other customers at the bistro had left a few minutes ago.

The magnetic pull that had caught Marley's attention when Cressida first knocked the chair in her path appeared again, growing stronger, tugging on her awareness. It bore a trace of the blue shine of flux, the yellow glow of the energy Cressida had poured into Anson, and Marley understood. She was drawing power. Not just soaking in the sun but actively using it to collect energy.

She was going to attack.

"Cressida, please, just think about this." Marley raced to reconnect with the lucid part of the goddess before it was gone completely. She might not have a chance in hell of changing anything, but she had to try. "Most of those men in the Pritchard

Building were dying. Anson died. Some of the Deimons do not have good intentions for the power you're giving them, and there are members of Numina who would use your power to leech other goddesses. You— "

"Let them!" Cressida's eyes glowed furiously. "They cast me out, blamed me for things I had no control over. Every self-righteous bitch who turned her back on me should suffer."

"Then why did you come here?" The air around them was no longer still. Across the street a flag hung limply from a storefront stand, but wind kicked up from Marley's feet and tossed her hair into her face. A smoothie cup tipped over and clattered to the ground. "Why warn me to stop? You don't care if I go insane."

"I care if you take my outlets!" Cressida yelled into the increasing wind.

A few people approaching on the sidewalk had stopped to stare. A couple turned and hurried in the other direction, but others came closer, watching avidly.

"When you take my power from them, they can no longer accept more. I am not responsible for damage they may do, Marley Canton, *you are*."

She flung her hands up, energy pulsing out of them. Marley dodged, and the wave hit the table, which skidded several inches before tipping, rolling onto its side, and taking out two chairs on its way to the ground.

"That's why you told me your story." Marley stepped around the table, slowly approaching Cressida. "You wanted me to be sympathetic so I'd leave you alone." She tried to sound as if it had worked so the goddess would let her come closer.

Cressida's hands lowered, hovering at waist height. "I'm not harming anyone," she said. "I'm not a parent or teacher. It's not up to me what they do with the power I give them. All I want is to be able to live without the agony."

"I understand." God, this was stupid. Marley took another step as though she were approaching a growling dog. “I want to help you find a way. And I think I have one.” She didn’t. She *knew* she couldn’t remove energy unless it didn’t belong to the person. She’d touched her sister and Riley with no effect. She’d even touched Cressida at Chris’s apartment.

But maybe she could make the goddess hesitate, stop to consider it, just long enough for Marley to take her down. If she could knock her out before Cressida could act…

She lunged the last few feet and clamped her hand over Cress’s wrist. In rapid succession she yanked the woman off balance, kicked one leg out from under her, and swung one of the heavy iron chairs at her head.

It almost worked. Cressida went down on one knee and the chair came within an inch of her temple before it halted in midair and tumbled harmlessly to the sidewalk.

Cressida rose and wrapped her free hand around Marley’s arm, her teeth bared. “There is no easy solution, you stupid bitch. Nullifying? Leeching? You delude yourself. My way works, and you will no longer interfere!” She sent a pulse of energy through their clasped arms and into Marley.

She gasped when the pulse hit her body and spread, sinking in heavily, a wave of pleasure tingling in its wake. Was this what the Deimons felt? The addicts? Tears gathered in her eyes, and she clamped her teeth together to keep herself from begging. She didn’t know what she would be begging for—another dose or for her to stop. Because hard on the heels of the pleasure came a roil of green clouds across the sky, a dull roar in her ears that may or may not have been real.

Cressida cackled and did it again. This pulse was bigger, and it burned before it died. Marley’s nerve endings shuddered in tiny orgasmic spasms, and seconds later, screeching green bats swarmed around them. She was on her knees, head bowed, no longer holding Cressida’s arm, but her own was raised over her head, gripped by the goddess, who bent to hiss in her ear.

"I tried to appeal to your common sense, your self-preservation, your compassion. Your refusal will have consequences you can't even imagine. Your sister, her lover, your friends, their children—every goddess, every Numina, they are all mine now. You feel my power, my strength?"

Another pulse. Marley convulsed, her jaw locking. She could barely feel the despair generated by Cressida's words, so caught was she in the throes of taking in so much delicious…hateful, horrible energy, inert as it may have been.

"I could have been different." Her grip loosened, her voice a whisper now. "But we are what we've become, aren't we, Marley? Too bad."

She released Marley and straightened. The wind died as murmurs around them grew louder. Barely able to draw breath, she forced open her eyes, squinting through the haze and still-fluttering forms she knew didn't truly exist. A crowd had gathered. Why hadn't anyone tried to interfere? But then someone muttered something about cameras and parabolic mics, and Marley remembered that they were in LA.

"Thank you, everyone, for helping make that scene perfect in one great take!" Cressida's voice rang out around them. Applause followed, though Marley saw a few people frown at each other, a couple pointing at her.

Get up. Let them believe it. Don't be a victim. The last bit rang false even in Marley's own head. She already was a victim. But she pushed to her feet, using a tipped-over chair for support as she struggled.

"You'll all be receiving releases to sign so you can be shown on film, but in the meantime, thank you again!" Cressida whirled and strode away, the crowd parting for her.

By the time Marley had gathered enough strength to follow, she was gone.

CHAPTER FOURTEEN

The compounded income streams will ensure stability and sustainable growth as targeted assets increase.
—AS Services business plan

The spectators had dispersed pretty quickly. Marley heard someone arguing that no one had taken contact information for the releases. Someone else babbled about the special effects. She could feel eyes on her, people avidly watching, maybe trying to figure out if they'd seen her in anything before. Her head throbbed, her vision was blurry, and she thought she might throw up any second. She had to get out of there.

She staggered around a corner into an alley. The stench hit her flat in the face—sun-cooked garbage in an overflowing Dumpster, combined with the sharp ammonia of cat urine. She lurched a few steps, heaved, and her breakfast splattered the cinderblock wall behind the trash bin.

Gasping, she dragged herself back to the street and weaved down the sidewalk. She had no idea where she was going. Just away. Away from the onlookers and any police a smart one might call. Away from the Fiametta, where Sam and Riley and Gage were. They couldn't see her like this.

The world was still green, the color a combination of Cressida's natural power and what it became when it was flux inside someone else. No amount of shaking her head and blinking improved it, but at least it wasn't foggy anymore. The muscles in her arms, her torso, and her legs protested sharply with every step, and after a few blocks, she couldn't keep going. She found a small park with a bench facing a children's climber that was mercifully empty and sank down onto it, folding over until her head rested on her knees. But her heaving breath smelled horrible when it bounced back off her jeans into her face. She opened her knees and braced her forearms on them, her hands pressed against her forehead.

God, oh, God, this sucks.

How had it come to this? She'd never gotten sick before, even in New York after Anson was killed. Her stomach lurched, and she dry heaved. It was because it was Cressida's pure power—that had to be why. She needed equilibrium. Flux could do that. Yes. She'd just find one of the Deimons or even one of the receptacles and nullify him. Then she'd be okay. It wouldn't hurt, it would just feel good. Those full-body orgasms…

Jesus. This wasn't her. This was addiction. What the hell was she going to do?

She rocked, watching the ground at her feet waver and blur out of proportion with the motion. She forced her mind to go blank, not to think about how she felt or what had happened, just to concentrate on improving. Getting better. She would get better. She *had* to.

And slowly, way too slowly, she did. The ground no longer moved, even after she stopped rocking. The grass was green because it was supposed to be, the shredded tires under the climber were black and white, her jeans were blue, the bench was brown. She sat up, and the air was clear, no wispy bats to be found.

Bats, for god's sake.

Where the hell was she? She looked around. The neighborhood was quiet, residential, but there was still steady traffic. She pulled out her phone. A couple of hours had passed since Gage had texted her that he was at the condo in the Fiametta. He'd texted her again more than half an hour ago, saying he was done and heading back to the rental. She had one from Riley, too.

They'd all be back at the apartment already, wondering where she was.

Even as she thought it, her phone buzzed. Gage was calling. She couldn't answer it. He'd know something was wrong. She wasn't even sure she could talk. Her throat was so dry, and fatigue dragged at her. But she had to get back, to tell them what happened. Everyone had to be warned. Marley had screwed everything up completely, and now "everyone could be at risk" had become "everyone is in immediate danger." Starting with the people closest to her. And from the extent of Cressida's threat, not ending until the goddess was dead.

She pushed to her feet with a moan and called up the GPS app on her phone to key in the apartment address. Once it identified her position, an arrow popped up on the map, and she started walking.

• • •

Ten minutes after he left the Fiametta, Gage arrived at the crappy rental unit alone, laboring under a weight that had grown on the walk back. He'd bolted past Sam and Riley, not ready to talk about what had happened. They'd obviously been able to tell, though, because they hadn't caught up with him. He dropped his keys on the counter and opened the refrigerator. Why didn't they have any beer?

The front door opened. He twisted to see if it was Marley, but only Sam and Riley came in. The heaviness intensified.

"I texted Marley," Riley said. "No answer yet."

"Same here." Gage straightened and shut the fridge. "Did you guys hear anything from her while I was inside?"

They shook their heads. All three of them took out their phones to double-check, but that only led to more head shaking. Gage cursed.

"So we don't know if she ran into someone or got hit by a car or what. Aiden was expecting me. He said Cressida knows everything."

"Everything?" Sam repeated.

"Something like that. Knows more than we think." He squeezed the phone. "She might have found Marley. I'm calling her." But she didn't answer her phone.

Nearly an hour later, there was still no word. Gage and Sam had searched the area around the Fiametta, checking in every few minutes with Riley, who'd stayed at the apartment in case Marley returned. There wasn't a trace of her anywhere, except that a waiter at a bistro said he served green-tea smoothies to a redhead and another woman. He couldn't confirm by her picture, though, and said he thought some low-budget indie filmmaker was shooting a scene on the sly. If he was right, the redhead wouldn't have been Marley.

"Anything?" Gage stood behind Sam, who sat on the couch checking hospital intake lists and police reports.

"Not yet. It's not instantaneous, and stuff doesn't always get entered right away." He looked over his shoulder, spotting Gage's fist. "Dude, you have to calm down. You're not going to find her by punching holes in the wall."

"It might make me feel better, though." He shook out his hand. The knuckles cracked. "What about—"

A *thud* at the door. The knob rattled, then snapped when the door opened under pressure. Marley staggered through, almost falling over when she pushed it shut. "Here I am." Her chest heaved and her T-shirt clung to her sweaty body. She glanced around at everyone, her eyes the color of aging newspapers. "Why are you looking at me like that?"

"What happened?" Gage pushed past Sam and Riley to guide Marley to the couch. She collapsed onto it, her head creasing the cushion into a deep V. Gage sat on the coffee table in front of her but didn't touch her. Her whole body shook, and she moved like she'd been trudging through the desert for days.

"Long story." She lifted a hand, the motion limp.

"We've been trying to reach you."

"Phone died." She licked dry lips and winced. "And I got a little lost."

"Can you get her some water, please?" Gage asked Riley. He didn't want to move away from Marley. He watched as her breathing slowed and her face grew less pale. But the yellowed color in her eyes didn't change.

She accepted the glass from Riley and guzzled the water. Once it was drained, she looked around at all of them again. "I hope you learned something helpful."

"I'm not saying a word until you tell us what happened. You ran into Cressida, didn't you?"

"I did." But her eyes pleaded silently not to push her, and Gage caved.

He cleared his throat. "I didn't find out anything good." He told them the little bit he'd learned from his meeting with his brother, about their business plans and the clients Cressida already had. And then he admitted how badly he'd botched things by telling his brother about the addicts.

"The receptacles," Marley murmured. "Phase three."

"What?"

She shook her head, still pressed deep into the couch cushion. "Sorry. I'll explain in a minute. Go ahead."

"He wants to take their place. He said he'll take whatever Cressida needs to give." He drew in a breath, the responsibility settling heavy on his shoulders. "I'm afraid of what it will do to him. Our mother committed suicide when he was a baby," he said for Sam and Riley's benefit. "We've always worried he might have the genetic predisposition. There's never been an indication that he does, but the flux—"

"Could trigger it if it's there." Marley dragged herself upright. "Okay, that's priority one, then. Get her before she gets Aiden, or if we can't get there fast enough, I'll get Aiden." She squeezed Gage's forearm and met his gaze with eyes still bearing a lemony tint. "I'll take it from him before it does too much damage."

Gage covered her hand in his. She no longer seemed jacked up, but a fear lurked in her eyes that he'd never seen there before.

"What happened to you?" he asked. "What did she do?"

She pulled herself to her feet and paced across the room, a little wobbly but becoming steadier with each step. Gage swiveled to take her place on the couch.

"Cressida and I had a nice chat." She described the rogue goddess pulling her into a bizarre conversation. "One minute she was as lucid as you or—you." She pointed at Sam and Riley. "The next she was raving. Back and forth for a while, but by the end, it was all forth. The sun has driven her insane." She told them everything the goddess had told Marley, including phase three.

"Those men were simply waste barrels," she said with disgust. "A place for her excess energy to go so she could ease the pressure and find some relief."

"Why was she telling you all this?" Riley asked.

"She acted like it was for my well-being." Marley paced away from them when she said this, and Gage wondered what she was leaving out. "But really, she wanted to appeal to my compassion. She wants me to stop nullifying and taking away her outlets. When I wouldn't play by her rules, she turned on me. And…God, guys, I screwed it up. So badly." She sank to her knees in the middle of the room. "She's coming after everyone. She hates goddesses anyway, for casting her out, not helping her, and now she's going to push her followers to become leeches. She's coming after all of you, and Quinn and Nick. Even the Numina." She raised tormented, still-awful-colored eyes to Gage's. "It all backfired. I'm so sorry."

He joined her on the floor, taking her hands. "Don't. It's not your fault. Blame could be liberally spread around but the bottom line hasn't changed."

"Except the threat is more concrete than it was before and that pushes our timeline." Sam sat back at his computer. "Aiden said there's a meeting tonight, right? He say where?"

"No." Gage was done talking. He pressed the back of his hand to Marley's forehead. It blazed with heat. "What did she do to you?"

Marley shrugged. "We fought a little. I lost. She sent a few pulses of energy into me. It was… Let's just say it was a little more than I'm used to handling at once."

"We can see it," Riley murmured.

Marley raised her eyebrows. "What do you mean *we*?"

"Your eyes." Gage touched her temple. "They're yellow. Or they were. They look almost normal again. But it's been hours since she hit you." He stood and bent to scoop Marley into his arms. "You need to rest, babe."

Marley scooted away and got to her feet, putting Sam and Riley between them. "There's no time to rest. We need to stop her now."

"As far as I can tell," Sam said, "there are only two ways to do that."

Riley looked at each of them with sad eyes. "One way. Because I don't want to hear it if any of you are capable of killing her in cold blood."

No one responded. Gage knew he was capable of killing if it meant saving the life of someone he loved, but that wasn't what they were talking about here. "And the other way?"

"Leeching her," Sam said.

The silence this time was twice as dense. "No." Marley stepped forward. "That's an unacceptable thing to ask of anyone. We don't even know if it's possible. She told Anson he couldn't take enough. She's always connected to the sun. It could kill anyone who tries, even if we could get close enough to do it."

"What do you suggest, then?" Gage demanded, frustrated. "I can't let Aiden—"

"I know. But if she gives him some, and I nullify him, he'll be safe. We need to make a list of everyone we know who has flux. Take them away from her. We'll have to contact Pettle and Vanrose and follow the connections until we get that dozen. Sam, you're good at that kind of thing." She spun back to Gage. "Can you get back into the condo? Because I think we have to take that list he found. If he can't get to them, he can't use them. Then we won't have to worry about always chasing, always being behind. If we take away her receptacles, her outlets—"

"It will just make her more desperate and dangerous." Riley stepped between them all and looked from Gage to Sam. "Are you guys seriously considering going along with this? Even setting aside the fact that if we take away what she has now, she'll just go further, target higher, and care less about the fallout, have you even thought about what nullification is doing to Marley?"

"Riley..." Marley's tone rang with annoyance and warning.

"No." She spun on Marley. "I'm telling them. I care too much about you, and they do, too, and that has to trump the big picture. It's *always* about the people we care about." She positioned herself in front of Marley, taking on the role of protector. "The flux doesn't just die when she nullifies it. It's building up in her system like the drugs we keep comparing it to. It's changing her, just like it was changing the Deimons. And I think what Cressida attacked her with today is worse than even that nullified flux."

"Changing you how?" Gage moved closer, watching Marley

tremble. Her chin lifted, but then her eyes rose to the ceiling and despair filled them. Her shoulders slumped.

"It's making me as insane as Cressida is."

The words echoed in Gage's skull and had only one meaning. A familiar image flashed into his head: a woman in a bathtub, drowned. He'd never seen his mother that way, but that hadn't stopped him from imagining it. Only now it wasn't his mother floating, bloated, gray-faced, but Marley. His stomach twisted, and his heart bled.

She would not be that woman. He wouldn't let it happen.

"Then that's it." Sam slapped the laptop closed. "We're done."

"We can't be *done*." Gage couldn't move. He wanted to go to Marley, to hold her, to keep her safe. But his brother filled his head—not the man he'd displayed today, the man he'd chosen to be, but the helpless baby, the laughter-filled child, the heart of his family. He couldn't abandon him, either.

Sam twisted and leaned forward, jaw tense. "What do you suggest?"

Gage stepped toward Riley. "If I understand leeching correctly, you could bestow some power to me, and then I could leech Marley. Would that halt the progression of her mental instability?"

"I don't know. It's not energy once Marley takes it. I don't know if it can be removed from her."

"Okay." Gage swallowed hard, making a decision he knew he couldn't go back on once he said it out loud. "Then I'll leech Cressida."

"No!" Marley shouted.

Sam and Riley didn't look thrilled with that idea, either.

"We know that's the only option. Even if Marley nullifies everyone Cressida has now, she'll find others. The more outlets we take away, the more desperate she'll be. Aiden's already prepared to accept it all for her." He knew this would work. It would put an end to everything. "I'll drain her completely, and—what did you call it?" he asked Sam. "Crack her vessel? Then she can't channel any more in, and she'll be cured."

"No way." Marley wrapped her arms around herself, shivering. "You saw what it did to Anson. He couldn't take a fraction of what she had."

"Totally different. He was a mess, and she was sending it into him. If I just take what she has, without her channeling more, I can drain her."

"And then what?" Sam asked. "We can't leave you like that. Marley would have to nullify you, and from the sound of it, that would destroy her."

"No. Look. The guys *use* flux. And then it's gone, right? Anson leeched goddesses, and then he had their abilities. He could use it. So why can't I leech her, and then blow the energy out of my body?"

"That amount of energy would be like a bomb." Marley remained huddled behind Riley, all tucked into herself. "You might not be able to control the discharge."

"I could teach him," Riley offered. "He'd need someone to start him off anyway, right? We can do a couple of trial runs."

"Okay, then." Gage nodded once, hard. "It's decided."

"It sure as hell is *not*." Sam put his arm around Riley's shoulders and glared at him. "Riley's never done anything like that. I'm not—"

"Letting me?" she asked in a dangerous tone.

Sam clearly knew better than to follow up with that. "We need Quinn. She took all the power back from Anson. She's the only one who knows enough about leeching to do this. And we could sure as hell use Nick in this, too."

Gage nodded. "Then get them. Whatever you need to do. Get them. The sooner we can do this, the better."

Sam returned to his laptop and Riley went to her phone on the kitchen counter. Marley had disappeared.

He found her in the bedroom, curled into a ball in the middle of the sagging bed.

"Marley."

She sniffed and turned her face harder into the pillow. "Go away, Gage."

"No." He sat on the bed, bracing his feet so he didn't slide off, and rubbed her back. "I'm sorry this is happening to you. Can you tell me what exactly *is* happening?" Maybe it wasn't as bad as she thought. How could she be objective when she was in the middle of it?

She rolled onto her back, her eyes swollen. The tears shimmering in them gave the white an opalescent sheen. He smoothed her hair back. She was so beautiful. He couldn't let this happen to her.

"I don't want to talk about it," she said. "Leave me alone." She rolled back to her side.

"No." He lay down on the bed behind her, curving his arm around her waist, pressing his face into her hair. "I'm not leaving you, Marley."

"Why?" she cried out, trying to roll again, to push him away, but he held fast. "You barely know me. Cut your losses."

"I can't." He tucked his chin over her shoulder and spoke softly but with a conviction that left him a little awed. "It makes no sense, but the last thing I want to do is 'cut my losses.' I haven't known you long, Marley, but I know you. You have infused me with something that is alive and wonderful, and it's not going to disappear just because you tell it to. So I'm not running." The words were a commitment that he hadn't expected to make, and fear tickled at the base of his spine. But what relationship was without fear?

Marley hadn't moved, and he traced moisture on her cheek. "Please don't cry."

"Are you doing this because of your mother? Because you

couldn't save her? So you'll save me?"

He thought about that through a few shared breaths—she deserved better than a knee-jerk reaction. "Maybe. I don't know. I do know I want to save *you.* And I will if I can. But not because of her. Because of you."

"Gage," she whispered, his name as full of despair as her eyes had been in the living room.

"Tell me. What's happening to you?"

It took a little more coaxing, but she told him about the hallucinations, the way her thoughts took her down unnatural roads, that she'd felt overheated all day when it was temperate outside. By the end, *he* wanted to cry into the pillow. But he hadn't changed his mind.

He shifted to let her turn over. When he could see her face, he was struck again by her eyes, so filled with regret and somehow, still, slightly hopeful. And something more. He remembered comparing them to marble when she closed off her emotions from him in the motel room after he'd stitched her side. Now he couldn't imagine them ever being cold and hard.

"You know," he said, heart thumping hard enough she had to feel it against her shoulder. "You haven't said you want me." He threaded his fingers between hers and stroked his thumb over the back of her hand.

"I do," she whispered. "I've been trying not to, but you make that very difficult."

He chuckled, and his heart rate slowed. "Good. Then there's nothing more to discuss."

"Oh, yes, there is," she protested. "There's no happy riding off into the sunset for us. I'm not letting you lee— "

He bent to kiss her, but their lips had barely met when there was a hard knock on the door.

"Guys," Sam called. "You've gotta come see this."

CHAPTER FIFTEEN

Word is that Vanrose's newest project is so awful, the man can't get a meeting with craft services.
—Hollywood gossip blog

Marley let Gage hold her hand as they emerged into the living room because she simply didn't have the strength to pull away. Everything he'd said had weakened her, so even though the walls bowed in on her in the hallway and the floor felt squishy beneath her feet, she couldn't muster the strength to refuse him.

If he could face fears that stemmed from childhood, from the worst event of his entire life, how could she be such a coward?

Sam and Riley sat watching the laptop, where a football player juked his way up emerald field turf. Marley squeezed her eyes shut automatically but then realized it was supposed to be that green.

"What is it?" she asked.

"Rewind it," Riley told Sam. He slid the marker to the beginning of the video and made it full screen. Marley and Gage stood behind the couch to watch.

"Pettle was well on his way to blowing out the competition for Rookie of the Year," a voice said over a clip of the running back

bowling over two guys much bigger than him, fooling another to dart around him, and then soaring up the sideline and into the end zone. *"He hadn't had an off game all season. So what happened Monday night?"*

The screen flashed to a new clip. Pettle went the wrong way and slammed first into a linebacker plugging the hole, then to his back on the ground. New clip, same result. Over and over, he hit the turf. Then he stood on the sidelines, helmet in hand, head bent as he listened to a coach, but he looked sick, breathing hard and gulping every few seconds.

"Some have speculated that Pettle has the flu that's been plaguing other teams, though not, reportedly, his own. Others blamed a bad game, inevitable for any player in the NFL at some point. But setting aside the extreme nature of this week's failure—twenty-four carries for twenty yards—a review of the past few games shows a marked decline in his performance."

They watched a few more examples of bad choices, weak moves, and big tackles.

"The flux obviously isn't working for him anymore," Riley said.

Marley could barely concentrate. She was struggling to come up with a way to keep Gage from having to leech Cressida. Even if it didn't kill him, even if he discharged it and she nullified anything that was left, that much power could still have a prolonged effect on him. What it was doing to her was bad enough. But she couldn't think logically. Her brain kept skittering down strange paths, concepts filled with impossible things like foggy scarabs chewing out the energy and even more disturbing images she flinched away from before they could be fully formed. Sound was fuzzy and distant, colors and lights dimming, her presence in the room drifting away.

It was like the moments before falling asleep. She yanked herself out of her head, relieved when voices resolved into intelligible speech, daylight returned, and Gage's warm, grounding hand was tight on hers.

The three who were actually watching the computer gasped, and Riley whipped her hand over the back of the couch to grab Marley's arm. Gage's eyes were on her, but she didn't turn to see what they looked like.

"Rewind it," she said, hoping they thought she wanted to watch again, not that she hadn't been paying attention. Or *couldn't* pay attention.

Pettle stood outdoors, other players moving around on a field behind him. People crowded around him, holding microphones and recorders over each other's heads and up close to his face.

He was responding to questions about his performance, his disappointment. "Some things can't be explained with the usual reasons. But every player has people to help him get better, help him get out of something that might be causing him problems." He looked directly at the camera. "Sometimes you just need the right person to nullify the damaging energy, if you can find them."

"Holy shit," she said. "Does that mean what I think it means?"

"He wants you to help him!" Riley jumped up as the video came to an end. "There's no other explanation."

"He doesn't know who I am." Marley stood, stunned. "So he's reaching out publicly. If Cressida sees this…"

"This could be it," Gage said. "Why Aiden and his partners haven't taken flux. They must know about this, even though my brother denied it."

"We need to contact him. How?" Marley asked Sam.

"Wait a minute." Gage tightened his hand and turned her to face him. "We have a plan. You don't have to nullify anyone anymore. Once Cressida is leeched, Pettle and the others should be okay."

"How are we even going to get close enough to Cressida to do that?" Marley pressed. "He might be able to help. He was her first client, the one she started with before this all escalated." She was excited, her brain clearing, everything feeling like it was slipping into place, where it was supposed to be. It wouldn't last—she had no illusions about that—but that just meant they had to act quickly. "Plus, you don't know that he'll be okay. We have to at least talk to him. He can give us another perspective on the whole thing."

Her logic unassailable, Gage nodded, though with obvious reluctance.

"Contact?" she reminded Sam.

"Let's see what I can get." He sat at the computer for a minute, new tabs and browser windows popping up like crazy. "I can send a message through his charitable foundation and his agency. Those might take a while to filter to him, unless he's monitoring them himself. I follow his page on Facebook and sent a message there, too. That might get to him faster. While we wait, I'll see if I can track down a phone number. That'll probably take time, though."

They stood staring while Sam went to work. "When was that conference recorded?" Marley asked.

Sam looked at his watch. "After practice today, so probably no more than a couple of hours ago."

"Well, we can't just stand here with our thumbs up our you-know-whats." Marley headed back to the bedroom. "If he comes through in the next half hour or so, we can set up a meeting. But we can't stay here longer than that. I told you Cressida can tell where we are if she's within half a mile, and if she sees Pettle's conference, she might come after us now instead of following through on all her other threats first."

Gage followed her, and they packed their things in silence. When Marley moved to leave the room to get her toiletries from the bathroom, he blocked her.

"I'm trying to keep myself from asking how you're doing every few minutes." He smiled and rubbed her arms. "But since I haven't actually asked recently… How are you doing?"

She tried to smile back. "I'm hanging in there." Her mouth was too heavy to keep curved. "It's only going to get worse, Gage. I can't let you watch it happen."

"That's too bad. I'm in this. I have a job to do now. And *I* can't let you go through it alone."

"He answered!" Sam called from the other room.

"Set it up!" Marley yelled back, not taking her eyes off Gage's. His body was close, warm, achingly familiar. "I don't know what to do," she whispered, "to keep you from being hurt."

Gage shook his head and drew her to him. "The only way to avoid being hurt is to not care, and it's too late for that." His mouth came down on hers, tender, hungry but gentle, everything he wanted to say obvious in the way he clung to her. His arms settled around her, trembling hands flat between her shoulder blades and at the small of her back. She closed her fist around his shirt, much as she had that first day while he'd stitched up her side.

When he broke the kiss, his whole body shook. "I love you, Marley," he finally said. "I don't care that it's only been a week, that these are extreme circumstances, that you think a future is impossible. I *love* you."

She started to cry and buried her face in his shirt. He held her tight and rocked her, his mouth pressed to the top of her head. They couldn't *do* this. He couldn't leech Cressida. But he had to. Someone else could do it, but the only one they'd trust was Sam, and he'd already been through enough. And it was Gage's choice, just like nullifying Darren Pettle was going to be hers, if that was what he wanted. They both had stakes in this, personal ones that went deeper than saving innocent strangers.

Was this how people with terminal illnesses felt? With so little time left and so much reason to want more?

She pulled back and raised her head, watching the silver swirl slowly through the blue in Gage's eyes as his pupils made minute adjustments to accommodate the afternoon's dimming light. He was waiting for her to say it back or maybe to deny it, and she didn't know which to do. If they succeeded, and Cressida was leeched and Marley had nullified everyone and either died or wound up institutionalized, which would better allow Gage to move on? Knowing she loved him or doubting for the rest of his life?

How would she feel in the reverse, if she somehow overcame the insanity but lost him in the leeching?

Putting it that way eliminated the question entirely.

"I love you, too."

They were deep in another powerful, painful kiss when Sam's phone rang in the other room. From the way he answered it, the caller was clearly Pettle.

The kiss ended. They held on for another moment, but there wasn't anything more to say. Not until this was done.

They stepped out into the main room as Sam hung up. "Half an hour. We're meeting at his place."

"Where's his place?"

"Brentwood."

Riley cast Marley and Gage a sympathetic glance. "I'll get our stuff together."

Sam could have drowned Marley in the empathy in his eyes. She didn't want it.

"What if Cressida saw the press conference?" she asked. "She might try to intercept us there or target him."

"Chance we have to take. She's unlikely to blast down his gates and kill his guards to get inside his place."

Marley wasn't sure about that, but there wasn't a safer alternative. "All right. Let's go."

Within minutes, they had the apartment cleared out and the rental car loaded, and twenty minutes after that, Sam drove them up a narrow driveway to a cobblestone circle and parked between a marble fountain and the wide, white stone steps fronting Darren

Pettle's Brentwood mansion.

Marley opened her door and stepped out, testing herself. The air was crisp and clean, scented with the flowers from vines curling up and around trellises bordering the steps and high front porch. Nothing was green or moving that shouldn't be. Marley's body was steady, her brain alert. For now. The rest of the group joined her, and they climbed the steps to where Darren waited for them.

He didn't look very much like an athlete in person. He didn't so much stand at the top of the steps as lean, both on a cane and on one of the towering pillars holding up the third-floor balconies. His Numina signature was one of the strongest she'd detected, though not as strong as Gage's. The flux level was low, sluggish, similar to what had remained in the men Cressida called "receptacles."

He straightened when Marley reached him but didn't smile. "Thanks for coming." He didn't hold out a hand to shake but scrutinized her eyes. "I have to say, I didn't really believe them. But they were right. Fascinating."

"Believe who?" Marley asked.

"My brother and the other kids. He didn't see you himself." He motioned toward the front door, where a young woman in a pantsuit stood. They all made their way slowly across the porch to the entrance. "So I figured it was all exaggerated. But if that wasn't, maybe the rest of it wasn't, either."

"Probably not." She glanced down at his legs. "What happened?"

He stepped up into the house, wincing when he pulled his bad leg behind him. The woman reached to help him, sleek and professional in her demeanor but affectionately concerned in her handling.

"Groin pull at the end of practice," Pettle said. "Not bad at the time, but these things tend to stiffen up. I'll be all right."

"Gives you a reason to be out a few games." Sam entered the dim foyer behind them. "I'm Sam Remington. We talked on the phone."

"Yeah." Pettle shook his hand. "Thanks for being so quick to contact me."

"We were lucky." Sam introduced everyone else. Pettle acknowledged each with a head nod.

"This is my personal manager, Divonne," he said next. "You guys can all call me Darren. Come on in."

They got settled in a violently scrumptious and comfortable living room and were served drinks from a rolling cart. Marley sank into plush cushions that made her think of five-star hotel bathrobes wrapped around memory foam. She could sleep here. She was so emotionally and physically exhausted now that given a few more minutes of stillness, she probably would.

The server made sure everyone had what they wanted and left the room, closing the pocket doors behind him. Darren's pleasant-host demeanor disappeared, and he hunched forward in his chair, staring at Marley. "You can take the flux completely away? Sam called it nullification."

She nodded slowly. "Yes, but why would you want me to?"

He snorted. "You saw the news, right? You know what's happening to me."

"I know you suck all of a sudden," she said, "but not why."

She'd earned a sharp look from the manager and reproving frowns from Sam and Gage. She had to be more careful about how she phrased things.

Darren didn't seem to mind. "I'm not sure, exactly."

"Is it addiction syndrome?" Sam asked him. "Has your tolerance risen and you need more to get the same result?"

The running back shook his head. "There's been no sign of that, and I've been doing this for a year. Same amount of energy every time. Same response by my body and brain. But after the dose I got last, nothing's worked right. I can't explain it. It's just… wrong."

Riley shifted. "I'm a goddess. I can read you, see if I can detect the flux and what it's doing to you. Have you had anyone do that?"

"I've had an MRI and CT scan, but nothing like you're talking about." He shrugged. "Go ahead."

They sat still while Riley checked him out. Divonne watched alertly, her fingers pressed to Darren's wrist, apparently keeping track of his pulse rate. After a few minutes, Riley settled back in her seat next to Sam. She looked up at her husband. "It's toxic," she said softly.

"Like Marley's was? In Quinn?" Sam's jaw flexed as if he wanted to chomp back his words. "How? That doesn't make any sense."

"What do you mean, toxic?" Darren asked.

Riley drew a deep breath. "The energy level isn't excessive. I thought maybe you had an accumulation, but I don't detect one. It's in line with what Aiden Samargo and Cressida both described. But for some reason, the energy you have right now has become poisonous. It's attacking your bodily systems. Not like real poison would," she added. She rolled her lips, thinking. "I don't see damage to your organs or tissues that can be repaired. It's more like interference with the less-concrete body functions." She looked to Marley, as if seeking confirmation.

Marley shrugged. "You see it differently than I do, but I don't have any reason to disagree."

"You're saying it's attacking me neurologically." Darren nodded. "Makes sense."

"It does?" Marley laughed. "I'll have to take your word for it." She pushed to her feet. "Easy remedy." She skirted a glass coffee table and Sam and Riley's legs and reached for Darren's hand. Four people shouted, "No!"

But it was too late. One stroke and the energy was gone.

Darren leaped to his feet and raised the cane as if to beat her back, but then his eyes widened. "Whoa."

"Good?" Marley asked him.

"Better." He tilted his head back and forth as if to unkink his neck. "Much better."

"Why the hell did you do that?" Gage demanded from behind her.

"He was sick. Now he's not." Marley raised her eyebrows at all the people staring at her as if she'd done something reckless. "What? That's what we came here for, right?"

"You should have allowed him to choose." Divonne had risen, too, and placed her hand on Darren's shoulder. "You just ended his career in a single second. Do you have any idea the consequences of that?"

"He chose when he asked me to come here." She eyed Darren, worried that she'd jumped the gun, scared that she hadn't thought this out beforehand. The impulsiveness, the lack of verbal filter had to be more symptoms of the flux's effect on her.

But Darren nodded slowly. "She's right. I had made my decision. I might have waffled, knowing what it meant, but I appreciate that you took the initiative." He reached to shake Marley's hand.

Gage tugged her back, his grip tense. "That's not the only reason you shouldn't have done it. We agreed you wouldn't. That it wouldn't be necessary."

Marley didn't remember agreeing to that and didn't want to discuss her condition in front of the others. "It was a small amount. I'm fine."

Riley grabbed Marley's other arm and closed her eyes again, assessing. When she opened them, she grudgingly admitted, "It doesn't seem any different, now that it's in you, than any of the rest of it."

"Right. Because it's *dormant*. It's not energy anymore, so the toxicity is neutralized, too. That's just logical." She decided not to mention that the snakes forming the legs of the coffee table were writhing now.

"It's not just me." Darren stared at his hands, flexing and squeezing them. "I was the first, so I thought when things started going bad, I could stop the others before it happened to them."

"He was too late for at least one," Divonne said, this time without such an edge. Instead, her voice was incredibly smooth and rich, matching her cocoa skin. "An old friend of Darren's. He was unable to get out of bed, barely able to move, and not in full control of his body. He was suffering something like localized seizures. We found out he'd doubled his dosage, getting it twice as often as Darren."

"That explains why he'd go toxic first. How long ago was this?" Sam asked.

"A few weeks. Right after I had my last meeting with Cress. He died on the way to the hospital. I don't know the results of the autopsy." He blinked hard and fast and cleared his throat. "I tried to tell Cress, but she hasn't returned my calls."

Marley battled back a sense of dread. "What about your other friends? Cressida said you'd referred at least a dozen to her."

He nodded. "Some of those are friends of friends, but yes. There are now eleven, after the one who died." He cleared his throat. "And after me. I've talked to several. Some already have problems. Others don't want them. I think they'll all want to see you."

"There's only one thing to do, then," she said. "Gather up your friends. Get them all here, and I'll take care of them."

"You can't, Marley," Gage growled. She was afraid to turn, afraid he'd see how much she agreed. She wanted it as much as she dreaded it. "She can't," he repeated to everyone when she didn't respond. "Nullification is destroying her."

She'd barely felt the little bit she'd taken from Darren, and it hadn't made things worse for her, at least in the moment. But she didn't know how she was going to face nearly a dozen more. And after that, all the Deimons would have to be taken care of, too.

They couldn't leave the flux in anyone now that they knew what it could do to them. She was the only one who could take it away, so she just had to face it head-on.

"We thought it was dangerous," she said to the room at large but looking only at Gage. "Now we know for sure. That's got to be the plan. I'll nullify them all. You leech Cressida." She pleaded with him to accept the solution, the shared responsibility. They couldn't save each other *and* the rest of the world.

He drooped but smiled. "Butch and Sundance."

She grinned. "Thelma and Louise. No, wait. I didn't like that one. Spike and Angel, facing the dragon."

Warmth engulfed her as he wrapped her in his arms and pulled her to his chest. "That works for me."

CHAPTER SIXTEEN

Sacrifice has never been a valued element of our business-focused culture. This has, perhaps, been an oversight.
—Numina board internal memo

Gage opened the door of the hotel suite they were now staying in and greeted Darren and Divonne, ushering them inside. "Thanks for coming. I don't think this will take long."

"Not a problem. We're glad to be here."

Gage ushered them through the massive suite toward the conference room where everyone else had already gathered. He glanced down at Darren's legs. "No cane?"

"Nope. I don't even have a twinge. Your friend should go into business as a healer."

Riley had healed Darren's groin pull before they left his house, but it was still his excuse for not playing in the football game tomorrow. He hadn't been on the practice field, as far as Gage knew.

"Jury still out on your future in the NFL?"

Darren shrugged. "Any player's career can end in the blink of an eye. I feel good. We'll see if I have anything left without the flux.

I'm prepared if I don't." He motioned to the door they now stood in front of. "Ready?"

Gage nodded, and they went in. He circled around to the head of the table while Darren and Divonne greeted the others and introductions were made. Marley, Riley, Nick, and Quinn were spread out around the big oval table. Nick and Quinn had flown in two days ago, and they'd pulled together so many details in such a fast and haphazard way, they were having this one last meeting to make sure everyone knew their roles and everything was in place for the plan they'd come up with. Quinn would fly back to New York on the red-eye tonight to meet with Gage's father, but Nick was staying for the battle to help even the odds. By tomorrow night, everything should be done.

"First, I want to again say thanks to everyone," Gage began when they all swiveled in his direction, "for coming out here and contributing to this mission. We all have a stake in the outcome but that doesn't negate the time, effort, and money contributed."

God, he sounded like a CEO addressing a company board. He glanced down at the list he'd written up, to hide his embarrassment. "*Ahem*. Okay, first is the location. Darren, you've confirmed the stadium?"

"Yes, sir." He rotated his chair, chin braced on his hand, elbow on the chair arm. "I have the keys right here." He dug in his pocket and set a large, round ring full of keys on the table with a clatter. "I went over after my session with the trainer this morning. It clearly hasn't been used in a long time, even by kids hanging out."

"Good."

Darren used to play high school football in the old facility, owned by a nearby college whose football program was now defunct. His connections and the money he'd donated to the school's athletic programs got him access. The stadium was surrounded by open space so whatever happened wouldn't hurt any innocent civilians or damage property. Plus, it was built to withstand the pounding of tens of thousands of feet and the bombardment of noise during concerts and other events, so even Cressida Lahr would have a hard time damaging it.

"Darren, you and your friends will meet us there at seven. Marley will take care of them first." He checked her reaction, but she didn't have one. She'd gotten good at wearing an implacable mask, and he worried how much it hid.

He turned back to Darren. "They've all agreed?"

"Yes, none of them want to continue like this."

"No doubters?" This wouldn't work if anyone backed out.

But Darren shook his head. "They're all in."

"Okay then. After they've all been nullified, we'll set up for the fake event the Deimons have been invited to. Sam, what have we got for the layout?"

Sam grimaced and wiggled his pen in the air as he talked. "We're compromising here with the facility. We need the privacy, the low risk of collateral damage it offers, but the size will be an issue. Containment. Darren has assured me the facility lockdown overall will be complete."

Darren nodded and indicated the slew of keys.

"So they won't be able to get out of the stadium itself," Sam continued. "But there's still too much space to deal with. We've collected some conference equipment for Darren's speech. Portable wall-type things, steel frames with curtains attached at the top and bottom. Sturdy enough, though not exactly a cage. We have a podium and speaker system, too." He consulted a legal pad. "We've sent out e-mail invitations to the Deimons using their message-board server and have a ninety-five-percent response rate. Chatter on the boards is excited. So far, so good."

Nick took over. "No one should be surprised to see Vanrose and the others. They have rumors about who is in the 'senior membership' and their presence should be seen as a bonus. Darren, great orator that he is…" Nick inclined his head at the football player, who tipped an invisible hat in appreciation. "He'll keep the Deimons enthralled while Marley slips through the crowd and nullifies them."

"There's not much chance I'll be able to do them all before they notice what's going on," she said. "So I hope your guys are up for containment."

"They are."

"There will be enough of us," Sam reassured. His quiet confidence almost convinced even Gage. "We won't let anyone get out of there without being nullified."

Marley nodded and twisted the cap off a water bottle, guzzling half its contents.

"At that point," Gage said, "Darren, you and your guys will shepherd the Deimons out of the building, hopefully before Cressida shows up."

"If she shows up," Quinn spoke up. "This is the part that makes me most nervous. She could come too early if she finds out about the invitation. Or she could be capricious and not show up at all."

"Vanrose has it covered," Darren insisted. "He's got it all timed. Even if she hears about it early, he'll keep her from arriving before we're ready. He's got connections in traffic control and law enforcement because of on-site filming. We'll be good."

"All right. That's the end of your part." Gage walked down the side of the table, holding his hand out. "Thanks again for coming down just for these few minutes." He shook Darren's hand as the player got to his feet.

"Like I said, not a problem. I wanted to hear it all for myself, and I'm leaving you the keys, just in case." He clapped a hand on Gage's shoulder. "Thank you, man. Really. We all appreciate this."

"Sure. I'll see you out."

"Nah, we got it. See you tomorrow."

Gage watched them leave, making sure the door was tightly closed behind them before resuming his position. There was no reason to let them know the details of the leeching process, even though they were aware that was the goal.

"Now the hard part. Cressida won't come alone. She's likely to have Chris, Tony, Brad, and Aiden with her. Probably not more than them, because—"

"She's an egomaniac and she doesn't need more," Marley finished.

"Not how I was going to put it, but yeah." He tapped his pen on the table. "So, can we handle them?"

"You deal with your brother. Sam, Riley, and I got the other three partners. No problem." Nick spoke with a cockiness Gage never would have tolerated from anyone who worked under him, but over the past two days he'd learned that Nick was more than capable of backing it up.

"And I won't exactly be on the sidelines," Marley added. "So we'll have the advantage." Everyone stared at her. "Numbers wise."

"Riley, you're sure you'll have enough metal around?" Gage had already been told his concern about Riley holding her own against the guys was sexist and unnecessary, that she was more powerful than Nick and Sam put together. Still, he had to be sure.

To her credit, she didn't get annoyed. "Yeah, the frames for the walls we're putting up are all steel. I just need them nearby. I don't need direct contact like I used to. Plus the stadium itself is full of metal. Prepare to be amazed." She spread her hands and widened her eyes as she dragged out the last word like a carny. Everyone laughed.

"The ultimate goal is for me to leech Cressida," Gage reminded them, nerves twisting his gut. "So I have to get to her, and she has to be neutralized. Sam?"

He looked up from something he was scribbling on his pad. "Yeah. Got it." He reached under the table and pulled out a small case. He unzipped it and held it open for everyone to see two small metal tubes, a couple of tiny, feathered darts, and a vial full of faintly yellowish liquid. "Sedative."

Nick looked skeptical. "I'm cool with blowing a dart at her, but what if I miss?" He was the one Cressida was least likely to pay attention to since he hadn't been involved until now.

"I'll have one, too, doubling our chances. And if we both miss…" Sam flipped a section of the case. Four syringes were strapped in underneath. "Insurance. We can pass these out. But they're not ideal because we'll have to be very close to use them."

"All right, then." Nick aimed a finger at Gage. "Then you're up."

Quinn had been the only one who'd ever actually leeched someone, pulling all the stolen power from Anson. She and Riley had worked with Gage yesterday, giving him tiny amounts of power, letting him get the feel of it and practice expelling it. Quinn had explained how to find, connect with, and draw Cressida's power out of her. Tomorrow Riley would bestow a bigger amount on him, and he'd use that to connect to Cressida's well of power and draw it out.

He blew out a breath. "Still a lot of questions we can't answer until it happens."

"Since her source is the sun," Quinn said, "she's always taking in energy. Will that make it impossible to drain her completely?"

"That's why we're doing it at night," Gage answered. "Minimal inflow."

"Can you take it all in?" Riley asked next. "Anson couldn't."

"I'm pristine." Gage flashed them a smile he didn't really believe. "Anson was a mess. I'll have more room to hold it."

"And finally," Nick said, "can you discharge it without blowing the whole place up?"

"I know how to control the stream." He'd practiced with Riley and Quinn's energy. "Like pinching off a hose or a balloon. A little at a time."

Everyone nodded, and there was silence for a beat.

"Any questions, comments, issues, things we missed?" Gage asked. They all shook their heads and began gathering things up. "Thanks for tolerating me taking over, everyone."

Quinn came over and gave him a hug. "You're taking on the biggest challenge here. It makes sense for you to lead. Good luck." She backed away, eyes flashing. "I wish I could be there to help."

"You just keep my dad from flying out here. That might be the hardest part." Gage's vague, reassuring e-mails and text messages weren't cutting it anymore, and his father had threatened just that in his last response this morning. Quinn had set up a one-on-one meeting with him, ostensibly to discuss stalling the summit, but she was going to tell him everything that had been happening. By the time she finished, it would be too late for him to get out to LA and interfere. Whether they succeeded or failed, he'd need to know the details. Gage would deal with the fallout afterward.

If he was able.

Marley hadn't looked in Gage's direction for the last half of the meeting. In fact, she'd been quiet for the last two days, and Gage was afraid she was dealing with more effects of the flux. After the massive doses Cressida had given her, they seemed to be lingering in a way the others hadn't.

She still sat in her chair, staring into space, after the others had filed out. Gage half sat, half leaned on the table next to her and waited for her to focus on him. It took a while.

"Sorry." She glanced around. "I guess we're done."

"For tonight. You hungry?"

She put her hand on her stomach, a little furrow forming between her brows. "Did I eat anything today?"

Gage had grown used to the tightness in his chest and only noticed it at times like this one, in the little ways she showed she wasn't okay. "Yeah. Dinner was steak, baked potato with sour cream, green beans, salad. Room service."

"Oh…yeah." Her mouth lifted at the corners. "Chocolate mousse. Sorry. So yeah, I'm fine. I'll just get some water."

"I'll get it." He took her hand and lightly tugged her out of the chair. "I'll bring it to the bedroom."

"Okay. Thanks." She wrapped her arms around his waist and briefly laid her head against his chest before leaving the room.

Gage sat there for a second, trying to find his breath. Moments like that were what killed him. She went both ways, one minute closing herself off, acting cold and aloof as if she thought that could protect him. The next she'd reach out, touch, connect, and he'd feel what they could have if they were just given a chance.

He hadn't yet accepted that they didn't have one. Logic and evidence all pointed to one or both of them dying or being too messed up to live normally. But events didn't always unfold logically and what they were dealing with defied all the rules.

The problem was that both Butch and Sundance and Spike and Angel had ended on the verge of attack, allowing the illusion that they could have survived. No one had to actually endure the battle itself. Still, Gage had no trouble envisioning a happy ending for everyone, even if he couldn't work out the details.

But in case he was wrong and they didn't find a way to survive together, he was making sure this last night with Marley was enough to take them through forever.

• • •

The suite was silent and mostly dark when Marley left the conference room. A light in the kitchenette and another by the door to the hall were enough for her to pick her way through, but she wished someone had left another, brighter light on. The shadows taunted her, growing along the walls and looming threateningly over her head. She knew it wasn't real, but that didn't stop her from jumping when one of them shot at her across the floor.

Nick and Quinn's door opened, and Quinn came out with her carry-on over her shoulder. Nick rolled her suitcase out behind her. He spotted Marley, kissed Quinn quickly on the mouth, and said, "I'll go get the car and meet you out front."

"Thanks, hon." Quinn watched him until he was out the door.

Marley hated her for that.

No. She didn't hate her sister, for God's sake. She was glad they'd had years to love each other, to share their lives. She just wanted what Quinn and Nick had for herself, too. It wasn't Quinn's fault Marley couldn't have it. It was completely her own.

"Thanks for letting Nick help us."

Quinn smiled. "Like I could have stopped him. I hate that I won't be there tomorrow."

"Your part in this is just as important."

"I know. I just don't like being out of the fighting. You know."

"I do." She let Quinn hug her. "Have a safe flight." But her sister didn't let go, and a second later, she heard a sniff. She pulled back sharply. "You're crying."

"No." But Quinn swept her hand under her eye. "Ow. You hurt my arm."

"Liar. I just wanted to catch the tears before they dried up. You never cry."

"Only when I have good reason." She placed her hands on either side of Marley's face. "I know I have no right to say this, but I'm proud of you."

Dammit, now Marley was going to cry. She went in for one more hug, then pulled away. "Good night, Quinn. I'll talk to you tomorrow. Or maybe Monday. We'll see how it goes."

Quinn laughed and headed out, then Marley escaped to her bedroom. Where she stood in the middle of the floor, unable to remember why she was there.

Gage came in and handed her a tall glass of water. "You okay?"

"What time is it?"

He checked his watch as he locked the handle on the door. "Almost ten. Did you lose time again?"

"No." Thank goodness. She hated the periods when the day skipped ahead and she hadn't been part of it. Bad enough to have the cliff racing toward her. She didn't want to miss any of the moments getting there.

"Why don't you get ready for bed?" Gage squeezed her shoulders, loosening the tension in them.

She moaned. "That feels good."

"I'll give you a massage. Relax you so you can sleep without nightmares."

She hoped that wasn't all he was going to give her. "I'm going to take a quick shower."

"Okay. Take your time." He kissed her temple and released her.

If this was her last night with any shred of sanity, she was clinging to it with both hands. She wanted this to be special, and she also needed to go into tomorrow being able to see reality. So she kept her eyes closed while she showered, focusing on the water, the way it struck her skin and glided down, the warmth and slightly metallic scent of it. The gurgle of the drain, the smooth glide of the soap. She didn't allow any other thoughts in, and by the time she twisted the knob and opened the curtain, she was calm and centered and no shadows taunted from the corners.

She did the same with the rasp of the towel as it soaked up beads of water, the gritty mint of the toothpaste, and the prickle of her toothbrush on her tongue. She rinsed her mouth and drank down all of the water Gage had brought her, tucked the towel tightly around her torso, and stepped out into the bedroom.

"Oh, Gage." She brought her hands to her mouth, fingertips touching, and the room blurred for a second. Not a crazy blur, but a watery one, because once again tears had filled her eyes.

The room was lit with a golden glow. Flickering candles would have wreaked havoc on her senses, but this came from well-placed, disc-shaped lights. He'd somehow done it so there were minimal shadows but the room wasn't bright. Lilacs filled jars on the dresser and nightstand, their sweet scent just right, not too light, not too strong. The bed had been turned down, a pillow placed for her massage, and Beethoven's Ninth played from an iPod plugged into the clock radio.

She walked over to the bed, where Gage stood, and brushed her fingers over a lilac stalk. "How?"

"How did I know that it's your favorite?"

She nodded. "And how did you get freaking lilacs in October? I thought that was impossible."

"I asked Quinn, who asked your mother. And nothing is impossible." He cradled her face in both hands and stared into her eyes, his almost shining with that silvery blue. "Do you hear me? *Nothing*."

She blinked back tears again, but that was the last of them. She'd regressed since Cressida's attack and her breakdown afterward, feeling sorry for herself and letting everyone do the bulk of the planning. If Gage could believe, truly believe that tomorrow didn't have to be their last, then maybe it wouldn't be.

But only if she believed it, too.

"You're right."

His smile was huge, genuine, and everything flipped. Fuck despair and dread. She was all about determination and…some other positive D-word.

"Lie down." Gage lifted the sheets and let her climb onto the bed. She pulled off the towel and wrapped her arms over the pillow, tucking it under her chin and closing her eyes. She heard a *pop* like a flip cap being opened, then a squirt and another pop. More lilac filled the air, this time oily and warm. Then Gage's hands were on her, slick and sure, digging into her shoulders and gliding down the length of her spine.

She continued her focus exercise, all her attention on Gage's hands as they stroked her arms, back, butt, and legs. Once he'd relaxed her muscles into noodlehood, each stroke drew a different sensation. His fingertips trailed up the back of her calf, her knee, her thigh, and fire followed them, arrowing right to her core.

"Roll over." His voice rumbled through the dim room and into her chest.

"No." She sat up instead and got off the bed.

"I'm not done." He held his oily hands out away from his body, his gaze sweeping down hers.

"It's your turn." She stepped closer and began unbuttoning his shirt so he wouldn't get oil on it.

"No, I—"

"Shh." She slowly pulled the shirt down his arms and over his hands. "Tomorrow's going to be hard for you, too. You should be as relaxed and focused as I am. Stand up."

He obeyed, hands still upraised. "I don't need a massage. I wanted to do this for you."

"And you did." She knelt to undo his button and zipper, looking up as she pulled his jeans and boxer briefs down. She carefully uncovered his erection, which flexed in front of her mouth. She licked her lips.

"Jesus, Marley."

She smiled and rose again but stepped back when he reached for her. "Lie down."

He grumbled but followed her order. First she plunged her hands into his hair to massage his scalp. He gave a long, rough groan that vibrated in the pit of her stomach. She dug into every inch of his head, rubbing away the tension along his hairline, stroking her fingers with gentle tugs through his hair.

"Okay, I forgive you," he mumbled into the pillow. "God, that's good."

Instead of getting fresh oil, she picked up his hand and massaged it with both of hers, transferring the oil to them and rubbing it into his skin, between both their fingers, down to his wrist and then repeating on the other side. Then she moved to his neck, shoulders, back, all the way down his body, just as he'd done with hers.

She worked her way back up, pleased that he was as limp and languid as she was, and when she reached the base of his skull he rolled across the bed, catching her and stretching her out on top of him. He was hot and hard, and his erection felt even bigger than before as it pressed against her belly.

Her fingers traced his hairline, each eyebrow, lightly over his eyelids, closing them briefly, then the strong length of his nose, his cheekbones, his jaw. She loved everything about his face. Everything about him. She lowered her head and pressed her mouth to his, tasting slowly, savoring. He let her take the lead, only opening his mouth when she opened hers. Their tongues touched in the open space between, swirled, then plunged. Gage gripped the back of her head and ate hungrily at her mouth, the other hand sliding down her spine, pressing her close. Marley spread her thighs to straddle his hips, rocking until he penetrated her, taking him deep, deeper. They moaned together, and his hands moved to her hips, taking up the rhythm, thrusting up into her as he pulled her down.

Her entire body tingled. The tingles coalesced and tightened, pleasure rising. She gasped and arched, and Gage pushed her back to ride him hard. She shattered, biting back her cry, fingers digging into his chest as she shuddered. She could feel him watching her, sense his own climax approaching, and clenched.

He lurched upright to stifle his shout against her shoulder, then rolled on top and thrust into her again and again, the position just right, every thrust hitting her clit and dragging her to another peak. She bit his shoulder and clutched his shoulder blades and clung desperately to the feel of him against her, inside her, and the sound of his voice whispering her name.

CHAPTER SEVENTEEN

You are cordially invited to a special session with the senior membership, featuring Darren Pettle, who will discuss how Cressida Lahr has affected his life and career.
—Invitation to Deimons

Marley stared up at the outside of the football stadium, a little awed despite herself. The deserted parking lot was dark and silent except for the occasional whistle of wind around the girders. It made the place seem even more massive than it was. But it hunkered, solid and sturdy, and gave her confidence.

An engine purred behind them, and Darren's SUV pulled around their group, parking across several spaces. He got out of the driver's seat while Divonne slid out of the passenger's side. Two men followed from the backseat, and seconds later two more vehicles pulled up. Within moments, Marley and her friends were surrounded by Cressida's original crew.

And none of them looked happy.

She recognized the producer and a couple of actors, as well as some of the businesspeople on Darren's list. Most of them showed signs of illness or fatigue. A few leaned on their vehicles, and more than one locked onto Marley with expressions of hope.

"Let's go inside," Darren said. He accepted the key ring from Sam and led them to the gate, turning the main lock with a *clunk*. Two more locks, an inside gate, and a door later, they emerged onto the football field. Another *clunk* and a bank of overhead lights went on, casting an eerie, uneven light over the expanse.

The grass looked gray in this light, with bare patches dotting the hundred yards between goal posts. Darren paused next to Marley and sighed. "Lotta good memories here. Sad to see it like this."

"How do you feel?" she asked him. "Physically."

"A thousand percent more normal." He laughed and shook his head. "It was good while it lasted. Not that I'd do it again, but…"

"Yeah, I get it." They watched his friends gather into clusters. One coughed hard enough to double himself over. Another visibly shook from the effort of standing. "Is this going to work? They don't look strong enough to contain the others."

Darren nodded. "They'll be fine in a minute." He glanced at her. "You ready?"

She almost said no. The star-strewn sky whirled overhead, the moon seeming to swell. The equilibrium she'd achieved last night hadn't lasted through today's preparations. But she knew what was real and what wasn't, hadn't lost any time, and was as functional as she could be.

"Yep," she said. "Let's get started."

"Hey, guys, line up!" Darren waved his friends over. They stood single file in front of Marley, all somber and silent. She worried that some of them didn't want this, that they'd have to fight earlier than anticipated. But when she asked each one if he was sure he wanted this to be done, they all nodded without hesitation.

Even though nullifying Darren had been easy, she'd been apprehensive about doing so many in a row. But taking in so much of Cressida's pure energy had rendered this tame. The first one she did, she could only tell it worked because of the guy's body language. His posture straightened and his eyes cleared. The next two must have been newcomers to flux. They hadn't seemed as damaged as the others before she'd nullified them, and after she took the flux, their skin seemed duller or paler, their movements lethargic. But they still thanked her.

The lack of desperate need for what she took relieved Marley. Unlike the other day after Cressida's attack, she had few signs of addiction.

Marley smiled at the fourth guy and reached out for his bare arm. This time, she had to suppress a gasp when her hand brushed his warm skin and tingled. A sizzle shot up her arm and then disappeared.

She braced herself for the next two. The burn turned into a wriggle, almost crawling into her body and diffusing before it solidified and the sensation faded. Her chest tightened until she could barely breathe. Dark spots danced in her vision. She gritted her teeth and pushed it all back, annoyed. This was just the appetizer. She couldn't let it take her over.

Her head spun and she swayed on her feet, but she held on until the last guy thanked her and moved on for instructions. Then strong hands caught her shoulders, a hard body keeping her upright until her head cleared. Gage's arm came around her shoulders, his familiar touch grounding her, giving her something to focus on. Slowly, the pressure in her chest receded and her vision cleared. Mostly.

"Come on," he said. "You need a break." He led her outside the curtained circle. She sank gratefully onto a metal folding chair. Gage handed her a bottle of water. The sweat made the outside of the plastic slick. The bottle crunched when she tightened her grip, water slopping onto her hand. She could have sworn it turned to steam.

Gage crouched in front of her, his hand on her leg, maintaining contact without touching skin while she drank the water. Riley had already given him power—it would be disastrous if Marley accidentally nullified him before he could leech Cressida.

The cold wetness slid soothingly down her throat. The rings around her lungs sprang open and dropped away. Her vision sharpened, her ears popped, and she could smell the dusty grass under Gage's familiar scent. She smiled at him, a little shocked at how soft she felt right now. She needed to be the hard, cold, kick-ass bitch she'd been before she met this man. But after last night, she thought maybe she'd managed to merge the two. Just in time...

She refused to finish the sentence. "Just in time" was sufficient.

"How are you holding up?" Gage asked softly. His blue eyes were bright, intense. Even more than the first day she'd met him.

"Fine." She hovered her hand next to his jaw. A different kind of electricity zipped between them, and she shivered. "Thank you."

"I—"

An air horn blasted, a one-second warning from the ramp at one corner of the stadium.

"They're here." Marley stood and glanced around. "Where's my robe?"

Gage grabbed it from where it hung over the corner of one of the curtain supports. He helped her into it and draped the hood over her head, adjusting it so her face was hidden. Marley held perfectly still while he did it.

She felt ridiculous. And hot. This getup belonged at Comic-Con, not here. But she needed a few moments of disguise so she didn't have to chase after every jerk she nullified. "Can I have some more water?" she asked Gage. He retrieved another bottle from a cooler and handed it to her. While Marley drank, they peered through one edge of the curtains.

Four of Darren's friends came to the barrier and fanned out, in position to grab runners. Sam, Nick, and Riley joined Gage and Marley, staying out of sight while the Deimons funneled in.

Some stared around as if they'd never been in a football stadium before, gaping up at the stands. Others wore the trademark boredom of the entitled, while the rest focused on glad-handing with the stars around them. Marley counted twenty-three in all. After the last one stepped onto the grass, Divonne closed and locked the gate. One kid noticed and frowned, nudging his friend, who looked over his shoulder and shrugged. The first dragged his feet a little as he followed his friend into the group.

They mingled for a few minutes with general chatter. Marley heard one guy mutter about the lack of refreshments. They'd talked about whether they should have any, for authenticity, and decided to minimize the potential weapons. Even a red Solo cup could hurt when full of liquid and flung at fifty miles an hour by an enraged goddess.

Five minutes ticked by, every second thundering in Marley's ears. She shifted from foot to foot, one hand clenching around the chill metal in front of her. Finally, Darren's guys started organizing the Deimons in front of the makeshift stage and podium. Marley closed her eyes, envisioning herself gliding along the rows. Brief, fast touches around the perimeter, so she didn't get trapped between them. The ones down the center would be the most difficult. By then, everyone would know what was happening.

The sound system squealed. Marley opened her eyes to see Darren smiling apologetically from the podium, adjusting the mic. Tapping into the main sound system was probably overkill, but the volume would help disguise Marley's efforts.

"Good evening," Darren said. "You've been asked here today to be part of an exciting new phase of the program. But first, I want to talk about what Cressida Lahr has done for me."

"You ready?" Gage murmured near Marley's ear. His body was warm and hard behind her. She didn't want to move. Wanted to stay just like this, with both of them whole, unbroken…mostly.

She turned and stepped away, desperate enough to kiss him

that she could blow everything. “I love you,” she whispered. He reached out, but she moved farther back, not trusting herself. She zeroed in on his signature, locking on so she’d know where he was on the field at every second.

But it was different from before, jarring her. Riley had given him her power while Marley nullified Darren’s friends, and it had altered his signature. It drove home how far they still had to go.

“In this new world,” Darren started, his voice booming overhead. The words were Marley’s signal, but she didn’t move. How could she leave Gage? He stared down at her, the glow in his eyes sharpened with sorrow.

“You have to get out there,” he told her. “We’ll be okay. I promise.” The words rang with conviction, and she remembered that she’d promised to give him no less.

She whirled and slipped through the curtains. Most of the Deimons had worn short sleeves, bless them. Or bless LA’s perfect weather. Determination firmed her jaw and made every step decisive. With a few strides, she was behind her first target.

Step one of the plan had been difficult because of her fear and resistance, but not this time. The faster and easier this process went, the better it would be for everyone. For Gage.

She shook back the soft, heavy robe from her hand and swept down the back row, brushing against the Deimons in the first half of the row so quickly they didn’t even notice. Kudos to Darren for his riveting speech. One, two, three-four-five. The flux snapped into Marley and solidified.

She’d reached the end of the row. No one had shouted yet, but a couple of gasps and mutters reached her ears. She turned the corner, quickening her step. The mutters got louder, but the ones in the back couldn’t see her, so the ones next to her weren’t prepared. A heavy oiliness slithered into her belly, making it harder for her to reach out, but she forced herself to keep going. *Only three on this side.*

Three more stood in front, with one in reach in the row behind. Eyes fell on her, shocked expressions, anger. *Now* came the shouts.

"Null!"

"She's here!"

"Traaaap!" came a high-pitched shriek as pandemonium struck.

Marley lunged for one young kid staring at her with his mouth in an O, frozen. *Nine.* Two of Darren's guys moved in, bumping the three in front together. Marley slapped her hands against two elbows and a jaw. *Twelve.*

But that still left nearly half of the group to go, and no one stood still anymore. She whipped off her robe, now more an impediment than an aid. The Deimons closest to her tried to escape, but ran right into Darren's guard. Marley had to stick her hand down the shirt of the first, one of the few who'd worn long sleeves and was smart enough to pull his hands up into them.

She got him, but oh, it hurt. The wriggling sensation had barbs now, digging in while it tried to get to the main mass inside her. She took a deep breath to combat the sting, but a cloud of aftershave choked her. She couldn't breathe. It, too, turned solid, dragged her lungs down, crushing her heart.

No. She staggered and forced the illusion away. Everything was chaos now. Ten left. Some had run, both the nulled and the fluxed. Marley struggled to focus, to pinpoint who she still needed to get. A roar thundered in her ears, and she spun just in time to block a punch with her forearm. The blow reverberated through her bones, a shock but the only pain on the surface. This guy was already nullified. That was why he'd dared come after her. Marley didn't have time for him. She swept her left foot behind his ankle and jerked his leg out from under him, moving on before he'd even hit the ground.

"Over here!" Vanrose shouted, gripping a struggling weenie by his collar. Marley shoved between two nulls and touched the kid's face. He collapsed, crying, and Vanrose let him go.

Some of the Deimons had rallied now, blocking Marley's way to the interior of the group, where six of the nine remaining huddled. She closed her eyes for a second. The other three were scattered. She'd have to rely on the locked gates and her allies to catch them. This batch was right in front of her.

The three biggest Deimons bared their teeth at her, fists clenched and muscles bulging. These were some of the first she'd touched, so they, too, had nothing left to lose. She had a brief flash of admiration for their loyalty, and then she stepped forward.

A couple of even bigger bodies cut in front of her. She had to stop so quickly to avoid hitting them that her toes crunched into the front of her boots. Sam flung one guy out of his way, while Nick cheered and landed a right hook on another. Marley dashed through the gap. A hand scrabbled at her arm. She twisted away and reached out.

Touch. Touch. Touch.

Bodies surged against her, overbalanced, and they all collapsed in a slow-motion pile. Limbs and tiny alligator logos on polo shirts blurred. Marley grit her teeth and strained her body, stretching, reaching. Someone had lost a shoe, and his smelly, socked heel caught her on the jaw. An elbow dug into her ribs. But one by one, her fingertips stroked skin, and the remaining faint signatures blinked out.

Three left. She wasn't sure where they were. The pile around her surged and grabbed. Her damaged awareness turned into a sea of writhing snakes, biting her, wrapping around her. *No. Not real.* She rolled to her back, still on top, but couldn't get to her feet. Someone's hip banged against the back of her head, and she sank into a gap.

"Sam!" she yelled. Seconds later he had her by the wrist and hauled her up.

"Thanks," she said, breathless. She blinked through the now-familiar green haze. "Where are the rest?"

"Over here." But he didn't just point the way, he hauled her up by the waist and freaking *carried* her to where Gage and Riley stood over three disheveled boys. They slumped on the ground, each with one wrist zip tied to the curtain frame.

"Nice," she approved. "Sorry, guys." She reached down to nullify them.

"Wait!" One of the young men flung up a hand but then recoiled so fast his head smacked the post behind him. "You don't want to do this."

Marley blinked at him through the green film over her vision. Every word he said echoed in her ears. She could hear some kind of bird of prey up in the rafters and the scrape of feet outside on the pavement. Every part of her body felt simultaneously heavy and strong enough to handle the weight. So no, she didn't want to do this. But she was almost done. Three more, and it was over.

"Why not?" she asked anyway.

"It's not yours to take. It's not fair for you to have all the power."

"Wrong answer." She bit back a cry when his nullification burned its way into her body and did the other two at the same time, just to get it over with.

Nick caught her when she would have sunk to the ground next to the despondent Deimons. "Not yet," he murmured. "Hold on." He held her up and shifted to look out across the field.

"We did it," she said, stupidly. Because that was just phase two. "They're all nullified."

"*You* did it." Gage handed Nick something wet and cold that he pressed to the back of Marley's neck. "You were amazing."

Amazingly tired. She leaned against Nick, wishing he were Gage.

"Status?" Gage's voice rumbled into Marley's body, even at a distance. She shifted to take her weight off Nick. The green film, visible against the back of her eyelids, was fading.

"Pettle and his guys are moving them out."

The plan was to get them all out of there before Lahr arrived. Marley had something to say about that, but her mouth was glued together. She sank away from awareness.

Until it smacked her so hard she gasped, her body stiffening her upright, away from Nick. She twisted to face the entrance to the field but couldn't see it through the curtained frames. "No. Oh, no no no no."

"What?" Gage called behind her, sounding frightened.

But Marley was already halfway across the space, trailing the last few nulls being nudged out by Darren and two others. She reached for the barrier in front of her, but she never made contact. A wail echoed through the stadium, accompanied by a wave of energy that blew the makeshift walls across the grass. And Marley with them.

She flew through the air, stars spinning, and landed hard on her back. She screamed when a metal bar came down on her right arm, pinning it to the earth before tumbling away behind her.

Gage. She had to find him—and Sam and Riley and Nick. They'd been close, too close to the blast. She forced her head up off the turf, using her abs to pull herself up to sit because she couldn't use her numb, limp arm. She didn't see Gage or her friends anywhere.

But she did see Cressida Lahr. The goddess stood twenty yards away, her hair waving wildly behind her. Her entourage stood along the sideline. Brad and Tony on the outside, Christopher and Aiden on either side of Cressida. They stood with their hands up, palms outward, feet braced. And they shimmered. A heat illusion, but it was tinged with yellow and practically crackling with energy. Protected by the goddess.

But that wasn't all. They weren't clean anymore. Flux penetrated so deeply into them that Marley could no longer read their Numina signatures. She'd never seen that much stolen power in anyone, even Anson. Cressida had fluxed them and turned them into weapons.

And they were aimed at the people Marley loved.

CHAPTER EIGHTEEN

Rendering of value to zero.
—Definition of nullification

Marley's fatigue disappeared. Any desire to panic faded. She stopped being aware of the pain in her body and called upon every ounce of control she had to rise slowly, but without giving away any of her deficiencies.

She strode forward, glad she'd worn the boots that gave her a couple of inches and made her feel powerful. Illusions—or delusions—could work in her favor as well as against her. Hands loose and open at her sides, she squared off with Cressida with less than ten yards between them. Christopher and Tony were on Marley's left, and Aiden and Brad on her right. She detected the same level of flux in all of them, as if the goddess had used a measuring cup to dole it out. A house-sized measuring cup.

The guys didn't seem to be suffering any ill effects from that much illicit energy. In fact, they practically glowed with good health and exhilaration. They stood strong and sure, albeit in ridiculous superhero poses that betrayed their immaturity and video-game habits. If she were facing them on her own, without her ability, she'd be scared, but they couldn't attack her directly. She'd just nullify them.

Which meant they'd attack her friends. Yeah, that was scarier.

Movement flickered in Marley's peripheral vision. Wouldn't it be great if Nick darted Cressida now, and in the confusion, she was able to nullify everyone without a fight?

But everything was too open. He'd never get the dart prepared without someone spotting him and interfering.

"Hello, Cress," she said.

The goddess narrowed her eyes at Marley. Her mouth tilted in a very unnatural smile. "I thought you were smart."

"Never said that."

"I thought you'd have some sense of self-preservation."

Marley laughed. "I'm far too dysfunctional."

The goddess sank back on her heels, her hair settling, and tilted her head a bit. "Okay. I really thought you'd be too scared to be this stupid. Don't you understand what you're up against?"

Hell, yeah, she understood. The birds of prey she'd heard had turned into six-foot smoky dragons perched on the rails in front of the stadium seats. Rage bubbled inside her, but unreal, detached from the part of her locked on Gage's location and the shredded remains of her sanity.

"Of course I do. You're the most powerful goddess on earth, and now you've made these guys the most powerful Numina." Letting them get overconfident couldn't hurt. "We don't want to fight you, but we have to protect people who are being hurt or who could be hurt."

The outside gate clanged—probably Darren getting the last of the kids out—and Cressida seemed to swell with renewed anger at the sound. "You've taken every receptacle, deliberately and maliciously. You've doomed me!"

"Not every one," Marley contradicted. "We're missing…" She turned to look over her shoulder. "How many didn't come tonight,

Sam?" She was relieved to see him standing alone a distance away. He didn't look hurt, but he did look pissed.

"Six that we know of," he answered. He stood like a gunslinger poised to whip out his revolver, but she knew he didn't have a gun. He did, apparently, have a plan. Always did.

She craned her neck a little farther and spotted Riley to Sam's right. A thin trickle of blood had traced its way along her hairline and in front of her ear. No wonder Sam was pissed.

Marley faced front again. She wanted to look over her other shoulder, confirm that Nick and Gage were ranged out on her right side, but putting Cressida in her blind spot again would be a bad idea. She could assume Nick was where he was supposed to be, and Gage was like a beacon in her awareness. Not just the Numina part of him, or the boost he'd gotten from Riley, but the man who'd become everything to her.

"Six that we know of," Marley repeated. "I'm sure you have other guys in other places, but we did what we could."

"It's not just *them*, and you know it. You broke my most important partnerships."

She had to be referring to Darren and the others. "They chose to be nullified." Marley clenched and stretched her right hand. The numbness burst into pins and needles all the way up to her shoulder. She liked the pain—it was real. And now she wasn't giving any more attention to things that weren't.

"You were killing them," she said. "They didn't think the prize was worth it."

"Liar!" Cressida made a sharp movement, and Brad swung into action. He wound up like a baseball player and whipped a ball of energy at Marley. She turned into it, arms out to her sides, chest up, and laughed when it struck and disappeared. She *had* to laugh to hide the pain, this time so searing she almost looked down to see how big the hole was. But she refused to let it show.

"Keep it coming," she taunted the disgruntled-looking lackey.

But he didn't try for her again. He ripped an aluminum bench off the concrete where it was bolted to the ground behind him and flung it across the field.

Marley gasped, spinning to watch the bench flip toward Nick, helpless to stop it. But it halted in midair and crashed to the ground, folded in half.

"Gotta do better than that," Riley said with a grin.

And the battle was on.

Cressida's four took off across the dry grass, each aimed at one of Marley's allies. Marley chomped down her scream, knowing it would do no good, just like *she* could do no good. She circled to Cressida's side so she could keep both the goddess and the action in view but also try for an opportunity to use the sedative. Cressida didn't make a move on her, just folded her arms and watched, smiling.

Marley wasn't worried about Riley, who had comparable power and a lot more experience using it than the Numina did. Sure enough, she sent Christopher flying up into the stands. The seats clattered when he fell against them, leaving her free to defend her husband, who was doing surprisingly okay on his own. He'd ducked and dodged most of the energy sent his way, and what did hit him didn't appear to have done much damage.

Tony, the fool, kept on coming. Sam met him partway and knocked him out with a thunderous punch. Marley couldn't help a surge of pride. She could nullify Tony while he was down, but she'd barely flinched in that direction when Cressida's hand closed around her wrist, long nails digging into the tender flesh on the underside.

"Leave him." She pointed her chin to the other side. "This one's interesting."

Brad was faring better than Tony had as he and Nick slugged away at each other. Brad had to be putting flux behind his punches, but Nick shook them off while every one he landed sent Brad staggering.

What Cressida was talking about, though, was Aiden and Gage. Aiden approached his brother with bravado, but even with the other fighting going on, Marley could hear him cracking his knuckles. Gage stood tall and steady, the anguish in his eyes obvious.

"I don't want to fight you," Aiden said. "Call this off. Leave us be."

Gage shook his head, his eyes never leaving Aiden's face. "I can't do that, Aid. It's too late. You chose your side, and it's the wrong one. Too much harm is being done. If you think I won't fight back, you're wrong."

Marley's heart broke when Aiden leaped at Gage and he sidestepped. Maybe he would fight back, but he really didn't want to. He still hoped he could get through to his brother somehow. Aiden used his momentum to swing around and plow into Gage's side, taking him to the ground. Dirt and grass flew into the air, evidence that Aiden, at least, was trying to use the flux against Gage. Marley didn't think Gage would even be tempted to use the power Riley had given him. He was saving it for something bigger, but he also didn't want to hurt his brother. Under the goddess's influence, Aiden might not have the same restraint.

Marley had to stop this. She twisted her arm out of Cressida's grip, the movement turning the other woman to face her. Her hand itched for the syringe in her boot. "This isn't about them. It's about you and me. So let's have at it."

Cressida rolled her eyes. "If you insist."

They lunged at each other in unison, locking hands around biceps and leaning into each other like wrestlers. Marley didn't have any power, but despite the encroaching insanity, she still had strength and control on her side. Cressida dragged and shoved but didn't budge Marley more than a few inches in any direction.

What was she doing? She had all the power of the sun at her

disposal, and she was *wrestling*? Cressida knocked Marley back and followed the push with a wave of energy. Marley held her breath, steeling herself for the combination of pleasure and pain. She *would* weather this and anything else Cressida gave her.

But it didn't happen that way. When the energy sank into Marley, her vision tinted green again, and her muscles tingled and tightened, but it didn't hurt like the nullifications had. And it definitely didn't have the strength of the pulses in the bistro or even the strikes she'd given Marley in New York. Cressida swung both arms to one side, then swept them up and out like a wave. Marley leaned into it, and the same thing happened.

And then she understood. Hope flared, bright and clean, almost clearing the haze. Cressida had loaded her team with so much flux she'd depleted herself. Maybe not enough to have a significant impact on her mental condition but enough to weaken her.

They could win this. And maybe do it without anyone dying.

Marley stopped playing defense and charged the goddess, yelling like they taught in her self-defense classes. It seemed the right thing to do. But she'd miscalculated. Cressida might be weaker, but she wasn't helpless. Instead of sending another useless wave of energy at her, she followed Brad's lead and used it to rip out a couple of seats from the front row. They tumbled through the air at Marley. One only grazed across her thigh, but the other came at her head. She managed to catch it with her hands, but the momentum took her to the ground and the impact knocked the air out of her lungs. Dry grass poked through her shirt into her skin, making it itch and burn until a conflagration roared around her. *Unreal. Ignore it.*

Chris must have been partially trapped under the seats until Cressida ripped them out because he followed them, leaping over the rail and landing twelve feet below. Riley was ready for him. She sent one of the seats back at him, pinning him to the wall. But her distraction left Sam vulnerable. Tony, recovered, stuck out his foot and tripped Sam. Marley could almost feel the ground shake when he fell. His head bounced off the ground, and he lay still.

On the other side of the field Nick was on his knees, Brad's arm around his neck, the flux enhancing him enough to do what he normally would never have the strength for—suffocate Nick. Marley thought of Quinn in New York, with no clue what was happening here. She could *not* go back and tell her sister that Marley had let her husband die.

But the fight was on too many fronts. Whichever way Marley went would leave the others vulnerable, and Cressida could join the attacks on any one of them at any time.

But she didn't attack anyone. She tilted her head back in a melodious cry, flung out her arms, and *rose into the freaking air*.

Wind swirled as it had by the bistro, and she hovered a foot off the ground. Real or illusion, Marley couldn't tell. Cressida's voice reverberated around the stadium, the steel and concrete and plastic becoming her loudspeaker.

"Honor me, my sons. Claim your tributes. Thrive on the souls of your enemies. Together we shall be powerful enough to rule all."

Marley struggled to her feet. "You've got to be friggin' kidding me." But the guys ate it up. Aiden, who hadn't seemed to be putting much effort into his attack on Gage, fought more vigorously. Gage couldn't simply deflect and avoid anymore. He swung a fist into Aiden's ribs, his expression more pained than Aiden's gasp.

Cressida cackled and glared down at Marley. "I warned you. I tried to help you. You defied me, betrayed me, and now you'll pay." She pointed but not at Marley. Several feet away, Riley screamed and crumpled.

"No!" Marley clenched her fists. *No*. She would not react like Lahr wanted her to. The goddess wanted to go after Marley's team? Fine.

She dashed across the grass, putting all her concentration into her speed. Tony was closest. He stood next to Sam, kicking him even though he was clearly unconscious. The guy didn't see Marley coming until the last second. She had only one chance. She jumped, getting a couple of feet into the air, and was right on target. Tony's eyes widened when he realized what was about to happen, but he couldn't get away. Marley hit him, taking no chances. Cheek to cheek, hand to hand, hand to throat.

The flux screamed into her so fast it was like her body had sucked it in. Tony grunted and fell, taking Marley with him. She couldn't move, couldn't breathe. Her body was paralyzed, shocked by the enormity of the flux she'd altered. Every cell burned as if it had been plunged into boiling water.

She shuddered, fighting to take in air. The intensity faded, leaving her limp.

Get up. You're not done.

She rolled to her side and glanced at Tony. He was unconscious now. Sam was awake, too alert for the head injury he should have had, so Marley knew he'd been faking. He spotted Riley and rage took over his expression, but he didn't go to her. Instead he took the zippered case out of the back of his jeans and opened it. After a few seconds of frantic fiddling, he raised a copper tube to his mouth and blew.

A tiny dart flew through the air toward the goddess. Marley watched in despair as the wind took it far off course, missing Cressida by so much the goddess didn't even notice it. Maybe Sam did have a head injury, after all.

Christopher was next closest to Marley. When Riley went down, he was free, though he seemed uncertain what to do next and Nick needed her help more in that moment.

Sam was with Riley now, checking her pulse, and Chris headed their way but warily. He obviously hadn't expected the fight to be so even. Marley got to her feet and ran toward Nick. Brad didn't see her coming he was so intent on choking the life out of her brother-in-law. Nick had at least gotten a hand up around Brad's forearm, and while he didn't have the leverage to pull it away, he'd gotten a little air. His color wasn't so red-verging-on-purple.

As Marley ran, Nick heaved himself to his feet and used Brad's weight to pull them both backward until they hit one of the curtained frames. It fell, and they landed on top of it. When Brad lost his grip Marley was there. She didn't go easy on him. She closed her hand over Brad's face and squeezed, almost enjoying the cool rush of the flux this time.

Nick sprawled awkwardly across the metal tubes with one hand at his throat. Marley bent to him. "Are you okay?"

He nodded, wheezing, and curled his body to try to get up. Marley helped him to his feet. He stared across the stadium. "Son of a bitch." His voice rasped. "Sam missed." He fumbled at his back pocket, where Marley assumed he had the second dart.

"Don't bother. The wind took the first one. You'll never be able to compensate for it." She yanked up her jeans and reached into her boot for the syringe. "Plan B."

Nick coughed and braced his hands on his knees, still laboring to breathe. He gestured at Cressida, who appeared to be lost in the funnel of air around her, her eyes almost closed. She didn't seem to have noticed that Marley was up on the scoreboard, with Brad and Tony taken care of.

But maybe her threat at the bistro had been all rage and bravado. Maybe she wanted all of this to be over as much as Marley did. She'd just been fighting for so long, she wasn't capable of surrendering.

"I'll get her."

"Wait!"

She ignored Nick's rasp and ran across the field. She hesitated when she passed Gage, struggling with Aiden in a slow-motion fistfight, but there was no time. She had to tackle Cressida while she wasn't paying attention.

The wind buffeted her as she closed in, plastering her shirt to her body and raising her hair straight up in the air. But the gale was only as strong as it had been at the bistro, and it wasn't going to stop her.

Nothing was.

• • •

This was the most ridiculous fight Gage had ever been in. Not that he'd been in many. Most had been with his brother and had been fiercer than this one was so far, probably because they'd actually *wanted* to hurt each other back then. The main difference, though, was the magic.

Riley hadn't given him much. Just a taste, she'd said, only enough to make him strong enough to leech Cressida. Still, it stirred in him constantly, a frantic energy eager to be used. He struggled to keep himself from using it against Aiden. It would be so easy to form a shield or bind his brother. Except Aiden was holding back, too. He pummeled Gage with bursts of energy and with his fists, and used the power to bring whatever loose objects were at hand into the battle, but he didn't do anything that caused any damage. That told Gage at least part of Aiden didn't want to be here doing this.

Gage let him land a few punches, mostly defending, but when Aiden let down his guard, Gage hit him just hard enough to remind him of the stakes.

"Look around," Gage half pleaded, half ordered. He gripped Aiden's shoulder. "Your team is losing. If you kill any of us, you've ruined your life. If you kill me…" He left the rest unsaid, holding Aiden's uncertain gaze for long seconds.

"I don't want to kill anyone," Aiden said. Gage almost let himself be relieved, but suspicion halted it right before Aiden continued. "It's not murder. It's self-defense."

"Against what?" He let go of his brother and lifted his hands in the air. "How could you possibly make a case for self-defense? You weren't invited here—you just showed up. Your guy made the first move, the first attack on Marley and then on Nick."

"Preemptive moves. You all want Cressida dead."

"That's the last thing we want." Rage that had been buried so deep Gage hadn't even been aware of it exploded into him. "We've done everything possible to protect people, including you. Including *her*. You have no idea the sacrifices people are making. You *asshole*!" He swung. Aiden's cheekbone crunched under the blow, and Gage's knuckles split open. He didn't care. When Aiden fell back, Gage followed. Blood spurted from Aiden's nose at the next punch. The one after that crushed his lip. Aiden couldn't block the hits or get leverage to make any himself, and an instant later, Gage was shoved up and back without being touched. He shifted to launch himself back at his brother, and then he saw Marley and froze.

Cressida was hovering a few feet off the ground, pieces of grass and other tiny bits of debris swirling around her. Marley propped the busted seats against the wall and climbed up onto the rails in front of the seating area. She held the rail, leaned out, crouched, and leaped.

The instant she touched Cressida, the wind stopped. They crumpled to the ground in a heap.

"Marley!" Gage ran across the grass, but his legs were heavy and the distance stretched ahead of him. A nightmare made real.

Gage heard his brother running behind him, but Nick beat them both there. He slid to a stop on his knees, thrust the needle in his hand into Cressida's neck, and pushed the plunger.

"Nooooo!" Aiden screamed. He plowed into Gage and tumbled to the ground next to her. "You've—"

"Sedated her," Nick growled. "So we can put an end to this once and for all."

Gage stood helplessly by as Sam helped Marley to her feet. The fall hadn't been that far, but she still could have broken an ankle. "Are you all right?"

"Fine." She circled the group, approaching Christopher. He stood over Aiden and Lahr, not even noticing when Marley laid a gentle hand on his arm. Then he shuddered and looked at her, his face almost expressionless.

"You've got to do this now," Nick said to Gage. He held up the syringe. "She's too powerful for this to work very long."

"I know." But Gage moved away to intercept Marley. Her eyes weren't the same aged-newspaper yellow as the other day. Now they were a dull gold, almost brackish. Her movements were slow, heavy, like she could barely move her legs. She went straight for Aiden but only took a few steps before her legs buckled. Gage caught her under the arms, before her head hit the concrete. "*Marley*."

She twisted her head and blinked up at him. Her eyes were glazed. She had to grab his shirt to keep herself steady. "I have to get Aiden," she whispered.

"I know." His voice cracked. He didn't want to let her, but even though Aiden was his brother, he knew they couldn't trust him with so much power. But a second later, her body went limp. Her head lolled against his shoulder. He called frantically to Nick, unable to check her pulse.

Nick hurried over and lifted her into his arms. "She's breathing," he said. "Finish it."

Gage couldn't stand watching her being carried away. A deep breath steadied him, and he turned, brought up short by his brother, held immobile by Sam. Tears streaked Aiden's face.

"This is wrong," Aiden cried out. "You can't do this to her!"

"What do you think we're going to do?" Gage couldn't dredge up any emotion. He was so tired.

"You just told me you were trying to keep people from being

killed. How can you—"

"For God's sake, I'm not going to kill her!" Okay, maybe a little emotion. "I'm going to leech her!" The words rang out, too loud.

Aiden stopped struggling. "What do you mean, leech her?"

"I mean I'm going to drain her of all of the energy she's stored. If I can get it all, it will damage her vessel enough that she can't absorb any more."

Aiden drew in a short, startled breath. "It's a cure?"

Gage lifted a shoulder. "Depends on how you look at it."

His brother looked down at Cressida. She wasn't completely unconscious, but she clearly had little control. Her eyelids lazed half-open, and her movements were minimal and aimless.

Aiden turned back to his brother, his expression clearer, more shrewd. "You keep telling me flux is dangerous." He looked at where Nick held a still-unconscious Marley. "What is this going to do to you?"

Surprised that he'd asked, Gage didn't take the time to answer. He just bent over Cressida.

"Can you hear me?" he murmured near her ear. She nodded. "I'm going to leech you, Cress." It seemed smart to use her nickname. How much more personal could you get than what he was about to do? "Do you understand what that means?"

She nodded again. Her hand rested on his arm, and her eyes opened slightly wider. Her gaze bore into his, weaker than he'd seen before but lucid enough to convince him she understood.

He closed his eyes and rested his hand on Cressida's abdomen. Then he tuned in to the energy inside him, getting a feel for it. Its properties, its strength. It was shiny and hard even while fluid, flexible yet strong enough to hold up a building. Like the metal that was Riley's source. He held on and reached outward, imagining part of him traveling into Cressida, seeking her energy.

It walloped him upside the head like looking suddenly into

glaring sunlight. He actually flung his free hand in front of his face, even though the sensation was wholly nonphysical. But it was *right there*, so much of it, so easy to touch. To take. Gage drew on it like sucking through a straw, just as Quinn had explained to him. At first it flowed without resistance, gold and light, filling him. Elation rose and popped and rose again.

Gage tried to direct the energy down into his body to make room for more. He drew harder when the light dimmed, the energy thickening. Sweat beaded on his forehead, and he leaned forward to place his other hand on the goddess. *"Don't lose the connection,"* Quinn had said. *"It might not be possible to get it back."*

Now the energy was sludge, heavy and slow. It glopped and settled inside him. He felt sick, and a headache started to pound in his temples. The gold darkened further, and Gage could sense that it grew black the deeper he went, toxic. He hesitated, knowing instinctively that it would burn, and worse. The stream slowed, reversed. He almost let it.

But then he thought of Marley, who still had to nullify Aiden. He couldn't let this all be in vain. He grabbed on and drew harder, hauling back. His lips drew back from his teeth and he vaguely heard a keening growl that came from his own throat.

Then something shifted. The energy split, some pouring faster into Gage, the rest going—out, into someone else. It had to be Aiden, the only other one capable of doing this.

His brother hadn't abandoned him. Gage focused. The blackness reached him, and hell, yeah, it burned. The heat of the sun scorched him all the way through, even before the toxic energy was internalized. He screamed, grit his teeth, and pulled harder. He sensed Aiden doing the same next to him. The last bit parted and slid inside them both with a whip-crack that Gage thought might have severed his spine. His body convulsed, muscles cramping, and he clenched his jaw to keep the screaming under control. Except he could hear it anyway, feel it in the rawness of his throat.

Discharging the energy he'd taken in was not an option. He couldn't remember how he'd done it, but even if he could, it would never work. Riley's and Quinn's powers were civilized compared to this raging mass. It battered him, thrusting daggers into soft organs until he bled. He had no control, could get no purchase on the energy to try to release it. He was its victim, completely.

The screaming diminished. Gage didn't realize Aiden, too, had been screaming. Until he stopped.

No. Don't let him be dead.

Gage forced open his eyes and stared up at a star-strewn sky. Marley stood there, devastatingly beautiful, devastatingly sad.

"I love you," she said and touched his face.

CHAPTER NINETEEN

As far back into the past our history stretches, so does our future ahead. Unknown, and brilliant.

—Numina manifesto and Goddess Society charter

Everything stopped. The energy disappeared, taking the pain and cramping and urge to scream with it. Gage lay on the hard ground, panting, bruised, but whole.

"Marley!" He shot upright, his heart cracking. There was no way she could have survived what she'd just done. He stared wildly around. Aiden stretched out on the ground beside him, propped on one elbow, retching. Sobs racked Cressida, who lay with an arm over her eyes. Sam stood over them both, but neither was a threat at the moment. Nick was a few feet away, a hand outstretched, his expression tormented as he called Marley's name.

And then Gage saw her. She'd backed away against the wall. Her eyes rolled back in her head. And her body…glowed. Faintly at first, almost like she was backlit, but then the glow intensified at her fingers, her head, and then her entire body. It got brighter, then darker, shining yellow but streaked with black. Green eddied through it as the glow expanded outward, swelling. It reached an invisible border and filled, growing denser.

"Everyone get back!" Sam knocked Nick away, getting him moving, and bent to haul Cressida into his arms to carry her away. He laid her next to Riley and tried to shield them both.

"*No*. Marley!" Gage pushed Aiden. "Move, Aid. Get clear." But he didn't follow his brother. He wasn't running from Marley and leaving her alone. She'd saved him, saved Aiden—saved everyone. If this was the end, he was going with her.

He had to close his eyes when he got close. There was no physical manifestation of the glow. No heat or change in air pressure. Just the bright, awful light. His hand found Marley's. He followed her arm up to her shoulders and gathered her to him. "I love you, too," he murmured, his heart falling to pieces as she seized in his arms.

And then it shattered. The boom was silent, but it rocked Gage on a metaphysical level. The glow disappeared, and Marley went limp. He cradled her to the ground, fearing the worst. He rocked her, murmuring her name over and over, willing her conscious.

A sigh whispered past his ear. He stopped rocking. A breeze kicked up—a natural one, fresh air, not the frenzy whipped by Cressida. It was cold on his face, drying the moisture trailing down his cheeks. He loosened his hold on Marley, and her head fell back over his arm. He could see the pulse throb beneath her jaw.

"She's alive," he croaked, raising his head to see Riley, Nick, and Sam gathered around. "I don't know how bad she is, but she's alive."

"Call nine-one-one," Sam said. Riley quickly dialed as he pulled a fistful of zip ties from his pocket and secured Aiden and Cressida to the long bench where the others were already tied. Nick had his phone out, too. He paced a few steps away, talking fast.

Gage shifted Marley, making sure she wasn't positioned

awkwardly, and watched her face. She was still unconscious but breathed steadily now. A mental litany ran nonstop in his head, begging and promising and praying. He didn't care what happened next, as long as she was all right.

Riley crouched next to them. "Ambulance is on its way. Nick's talking to Quinn. She and your father landed about fifteen minutes ago. They brought a Society security team and whatever the Numina equivalent is. They'll round up everyone here and deal with them."

Gage grabbed Riley's hand and tugged her closer. "What's wrong with her? What do you see?" He knew Riley would have scanned Marley for injury. "Is there anything you can heal?"

She shook her head, her eyes on Marley. "I don't know what's wrong. There aren't any physical injuries. Not like the ones Quinn healed."

"The vessel? The inert flux? Whatever you saw before, what does it look like now?"

She turned wondering eyes on him. "Gage, I don't see anything. I don't know what happened, but it's gone. There's no trace of the flux, no void, no original vessel."

The hope he'd held onto swelled. "Are you saying she's going to be okay?"

"I don't know."

But he did. She had to be. They couldn't have survived like this only to have her fade away with no discernible cause.

He stayed like that for god knew how long. Eventually Quinn and his father arrived with a dozen other people. His father strode across the field in his business suit and distinguished silver hair, commanding just by his presence. He directed a handful of men to take custody of Chris, Tony, and Brad, and he spoke to Aiden at length, hugging him before allowing him to be taken away, as well. Then he approached Gage, crouching beside him as Riley had.

"Quinn told me everything." There was no censure, only pride mixed with regret. "Are you well?"

"I don't know." Gage couldn't objectively assess how he felt. Everything was about Marley. "Where are the paramedics?"

"Nicholas tells me they were delayed in traffic. They should arrive any minute. I'm having the boys transported to the hospital for assessment before we return to New York. But I'll stay as long as you need me."

"That's all right." Gage rotated his neck, wincing at the stiffness that had settled in. "I'll be okay." As long as Marley was.

His father studied her for a long time, worry furrowing his brow. "Quinn tells me she was having…issues similar to your— "

"They were nothing like Mom's. And they're not a concern now." How could they be? If the flux was completely gone, there shouldn't be anything to cause hallucinations or worse.

And the energy *had* to be completely gone. It had blown outward, dispersing. There was no other explanation. Maybe it was the coalescing of every bit of Cressida's stored energy with all the energy she'd given to others that Marley had collected. A kind of chemical reaction.

But it didn't matter. All that mattered was that she didn't leave him.

Gage could hear an ambulance approaching the stadium, siren blaring, followed by a second one a moment later. After a few minutes, the paramedics wheeled in two gurneys. One came straight to Gage and Marley.

"Can you tell us what happened, sir?" one asked as they gently took her from his arms and laid her on the ground, checking her vitals.

He laughed weakly. "No, not really."

The one with the stethoscope gave him an odd look. "Did she hit her head?"

"No."

"Complain of chest pain, shortness of breath?"

"No."

"What kind of physical trauma has she had?"

"I think she got hit in the arm, fell on her back. She was moving around okay, though."

They checked her spine, her arm, tested her ankles after he said she fell from a few feet's height. Finally, looking stumped, they declared it shock and bundled her onto the gurney with a saline IV attached to a pole.

"I'm coming with you." Gage's feet were asleep, but he staggered after them without waiting for the feeling to come back.

The paramedic turned and put his hand on his chest. "Are you family?"

"I'm her husband," Gage growled so ferociously the man backed away.

"All right, okay, calm down. It's just policy."

Gage followed the man into the ambulance and held Marley's hand the whole trip.

It was more of the same at the hospital, questions he couldn't answer, stumped medical professionals, a declaration of "stable but unresponsive." She was admitted and finally settled into a dim room, hooked up to several beeping, flashing monitors.

"I'm supposed to tell you to go home," said a tall, imposing nurse. "But I think you'll rest the same here. The chair reclines and the bottom lifts up so you can stretch out."

"Thank you." After she left, Gage positioned the chair so he could touch Marley's arm, hold her hand. He closed his eyes, prepared to wait for her.

For as long as it took.

• • •

Marley didn't know how much time had passed when she opened her eyes and found herself in a hospital room. It was sunny outside, so at least half a day. But she had an IV in her left arm and bruising on her right, so this must not be the *first* day. She also had…*ugh*, a catheter.

There was no one else in the room, but she recognized a leather jacket over the arm of the chair. The coat Gage had worn when they first met. The chair was positioned right next to her bedside, away from the monitors. Flowers in vases and baskets filled the windowsill.

A remote dangled over the bedrail, and Marley found the button to raise the head of the bed. That's when she heard a toilet flush and saw that the door to the bathroom was closed. She couldn't sense anyone behind the door, though. Water ran, then shut off. A moment later the door opened.

Marley let out her breath in a long, slow stream when Gage walked out. He stopped short when he saw her sitting up, and then a grin spread wide across his face. "You're awake!"

She winced. "How long was I not?"

He shook his head and came around to sit in the chair, immediately taking her hand and resting his other on her leg. "Days. Maybe weeks. I've lost track. How do you feel?"

It was her turn to shake her head. "Amazing. I've never…" She frowned. "Where is everybody? Are they okay? I didn't blow anyone up, did I?"

"No." He patted her leg and squeezed her fingers. "Everyone's okay. Riley, Sam, and Nick weren't hurt much. Just from the fighting. Riley healed Sam's concussion and Nick's bruised windpipe pretty easily."

"And you?"

He shrugged. "No one can find anything wrong with me."

Which didn't mean nothing *was* wrong. "What are you feeling?"

"Lonely." He smiled again, the silver bright in his blue eyes. "I missed you like hell."

Her heart swelled, but she refused to let him see her reaction.

"I mean from the energy you leeched. The amount you took in should have killed you. *Would* have killed you if Aiden hadn't helped."

"I know. He's being detained, but when that's settled he and I have some work to do on our relationship. Dad, too. But it'll work out."

"You're evading."

He sighed and rubbed his thumb over her knuckles. "I know. I just don't have an answer. I'm okay. I don't feel ill or have hallucinations or any obvious effects. There's an emptiness, I guess. But that might be because I didn't know what was going to happen with you."

There was one more thing she had to know. "Cressida?"

"Taken away by the Society security team. Quinn says she's completely powerless. I think they might have hospitalized her back East. She's no threat to anyone anymore."

"Good." She let her head drop against the pillow. She'd just woken up and yet she felt so tired.

"Your turn, Marley. What happened? You glowed. There was some kind of explosion, only with no physical blast. You collapsed and have been in a coma ever since."

She closed her eyes, remembering, and decided that this would be the last time she did. The memories crowded into her mind as if they were happening now, and she did *not* want to relive any of that. The horror of Gage's pain, so much worse than when it was Sam because she loved this man beside her so much.

"I passed out, but not for long. I came to with Nick holding me, and you were leeching Cressida. Aiden saw that you were losing it. We all did. I think I cried out. I don't know. I could barely see, barely feel anything but the energy I'd already nullified. It weighed me down, but when you both collapsed, I knew there was only one thing to do. I touched Aiden and then you." And then she'd descended into agony. She wasn't going to tell him that part. He didn't need to know that she would have gladly died, even killed herself, to escape it.

"There was so much in me already, I don't think I had the capacity for more. It didn't fully change. The part that didn't... Well, the only way to describe it is like mercury. The parts all rolled together, coalesced, and that increased it beyond my capacity to hold anything. It blew out of me and stripped whatever was holding it along with it." She tossed up her hands, then let them fall back to her lap. "And that's it. All I remember until I woke up a few minutes ago."

Gage's hand tightened. "And?"

"And what?"

"Ghosties, ghoulies, green mist?"

She shook her head. "Nothing."

He breathed out a "thank God" and bowed his head over their joined hands.

"What's going to happen to the ones we missed?" she asked. "The Deimons?"

He shook his head. "Not our problem. We're done. My father will figure that out."

She had to admit, that sounded fantastic.

The door to the hallway opened, Riley and Sam bickering as they came in.

"I'm just saying, Katie has run the bar on her own for too long," Sam said. "I want to get home."

Riley talked over him. "Then go home. I'm staying until Marley's—" She gasped and then beamed. "You're awake!"

"So you can go home," Marley said, laughing as Riley dashed over and hugged her.

"You look good," Sam agreed, flashing a dimple. "I'm sorry. I wasn't being..."

"No, it's okay. You guys were supposed to be on your honeymoon."

They all laughed. Sam handed an In-N-Out Burger bag to Gage and after three rounds of good-byes, they left Marley and Gage alone again.

He wedged the bag between two vases on the windowsill and wrestled the rail down so he could sit on the bed next to her. "You'll probably be discharged tomorrow, if the doc doesn't see anything today."

"Good. And then I can go…" Hell. She didn't have a home.

"Marley." Gage waited until she looked at him. "What about us?"

Her heart tripped over itself. "You tell me."

He rolled his eyes. "I wanted you to tell me."

She crooked her finger until he leaned in, then wrapped her hand in his shirt and pulled until he was close enough to kiss. As soon as their lips met, sweet assuredness filled her. He smelled the same, tasted the same, but there was no fear, no resistance to block the pure, unadulterated love that had *not* disappeared with everything else.

When they came up for air, Gage stroked her hair back from her face. "Will you come with me to New York?"

She nodded. "But I don't know how to live a normal life. I have no idea what to do."

"We'll figure it out together." He kissed her again, this time keeping their foreheads touching when he stopped. "You know, it feels pretty damned good to have a future again, no matter how uncertain it is."

"No, that's not right."

He backed off an inch or two, frowning. "What?"

"It feels damned good to have a future *with you*."

Neither of them said anything more for a very long time. They just smiled.

Acknowledgments

First thanks, as always, go to my editors. Kerri-Leigh Grady had valuable input at the beginning of the process and invested a great deal of time and energy into making this series as good as it could be. Danielle Poiesz took over and whipped me…I mean, guided me into whipping this book into shape. If I failed in any way in making it a compelling, interesting read, it's all on me.

I also thank Erica Poiesz for her time and input on the most challenging aspect of this book, and thanks to Kat Carlson and Misa Ramirez for their suggestions of indie rock bands that rich guys in their twenties might listen to. Danielle Barclay and Anjana Vasan also get my gratitude for their assistance and support for publicity and marketing. You guys are fantastic.

I cannot adequately express my joy and satisfaction over the completion of this trilogy. It began with the most fun I've ever had writing a book with *Under the Moon*, and ended with the most challenging, frustrating, and even kind of frightening with *Sunroper*. All of it together has been the most rewarding experience of my career. Every moment along the way has been bolstered by the readers who discovered me through these books and said wonderful things about reading them. I appreciate every one of you, and especially the bloggers and reviewers who took extra time to voice their thoughts on these stories.

EBSABS